DOMINUS

TERINA ADAMS

Cedar
Thanks for the courage to get this far

Author's Note

Lover of young adult science fiction and fantasy thrills and adventure?

You've downloaded the right book.

Fall into Sable's tale but be careful you don't fall too far or you may be left wondering where your world ends and her world begins.

If you would like some ya sci-fic fantasy action in your inbox now, join my newsletter at terinaadams.com and receive three stories free.

Happy reading

Chapter 1

AJAY SQUEEZED MY HAND TIGHT, as tight as the day *that* murderer was taken from our home. Shame it wasn't from our lives. I turned him to face me and ran a hand over his hair to straighten the curls like Mum had always done as the bus came into view, belching black smoke as it accelerated away from the last set of lights before our stop.

"Do I have to?"

Staring down into his brown eyes, I saw my father looking back at me. I turned away for a moment, eyes closed, a quick swallow, before turning back to him, lips pressed together. The lecture waned on me, no doubt on him too. I placed a finger to his mouth at the first sign of a quiver and bent to his height. "Six hours. That's all. And I'll be here when you get off."

"But I don't have any friends."

"It's been two months. Friends worth having take time to build."

"They're all mean."

"Have you given them a chance?"

He dropped his eyes to the paving, but I returned them to me with a finger under his chin. "I want you to do something for me today."

Ajay's moody face appeared, an expression of sullen resignation. "What?"

"Ask one boy a question about himself today. About his favorite TV show, favorite sport, favorite movie star, favorite pet, favor—"

"I get the picture."

The falsity in my smile hurt. "I bet you haven't thought of doing that yet." I gave him a playful jab in the stomach.

He swiped my finger away. The smile now hurt my cheeks.

The bus squealed to a halt with a jolt. The doors jerked open, cutting off my chance to say yet more hollow reassurances. A good thing as they hurt me to say them as much as they closed one door in Ajay's heart.

I straightened, my hands on Ajay's shoulders. "I'll be right here when you get off." I bent again to whisper in his ear. "I might even have a surprise for you."

He slouched out of my hands and up the steps to the bus without looking back. If only I could say something different, something that would earn me his smile. As usual he took a seat on my side of the bus, where he stared down at me with dead eyes as I waved him away. The routine was the same, his expression unchanged for the last two months, mine neither.

I inhaled, then held my breath against the black smoke belching from the bus's exhaust as it joined the rest of the rush-hour traffic.

Every morning, five days a week, I was the bad guy. For two months, I'd tried to make up for it by being the cheerful welcoming committee of one at the end of the day. Hard to do when the cheer was far from touching my heart. The hours in between, I'd gone from schoolgirl to thief. Ajay didn't know this. Mum didn't know this. I kept my lie, kept pretending, kept smiling, but only when I was around my family—what was left of it.

Adults were wrong; passing time did not heal.

With a break in the traffic, I crossed Northcote Street, heading for a small convenience store two blocks down. My air became the churn of cheap perfume, cologne, tobacco, and leather as I dodged and ducked through the steady stream of oncoming pedestrians.

Weaving around one young guy in torn denims, I collided with a heavyset man wearing a white shirt, white until his coffee decorated it brown across his chest. The stain spread like blood would seeping from

2

a gunshot to the heart. I dodged around him and kept going, closing my ears to his abuse.

At the store, I turned my back, facing out onto the road, and stared at nothing while my pulse racketed up a notch. One week ago, I'd stood in front of the open doors of my bus while I fought an internal war. Four months and I would've graduated from high school. Then what? I couldn't go to college without money. Getting a job was my only option, which meant there was no point in going to school, not when we struggled to survive, not when the rent was due, the gas bill went unpaid, and most days I couldn't find enough for Ajay's lunch.

I exhaled as I turned to face the store, peering through the glass to the young guy behind the checkout, head buried in a magazine, leaving the bush of his hair spiking over the top.

My arced adrenaline made my stomach churn. Before I pushed through the door into the shop, I spied my reflection. The girl staring back looked only marginally familiar. The difference was in her eyes and the angular jut of her cheekbones. She looked older, harder, weaker. But the biggest change was inside. One day I was someone; the next I was someone else, someone I didn't want to be.

The magazine stayed in place when I entered, while his head bobbed to a silent beat. Earphones and magazine, it couldn't be more perfect. My eyes flicked to the mirror at the end of the first aisle, raised high enough to scan over the top of this one and into the next, possibly the next after that. Ignoring the cleaning products, matches, candles, foiled barbecue trays and tongs, I hurried to the end of the aisle on whisper-quick feet, fighting against my adrenaline, which wanted me to run.

At the back of the shop, I paused behind the shelving separating the two aisles and forced in two breaths. I had to be smart, rein in the jitters.

I picked up a can of beans on special, staring at the label, surreptitiously casting a few fleeting glances to the front of the shop. From this angle, the guy was out of sight. A quick glance behind me at the mirror and I saw the small speck of him right up the back—I should say front —of the shop.

Beans would be useful, but at this price, they were something I could afford to buy. I skipped the next few aisles until I found one useful.

Only a handful of items I took at each trip, anything that ate into our grocery budget too much. And I visited the shops once. Only items small enough to fit into my lunchbox I slipped straight from the shelf into my backpack.

Up the next aisle, I slid my backpack from my shoulder. The silence in the convenience store increased the decibels of my zipper as I inched it open and rested it between my feet. I swiped a tube of toothpaste and hid it away in my empty lunchbox. The bristles on Ajay's toothbrush were horizontal, so I grabbed one of those as well, sparing no time to decide if he should have sensitive, medium, or hard bristled. Lid closed, I returned the lunchbox to my backpack. Batteries were next, in case we delayed payment on our electrical bill.

I craned over the aisle to the checkout, but the kid with the spiked hair remained buried behind his magazine. Hold out, luck. I ran the sweat from my palm down my denims, then swapped hands and did the same with the other.

At the back of the shop, I moved a few aisles farther along, hunting for the batteries, and found the shelving for the chocolate instead. This would put a smile on Ajay's face. Chocolate-coated licorice was his favorite, had been since the day Dad returned from a business trip with a tin full of it. I'd loved it too until the memories made me feel sick whenever I smelt it.

I knelt to take my lunchbox out again. All I saw was the smile on Ajay's face as I chose the longest one on the shelf. His eyes would pop. Those cute dimpled smiles of his were long gone, two months on, and I'd forgotten how much they warmed my heart. But the damn thing wouldn't fit in my lunchbox. That one would have to go down to the bottom of my bag under my sweater.

"I would've gone for the Hershey."

I jerked, dropping my lunchbox, which clattered across the smooth floor and under the chocolate aisle, spilling the toothpaste and brush.

Eating my heart, I looked over my shoulder to a young guy dressed in black, but not the spiked-haired kid from behind the checkout. Black from neck to toe, even his hair, which was a mess of shaggy loose curls. The dark shadowing around his jawline made him look older than his smooth skin implied. He reclined on the opposite shelves, elbows resting back on stacks of savory crackers.

I gave a stupid little half laugh, which revealed my nerves more than anything, then turned back to the toothpaste and brush.

"Do you often take your toothbrush to school?"

I closed my eyes. *Go away.* "It's a spare." I heard my nerves in my voice.

I scooped both the toothpaste and brush and shoved them to the bottom of my backpack, then retrieved my lunchbox. The lid wouldn't fit on, the snap locks refusing to close. It took a few tries and my heart crawling up my throat to snap them closed.

All packed, I straightened.

"You going to get your chocolate bar?"

It lay between us on the floor, between my trainers and his thick-soled boots. I bent to pick it up and returned it to the shelf.

"Changed your mind?"

From here his eyes looked black, blending with his black lashes and olive skin. My heart banged to get out of my chest, and my legs itched to be gone. Even so, I couldn't help think him good-looking, like dark, smoldering good-looking, but the flat stare of his eyes, the hard line of his mouth, the heavy vibe that emanated from him, and I wanted to back away. There was nothing in his demeanor or expression that made him appear welcoming.

"Yeah."

"You don't look like you need to steal, but I guess your clothes may have been lifted too."

My organs fell through my body to the floor. It was as though my feet were stapled there as well. "I don't know what you mean."

The back of my neck prickled from his blunt stare. Eyes like bores, they tunneled through into the core of my lie, my shame. The heat rushed up my throat. *Asshole, go away.* Goading me like this. If he wanted to turn me in, he should do it now. Get it over with rather than taunt me. *Christ, I hope he doesn't.*

"I gotta go."

I made to move past him. He pushed off from the shelving, a cat ready to pounce. The swift grace of his sudden movement and I backed up, my heart like a jackhammer as he squared on to me, placing himself in the middle of the aisle.

"You sick of our conversation already?" There was a faint sneer to his question, matched by the hardness tensing the corners of his eyes and around his lips.

"I wasn't aware we were having a conversation. Not really. Not a proper conversation." And that didn't sound casual at all, not when I practically swallowed my last sentence.

"Didn't your dad teach you any manners?"

Oh, god. "Can you just let me go?" I had to sound stronger than this. No ninny voice, no slight quiver at the end. I clenched my fists. "I have to get to school."

He smiled, no…sneered, dropped his head, and looked at the floor. Released from those viper black eyes, I heaved a silent shuddering breath.

He inched his head up, eyes finding mine through another of his piercing-dart stares. "That started twenty minutes ago."

"And I'm getting later by the minute."

Slinging one strap of my backpack over my shoulder, I walked toward him, angling for the small gap between him and the chocolates, but he sidestepped to block my path.

I pulled up. "What do you want?" This time, with another sudden spike in my adrenaline, I found the anger I needed.

"I want to know how cunning you are."

Jesus. This guy was a loon, a creepy loon.

"Why would you want to know that?" My hand found my hip.

"Can you be trusted? Are you loyal? Willing to do what it takes regardless of what it means to you?"

I opened my mouth but slammed it closed again. Don't make conversation with unstable people, especially unstable people who look like they know how to wield a knife. "Get out of my way, please. I'm late already."

He nodded, pretending to assess what I'd said when really he was enjoying himself. "Jax."

I gave him a blank stare, blank because my mind was blank. Was that his name? He bothered to give me his name? Not good. People gave names when they excepted to meet someone again.

You're not getting mine, asshole.

"You need to know it." That sounded semi-permanent, as in *let's hang out.*

I swallowed. "My parents will receive a call from the school if I'm late. I'll get in big trouble."

Parents. The word had come out so easily. I swallowed my correction.

Clean clothes, no holes, he wasn't a street kid. His black tee shirt looked good quality and the gold ring on his pointer finger would have cost a few hundred. Could be a drug dealer, then he'd be rich, if he was any good. There would be a knife tucked down the back of his black denims, or a gun. The idea of either and the sudden tingle that swooped through my body paralyzed my limbs.

"Parents? You look like a single-parent home to me."

"You look like a no-parent home to me."

The creepy twitch at the corner of his mouth, threatening a smirk, slid away like an avalanche, leaving a dark coldness behind, so cold, so dark I involuntarily backed up a step.

"Is that so?" Calm, quiet, sharp as a knife.

I shook my head. "No, not really, I was just saying stuff."

His eyes said he was capable of anything. It was possible to feel the rage of someone else. It was a living emotion, suffocating in its tangible nature. Seen through the eyes of a stranger, and it became the flash-fast fist, the slice of a blade, the sudden pulled gun, the end of my life.

I flicked my gaze away from the stab of his eyes, which were nothing now but the steal of a knife, down to the floor, but they were arrested halfway by the black tattoo on the inside of his forearm. A vast labyrinth of thick black marks with no apparent design. What happened to skulls or girlfriend's name? Who'd decorate their arm with such an ugly tattoo?

He turned his forearm inward, hiding it away. I snapped my eyes up to his.

"You like?" He said.

Despite my nerves, I'd thought him good-looking, but the smirk ruined everything. The guy was an arrogant ass who liked to scare people. Mystery as an allure worked as long as the person was actually nice. This guy was the opposite. "It's ugly."

"It's not decoration."

It was a gang thing. It had to be a gang thing. *Get out now.*

No way was he letting me pass him, so I spun and fled toward the back of the shop, rounded the shelving and up the next aisle, squeaking my trainers on the smooth floor as I went. *God, so stupid*, hardly an escape routine, but what could I do?

At the end, I found Jax leaning one elbow against the counter. The fuzzy-haired kid had dropped his magazine and was eyeing Jax, then me. Jax was back to that cruel smirk.

My mouth twitched a small smile at the kid as I strode past the counter, practically wetting myself.

"You might want to check her bag." That drawl, that arrogant voice, sliding out like silken thread.

I froze, spun, faced his horrible sneer. The cruel smile was in his eyes, black insanity, the devil's henchman. "Leave me alone."

This time my gaze was stolen by the tattoo just below and behind his right ear, but my eyes soon snapped to his with no time to work out what it was.

I promised Ajay a surprise, the promise the only thing that would get him through the day. This guy was making me break my promise, so now it was my turn to share the venom. We locked weapons, our eyes, in silent threat, and I swallowed the lump in my throat. Fear is powerful, anger just as big. The two together…

Those black eyes did not leave mine. Who would back down first? The predator or the prey? Ticking seconds turned into snail-crawling hours, our only distraction the nervous throat clearing of the kid behind the checkout.

Jax dropped his eyes, not to signal defeat but to claim his victory with a languid walk of his eyes up my body, the sort a guy gives a girl to put her in her place. There was nothing on his face to indicate he took pleasure in what he saw any more than in the conquest of an enemy.

"I was disappointed with our first meet." He jerked his head in the direction of the aisle. "I'm happy to say things have changed."

Two steps and I closed the distance between us. "The only thing that's changed is how close I am to leaving you behind."

He rolled his tongue along his inner left cheek, relaxing farther onto the counter. "This will be an interesting game."

I threw my backpack on the counter, pinning the fuzzy-haired kid with my glare. "You want to check my bag?"

"Umm…well…I don't know."

Jax swiped the bag across to him and yanked the zip undone with a violent tear. "Delve deep," he said as he shoved it across to the kid. His black eyes drifted to me, a challenge.

There was nothing left in me, the collapse when faced with the inevitable. I closed my eyes, the only way to escape this mess, escape him.

Chapter 2

THE ONLY OTHER time I'd traveled in a car down this road was in the back of a taxi another lifetime ago—two months to be exact. Unfortunately the scenery had yet to change from the wastelands of desolation to the architecture of the privileged few, who'd been us in that other life, the one that came before the destruction of everything I knew, including my trust, faith, and love.

The view was worse this time because it came from the back of a police car. They had rung home, but I never expected Mum to answer. And she didn't. They couldn't have had much else to do with their day because I was bundled into the back of their car and escorted home. All of this for a tube of toothpaste and toothbrush. But I missed my chocolate-coated licorice bar. Asshole, I wouldn't forgive him for that, along with all the other weird, creepy things he'd said. At least riding away with the cops got me away from him.

With the windows up, their colognes mixed, clashed, and filled the small space. Oceanic wilds, salt spray, lashing winds, that's what my dad's cologne made me think about, the only one he ever wore, an expensive brand. Nothing like the cloying smell of fake citrus and lavender filling the car right now.

We turned onto my street, and I pressed back into the seat as I watched the houses flick by, seeing it from the cops' perspective, the way I'd seen it when we first arrived. Unkept gardens, broken fences, car bodies, and scrawny dogs with rib cages protruding like piano keys. In the rearview mirror, they would see a young woman with no future, possibly popping pills, perhaps a jailed boyfriend and a hooker for a mum. They would never know about the private school, the driver, the mansion, the yacht, the clothes, the parties, the belief life would always hold, and family wouldn't change or betray or kill.

"Fifty-five?" The cop looked in the mirror as he asked, so I nodded.

"Good-looking neighborhood," said the cop in the passenger seat.

I stared at the back of his neck, the only thing visible from the small gap between the headrest and the seat. No surprise to hear the derision in his voice. Circumstances had forced me into that shop, and my aspirations were pathetic, but I was still the girl chauffeured to school another lifetime ago, still the girl who tried to be the best in whatever she did to please her dad, and who failed every time. That girl remained inside of me, trapped with no hope of ever being free.

The cop swung into my driveway, pulling up to the house because there was no car of our own to fill the space. Once the engine was off, I climbed out and dodged the cracked paving to our door while listening to the sounds of the cops' boots smacking along behind me. They weren't going to drop me and go, like a stupid part of me had hoped.

On entering, I saw the cushion foam sticking out of the hole in the cover, the frayed upholstery on the armrest, the deep grooves running tracks across the wood coffee table, and the stain in the worn carpet. We didn't even have a TV and the built-in shelving on the far wall was empty. Cleaning made no difference to the appearance of the place. I shouldn't even bother.

I forced myself to leave the door open for them to enter and swept my eyes to the corners of the wall, where the wallpaper peeled back in thin sheets, and the linoleum floor at the entrance to the kitchen, which was worn down to form brown smears.

The two cops stood in the middle of the living room, the shorter one looking at me. The other, whose belt was stretched tight across his wide waistline, cast a look around the room. I saw what he saw and more, caught the smallest lip curl and the thoughts churning in his mind, the judgments already formed.

"You said your mother was home," said the short cop with the flat nose.

"She'll be in her room."

Without waiting for the prompt, I headed down the narrow hall, seeing yet more wallpaper peeling, more stains on old carpet, more of everything that had not been in my life before but was part of the real me now.

Stale air wafted out to greet me when I opened the door to Mum's bedroom. The drapes were thick and heavy, creating a blackout, which helped her fall into herself and disappear. I shut the door in case one of those cops got nosey and made my way across the bedroom in the dark.

"Mum." I moved my way up the bed, patting the edges as I went. "Mum."

She stirred when I found her hip and gave it a gentle shake. "Mum, some people are here to see you."

She made soft sleepy sounds, murmurs, then grunts.

"You need to get up."

"Sweetheart." Her voice was croaky and rough.

I fumbled for the lamp on the bedside table, which had already been in the house when we arrived. The shade hung on a slant to the left like it had been knocked off too many times, but the thing still worked.

"Cover your eyes. I'm switching the light on."

The gentle yellow glow was too much for her eyes and she rolled away, her forearm over her face.

"Mum, you have to get up."

"What time is it? Is Ajay ready for school?" she mumbled.

"Ajay's at school already. It's going on ten."

"So late. I should be up." Her warm hand found mine. "Sorry, hon, you got him to the bus. Has he got lunch?"

She slowly inched herself up to sitting. Unveiling herself from the covers brought out the sour smell of her unwashed body. "How was he?"

"Better each day." I brushed the hair that had loosened from her braid out of her face. "Everything will get better each day."

Mum clasped my hand in hers and drew it onto her lap. "My beautiful girl." Her warm hand soothed my cheek. "You're the only one holding us together." The last words wobbled under the strain.

"And I will."

She sucked in her bottom lip as she shook her head. With more light in the room, I'd see her tears.

"It's okay, Mum."

No, it wasn't okay. There were two cops in the living room waiting to speak to her about her thieving daughter.

"There are some people here to see you."

Mum brushed her hair from her face, her expression stunned silence. "What? Who?"

"Some cops."

She palmed her mouth. "Sweet Jesus, will it never end?"

"They're here because of me." I shifted closer to her. "It's all right. It's nothing."

"You? Why?"

"I was caught stealing some toothpaste."

"Stealing? I don't understand, Sable." Then suddenly, as if reality caught up with her, "Why aren't you at school?"

"Just come out, please. Let's deal with the cops. It's a formality. That's all."

Less than an hour ago, I'd been nailed by a different kind of stare. Mum's kind hurt worse, broken and defeated, oozing the misery of our combined pain.

"You should be in school. I don't understand why——"

"Please, Mum, let's get rid of the cops first."

I stood, willing her to get out of bed. In two months, she'd withered away, her once curvy figure now hard angles and juts. With no hips, the pajamas slipped low on her waist, forcing her to tighten the thread.

I turned away to spare us both and headed for the cupboard. All her dresses lined the small cupboard, packed in with no room to spare. This far from the lamp, I couldn't see whether my hands found an evening gown or a light summer cocktail dress.

With the soft pads of her bare feet crossing the room, I turned to find her robed and leaving the bedroom.

"Mum."

"Hmm." She turned to me, her shoulders slumped, curving her into a C.

"I thought…" I looked at the dress in my hand, a soft blue with fitted bodice, which perhaps wouldn't fit her now, cinched waist and loose flowing skirt, something styled from the fifties Dad had adorned her in. "Never mind."

I knifed my hand through the throng of dresses and rehung what I'd taken out, then followed her out the door. In the light from the living room, funneling down the hall, I couldn't help but look at her bare feet. Gone were the manicured toenails. If the dress called for open-toe sandals, she painted her toenails the color of her dress for that special occasion or muted colors on every other occasion to match anything she wore.

The cops hadn't moved while we were away, perhaps scared they'd catch something. They both turned in our direction as we entered, eyes settling on Mum, words delayed, making me see things I normally paid little attention to now, like the deepening of the shadows below her eyes, the regrowth line down the center of her scalp like a runway covered in dirty snow. The scrutiny in their eyes became my own.

"Mrs. Wellcrest."

"Yes."

She was smaller than me and grew smaller still in this room filled with the living when she had one foot in with the dead. When had her face become so lined, her cheeks hollowed, her complexion ashen?

I should've offered to do her hair, at least, to spare her the embarrassment of her scraggly mess, which had worked loose from the braid, something I'd done for her one week ago. But she didn't look embarrassed. I'm sure she didn't even realize how she looked. Two months and she existed, nothing more.

"Mrs. Wellcrest, this is about your daughter."

"My daughter is a good girl."

The two cops shared a look, and I caught it too, the cynicism, the joke. A withered old woman in a desolate house. Two couches, one coffee table. In the kitchen, they'd find a table, three chairs, kettle, and little else.

"Mrs. Wellcrest, your daughter was caught stealing."

She bit her bottom lip as she sank to the couch, me sinking beside her. "I am so sorry. We can pay for the items." For the first time, she brushed a strand of hair flat as if, for a moment, she remembered she'd once been different to this.

"That won't be necessary as they have been returned to the shop. No charges have been laid at this point since the total of items was less than ten dollars. But it is imperative your daughter is made aware of the consequences of her actions. Had the amount been greater, we would have no choice but to take further action."

"I understand, yes," she said in a small voice. Mum had withdrawn into herself, concaving forward.

I stared at my hands in my lap, then to Mum's robe and the brown stain above her left pocket, then farther to the gaping V where the two halves of the robe crossed at her chest. In the gap, I saw the missing button on her pajama shirt, saw down to the jutting bones of her clavicle. She barely ate, no matter what I bought her.

The cops' eyes drilled Mum down. I read the insinuations, trailer trash, junky, discarded prostitute, unfit mother. What they didn't see, buried deep in the depression, was beauty. She'd always been beautiful, with a lush mane of hair, light brown when it had been natural, then a glorious, glossy dark brown after it came from a bottle.

I dropped my eyes and slumped forward. If only the couch would swallow me.

"I can assure you this won't happen again."

The cops shared a look, unconvinced because her voice lacked conviction. The robe and pajamas would not have helped, neither her wild tangles and obvious still-in-bed look at ten in the morning.

"Your daughter is forbidden to enter Dram Truckers convenience store for the next six months."

"Of course." Mum patted my knee. "She won't be needing to go back. We don't shop there."

"If she is caught shoplifting again, charges will be laid."

She nodded, clutching her robe closed with one hand, squeezing my knee with her other.

"Her name is recorded. We will be keeping an eye out for any further misdemeanors."

Like birds diving in to pick at the scraps, the cops would not relent. They'd made themselves clear after the first sentence but still they hovered around, diving in, withdrawing, diving in again, pick, pick, pick. The highlight of their day, demeaning and degrading because it made them feel better that others were so low.

"I suggest you keep a close eye on that one," the short cop said, pointing his finger at me. "Any mark against her name will affect her college admission." One side of his mouth quirked back in a smug smile as he glanced to his partner, who mirrored his expression. Said because they knew damn well I wouldn't be going to college.

Final judgment pronounced, taut silence snapped, they left us alone. When the door closed, Mum collapsed back onto the couch. I copied her and stared ahead at the surface of the table. Snuffles beside me and I looked across to see Mum had covered her face with her hands, her shoulders bouncing in rhythm to her sobs.

I took one of her hands and kissed it. "Come on, Mum, please. It's all right. We're going to be all right."

She palmed her mouth, the tears rolling over her fingers. "Your daddy wanted you to go to college."

"A job's more useful."

"Is that why you're not at school?"

I looked away, relaxed our joined hands between us on the couch. "There's no point. I'm old enough to help financially."

When she didn't respond, I looked over to see her silently crying again. "My baby," she said, snuffling her sobs back into her mouth. "You shouldn't have to do that. I've found it hard."

"I know, Mum. And it's fine. I don't blame you at all. Neither does Ajay."

"I've let you down."

"No, you haven't, not you."

"Please, honey, don't punish him like this."

"Who else can I punish? We're not the ones who did all those things. It wasn't us who killed someone."

She shook her head. "No, they are lying. All of them. Your father

16

never did those things." She clasped my cheeks between her hands, her face turning red with the tears. "He loves you, Sable."

I couldn't do this, couldn't express my fury at the man I had loved for seventeen years, not in front of Mum. No matter what the evidence showed, she stuck by him. Even when they ripped us from our home, stripped us of all our possessions, reclaimed the proceeds of crime, his supposed innocence stayed in her heart.

"How about I make you a cup of coffee?"

She nodded, unable to talk.

At the edge of the couch, I looked down on her. She looked like a child, small, fragile, and alone.

Halfway across the living room, my cell rung from inside my back-pack. Frozen, I stared down at the bag. In two months, that cell had never rung. My old life was left behind. Old friends shunned us and we weren't about to make new friends in a place like this. Who would be calling me?

The chimes stopped but still I stared down at it like the thing ticked. Curiosity won out, and I scooped my backpack off the floor and headed for the kitchen. I threw it on the table and stared at the pocket where I always placed my phone. A wrong number or sleazy sales call?

The number I didn't recognize. Whoever it was had left no message. Cell still in my hands, it chimed as the text appeared across the home screen.

Soon

J

I threw the cell down onto my backpack. It landed faceup, the message staring up at me. J? Who the hell did I know with the initial J? I backed away from the table as the cell screen turned black. Unless it was... No, that was impossible. *This will be an interesting game.* He'd said those words. *Not possible.* A stranger could not have my number.

Chapter 3

"Why are you dressed like that?" Ajay stood in the bathroom doorway.

I stared at him through the mirror. "I have a job interview."

He came in and slouched down on the side of the bathtub. "What's it for?"

"It's a clothes shop."

He rolled his eyes.

"Once I'm working, I can buy you a chocolate-coated licorice bar every day as a surprise."

"It's not much of a surprise if you've already told me."

"Treat then."

"When do you start?"

"I haven't got the job yet. But I'm confident." I spun to face him. "What do you think?"

Ajay flicked his eyes over me without much enthusiasm. "You're all right, I guess."

I headed over and ruffled his hair. "You've had breakfast?"

"Hmm."

I crouched down in front of him. "Best stay out of Mum's room.

When I get back, we'll go shopping, okay? If I get the job, maybe I'll buy you something small as a celebration."

He nodded.

"Done your homework?"

"It's Saturday morning."

"You could play in your room, or read. Just try and keep the noise down. Promise when I get back we can go to the park on the way to the shops."

He nodded again as his head dropped to stare between his knees. I lifted his face with my finger under his chin. "Give me about two hours, then I'll be back. Got it?"

"Sure."

I took his hand and pulled him up and out of the bathroom with me.

"Later," I said as I swiped my backpack from the table and headed out the door.

The bus stop was a ten-minute walk from our house, then another twenty minutes' ride. I'd be back within the two hours, but Ajay would be counting, so I'd made sure to give myself plenty of time.

Saturday morning the bus was nearly full. I spied one spare seat by the window toward the back, which meant disturbing the old guy who'd taken the aisle seat, so I decided to stand behind a woman in a paisley dress surrounded in a halo of cheap floral perfume.

The lady beat me off the bus, then bathed me in her floral perfume as we both waited for the bus to pull away from the curb. Beside me was the newsstand's bulletin board announcing the front-page news. The words 'two young teenagers' and 'mysterious deaths that defy any logical explanation' caught my eye, but before I could read any more, the bus left, clearing my way to cross.

I ducked between slow-moving cars but couldn't get a good run because of my heels. An upmarket clothes shop called for a sophisticated look, and it was good to throw on a nice outfit again.

I skipped up the curb, but my left heel caught on a crack in the paving and sent me tumbling to the side. Strong hands caught me before I hit the ground and I collided with a man's chest.

"A woman falling into your arms first thing in the morning has to be good luck."

"Sorry." I straightened out of his hold, looking up into his face. God, the new gym teacher.

"Sable, isn't it?"

"Yeah, Mr...."

"Holden." He held out his hand for a shake.

"First or last name?"

"First. My last name's a mouthful."

My first month of being a new student at Forrestfield High saw me with a detention because the old guy who was supposed to be their gym teacher took an instant dislike to me, then disappeared within the month to be replaced by Holden. Record numbers of girls turned up to participate in every gym class in Lycra rather than the school-issued baggy shorts and tee shirt.

He still held my hand from our shake. Awkward. "I better keep going." I withdrew my hand from his and bent to retrieve my snapped heel, but he beat me to it.

"Looks like a job for heavy-duty superglue."

I couldn't turn up to the interview wearing only one shoe.

"You weren't going anywhere important, I hope," he said as he held the broken heel up with a humble smile.

"Just a job interview."

"Job? Is that why I've not seen you in gym this last week?"

He was looking out for me? Nah, couldn't be. I revealed myself early in gym class as being inept in coordination, strength, and stamina, basically anything to do with sport, despite the pressure my dad placed on both Ajay and me to be the best in anything we did. For Ajay it came naturally. I was the opposite.

I shrugged because what I did had nothing to do with him.

"Will you be in gym on Tuesday?"

His point for asking was...?

Holden wore casual olive-green cotton pants and a white cotton shirt, top button left undone. His blond hair was cut short at the sides and back, with long layers on top, which were artfully tousled thanks to styling mousse. Money breathed from his cologne, a nice blend of mulled spices. In short, he looked expensive, a guy my mum and dad would've welcomed to our dinner table in that other life I once had. We didn't even have enough chairs at our kitchen table for extra people now.

I held my hand out and looked at my heel resting loose in his palm.

"You still going to the interview?"

"It's not my fault the paving needs fixing."

He chewed on his inner cheek while he weighed the heel in his palm like he was deciding if it was worth selling. "There's a party tonight—"

"You're my teacher."

"Something tells me you're not going back to school."

"I'm babysitting my brother."

"He can come."

"To a party? Hardly, he's ten."

"It's not that sort of party."

He couldn't mean it. Not really. Gym class was full of girls better-looking than me. And what about women his own age, women who were worldly and sophisticated and didn't have peeling wallpaper, cracked linoleum, and not enough seats at the kitchen table for guests? "How old are you?"

"Do I look too old?"

Too old for what?

"I'm twenty-two. Too young to be your grandfather."

I ducked my head to hide my smile. He was asking me out on a date. This was a date. I'm sure it was a date.

"It's not a date."

I flicked my eyes to his.

"Well…I guess it depends." He had a cute smile. I'd never noticed that in the few times I'd met him before. I'd also never noticed how blue his eyes were, like the deepest part of the ocean.

"Depends on what?"

"If you want it to be a date. My intention was for this to be a friendly, get-to-know-each-other night out."

"Sounds like a date to me."

"Then that's what it will be."

"No. I wasn't meaning I wanted it to be a date."

His lips twitched into a smile. "Will your brother be coming?"

"I haven't decided if I will come."

"It's at the beach. It's going to be a nice night. Bonfire, good food. I'll introduce you to some friends. If you don't drive, I can pick you up, and you'll be home before pumpkin time."

"I don't think so." No way was he picking me up from mine.

"You don't want me to pick you up?"

Does he read minds or what?

"It's not a good idea."

He fished into his pocket and pulled out his billfold, then presented me with a card. In bold block text, it read Dyno Mixed Martial Arts.

"It's my club."

"I thought you were a gym teacher."

"Fill-in gym teacher. This is my real dream. You can meet me there if you don't want me to know where you live."

I could feel the heat creeping up my neck. Damn him, he was stubborn. What did it hurt? Only getting involved with some guy wealthy enough to own a club at twenty-two, whose clothes would cost our food budget for the month, or more… Now was not the time for distraction. Or maybe it was the perfect time. "What time?"

The dip on his left cheek when he smiled could be confused as a dimple if a girl got fanciful enough. "How 'bout six? It doesn't start until eight, but I'd rather you not ride the public transport by yourself at night."

A gentleman. *Take it slow.*

"Fine, I'll see you then."

"We could exchange numbers. That way if anything happens, the other's not left stranded."

This had been his ploy all along. I recited mine as he punched it on his cell, then he phoned me.

"Done." He handed me my heel. "I hope you're successful today."

So do I. "Thanks."

I didn't look back as I hobbled away. Not until I reached the corner, then before I disappeared around, I snuck a quick peek back to see he'd disappeared. I glanced down at the card. Was it weird that he should ask me out when that was the first time we'd spoken properly? Twenty-two wasn't a gross age gap.

I slipped the card in the front pocket of my backpack, then rummaged inside for my cell. The clothes shop was across the street, yet I had fifteen minutes until my interview. Nerves made me remove my other shoe and keep walking.

At the end of the street, I was about to turn back when I saw a group of young people leaving the central cemetery. The guy in black walking alongside a woman wearing tight-as-tight denims and thirteen-inch heels—at least—caught my eye.

Jax.

He couldn't be. From this distance, I had to be wrong. I stood, transfixed, watching the three of them disappear down the street. They all wore varying shades of dark clothing, each blending in with the person beside them. This had to be the gang I'd thought him a part of, a gang of three, hardly menacing. And what were they doing leaving a cemetery, unless they were into some creepy satanic practices?

He had my number. How? No way was his sudden appearance at Dram Truckers yesterday coincidence, and the message last night a warning? *Soon.*

The smaller they became in the distance, the greater the tug in my body to follow grew. What else did this creep know about me? My address? Had he followed me? *Oh, Jesus, Ajay.* Did he see Ajay and me at the bus stop?

Soon, all right. Only sooner than he expected. I'd likely not get the job in one shoe anyhow.

By now the three of them had rounded the corner at the end of the cemetery and moved onto Barrack Street, where the rail line ran. If they planned on catching a train, I'd given them a good head start.

I ran the length of the street, shoes in hand, to the corner. The group had disappeared, across the street to the underpass most likely. The lights of an oncoming train glinted in the distance, so I legged it across the street in front of a truck and felt the wind of its passing on my tail.

The first lot of stairs I took two at a time. At the top, I grabbed the railing and swung myself around to duck back down the stairs a couple of steps. The four of them waited on the other platform, looking to catch the train heading in the opposite direction.

I headed back down and moved farther into the underpass tunnel. At the bottom of the stairs to the second platform, I waited, swallowing my pants. With only them on the platform, I had nowhere to hide.

What the hell was I doing here, back against the cold brick wall in a train underpass, chasing after a stranger, skipping my job interview like this, which should be my priority? How about finding out who the hell this guy was and how he got my number? More importantly, why me?

The low-sounding horn of another train tensed my muscles. I climbed the steps, stopping before my head drew level with the platform. Rising on tiptoes, I peered out to see the three of them had moved to the edge in preparation to board.

As the train slowed to a stop, I climbed the remaining steps. With the last of the three entering the first carriage, I sprinted across the platform, dodged a woman exiting the train, and slipped onto the next carriage along.

The train shunted away as I looked ahead through the glass window to the adjoining carriage. I couldn't see them so took the first seat closest to the door by the window. That way I could keep watch at each station in case they got off.

My pulse raced as I eased myself back into the seat. What was I doing? If I got off at their stop, Jax would see me. But why chase them if I wasn't going to confront him? I'd acted without thought and was now heading to god knows where. Ninety minutes was all I had before I should be home so as not to disappoint Ajay. I closed my eyes and banged my head back onto the headrest. I'd lost my mind.

Someone sat beside me. I looked out the window as I straightened and automatically shifted a little farther toward the window.

"What is it about us that lures you?"

Sweet Jesus.

I turned to stare into his black eyes. Too close, I leaned back, pressing myself into the corner of the seat. Like I remembered, he was good-looking, but his hard, unwelcoming expression made his features look angular and chiseled from unyielding rock rather than classically handsome.

"Excuse me?" I'd been caught, but it didn't mean I had to confess.

"You're following us. Why?"

"This is my train."

He looked ahead, releasing me from the prison of his stare. Dead-pan, nothing about his features gave his thoughts away.

"How do you have my number?"

He inched his head around to face me again. "Pretty please."

"What?"

"If you want answers, you have to say the magic words."

He had to be joking. "It wasn't a coincidence you were at Dram Truckers yesterday, was it?"

"Is that what the shop was called?" He slouched back into his seat. "Was your mum upset when you turned up in the back seat of a cop car?"

"It's a joke to you, isn't it?"

"I'm not so easily amused." By the flat press of his lips, I would agree.

"Why me?"

"Don't get excited, you're nothing special. But I want you all the same."

No way. "I'm out of here."

I grasped my backpack and went to stand, but his hand gripped on to my elbow. I jerked around to face him, wrenching my arm from his hold. "Don't touch me."

His response was another of his penetrating stares. I wanted to smack the walled look off his face and then see what sort of expression he would give me.

"You keep raising the stakes. Increasing the challenge, but in the end, Sable, you will only be as good as I allow you to be."

My name coming from his mouth had my heart freezing to its core. I had not given him my name, just like he should not know my number.

"How do you know?"

"You are important to us."

"Us, your gang."

He snorted a short, hard laugh. "Yeah, my gang." He announced the word like he thought it a joke. "I want to show you something. Are you willing?"

"Wow, you're being civil."

"Just this once. And only because I know you won't refuse."

"You arrogant asshole. I'm—"

"After answers."

"I wasn't going to be so polite, but yeah, I want answers. But I'm not going anywhere with you or your gang."

In his slouch, he steepled his fingers and eyed me over the top of the small pyramid he'd created. "I can reveal the truth for you. Unravel dark secrets."

"Being mysterious is not alluring."

"Is that what I am?"

He was impossible to have a conversation with. A brick wall of arrogance. "You're the biggest wanker I've ever met."

He huffed a laugh. "I'll message you the location."

"I'm not interested."

"What about your answers?"

"You're only saying that to get me to agree."

He leaned in close. I pushed back until I was pressed up against the window. "I really want to bust your reality apart." If a voice could be a weapon, his was the sharp steel of a blade. "Tick tock, Sable, don't waste time. It's not a luxury we have."

"You're insane."

"I wish it were true. It would be more peaceful that way." He lurched to his feet. "Don't turn your phone off."

End of warning, he headed back the way he'd come.

Chapter 4

I KNOCKED ON THE DOOR, then pushed through to find Mum standing beside her bed wearing a light sweatshirt and loose pants. "You're dressed." I stayed in the doorway, tray in hand.

"I thought I would make some dinner." She brushed at her hair, pushing the untidy mess out of her face.

I held the tray up in front of me. "I've already made some."

"Is it late? I should've come out early. What about Ajay?"

"He's eating."

"But we should sit up as a family." She patted her hair again.

"Sure, if that's what you want." I hesitated in saying the rest of what I needed to say. "But I've already eaten."

"You have."

She came over to me in the dim light of her lamp and placed a hand on my cheek. "My darling, thank you." She glanced at the tray. "It smells good."

The shock of seeing her up was replaced by a lump in my throat for all the days we'd lost her, all the small moments we'd missed while she descended into her darkness.

Mum had never experienced independence. She married Dad young once she discovered she was pregnant. He was an adoring yet domineering man who treated her like an exotic bird, albeit a caged one, and she loved it. He treated us all like that. He earned the money, made the decisions, dealt the discipline. But he was fair and giving and we'd all adored him. With him gone, the heart of our family went too, our family's foundation sucked down a black hole into oblivion.

In my heart, the love for him had turned to venom. He'd lied to us for seventeen years, pretending to be an upstanding successful businessman when really he was a crook and a murderer. I watched a stranger being led away, stripped of dignity, cuffed, sandwiched between two guards, a stranger whose face I'd seen every day of my seventeen years, a face I'd loved. As Dad became someone else, so too did we. He became the liar, the crime lord, while we became the destitute, the shamed.

Mum acted like she didn't know about everything Dad had done, but she couldn't be that naive. However, there wasn't enough hatred in me for the terrible lies told to extend to Mum as well.

"I should be eating this at the table with my children, not on a tray hiding in my room," she said as she wiped at her eyes.

This was one in a handful of times since we moved into this rental she'd pulled herself together enough to leave her room. Usually the only times were to visit Dad in jail. Visit over, the devastation would bleed her raw all over again, sink her low in the reality of our life, and suck her back under her covers. It was great to see her up, but I couldn't hold the hope in my heart that this was permanent and that she would not collapse back into her shell.

She rested a hand on my arm. "You're my sweet girl."

"I need to wash a few things tomorrow. I was thinking we could strip the beds and throw the linen in as well."

She withdrew her hand and forced a smile. "Of course. But I'll do that."

I wasn't even sure if she knew where the laundry was in this house. "Yeah, fine."

"Honey." She tugged gently on my arm, encouraging me to sit on the end of her bed next to her. "I have been so selfish these last few months."

"No, Mum. You haven't."

"Shhh." She patted my arm, forcing a wan smile. "There's no good in pretending. I have been a terrible mother."

"Not true—"

"Honey, even though I haven't acted like it these last few months, please treat me like the adult I am. You know the truth. I've let you and Ajay down. But"—she held up her hand to ward off my interjection—"things are going to change. They are. I promise." She wiped the tears. "I can't keep doing this to the two of you." The tears wobbled her voice. "This is not what your father would have wanted. He wanted you to finish school. He wanted you to be the best. It would kill him to know how we live. It's killing me too." She swallowed, then gave a sniffle as she straightened. "And so this is the start." She patted my thigh. "We're going to live as a family." She turned from me as a sudden burst of emotion choked anything else she could say. When she pulled herself together, she turned back to me. "It's going to be all right, Sable. Everything is going to be all right."

"I know it is." But I didn't. In my heart, everything was falling to pieces but in a different direction from the fall I'd felt when Dad had gone to jail. How could I have not known this man, my father? His had been a wicked betrayal, which left me questioning who I was. The daughter of a murderer. Was I as tainted as he?

The ghost of his actions would forever live with us, but he was in jail, locked away from us. If not for the visits, I could pretend he no longer existed. Not so Jax, the creep who for some reason decided to target me. He could only have gotten my number through illegal means. And what did he want to show me? Nothing I would want to see. I had to shake the guy. But how?

"I'm going somewhere tonight."

"Oh, you are?"

"With a friend." *A male teacher from my school, actually.*

"That's wonderful, darling. I'm glad to hear you've made friends. Your daddy would be happy to hear as well. Yes, of course you should go."

"Thanks, Mum." I leaned over to hug her and upset the tray but was quick enough to right it again without losing any of the food onto her lap. "I'll be back before twelve."

Her eyes flicked between both of mine. "I know you will."

Dad would've grilled me. He would've known exactly who I went with and where I was going. Mum's naivety and belief in everyone's good virtues meant she wouldn't ask.

I stood, trying to push aside the heaviness in my stomach, like an iron ball rolling down my throat and sinking everything through to my feet. I wouldn't tell her about Holden because she would tell Dad, and I would be fried under his fiery glare and made to endure a long lecture about how boys would only distract me from my potential at our next visit. But withholding the truth was a lie and hadn't we all been lied to enough?

Not a lie this time but a secret, that I was being stalked by a creep, possibly a dangerous creep, who'd gone to great lengths to get my number and now wanted to drag me into something that couldn't be legal, like my father's secret life. I would withhold this information because I had to spare her the burden of knowing. She needed to get better, stronger.

Jax wanted to force me to develop a dangerous secret life of my own, and I was powerless to stop him.

HOLDEN CAME UP BESIDE ME, in his hand an offering of alcohol to toss into the communal tub, which was what you did at these sorts of parties. I had to take his word for it.

"Ready to go?" he said to the drum of a heavy beat coming from over the sand dunes.

I walked alongside him down the narrow path to the beach, conscious of his hand hanging loose beside my own. We weren't up to holding hands because this wasn't a date, or was it? We'd not been clear. And did I want to date him? Relationships were not something I thought about. Dad had been dead against them. Apparently I needed to find my way first, establish myself in this world before I allowed myself to be distracted by someone else. And who'd want to date me now? It would mean revealing so many secrets too embarrassing to reveal. I wasn't ready to open my life up for scrutiny.

So what would happen at the end of the night? Would Holden expect a kiss? A feather touch on the cheek, or maybe the lips, at the end of tonight was probably safe enough, but definitely nothing else.

I flicked a glance at Holden, thankful the moonlight kept the heat in my cheeks hidden. While looking, I couldn't help but notice he had a decent set of lips, which flared a rapid jig of my pulse at the thought of his breath mingling with mine.

Over the shrubs and dunes obscuring the beach, the occasional flame flicked skyward, releasing a few glowing sparks. As we neared, I dropped behind Holden as the path narrowed further. Around one more dune and the party came into view.

"I thought you said Ajay could come."

This was not a child's party. A couple of Ford pickup trucks were reversed so the rear bumpers faced the fire and people lounged on couches strapped on the backs beside large speakers that pounded out a bass beat and not much else.

"I took the risk in believing you wouldn't want to take your brother out on your date."

I swallowed my inhale. So he thought this was a date?

"Fancy a drink?"

"Maybe later." No way was I heading home with alcohol on my breath.

"I'm sure I can find some soda. I'll be back."

Embarrassing, but at least he didn't seem to care. He headed around the other side of the fire to a large tub half-buried in the sand. He placed his share in the ice, then straightened and palm slapped a couple of guys hanging around the drinks.

I glanced around me, fidgeting with the ring on my finger. Everyone seemed to know someone here except me, and Holden looked comfortable laughing with some guys by the drinks tub. I sucked at starting conversations with strangers and had little experience mingling at parties thanks to Dad. At least I was hidden within a crowd of people engaged in their own conversations. A lot of the girls were dancing, dressed in slinky dresses or short-shorts and crop tops, making me look out of place in my denims.

I scanned those around me, then looked across the fire only to have my heart seize up then lurch a few rapid beats when my eyes found Jax. My throat constricted into a thin tube, making it hard to breathe.

I spun away from the fire before our eyes met, the shakes running throughout my body. Oh my god, he was here. Did he know I would be here? No, that was impossible. This was just a wild coincidence.

Using the people around me as camouflage, I dared another look. He spoke to a short, petite girl, who, from the back, looked like a child. The firelight threw shadows on his expression, making him appear to frown down at her. Given the way he'd treated me through our last two meetings, I wouldn't be surprised if he was grilling her with his unrelenting hard stare. If he was alone, I would march over and demand he give me the answers to all my questions.

"So, what do you think?"

Lost in my scrutiny, I jumped at the sound of Holden's voice.

I turned to him, wanting to erase the guy across the fire from my thoughts. "Who do you know here?"

Holden stood alongside me, turning me inches to the left with his hands on my shoulders, and I shouldn't be conscious of their size and warmth and the fact he left them there for longer than was necessary after he had me facing where he wanted me to look.

"The group of guys standing by the tub of drinks. They're regulars at Dyno. Duke, the guy with the blond hair tied in a ponytail, is one of my instructors."

With his hands still resting on my shoulders, he turned me farther to the left. "Hendrick and his girlfriend are also regulars." This time he pointed, lining his arm up with my eyes.

"Is this a Dyno Martial Arts party?"

"Not quite, but there's a few here. You should come some time."

"I know nothing about martial arts. And you must've seen how inept I was in gym."

"Firstly, no one knows anything about martial arts until they start. Secondly, ineptitude is the result of lack of discipline and training. Both of which are in your control."

"You sound like someone I know."

"He's a smart guy."

"What makes you think he's a he?"

"Am I wrong?"

"The he was my father."

He stroked his chin while he quirked an eyebrow. "Not sure I want to remind you of your father, although they do say girls grow up to marry men like their fathers."

Jesus, did he just say that? "I'm looking for the opposite."

"Father issues?"

I glanced at the fire. How did we get onto this conversation?

"Got it, drop the subject."

He scanned the fire as if looking for a few more people he could point out when his brow creased into a heavy frown. I followed his gaze to find Jax at the end of it. Jax? No, it couldn't be. There were enough people around Jax that it could be any one of them who'd made his brow furrow up in annoyance.

"Come." He took my hand. "I want to introduce you to some of the guys."

I should think of his hand taking mine and holding it firmly while he led me away, but instead I agonized over sparing one last look toward Jax. An invisible elastic stretched taut between us as Holden led me farther away. I needed to know his secrets. At the very least his reasons for pestering me, which had to be bad.

Unable to stop myself any longer, I risked another glance in Jax's direction only to see the petite woman had been replaced by another with long, flowing raven hair. From behind, her snug denims hugged her ass. Long legs stretched longer with a pair of expensive-looking high-heeled boots. Boots on a beach?

I wanted to ask Holden who they were since he so obviously knew them, but remained tight-lipped as he led me away. I'd say he wasn't keen for me to meet them.

Chatting with Holden's friends consumed a large part of the next twenty minutes. I kept quiet the whole time, having nothing to say that would fit with the conversation. Holden talked and laughed like there was nothing lurking behind us that needed constant attention, unlike me. Knowing he was there, just over the other side of the bonfire, stabbed at the back of my head.

In my periphery, I could see someone approach. I turned to see the raven-haired beauty stride our way. My breath stalled. I glanced away to hide my stare only to find Holden's eyes glued to her approach and hers likewise on him. Her mouth curved up in a killer sexy smile. The three of us were locked in this dark pantomime, although I was the spectator rather than a participator. The invisible bond that linked the two repelled me to the outside. Holden was safely ensconced within the shield of their private moment, this mysterious woman and him, with me shut out. His eyes never left her. The time ticked. She passed, maintaining eye contact with him as she went. Holden kept looking. The woman's mouth curved up into another seductive smile.

On the woman's passing, the spell broke. Holden un-paused and looked down at me as if just waking from a dream.

"You know her?" I tried to keep my voice light. I would appreciate an explanation for his behavior, but since we weren't dating for real, he didn't owe me one. More importantly I wanted to find the link between him and her, then all the way to the end—to Jax.

"That's such a long, complicated story. I can't go there right now. There's nothing between us except tortured memories."

"You didn't look tortured." I had no right to interrogate him like this.

"Shocked is the accurate word. I haven't seen Elva in some time, which is a good thing."

"If you know each other, why didn't either of you say hi?"

"The way our relationship ended wasn't conducive to warm welcomes further down the line if we ever ran into each other again."

I wanted to say something along the lines of *she didn't appear to think so* but held back. Time to stop the conversation there. Truth was, I didn't care what Holden thought about her. I didn't care about his and her relationship history. I only cared about them, or at least one of them, Jax, and if she was linked to him, then she was part of my worries as well.

Holden turned back to the group we were with and picked up the thread of the conversation as if it had never been broken.

The fire was large enough to create some sense of distance, but an invisible thread wound its way from Jax to me. Resisting the urge to look became impossible, but I feared turning only to meet the dark depths of his eyes.

Finally, the war in my head won out. I scanned the distant side of the fire to see he was no longer there. A little further searching, I found him lounging on one of the couches at the back of the truck, one leg slung over the arm rest. His expression distanced him from those gathered around. While they laughed, he stared ahead into the fire with the look of someone whose mind was elsewhere, his face an unreadable mask.

I wanted to read it, search through the thoughts that masked his hard features, and know what encased him behind an invisible wall. A series of tattoos ran the length of the back of his arm, snaking all the way down to his fingertips, much like the one I'd seen on the underside of his forearm.

After a while, he raised his drink to his lips. I followed the swallow as his Adam's apple went up and down and resisted the urge to swallow myself. A shiver ran down my spine. I remained within this dark web of fixation. I'd lied to him on the train. There was a mystery about him, a cruel mystery, probably a dangerous mystery I wanted nothing to do with but for some reason felt compelled to follow.

A distant musical laugh and my attention snapped to the woman beside him, Elva. From the back, she was a woman to make every other jealous. From the front, she was something else. A total knockout. Everything about her was perfect, from her straight nose, glossy thick hair to her plump lips and fine chin. She sat close to Jax, the sides of their bodies touching. It made sense he would have such a beautiful girlfriend. But to be his girlfriend, she would be into the same stuff as him.

I turned back to Holden, scrutinizing his profile. There was little I knew about him, but he was friendly, quick to smile, and so far seemed warm and inviting. The golden boy with an entrepreneurial flare. Dad would've loved him. Jax was the opposite. Danger oozed from every pore. A gang leader, drug dealer, or pimp, he could be any or all. I had to know why he was targeting me, make him stop. If he knew my number, he might know where I lived, and then he would know I had a younger brother, an easier target for whatever sick ideas he had in his mind. I had to talk to him.

"Can you excuse me for a moment?"

Holden looked about to ask a question. I watched the query form then slip away. "Don't get lost."

I nodded then weaved my way through the throng of people, which seemed to have grown from when we had arrived. The music continued its crazy bass beat. More women joined in dancing to the tune, while the fire crackled, sending up sparks to the clear sky. Every so often, the gentle breeze would shift, driving the smoke in a new direction. I walked through one chimney of smoke, hand over my nose and mouth, while I headed for the trucks only to see the space next to Elva vacant.

I turned to the fire, scanning the faces.

"Is it me you're looking for?"

I spun away from him. "Only because I demand answers."

"But if I gave you answers, I'd lose my leverage."

"For what?"

"You'll find out."

"I'll call the cops."

"But would you? My guess is you wouldn't want to be on their radar any more than you have been already. And if they start digging into you, what might they find?" The firelight danced in his eyes—the lair of the devil.

A coldness swept through my body. It felt like my insides were rattling through a mini earthquake. "What are you talking about?"

"Your naivety is a crime."

"I'm sick of this. I'm sick of you. If you dare threaten me, threaten my family, I will do what it takes to hurt you."

In the silence of his stare, the air between us turned to spikes.

"I don't know how much clearer I can make myself." As the quiver inside my body, ramping up my pulse, moved to the outside, tremoring my hands, I moved past him, determined to get away. I'd said more than I thought I would dare.

He snapped out his arm and latched on to my elbow. "I haven't even begun to threaten you." His low voice was laced with a deadly warning, as were his eyes, even in the golden light of the fire with his face partially shadowed as he looked away from the fire at me. There was no mistaking his intention in saying those words.

He let go, raising his hands in surrender. "Besides, it's not my intention. I only want to blow your mind."

Drugs, I knew it.

"Forget it. I'm not interested in anything to do with you." I turned to leave.

"Sable." The steady calm of his voice ran a chill down my sweatshirt. I looked over my shoulder.

"I would respond to my message favorably if I were you."

"You haven't sent me a message."

"Not yet, but I will."

Chapter 5

Mum had returned. She stood in the kitchen, showered and dressed. The miraculous change was mirrored by the fresh smell of her coconut soap and the sun shining through the kitchen window, lighting the room with its warm glow.

Her cheeks were hollow and her hair hung limp but she smiled when I entered for breakfast. The first real smile I'd seen in two long, dark months. All the same, I regarded her warily, not sure how to take this sudden turnaround. "I didn't hear you get up."

"I wanted to be quiet. Thought I would make you both breakfast as a treat."

"You don't have to."

"But I want to." She came over and placed a hand on mine. "You've held together what's left of our family long enough. It's time I became the mum again. My children need me. You need me." She swept me close. "When the police turned up the other day, it was the wakeup call I needed." Gently pushing me to arm's reach, she said, "I know you, Sable. I know you would never have done what you did if things weren't so bad." She closed her eyes. "It's all my fault."

"Mum—"

"It's all right, sweetheart. This is what I needed. The raw slap to bring me back. It will be all right now. Things are going to change. Things are going to be good." She gave me a kiss on the head, then set me free.

I slipped into one of the gray plastic chairs we'd picked up from a garage sale after we sold our more expensive dining room set for cash, and watched Mum open cupboards, looking for anything she could throw together for breakfast. Since I'd been the one to unpack our meager belongings, Mum had no idea where to look.

Giving up on the cupboards, she yanked open the fridge and peered in. There was little inside because I could only carry so many shopping bags home on the bus. "I see milk, eggs." She looked over at me with a keen grin. "Do we have flour? I could do pancakes."

Whatever she saw on my face made her smile leave. Perhaps it was nothing more than the sudden realization she was asking her daughter about what food was in the house. Her shame eclipsed her enthusiasm of moments ago.

"Cereal's fine."

Mum backed up to give me room while I whipped the cereal out from a low cupboard, then bowls and spoons to save her searching again.

"We have milk." She moved past without meeting my eyes. "At least I know that."

To help her forget the embarrassment of how little she knew about her kitchen because she'd struggled to climb out of bed the last two months, I asked her a question. "How are things going to change?"

"I'm going to get a job."

Mum had never worked before if you didn't count hosting parties, organizing gala dinners and charity auctions, or arriving looking the million-dollar wife on Dad's arm to every function they attended.

I tried not to appear incredulous. "Doing what?" I tried but it didn't work.

Mum waved her hand in the air like she was having a hard time with the answer.

"I could be a waitress…or one of those people who answers phone complaints." She sounded defensive. She blew out her cheeks because she'd run out of ideas after two. She was trying, and I was making it hard for her. Out of bed before midday was a great turnaround for her, and my interrogation would do nothing but ground down her first steps back into her life. She needed my support, not my skepticism.

"I don't know, but I'm sure I'll find something. Some of your father's old contacts should be able to help me."

"You've got to be kidding me." I'd heard her wrong, surely.

"What's wrong with that?"

"You need to ask me that? Mum, Dad's in jail because of the people he knows." And a lot more, but none of it was necessary to delve into right now. "Don't go there, Mum."

"I'm not meaning anything illegal."

"That's all those sorts of people know. They'll drag you into their world before you know what's happened."

"You don't have to worry about a thing. I can handle myself." She turned from me and busied herself with the kettle.

She was thin now, thinner than normal. Something she couldn't disguise under her dress. She looked so frail, a child in need of care from someone capable. I wasn't ready to be capable. I didn't know how to be capable, but I was the only one who seemed to be half functioning, and that's saying something since I felt like I was riding on a landslide most of the time.

"Maybe you should wait and see what Dad can do to help."

"It's too dangerous. He's already in too much trouble. They'll be keeping a close eye on him. If he's caught…" She shook her head. "No, it's up to me. I need to be responsible."

"But you don't know how to be responsible." What the hell? Where was my filter?

Dad had never left anything important up to her. To be honest, it probably had more to do with his obsessive need to be in control of everything than the little trust he placed in Mum's capability. Nonetheless, Mum had no idea how to stand in this world alone.

Mum's hand froze mid-scoop of the coffee as our eyes locked. Her expression amplified my feelings.

She was going to get herself in trouble, bad trouble, jailed, or worse, killed. Why couldn't she go back to bed? I couldn't believe I was thinking that.

I'd been numb the day strangers entered our home and carried off everything of value. Setting up home in a cheap rental, I'd shut down the emotions that didn't help, like fear, shame, and my deep well of sadness. I'd endured the humiliation of shopping secondhand for the extras we needed to make this place livable. In a short space of time, I'd learned to ignore any emotion that made me feel weak. I'd fed on my anger of Dad's betrayal and gained the strength needed to keep my remaining family going. But in the last two months, I'd never felt so caged as I did right now. I was powerless to stop Mum. There was nothing but pain on the road ahead if Mum continued on this path.

Dad could do what I couldn't. He was the only person I knew who could stop Mum's destructive determination. But there was a big hurdle to telling him. I was underage, which meant I couldn't see him without an adult accompanying me.

Before I could reply any further, a message arrived on my phone. I fished it from my back pocket, expecting it to be Holden since he'd continued with his invitation for me to visit his club on the way home last night, and I'd relented and agreed.

Saturday

I stared at the screen. Holden's name was in my phone. Had it been him, I would see his name. Instead it said unknown. Jax. He'd done as promised.

"I could walk you both to the bus stop today. How's that sound?"

I could tell by the way she drove the conversation onto safe ground she'd decided our argument finished. Not as far as I was concerned, but all I could think about was the text. Meet him Saturday for what? I should delete it, but I was too afraid of what he would do if I didn't respond.

I took a deep, shaky breath.

"What's wrong, honey?"

I jolted. "Huh…what? Nothing."

"You don't look happy. Who's the text from?"

"It's nothing. Friends. School." I shrugged then lowered my phone. "Look, Mum. We need to talk about your job idea."

She sighed and grabbed another cup from the cupboard. "There's nothing to talk about. Everything will be fine."

Dammit. She wasn't going to listen.

I glanced at the text. This Saturday. For what? I had no idea what to say to either Mum or Jax.

"Please promise me you won't do anything until we've talked some more about it."

"Honey, there is nothing more to talk about."

"Since our lives have changed drastically, I think it's time we change the way we functioned as a family, namely a democracy rather than a dictatorship."

"Sable, honey, don't be silly. I don't understand what's suddenly gotten into you."

"Fear and determination. It's amazing what they will make you do. I don't want to lose any more of my family."

Mum crumpled, that small frame of hers bowed forward from my verbal punch. When I was about to walk over and give her a hug, my phone signaled another message.

????

Impatient asshole.

"Mum, I'm sorry."

I wanted my apology to be sincere. Mum deserved that, but I was too distracted. *Damn you, Jax.*

"I didn't want to say that." I wrapped my arms around her neck, shutting out the feeling of her bones poking through her skin.

"It's all right. I have to stop pretending tomorrow will change."

"But it can, Mum. We just have to work together."

She kissed my cheek. I closed my eyes and held on for those extra few moments. When we let each other go, I headed for the door.

"Where are you going? I'm doing you breakfast."

"I'm swapping my outfit. I think the weather's going to change later on."

Clutching my phone, I evaporated from the kitchen. Once in the hall, the argument vanished as I stared at my screen. Biting my bottom lip, I typed.

Do I get to know what's happening first?

I chewed my lip some more.

No. Surprises are best.

What the hell? This wasn't a date.

Not for me, especially since it involves u. I know nothing about u.

I scurried to my room and shut the door before I dared read the next text that came through.

U'll know me in the end. Perhaps a little too well.

Oh, god, I didn't like the sound of this. He was going to sink me way deep in something I didn't want to be a part of. Perhaps I'd end up in jail like Dad.

I don't want to know u at all, so I'm going to say no until u tell me more.

Remember what I told u last night.

I leapt onto my bed and threw my phone onto the quilt so I could cover my face with my palms. This was so bad. But if I refused? How far would he go to bend me to his will? I glanced around my room, which no longer felt private. It was as though he could look out of my screen and into my heart, look into everything I held special.

I hope ur still there.

I snatched up my phone, inhaled, then typed.

Where and when?

Corner of Lincoln and Forty-Fifth Street. Eleven o'clock.

I might be there.

u better be.

Chapter 6

AJAY'S FOOT jiggled as he ran his hands over the tattered bear in his lap. Bear came to every visit, his fur now matted gray and both eyes had fallen off.

Mum sat opposite, looking in a compact mirror as she reapplied some lipstick. She'd tried her best, even pulling on one of the dresses Dad loved her in best. Why should we all strive to pretend everything was all right when he'd so thoroughly screwed any chance we had of happiness? Coming here was like playing a game, us acting out the motions and Dad having to guess the truth in our pantomime.

The plastic upright chairs in the visitors' room made the wait uncomfortable. The sterile smell reminded me of a hospital. It was as if they didn't want people around so they tried to make the whole experience unpleasant. The worst part was when they brought the dogs through to sniff for drugs. Big dogs with big black eyes, running their noses over our legs and into our bags.

The first time we came, Ajay became so frightened of the dogs Mum yelled abuse at the guard. I wanted nothing better than to shrink a couple of seats away and pretend I wasn't a part of the family. Instead I intervened to calm Mum down before we managed to get ourselves kicked out of prison. Mum apologized, flushed scarlet, and fell back into her seat. That was the start of her mental unraveling.

I spent time in every lead-up to leaving the house explaining to Ajay that the dogs were necessary for everyone's safety and had to stay, and that they were specially trained not to bite anyone, yet he still made a huge fuss about not wanting to go. Finally Dad had a private word with him about the visiting experience. Whatever he said worked.

A handful of people waited to be called through. A girl not much older than me slouched in her seat, her mouth working furiously on a piece of gum, picking her nails and looking like she wanted to be elsewhere. I understood the feeling.

I glanced at my phone to make sure Jax was not intent on pestering me any more than he had. Blank screen, good sign. Phone pocketed, I slid down into the seat, folded my arms across my chest. If only I could avoid these visits.

It had been too easy for my dad to fabricate a life. The lies became an infectious disease, fast spreading and difficult to eradicate. They flowed from his tongue with ease. The longevity of his lies would've impressed me if I wasn't so hurt and bitter.

When I was young, he would sit me on his knee and tell me stories about his trips overseas to meet prospective clients, oversee a branch of the company, or make important deals. He talked about the funny people in his business. Everyone had a quirky personality, weird habits, collected bizarre things, or owned exotic pets. The stories were designed to make me laugh, and I did, while gazing adoringly into his eyes and loving him with all my heart. He would tickle me if I dared tell him I didn't believe him, so I told him often for the love of laughing until I thought I would die, breathlessly begging him to stop.

In my mind, he created a magical world, embellished with vivid scenes. I wanted to travel with him, experience with him, be with him, and had right up until he was led from the courtroom handcuffed, sandwiched between two policemen.

Behind every smile he gave with every story he told was a wall of deceit. And now behind every thought I had of the man I didn't know was a heart of stone.

"Mrs. Wellcrest."

Mum lurched from her seat and motioned for Ajay and me to follow.

I took Ajay's hand and led him through the glass sliding door. On the other side, we submitted to yet more security checks, and as with every other time, Ajay was forced to relinquish Bear to the conveyor belt, under duress, to be x-rayed along with Mum's bag and anything else we carried. I managed to keep Ajay calm by showing him the insides of Bear on the screen, which never ceased to fascinate him. Once through, we were led to a separate building across a concrete courtyard, which would suck anyone of cheer.

He watched us enter. Seats in the spacious room were occupied by prisoners in orange and their families or friends, yet Dad managed to make himself appear the only one in the room. A broad grin broke across his face as Mum ran into his arms. The guards fidgeted and shifted their weight while nailing my parents with uncompromising glares. Ajay galloped after Mum and I followed with my head down, casting surreptitious glances at the others in the room, who were staring at my parents.

Dad knew not to hug me. He emerged from his embrace with Mum and Ajay, each still on either arm, and stared at me. There was my family, and then there was me, standing on the other side of the table. Two months ago, I would've been the first demanding the hugs. Now I was the interloper. I hated him. More so, I hated the feeling of my heart cleaved in two. I glanced away, pretending the people a couple of tables down were more interesting to look at. While I was raw, I couldn't look at him. He would read it, would know rejecting him hurt me. And I couldn't let that happen because this place was not punishment enough.

Dad released me from his stare and turned to Mum.

"How you doing, babe?"

"So happy now I'm here." Mum worked her way back into his embrace, standing on tiptoes to wreathe her arms around his neck.

After squeezing her tight one more time, Dad peeled Mum's arms away and sat down on one of the small plastic seats. He wanted Mum in his arms, but the guards would likely approach and demand, in not-so-quiet voices, they keep contact to an acceptable minimum.

Dad slung his arm around Ajay's neck and pulled him in for a rough hug and ruffled his hair. Ajay scrunched up his eyes and giggled. I slid onto a seat opposite, because if I remained standing, everyone in the room would look at me.

"How's school? You being a good boy?"

He nodded his head and cuddled Bear.

"Is Bear helping you get ready in the morning and helping you get to school by yourself?"

Again Ajay nodded and buried his face in the mangy fur.

"Ajay's become so independent. He makes his own bed, helps Sable with the lunches, takes himself to school."

Mum and Dad entwined hands. He ran his free hand through Ajay's hair again.

"I'm glad to hear." He glanced down at Ajay with unmistakable feeling.

I looked at the table. I didn't want to see any emotions on his face.

"And how's my girl?"

I stared into his eyes and managed a shrug. Mum sat on the right side of him, radiating tension.

"School going well?"

"Uh-huh."

This was the part I hated the most. He didn't deserve to have Ajay's continual devotion or still hold a piece of my heart, and I hated him for being able to tap into that rogue piece sequestered deep inside and pull it out whenever I was with him. I didn't want to feel anything but anger. All those feelings, like guilt, longing, and affection, kept the link between him and me alive.

In the beginning, I wanted to believe it was a mistake. I swallowed everything Mum and Dad said to me and raged against those who tried to pin the lies on him for revenge, or had the excuse been jealousy? I couldn't remember now. It took eight months, total invasion of our lives, and exhaustive investigations before the noose was tightened and neither Mum nor Dad could pretend anymore. Then the money disappeared, next the possessions, the house, everything that had made our home, including Dad. And the good emotions went too, sucked down the dark abyss that now encompassed my life.

"Concentrating on your schoolwork, maintaining your good grades. It's an important year, honey. Got to make it work for you."

I nodded my head. "Uh-huh."

Mum intervened by leaning forward and taking his attention. "I don't know what I would do without Sable. Truth is, baby, I've been struggling a bit with everything that's happened. Sable has stepped in and kept the family functioning." She glanced around and gave me a pained smile. "My girl." She gave my hand a squeeze.

"She's doing well at her new school. She has new friends and her teachers are impressed with her grades."

Mum did this when we visited. I had little to say, so she filled the silence and my grunts with the answers to Dad's questions. The first time we returned from a visit, she burst into tears, then demanded to know why I wouldn't speak to my father. With the deceit still raw, I couldn't answer. Mum yelled at me for being hateful and cold, then ran to her room. I disappeared into mine and cried until my wet pillow couldn't hold any more tears. Later that night, she crept into my room and cried a heart-ripping apology, asking me to find some forgiveness for him.

I couldn't. Not yet, maybe never. Beaten down, Mum no longer asked me to pretend my feelings and instead tried to fill the gap created from the love I'd withdrawn.

"That's good to hear. You can't go messing up this year, sweetheart. It's important. What happens from here will decide your future. And I want to see my girl going places. I want you to have choices."

He slid his hand across the table but stopped when he almost reached me.

"Thank you for being there for your mother and Ajay. It's important you all stick together. I'm not there to back you up, so you need to be there for each other."

I wanted to shut my ears to any kind words, but the lure of his gentle tone sucked me in. I was broken like my world, torn apart by conflicting needs; I wanted my dad back but he needed to know how much he'd destroyed me.

"Of course."

He smiled. "That's my girl."

He swept Ajay into another neck hug and kissed him on the head.

"So you coping financially? I'm doing everything I can from in here to try and lighten things a bit for you. It's taking time though. I've still got contacts willing to help out."

"No, baby, you shouldn't. I don't want you in any more trouble. We're doing fine. I'll look for work. Once Sable finishes school, she could also help out with the money."

"I don't want my girls working some diner to bring money home for the family. Give me time. I'll make sure you get enough flowing your way."

Mum pursed her lips and frowned but said nothing, instead played with his hands, which still rested in hers. She turned one over and ran a finger down the tattoo on his wrist, absentmindedly trailing the swirl like she'd always done.

Dad pinned me with a hard look. I knew what was coming, what always followed a look like that.

"You keeping away from boys?"

I rolled my eyes and sighed.

"Oh, yes, Sable's not interested in boys. She's home every day after school and focuses on her homework."

As if hoping to pluck the truth right from my brain, Dad continued to eyeball me. While staring in his eyes, I realized one thing; I was like him. The magnitude of my lie was nothing compared to his, but a lie all the same. Seventeen years and I'd never thought, never dared to hide anything from him.

"Who would want to be stuck with a girl whose dad's a criminal?"

He didn't even flinch at my jibe. Faced with his uncompromising wall of strength, I retreated an inch and sat back in my seat. To shy away from the force that was his will, I glanced around the room to a sea of orange, most with only one visitor. Dad was unique in having three, which made him seem loved. The gum-chewing girl slouched four tables down, still staring at her phone. I glanced across to the guards, sentinels at the door, eyes forever scanning for any misbehavior or rule breakers.

Dad's movement drew me back to our table, to him sitting opposite me, to his determined stare, then to Ajay and the solemn expression I saw on his face too frequently now.

"I mean it, Sable. Boys will only mess with your future. Keep focused, and know what's important."

Hands withdrawn from Mum's hold, he leaned over the table, reducing the distance between us, and for the first time, I noticed the strained look in his eyes, the tightness in his jaw. Dad had always held an aura of serene dominance. Ajay and I had learned young there was no getting around him, no fighting back because we were bent to his indomitable will. Ruling his family like a benevolent dictator, determined and unrelenting but fair and loving, made it easy to relent. I'd never seen stress mar his handsome face. I guess jail would screw anyone's equilibrium.

"I want so much for you. I want you to want the world. Don't get lost in something that will only bring you down."

I blinked, swallowed my breath, glanced away. The orange prison overalls became a dot pattern to my unfocused eyes. The relevancy of his words to my current predicament dragged a hot spear down through the center of my being. I was too shocked, too afraid to muster the courage needed to match Dad in his death stare, the one he used to force his will on me, perhaps even those within his crime world, the same he also used on his enemies, no doubt.

Too late, Dad. Too late. I was already lost. Jax would drag me into something I couldn't escape from. I just knew it. He was going to bring me down.

Chapter 7

WITH HANDS IN POCKETS, I jiggled up and down on the corner of Lincoln and Forty-Fifth to keep myself warm. I pulled my phone from my pocket to check the time, five to eleven. A bus passed, blowing my hair from my face as it went. Once it was gone, I saw him on the other side of the street, standing by the streetlight with his hands in his pockets, looking at me. How long had he been there? He neither waved nor made any indication that I should join him, just stared, still and quiet. Fine, if he wanted to play like that, I would stay put and make him cross to me. He didn't move, of course. He stood like a statue, staring at me.

"Stubborn asshole. Fine, it will only end once I go through with this." I stepped off the curb.

"What's this all about?" I said once I joined him on his side of the street.

"Anxious to start?"

"Anxious to get away from you."

He leaned against the pole behind him and folded his arms across his chest. "I like your honesty. In fact, I've been surprised by you so far."

"How could you be? You don't even know me."

"But I do. I know more than you think."

His arrogant confidence reminded me of Dad. It had been something I'd admired in him because, from my innocent point of view as a child, it appeared as if he was in control of everything.

"How about we get over the creepy innuendo and finish this?"

"At some point soon, I'm going to remind you you said that."

And I'd been so foolish to hope this would be a one-off meeting. "We'd better get on with it then."

He pushed off from the pole and led me down the street. "It's only a short walk."

"To where?"

He had long legs. When he got a pace going, I had to speed to keep up, not to mention this was the busy part of town, and the Saturday shoppers were in an equal hurry to get their bargains. I had to dodge the greedy while he seemed to sail through on a direct path.

"You know the Adolphy Tower?"

"Of course."

"There's your answer."

"We're heading to an apartment block?"

"You sound disappointed."

"Totally. Do you own an apartment there? I'm not going to your apartment."

"Nothing so mundane. No, we're heading for the roof."

"Now I'm worried."

"Good. Fear builds anticipation. Sharpens your senses, makes you alive."

"Great, an adrenaline junkie." And a drug addict and probably into really bad things.

"That's for kindergarten. What I do is so much better."

The Adolphy took up a large portion of the square corner from Forty-Fifth and Mayfair. Home to some of the most exclusive apartments in the city. The rooftop gardens were a well-known feature and popular tourist destination up until four years ago when the wealthy decided they'd had enough of people stomping all over their private garden and put a petition together banning non-apartment owners from stepping foot on the roof. The city mayor was quick to agree since most who owned the apartments effectively ran the city with their big political campaign payments and the like.

He pressed buttons and the door clicked open.

"Can I ask how you got the code?"

"No."

The inside of the tower was more impressive than the rumors—marble, pillars, polished everything so that you saw your reflection in all the surfaces. Giant pots, bigger than our bathtub, were filled with miniature ecologies of their own, and in the center, a huge mermaid spouted water from her open mouth into a pool the size of our whole house. I was stalled by all I saw, so Jax left me behind as he hiked it across the open space to the lifts.

Confined inside the lift, a fresh blend of woodlands and citrus spices permeated the air, a pleasant smell if not for the person who wore the cologne. I shut out the distraction and watched the numbers climb rapidly to thirty, pretending to be fixated while casting a surreptitious glance sideways at Jax, who leaned against the wall of the lift, watching me. Caught out. I resumed my number counting, conscious of his eyes on me. The unreadable mask of his face made it impossible to know what went through his mind while he stared at me.

Unable to stand being a deer in the headlights any longer, I found my courage, turned to him, and asked the first thing that came into my head. "They have any meaning?" I nodded to the tattoo on the inside of his left forearm.

"Yes."

I rolled my eyes. "And that's it, huh? I don't get any more. You're really one for great conversation." The digital numbers were more interesting.

"It's my guide when all is lost."

"Sounds significant."

Up close, the ink was more than squiggles. The design looked intricate. A good tattoo artist put it there.

He pushed off the wall, ignoring me, and looked at the lift doors. "It could end up being the difference between life or death."

The doors slid wide to an empty corridor.

I followed him out. "Are you trying to be Zen?"

He looked back at me. "I wouldn't know how."

Before he went any farther, I had another question. "And what does that one mean?" I pointed to a tattoo on the inside of the right wrist, one I'd not seen before.

"My enslavement."

"And the one behind your ear?"

"You have been studying me closely."

I turned away from his smug smile.

"It's a symbol of my strength, courage, and loyalty to my family."

"Wow, you really have some strange symbolism going on with your ink."

"What's the point otherwise?"

"I don't know, pretty pictures. Some people like the idea of using their body as a canvas."

"I draw for meaning, not pleasure."

"Whoa. You did those?"

"Only this one." He trailed a finger along the design snaking its way down his left inner arm. He turned his right wrist over. "I would never have chosen this one."

Jax headed down the corridor, leaving me to watch him depart. At the end was a door. It was quite possible that, when I passed through the door, I would never be able to turn back. Behind me the lift slid shut with a gentle *whoosh*. Jax stood with his hand on the door, looking at me, waiting for me to follow.

Something weird was going to happen. I couldn't put the feeling into words, but goose bumps ran along my back. I lost my traction. This was a terrible idea. *Get back in that lift.* But I couldn't. No matter that a sixth sense told me I would soon regret this day, my feet moved, one after the other, and carried me to him. He neither smiled at my acquiescence nor frowned in impatience at how long it took. He waited like he had all the time in the world.

Out in the day, I stopped in my tracks. This was not the rooftop garden I'd expected that had brought all the tourists, no flower beds, edible greens, or topiaries. Instead, looming from one end of the tower to the other was a huge hedgerow at least seven feet high. The magnitude astounded me. Perhaps not for something grown on the ground, but thirty stories in the sky, it was a dazzling feat of horticulture. A plane flew overhead, a mere speck as a backdrop to the giant wall of green.

"They never mentioned this in the tourist brochures."

"I'm sure the residents think of it as the eighth wonder of the world. Come, I've got something more to explode your mind."

No den of drug dealers up here.

We headed left to the edge of the tower. Up close, the hedge appeared as though the gardener used a ruler to measure the symmetry. Not a leaf or a branch ventured out of place. At the end of the row, which happened to be the edge of the building and a waist-high brick wall, Jax stuck his hand through the leaves, feeling for something. A clunk like a latch drawn and a part of the hedge transformed into a door.

"The surprises just keep coming."

"We're only getting started." He winked at me. The suddenness, coming from him, made me feel like I'd just been slapped. People winked when they were being nice, not threatening. This whole exercise was a threat. There was no innocence or fun in why he brought me here. And the last thing I would believe was a flirting Jax.

I stepped through the living door and was brought up short by a wall of green about a meter in front of me. Left and right, plus towering above, more hedgerow. The only thing not green was the concrete beneath my feet and the gray clouds drifting across the sky, which had the strange effect of washing the color from Jax's face, and mine too, no doubt, making him look like some nightmarish walking dead.

"What's this?"

"A maze."

"You've got to be joking. How big is it?"

"As big as the dimensions of the tower."

"What's it here for?"

"Fun. I guess the residents get bored playing with all their money and come up here to lose themselves for a while. The roof is made up of slates. Each slate grows a certain number of hedges. These can be slid around like Rubik's Cubes to create new corridors, which means the maze can be recreated over and over. Ingenious."

"How often do you come here?"

"Once I found it, a lot in the beginning. Now the novelty has worn off. But I like bringing greenies, like yourself, here."

"Greenie? Greenie at what?"

He walked backward. "So this is the idea. We're going to race each other to the middle."

"You brought me here to play a game of chase?"

"No, but that's how it starts."

I should've known that wink of his was not because he suddenly wanted to play nice.

"What's in it for the winner?"

"You agree to follow me."

"No way. I'll follow you nowhere."

I looked for the smirk in his smile and surprised myself in not seeing one, but neither was his smile warm or inviting. Nothing about him was warm or inviting.

"When I'm finished with you, you won't be able to back away."

I spun around, looking for the exit. All I saw was green. "How do I get out of here?"

"By playing the game."

"What if I don't want to play?"

"There are no choices."

"This is childish."

"No, this is the beginning. You have to follow through to the end."

How stupid was I? A lump welled in my throat, impossible to swallow. I clenched my fists as I stared at his perfect face, imagining the spot where my fist would meet his flesh.

"Once I play your stupid game, I'm out of here."

There was the smirk. I clenched my fists harder. All it would take was enough courage and conviction to kick him in the nuts, but I still would not find the exit.

"Like I said, Sable, this is the beginning of the game."

"You're going to cheat."

"I'll give you a hint. If you go that way, you'll head in the right direction." He pointed in the opposite direction to where he was going.

"How do I know you're telling the truth?"

"You don't. But you'll soon find out."

"That's not enough. I want a head start as well."

"I'll give you two minutes before I move."

"And I have to trust you on that as well."

"You have trust issues. That's good."

I hard stared him, hating the sight of him. I turned and ran. Maybe this was the wrong way, but by now I didn't care. He'd probably spent all morning memorizing the maze. Besides, what choice did I have?

I ran down a green corridor, around a hedge, only to find yet more green, another long corridor. Halfway along and I had a choice of two more directions to follow. Nothing looked promising, so I ducked left and kept jogging. The more turns I made, the farther I tunneled into the maze, my problems compounded. Everything that had happened the last two months licked at my heels. I increased my pace, my breath laboring. With each turn, each dead end, I felt like I buried myself deeper and deeper until I could almost feel the dirt and grit running down my throat.

I gasped a sob and staggered to a stop when a rustle came from close by, just the other side of the hedge. The hard sawing of my breath drowned the subtle noise. Did it mean he was a hand's reach away on the other side of the hedge? I inched over and tried to peer through, but the hedge was too thick for me to see.

Behind me, another crunching of leaves. Was this me wasting time? Or it could be a false lead, taking me away from the center. Cheating would be his primary goal. Lying, cheating, luring me into his twisted reality.

I rounded another corner only to see more green. This was some maze. Why couldn't I hear him? I had to be making a racket with my boots slapping the concrete while I ran. Perhaps he was already there standing in the middle because he'd cheated.

I got to the end, turned into another corridor that looked exactly the same. Was I going in circles? Hard to tell as I didn't even know which compass point I headed in. The end of another corridor and more choices, both equally likely.

Dammit. What a stupid game. Everything was the same green and gray. No variation to give me a hint at where I'd been or where I was going. How long had we been at this?

"Jax." Silence. "I want a clue. I'm going in circles here. I'm sure of it."

His voice came across the hedge. "If I give you a clue, it means you lose."

"It's not fair. You've done this before."

"You're willing to give up so easily?"

"I'm not giving up. It's only fair you give me an even chance."

"I would've pegged you for a girl with tenacity."

"I don't care what you think about me. I just want out. If you have something to show me, just do it, get it over with."

"You really shouldn't be in such a hurry. Frustration's part of the game. Learn to deal with it, push through, and become better." Christ, now he sounded like Dad.

"What if I just stand here and refuse to move?"

"Come on, Sable, you're disappointing me."

"Good, you can go find someone else more stimulating. I'm not interested in your games."

"I'm not interested in what you want. You must've realized that by now."

No surprise there. "And you have nothing better to do with your time than play these stupid kids' games. Great life that must be."

That brought me silence. What was better, the annoying banter or being cut off from the one connection to my escape?

"Follow the hedge to the end and turn right."

"Is this you helping me or leading me farther into the maze?"

"Do you trust me?"

Here we go again.

I did as he told me. "And what happens when I turn right?"

"You're going to come to another turn halfway down on your left. I want you to take that."

I obeyed. As I was nearing the end of the left turn, he instructed me to turn left again. A few more turns and I saw the waist-high brick wall at the end of the green corridor.

Stepping out of the hedgerow, I found Jax standing on the brick wall, on the other side of which was a thirty-story drop to the streets below. I stalled walking toward him, as if getting any closer would push him off.

"Should you be up there?"

59

As a taunt, he walked along the top. The wall was wide enough but that didn't stop my throat from constricting.

"Depends on your faith in your ability." He crouched and beckoned me over with a finger. "You've lived a very sheltered life, Sable."

An invisible wall descended between us, the crazy on one side, the terrified on the other.

"At least I know where my boundaries are."

"Do you? The problem with living a sheltered life is you never learn how good you can be."

"Ditto if you're dead."

"At least you tried."

"I'm not okay with that. Seems like a waste to me."

He straightened and began to walk again. I closed my eyes, unable to watch.

"You must have the maze mapped in your head if you managed to get me out." Distracting him seemed the best thing to do. I wasn't sure how far he was willing to take this...whatever he was doing, but I didn't want to be responsible for any reckless behavior.

"I wonder, how far would you be willing to go?"

"All depends on the risk versus the reward." His question did nothing to settle my nerves.

"Walking on this wall for a little fun."

"No way. Poor reward. Besides I'm afraid of heights."

"Crossing the tracks when a train's coming."

"I think I've done that one before."

"Directly in front of the train."

"What's the reward?"

"Admiration from everyone watching."

I snorted a laugh. "Sounds like a testosterone rush to me. I know I'm courageous when it counts. I don't need a group to tell me that."

"Russian Roulette?"

"You're freaky."

"How about killing someone to save your brother's life?"

My brain scrambled up. An ice swept through my body, leaving me shivering and faint.

His eyes implored me for an answer, as if it meant life or death.

"How do you know I have a brother?"

He shrugged and paced a couple of steps forward. I stared at his leather boots, willing them to stay steady, stay one foot in front of the other, and not to deviate.

"I make a habit of knowing things."

"You can leave him out of this." My words were injected with heat and came out forceful.

He barked a laugh. "You're protective of your brother. That's good. But don't worry. I don't mean anything by it. I would like to meet him sometime."

"Why?" Still with the steely tone. No one was allowed to mess with my little brother, certainly not someone like Jax.

"I had a younger sister."

"Had?"

"Yes, had."

As if someone had pricked me with a pin, my anger fizzled out. "I'm sorry."

He turned his back on me to stare out over the city skyline, his boots less than half a foot from the edge and a thirty-story drop below. "You never answered my question."

"Remind me what it was."

He turned to face me so his back was to the city behind, which made me feel sick. One accidental step back or wobble and he would be gone.

"Can't you come down?"

"You haven't answered my question."

"I forgot the bloody question."

He narrowed his eyes as he studied me. "You could last longer than I've predicted."

"I thought you were a mystery. Now I think you're insane."

"A mystery? You're closer to the truth with insane. But the right sort of insane. The sort that ensures survival."

"You need professional help."

"How far would you be willing to go? That was my question."

You're sick, you're sick, you're sick. But his eyes were sane. Intense, scary, but sane. I'd never felt someone's presence more, never been so acutely aware of their proximity and body language, never wished more for them to be gone but mentally begged them to stay, stay standing away from the edge, stay unmoving so they didn't fall.

"Not very far. Answer good enough for you?"

"Not in the least. Sometimes you don't have a choice. You gotta keep moving as fast as you can, as far as you can go, if you want to make it out alive."

He took a step back. Not enough to send him over the edge but enough to make me nearly wet my pants. "Jesus, what are you doing?"

"You've got to learn how to push the boundaries, Sable. Got to learn how to be the best. There's no guarantees, no safe ground. Only those who make a slave of their fear win."

"Jax, I don't like this. Please, just come down. This is officially turning into the worst time of my life."

He shook his head. "You'll look back on this day and realize it was the day your life began."

With that, he lifted his arms out to each side, arched his head back, and fell, a perfect backward dive.

Chapter 8

I was stone, but my heart still beat, a furious thumping rhythm. Breath frozen in my throat, palm covering my mouth, I stared. I couldn't even blink, nor turn away. My body would not carry me forward to the edge, backward to escape.

He'd done it. He had, hadn't he? That's what just happened. I wasn't dreaming? I wasn't in an altered state? I wasn't mentally insane? He'd jumped. He'd jumped.

Time condensed into one breath. I stared ahead to where his boots had been, standing over a crack that ran like a fissure across the brick work, to where he'd stood, now empty except for the skyline of buildings behind. The plane crossing the sky seemed to hover, suspended along with time, along with my breath, while my pulse thrashed through my veins in a torrential rush.

When my legs gave out, I collapsed into a crouch, arms wrapped on head, head between knees. *No, no, no,* that had not happened.

I hugged myself tight, a wall against the inevitable, the truth, then lurched forward onto my knees, palms slapping the concrete as what was in my stomach wanted out. It managed as far as halfway up my throat before I swallowed to clear the obstruction. An ant darted over my hand in a frenzied rush. I closed my eyes and felt the tickle of its movement, felt the tremor in my hands spread throughout my body. I opened my eyes and pushed back to my heels, raised my hands to watch them shake.

Another glance at the wall and I was still alone, abandoned. He was gone. It was the truth. He'd jumped. Time had not rewound, giving me a second chance to stop him.

I made myself stand, which took enormous effort because my legs refused to respond. The frozen fear of what I would find thawed from my body. When I started moving, time would no longer remain suspended. I would have to face the fallout.

Face it.

I closed my eyes and gave myself the leisure of two big breaths before I headed for the corridor and the lift that would take me down. Up here I was sheltered from the devastating aftermath that would no doubt be unfolding on the streets below.

Was this what he wanted? All his taunts. He meant to do this? Commit suicide in front of a stranger? *Blow my mind.* But not like this, surely? But why had he done it? And why in front of me? I was nothing to him. I didn't even know him, so why commit his final act in front of me? But perhaps I wasn't a stranger. He'd known about Ajay, which meant he'd bothered to delve into my life. Maybe, unbeknownst to me, there was kinship through tragedy.

The maze proved a problem again, but I managed to win free. Unlike the time coming up in the lift, I willed the digital numbers to slow down, but of course, they didn't. When the doors opened at the bottom, I remained inside until they began to close. I pushed the button to open them again and told my feet to move.

The cars passed like they did every other day. I looked up and down the street, then jumped out the way of a guy staring at his cell screen instead of where he was going. He apologized, but I had no words for him, only a vacant look. He passed, giving me the weird eye, which said he thought I was on drugs.

No sirens. No major emergency. I walked to the corner and looked down the street. Nothing. No crowds of people. No ambulance.

I headed back the way I'd come and saw him leaning against a bus sign. His pose nonchalant, as if a wayward street kid looking for trouble.

He eyed me with a wicked smile. The sort of smile that led to a wink and promise of more to come. I marched up to him with a scrunched fist and punched him in the jaw.

My fury obliterated the street and everyone in it; we could've been the only two left in the world, which meant it didn't matter who watched our unfolding drama and thought me a violent psycho. My knuckles smarted from the impact, but to hear the *thwack* and see his head snap to the side gave me an immense sense of satisfaction.

"Bastard. How dare you."

I spun to leave but he caught my arm and pulled me back. My body tensed as I shook his hand off.

"Don't, Sable."

I got right in his face. "You jumped from a thirty-story— How is this possible? Tell me. How are you here?" I didn't want to be this close, not now, but I was furious and confused and desperate for a logical answer.

"Illusion?"

I jammed my hands on my hips. "I don't want to be a part of your sick and twisted games. I'm out of here."

People in the street looked at me. Generated by a human form of rocket fuel, I was immune to anything embarrassing.

"Hang on." He tried to grab my arm again.

I lifted it out of his reach. "Leave me alone."

He held up his hands in surrender. "Okay, maybe it was a little over-the-top, but I have your attention."

I stared into his black eyes, looking for some sanity.

"You wanted to cross boundaries. Well, you just did. Hope you're feeling great."

"That's quite a fire you have in you."

"This is a game to you. Jesus." I closed my eyes and ducked my head, scrambling to find the right words, but the turbulence of my emotions messed with my thinking. There was nothing I could say that would change what he'd just done. "I don't care. Not anymore. What-ever you're trying to prove, I want nothing to do with it."

"Do you want to know how I'm still alive?"

"No." Dear god. "Did you slip me a drug? Is this a hallucination?"

"This is reality. Your reality now."

"It just keeps getting worse. Listen to what comes from your mouth. I don't want anything to do with you. I'm only interested in people who choose to care about the life they have."

He stepped closer, releasing the gravity of his stare, which felt stronger than a black hole's pull. "You have no idea how much I care about my life." There was everything scary about his tone. "I care about a lot of things, perhaps more so than you." The sincerity in his eyes held me captive.

The weight of my mood thinned the air and darkened the day. Why did I feel I was spiraling into a black hole with no end apart from one of Jax's making, that there was nothing more substantial than the sort of games he offered, and I had nothing within me to pull me away?

I looked away as my emotions boiled in my chest, threatening to rise up and engulf me.

"Your future's set now, Sable. I can give you answers."

"I don't want answers. Not anymore."

"I wish you would recognize that you have no choice. You were always going to end up here."

He pushed off the sign, brushed past me—"Let's go"—and headed off down the street.

"I'm not following you, Jax," I yelled after him.

"Think smarter, Sable. Think of your family."

The comment was a fist to my stomach. I rushed after him. "Are you threatening my family?"

"Never, if you come with me."

He was right. The understanding gouged a hole in my heart. What-ever mystery followed Jax, it would not relent, he would not relent, until he had me where he wanted me. Ajay was his guarantee I played nice, became his docile pet. And I would. I had to until such time as I under-stood who he was, what it was he wanted from me, what sick fantasy regarding me he'd created in his mind.

We caught a bus the next block down, Jax paying for us both. I gave no attention to where we were going because my focus was on him, without appearing to be focused on him. After the horrible shock of his jump, I felt flat, like my energy had been sucked away. The whos and whats were too many, the fear too great.

"This is our stop."

Twenty minutes had passed as we'd moved farther out of the city and into the old light industrial area, now transformed into a trendy suburb. Not the place I expected him to live. The warehouses remained but were refurbished into modern apartments, using mixed materials: wood, steel, and brick. With a new paint job and streetscape, meaning ample road-verge gardens, the developers increased their revenue and residents needed a bank vault of money to buy. So, what was Jax doing here?

An elderly man gazed up at us as we exited. He glanced over me and fixated on Jax. His eyes then followed the long tattoo down Jax's arm. A frown revealed his thoughts—a guy all in black, ink down his arm, tousled, messy hair, another useless piece of street trash. I wanted to think the same, but there was more to Jax than the surface.

Once the bus passed, Jax crossed the street, heading for the warehouse opposite. At the door, he punched in a code and, with the click of the lock, yanked it open.

"You live here?"

"Surprised?"

"I had you under a bridge somewhere."

"Sorry to disappoint."

I stalled. "I'm not going inside."

"You came all this way to refuse at the door?"

"I thought being on the roof of the Adolphy was uncomfortable enough. Now I'm not so sure."

"We won't be alone. The rest are inside."

"That's even worse."

"You want to get home to your family, don't you? Your mum will be wondering where you are soon. Maybe she already is. Your brother will be wondering too. Ajay, right?"

"You asshole." And he never included my father in the list of worried people.

"I just need a little of your time. To talk. Answer questions. Nothing bad is going to happen. I promise."

I glanced down the street and saw no escape, no hiding place Jax could not reach, so ducked under his arm into the foyer and followed him across to the lifts as the door shut behind us with a click. With the sound, I thought about prison, no escape and sealed fates.

The lift ride was over too soon.

"They won't bite."

I frowned at him. "I never said anything."

"You don't need to. Your body language is doing all the talking. That and the fact the lift doors have been open a couple of seconds now and you've been staring out but not moving anywhere."

Get it together, girl.

Jax led me into his apartment. I stood in amazement at the room such that the lift doors shaved my ass on closing. We entered into a spacious place, craning high with a huge vaulted ceiling, disappearing into the sky because of the skylights. A black steel banister segregated the mezzanine, which ran the length of the room, from the floor below. Comfortable couches, bean bags, and all manner of other cozy furniture littered the space. The punching bag in the corner was perhaps for those fed up with lounging around. With the discarded clothes and enough empty wrappers and drink bottles, the age category of the occupants was indisputable. But the rich aroma of something good baking was more in keeping with a family home.

"I thought you said the others were here."

"Elva," Jax yelled as he headed for the kitchen, an impressive display of brick, stainless steel, and granite, tucked in under the mezzanine. "You want a drink?"

"No."

He seemed relaxed, happy, in direct contrast to how he'd been so far.

Elva stuck her head over the banister. "What do you want? Uh-huh...I see."

That *I see* had to be referring to me, and the manner in which she said it didn't sound much like *oh, goody, a friend.*

She glided down the stairs one step at a time, slow and calculating.

"Holden's girl. My, my, my, aren't you naughty."

I wasn't going to bother correcting her.

She sauntered across the floor in yet another pair of stunning leather boots, looking like she'd been poured into her pantsuit. She eyed me all the while, taking in my jeans and shirt.

"I don't suppose Jax has bothered to tell you?" She looked sideways at Jax, who was busy cracking the lid on two cans,—even though I'd refused a drink—to involve him in the conversation.

"I can't say since I don't know what you're alluding to."

Elva looked down at me—without the heels she would be at least six foot. As if my comment was a call to arms, she squared on to me. "Jax and Holden are enemies. They hate each other." Her smile was shockingly seductive. "Which makes this"—she waved a hand dismissively at me and Jax—"kind of funny, don't you think?"

She sauntered a little closer, bringing her exotic perfume with her, mandarin and clover blended with other warming spices.

"Oh, dear. What are you going to do now?"

Jax came up beside her. "I think it's enough." He handed me one of the cans, winked, and said, "Don't worry. I won't tell."

Elva rested her elbow on Jax's shoulder. The heels brought her up to his height. "You won't, but maybe I will."

He moved away from her. "Cut it out, Elva." He motioned with his head for me to follow. "She won't. I'll see to it." Then he smiled. "Trust me."

It didn't really matter to me if she did. The two of them were still working with the false assumption Holden and I were an item. All the same, her snarly attitude made me uncomfortable. I didn't want to be here any more than she wanted me here.

"I think I should go."

He spun and stopped dead in front of me. "Why?"

He looked over my shoulder and frowned. "Time to leave, Elva."

I turned to catch Elva's smirk, which she didn't bother to hide.

"Sure. Anything you say, boss. It's too late now, though. Nothing will make it easier for her. You should know that."

Jax sighed. "Just go, will you?"

She spun and sashayed her way across the floor. At the lift, she grabbed a jacket that hung from iron hooks to the left. The smirk had yet to leave her mouth and she bestowed plenty of it on me before the doors enclosed her inside.

"Sorry about that. Elva's...Elva. There's not a lot more I can say." He headed over and threw himself into one of the slouch couches and slung a leg over the side. I stood, not wanting to get comfortable.

He watched me for a moment before taking a swig of his drink then sitting forward. "You want explanations, I guess?"

"It's the only thing that would stop me from leaving."

"So where do I start?"

"Is what Elva said true?"

"Yes."

"How do you know Holden? Why are you enemies? Is it because of Elva?"

"I'm going to forget everything you ask if you fire them at me like that."

I sat on the armrest of the couch closest to me. "Answer those and we'll move on."

"Holden and I go way back. We come from the same place."

"As in?"

His blank stare gave me nothing. He took a swig of his drink. "Not from around here. We've never liked each other. It's more to do with where we come from, different neighborhoods you could say, than anything personal. Like the Capulets and the Montagues. You know Shakespeare?"

"I'm surprised you do."

One corner of his mouth crept up in a half smile. He sat back.

"As for Elva... Yes, Holden and Elva had a thing. She was, let's say, a Capulet and he a Montague and never the twain shall meet. But they did and raised a few hackles along the way. It lasted as long as any ill-fated romance can. Messy in the end. Hasn't he told you any of this?"

I shook my head. Of course he wouldn't since we barely knew each other.

"Anyhow. I'm a Capulet. So there's nothing stopping me and Elva making it, right? Yeah...but we haven't. Not interested. Elva's...Elva. Not my type. So no, the ill will between me and your boyfriend has nothing to do with her."

"When you say messy, what do you mean?"

"As in, *is he over her* messy? Is that what you're asking?"

Why was I asking? There was so much more to know than messy personal history.

"You tell me. Is Holden the sort to pine over a lost love?" He goaded me.

I looked at the can of soft drink in my hand.

"I doubt it. Holden was over her long ago, from what I can gather. Different story for Elva. She never wanted to let him go."

He stared at me, as he always did, looking like he was gauging his reply—as he always did.

"Where Holden's concerned, you've got nothing to worry about. He's not the sort to stay in love, lacks loyalty."

I wasn't worried, but I refrained from enlightening him about my relationship, or lack of, with Holden. I didn't want him thinking I was alone and at his mercy.

"Everyone in your gang, are they from your neighborhood?"

He nodded.

"You said your sister was dead?"

"As are my parents."

Life in tough neighborhoods was like that. "Oh."

"They were murdered." It rolled off his tongue so smoothly I couldn't believe I'd heard it right. I didn't want to feel sorry for him. "When did that happen?"

"Six months ago."

"So recent." It would explain his joyless nature and hard exterior. And I couldn't help but feel the twinge of empathy for him. If anything happened to Mum and Ajay... I couldn't bear to think about it. They were all I had left in this world.

"The guy responsible is in this city."

"Did you come here because of him?"

"I'm going to make him wish he never messed with my family." A raw energy pulsed through his body and into me, the assault of withheld rage. I'd never been hammered by such a strong emotion as this before.

"You do that and he'll win. Killing someone is a hollow victory, especially when you're in jail."

His laugh was hard and angry. "Is that experience talking?"

"You seem to know me so well, what do you think?"

"I'm not talking about killing. He took something precious from me. So I plan on taking something precious back. Eye for an eye. Dying hurts the least, loss the most when it means more to you than life."

"Do you think you'll feel happy when you've succeeded?"

For once he wore his emotions on his face, but it would've been nicer if he'd left them tucked tight under his blank mask. A roiling darkness stirred beneath his calm exterior. He looked ready to explode, but he held himself in check. "Maybe not, but I owe it to my family. I can't let what he did pass."

"And by the end, you will be so twisted you won't remember who you are."

What would I do if in his shoes?

"My sister was young, innocent, like Ajay. She didn't deserve to be murdered. You care for your brother. Wouldn't you want to see the murderer suffer?

"Yes." It was nothing more than a whisper. I took a drink from my can to hide my emotions. He was right. I'd be crippled by anger and the pain of having my brother brutally taken from me. But how far would I go?

"My dad's in jail for murder." I stared at the can in my hand. Dammit, why did I say that? I hated Jax. He was a stranger, a dangerous one at that, and yet there was a mirrored hatred inside of us. Jax's dirty, raw emotions surfaced my own. We were both messy people, crippled by something beyond our reach or ability to control.

He nodded. "Rough blow."

He turned away as he said it and stared off into nothing, so I took the opportunity to scrutinize his expression. The mask he usually wore had slipped when we started this conversation, and now I was able to read the anger, but also something else humbling and fragile—his pain.

"They say he murdered a business associate of his."

"You loved him?"

"Yes, I did. Once upon a time ago. I can't now, though. Mum's struggling to cope. They seized all our assets. Everything's a mess because of him. He betrayed us. Now Mum's looking to use his contacts to get herself a job. She'll get herself in trouble and only Dad can talk sense into her, but I can't see him alone because I'm underage."

Sudden cheers from a room behind brought Jax back into the present. He returned his attention to me, settling those black piercing eyes on me. The intimacy of our conversation before, then to the way he looked at me now, eyes hardened, expression cloaked by his anger, and it felt like I was sitting here with two different people.

As if remembering something, he leaped to his feet. "Come. Let me introduce you to the rest."

He headed in the direction of the noise before I could protest. I didn't want to meet anyone else. Elva had been enough. What if all his friends were as prickly?

Jax looked over his shoulder at me as he pushed the door open. I slowed for a moment, seized by his expression. There was a finality within his dark eyes, an accomplishment achieved. He paused in the door, turning his head away, closing his eyes as he did so. For the time of my next breath, he hung in limbo. His body showed outward signs of his inner turmoil, shoulders rounded, head hung low. And for one second, before he entered the room, I read the sadness in his body language, all smugness gone, arrogance forgotten. Was this for his sister? Did the conversation churn up fresh pain? Looking at him, I saw defeat. Then the strange moment was gone as he entered the room, disappeared so fast I could talk myself out of believing it had been there.

The room was white, stark, and vast—white on the ceiling, walls, and all the spaces around a large rectangular mat in the center. To our right, two guys sat at a desk, a giant screen in front of each. Both wore headphones so neither heard our entrance. Gamers.

Jax tapped one of the guys on the shoulder. He jerked at the disturbance, then slid his headphones off as he turned around.

"Jesus, man, this is a crucial moment."

"Tyren, say hi to Sable."

Nothing like Jax, his smile welcomed and made it all the way into his brown eyes. He smacked the other guy's arm. "Pause, will you?" Then he leaped from his chair, extending a hand.

"Nice to meet you." He winked, engulfing my hand with his.

Both Jax and Tyren had olive skin, but Tyren's hair was shorn an inch from his scalp, revealing the same tattoo as Jax behind his right ear.

He hit the other guy on the arm again. "Hey, Salvador, show some respect. Say hello to the lady."

Salvador looked over his shoulder and did a double take. He pulled his headphones to his shoulders. "I know you."

"I think I've seen you in school."

"Yeah, that it's. You're new, aren't you?"

I nodded to fill my lack of fitting response.

"Salvador's a wicked marksman. I'm being crucified here. You into gaming?" Tyren's relaxed, talkative manner was in direct contrast to Jax.

"Never done it before."

He eyed Jax with a wicked glint. "Looks like you have a new recruit."

"What? Me? I don't think so."

Jax jumped to my aid. "Sable doesn't have time now."

"Probably the best. It's wickedly addictive. Once you start, you can't stop. Sucks you in."

"Then I definitely don't have time."

Jax began to back out of the room, which I took as my cue to leave too.

"Hope to see you again, Sable."

Not likely. But at least he seemed sane.

Without asking me if I wanted to go, Jax led me out the door, toward the lift.

"I don't know much, but it looks like you're serious gamers with that setup."

"We don't mind playing now and then."

"What's it called?"

"Dominus."

"Never heard of that one, but I'm not a gamer."

"I'm the GM. Dominus is a MMORPG we designed."

"What's a GM?"

"Game master."

"And you designed it? That explains your apartment. No one your age could afford a place in this area."

"I'm not the only one who designed it, and money's not our motivation."

"What is?"

"Play the game and you'll see."

"I'm not a gamer."

"Doesn't matter."

"I'm not interested in gaming."

"Have you done it before?"

"No."

"How do you know you're not interested?"

"Sitting at a computer, chasing the bad guys, or grabbing the pot of gold doesn't interest me."

"That's not what it's about."

"What is it about?"

"Play the game."

Would this guy let up? "You haven't even given me answers and now you want me to play a game. I don't understand you. Are you going to tell me about what happened on the roof of the Adolphy?"

"Are you going to play Dominus with me?"

"What about how you got my number and know about my brother?"

He stepped toward me and my pulse jacked. This was far too close for someone who was not my boyfriend. I became acutely aware of him and me, alone, a foot apart.

"Play Dominus with me."

"You brought me here for this?"

He allowed his eyes to speak, and for once, the black was no longer flat. Dad's death stare, uncompromising, unflinching, unrelenting.

"I don't understand any of this. It's like you're not even human. Your mind's so messed up."

"I need one of you, Sable. It's up to you which one."

"You're not making sense." A horrible tingle raced through my body, twisting my stomach into the tightest knot. I stepped away, gaining much-needed distance to breathe.

He had yet to blink. "Just one. And I'm sure you would want it to be you."

The coldness swept through me, turning my blood to ice. "You mean my brother, don't you? You want him to play your stupid game."

"No, I want you, but like I say, I have to have one of you."

I spun and raced to the lift, but unlike a store entrance, it refused to open for me.

"Next Saturday."

I turned back. "No."

He shook his head. "Wrong answer."

"You're crazy. What's so important about your game?"

"You need to play Dominus before you'll understand that."

I'd been expertly maneuvered, but to play an online game? This didn't make sense. What happened to the drugs and other illegal stuff? I should be grateful. Playing a game was safer, if not the weirdest request I'd ever heard come from a guy I'd expected to live in a dungeon and house a room of weapons.

Jax stood in the center of the room, hands flexed by his sides, legs hip-width apart, eyes trained on me like everything around us had faded to black, leaving me the only available view. This felt like a showdown, the final seconds to the fatal draw.

"I play on one condition. That you stay away from Ajay. You don't go near him. At all."

His reply was another one of his intense stares.

"And we play. That's all. When it's done, I leave."

Now the smirk was back. "Sure."

I shook my head. "God, you're smooth. You've been slick with your manipulation."

"No, Sable, you were always going to end up here. I've just fast-tracked your descent."

Chapter 9

I DIDN'T NEED his frown to know I sucked at this. Holden stood back and appraised my stance.

"I'm not getting it, am I?"

"You're doing fine. But you can do better. I know you can. I see it in the way you move. Your balance is great. You have a natural style."

"Is that your polite way of saying I suck?"

"This is your first time. No one's great their first time."

"But something is lacking."

"I wouldn't say lacking. I have to warn you, my expectations are high. I ask a lot from my students. We can take a break for now."

"I can't stay too long, so I'd rather keep trying." I'd promised to do something with Ajay this afternoon.

"This isn't a punishment. We can take five minutes. Mastering martial arts takes time. It's not only about learning the techniques. You must also learn to master your mind, for martial arts is as much about mental discipline as it is about the physical movements. The mental discipline is the hardest part."

"Does that mean you're going to make me meditate?"

He laughed, a warm, welcoming sound. "Not straightaway. But I'm serious about the mental discipline. Speed, agility, and technique are necessary, sure, but without the mental steel to see you through, everything else falls to pieces. You lock up, mind blanking out. And then it's too late. You don't want to be in that situation. I've seen many go down because they seize up, forget their training when the situation turns against them. That wouldn't happen if you had control of your..." He tapped his temple.

"Are you talking about marital arts tournaments?" I was trying to think of a time when any of his martial arts students and he would be in situations so dangerous they would fall apart.

There was a pause in his reply. "Yeah. Tournaments."

Holden assumed a fighting stance and looked at me, invitation in his eyes. I remained where I was, not sure what was expected of me. He motioned with a finger that he wanted me to follow his stance. I did reluctantly.

"Mental control is maintaining your focus even in the most desperate of moments."

He feigned an attack, and as a first reaction, I quick stepped back a few paces.

His brow twitched, threatening a frown. "What happened to the skills I just taught you? Don't turn skittish on me now, Sable."

Was he chastising me? "I wasn't expecting you to do that."

"Your opponent is not going to wait around for you to give the signal you're ready."

I'd caved under his repeated insistence I should come to his club and not because I had a keen interest in learning marital arts. To be truthful, I wanted to test our friendship, or whatever was budding between us, to see how far it could develop. Half of me was scared of allowing him into my ugly world; half of me wanted the distraction. Holden was good-looking, uncomplicated, and fun to be with, yet bizarrely intense when it came to his training. I had thought this would be relaxed and fun, but he'd turned into a mini drill sergeant; he'd turned into my dad.

Pushing aside yesterday and the weird moment with Jax was another important reason I agreed to come today. Elva said Holden and Jax hated each other, which made Holden an ally.

Curling his palms as invitation, enticing me toward him, he said, "Remember some of the skills I've taught you. Defend, counterattack."

I would've rather stayed back and out of the way, but I didn't want to disappoint him, so I stepped forward.

"Once you are proficient in your training, and that involves your mental proficiency as well as technical proficiency, then you start to fight on instinct. You stop thinking about your moves and just do them. You embody the knowledge of what it takes to survive."

"What happens when you're proficient in neither of them?"

"You learn to become proficient quicker."

This was what I wanted, right? After all, I'd opted out of taking a break.

I tried for another of the kicks he'd taught me; I couldn't even remember what he called it. Holden's counterattack was swift but gentle and would've set me on my ass if he'd not caught me before I crashed into the mat. It could've been a cozy moment, but he set me back. "Again."

If I'd wanted to test our friendship for possible potential, coming to his club was the wrong decision. His attention seemed channeled to the mat and technique.

I tried something different from my limited repertoire, to be rebuffed and sent spinning.

"Keep your focus. Believe in your ability."

"Since this is my first time, I don't have any ability at the moment."

"But you have enough. This is me going gentle. You should be able to match my moves."

Should was the only word I heard. Maybe Holden didn't mean it as a judgment, but I couldn't help but take it as one. Dad was good at expectations, but expectations only made me worse. I blew out a long and hard breath and eyed my opponent. What if I attacked first?

I tried for the first kick he'd shown me only to feel a sudden, short pain in the side of my ankle as Holden effortlessly blocked me. I jumped back, favoring my other leg.

He quirked an eyebrow as he eyed my foot. "Did I hurt you?" The tone of his question was neutral, if not tinged a smidge to annoyance. Perhaps reading something in my expression, he snapped out of his fight zone and relaxed his stance. "Sorry, it wasn't my intention. I'm used to sparring with my students."

Was that another judgment? "It's all right. Feels fine now."

"Let's take that break." He came toward me, resting his hand on my upper arm. "I'm being a jerk here."

"No, you're being passionate about something that has meaning to you."

Again with that warm and inviting smile. Holden was a contradiction. Training with him today brought out an intensity I'd not witnessed the other night, and that was all right. My dad was an intense man who held strong passions and ideals. I had always admired that in him, even if it did mean he'd placed heavy expectations on us, expectations I struggled to achieve, expectations that made me feel like a failure.

"Come, let's get a cool drink."

I followed him out of the gym and into the reception arena to the slimline fridge behind his front counter. Without asking my preference, he handed me a can of soda, then leaned back on his desk. The club had yet to open, which gave us the peace and quiet to talk and the space to do what we wanted.

"How long have you owned the club?" Hopefully I wasn't standing too close for him to smell my sweat, and I was not about to sniff my armpits to see if I did smell sweaty.

"Six months. It's been a dream of mine."

"How long have you been doing martial arts?"

"All my life. Or so it seems. It feels like I was born doing it."

"You must really love it."

"It's as much a part of me as my personality."

"It would be good to have something in your life you love that much."

He ran a finger over the stubble on his chin as he eyed me. "You've got something you're passionate about. You just don't realize it yet."

"If I don't realize it, how can I be passionate about it?"

"Because it's there inside of you. It always has been. Just because it's yet to come out doesn't mean it's not there."

"Hmm…I think that makes sense."

"One day you'll find out how close this side of you is to who you really are."

That was a weird thing to say, I think? I couldn't work out what was his point in all the cryptic talk.

"You have a natural talent buried deep inside, wanting out. All you need is the right trigger and the right person to guide you."

"Let me guess, you're the right person?"

It wasn't until he laughed that I realized my chest had tightened. He was going too intense too soon, not to mention a little weird.

"I want to be."

A hint stripped of subtlety. A warmth flowed up my neck into my cheeks. "How do you know Elva and Jax?"

Good job flipping the subject. Holden looked as though I'd told him I was pregnant with his child.

He shook his head and blinked. "I wasn't expecting that bucket of ice water."

"Sorry, you don't have to answer."

"How do you know Jax?" Although he kept his tone light, his eyes said his question was anything but casual.

"I met him at the party." I didn't owe it to him to tell the whole truth. We weren't dating, not really. But he'd hinted that he wanted to be. Hadn't he? Wasn't that what he meant when he said he wanted to be my guide?

Lips pressed together, a muscle twitching in his jaw, Holden looked at the wall opposite the reception desk, giving me the chance to flick a look at his grip on the can and the white of his knuckles. Amazing how much Holden reminded me of Dad, the mask, the same wall holding back the anger, which nonetheless pulsed out through his body language and the invisible vibration of energy permeating the air. He placed his can on his desk and pushed off. "Shall we head back through?"

Conversation over, he left the reception area, drawing me along in his silence and into the cavernous room filled with the all the equipment necessary to turn duds like me into skilled competitors.

Holden returned to our training mat and turned to face me. "I suppose he's told you we have history."

"Messy history. But I think he was referring to Elva. She said you and Jax hated each other."

"She? You spoke to her at the party as well?"

God, I was a hopeless liar. "It was after the party. I ran into them again."

If I'd shot him in the chest, he'd look less surprised. "This is a friendly warning, Sable. Please take it as one. Jax is not someone you want to be around. Him nor the people he's with."

"I'm not interested in hanging around them, but I'm interested in why you said that."

"They're dangerous. Jax especially. Please, Sable, trust me. Stay away from them. They're not for you."

A bizarre comment to tack on the end. "How do you know them?"

"We grew up together."

"Did you always hate each other?"

"Yes, it was inevitable."

I didn't believe in fate. "What about Elva?"

Like a sharp needle puncturing a balloon, the tension turning his body rigid dissipated. He finger combed his hair as he donned the look of a cornered animal. "Elva." He shook his head. "It was crazy, stupid of us."

"She still seems to harbor something for you if the way she looked at you the other night is any indication."

"She's a fool if she does."

"Love's not meant to be logical."

He groaned a breath. I couldn't tell if the groan was for my soppy sentiment or if he still felt trapped. "If you had said lust, you would've been more accurate."

I'm sure Jax said she would never have let him go. Typical guy, they rarely committed as much. But then what would I know? Just bathroom gossip in the school toilets, overheard conversations, which involved a lot of tears.

"But I'm serious, Sable, please promise me you'll stay away. You can't trust Jax. He's manipulative and cruel-hearted."

I should but I couldn't tell Holden about my conversation with Jax because I was embarrassed at how easily he'd conned me and manipulated me into playing his game, which was so weird. Why a game? But I could handle playing a stupid online game. I'd get beaten within minutes and he'd grow bored with having me as his gaming partner.

"Did you know his family was murdered?"

"He told you that?" Holden was acting freakishly intense.

"I thought it was too personal a thing to say to a stranger, but…" I shrugged. "He's on a vendetta."

Two strides and Holden was on top of me. The sour smell of his sweat rushed over me. "What else did he say?"

On instinct, I stepped back a few paces, which helped soothe my sudden amped heart rate and snapped Holden out of his bizarre mood. "I'm sorry. I didn't mean to scare you. It's… I never expected this. He shouldn't have been at the party. If I'd known, I would not have invited you."

"Why? Why would he care about me?"

"He doesn't. He doesn't care about anyone but himself. But he saw you with me and that's what's made you a target. He'd do anything to teach me a lesson."

Maybe so but he'd started pestering me before that night, before I'd met Holden.

It was all such a sudden shock, everything unfolding too fast. I didn't know what to believe, what to say, more importantly what to reveal. Reveal! Why should I think I had something to hide? Why should I think it needed to be hidden?

Dad went to jail and our whole life went to hell, but it didn't stop there. It seemed the slide to hell was longer and greater than I could've dreamed.

Chapter 10

THE COLD that penetrated chilled me down to my core. There were two people sitting on the bus seat. One small and one big. The small person was Ajay, waiting for me to meet him, but I was late thanks to an accident two blocks away. Ajay talked with his hands, waving them around like he did when he became excited about something. Sitting next to him was Jax, appearing interested in everything Ajay had to say. After Dad's stranger-danger schooling, Ajay never spoke to anyone he didn't know. He seemed to have forgotten that fact.

Neither noticed me until I stood directly in front of them. Ajay leaped to his feet and pointed a finger at me.

"You're late."

"You all right?"

He scrunched up his face like he thought I was an idiot. "Yeah."

I didn't want to alarm Ajay by lashing out at Jax, so I continued to ignore the one who had no right to be here.

"Sorry. There was an accident a couple of blocks back."

Ajay shrugged and quickly lost interest in our conversation.

I focused on Jax and schooled my voice to calm. "What are you doing here?"

"We have a date."

Ajay reacted with a jerk of his head toward Jax, his eyes narrowing. His big sister didn't do dates; she wasn't allowed to date. Now Dad would know as there was no way Ajay would keep this whopper of a secret to himself.

Jesus, how to get out of this one? "No, we don't."

"Did I get my days mixed up?"

This was not Jax, not this friendly guy with the casual smile. But the lie, now that was Jax.

I ignored him. "Come on, Ajay, we have to get home."

He pulled away from me. "But what about your date?"

"We don't have a date."

Jax rose from the bus seat so he was between Ajay and me. "Actually we do. I notified the prison we would be arriving in half an hour."

"You did what?"

"Are we going to see Dad?"

"Ajay…no…" Why was Jax doing this?

I glared at him. There were so many things I wanted to yell at him right now, but not in the street or in front of Ajay. I felt like I'd been maneuvered into this position. He'd manipulated me once again.

"If you want to make it, I suggest we get going."

Ajay punched the air. "Yay, we're going to see Dad." He grabbed my hand and pulled. "Come on, what are you waiting for? Jax's car is over here. I saw him pull up in it. It's real fancy."

I couldn't take Ajay. There were things I needed to say to Dad without Ajay present. And I needed to think hard about what and how I would say them.

I slipped my hand from his. "Ajay, you go ahead. I need to have a word with Jax."

Ajay rolled his eyes. "Boring. Just don't make it long."

I waited until he was farther down the street, heading for a black sports car, before I turned on Jax. "How dare you. I can't believe you're here. You're invading my privacy. Ajay's off-limits."

He remained calm through my onslaught. "I thought it was important. You need to save your mum, don't you? I'm of legal age, so you can come with me."

"You're out of your mind."

"I'm offering my help."

"I don't want your help. You had no right to speak to Ajay."

"Are you prepared to disappoint him? He's psyched about seeing his dad."

The stress of arguing with him made me feel weak. "I can't believe you did this." I covered my face with my hands as if it would make the moment disappear.

"I thought it would help."

"No you didn't. Since when have you acted altruistically? Besides, I can't say what I want to say to Dad while Ajay's around."

"I'll wait with him outside somewhere."

"And let him miss his chance to see Dad? He won't do that."

"How about I keep Ajay to start with while you talk, then he can come through."

His persistent solutions told me he wasn't going to back down. I needed to see Dad, help Mum ASAP, but, yet again, he'd manipulated everything to turn it in his favor. I had my solution, but I also wanted to claw at him for interfering. "You've got to stay out of sight. Dad can't see you."

"Sure, anything you say." I eyed him. Was he making fun of me with his schoolboy compliance?

"It's useless anyhow. Ajay will tell him."

"What's so bad about that? We're friends."

"You don't know my dad. I'm not allowed to have male friends."

"I'll have a word with Ajay, ask him to keep it a secret."

"No you won't. You have no reason to talk to Ajay again."

"So we're on."

I could strangle him right now. "How did you know where to meet Ajay?"

"I have my ways of finding things out."

"That's totally creepy."

"I'm here as a favor, that's all."

"I don't trust you."

"Good. Now you've got that out we can go?" Without waiting for me to reply, he headed for his car.

Of course it would be a sports car. Ajay leaned against the door, smiling a stupid excited smile as we neared. He might be ten but he was still a boy, old enough to be impressed by a fancy car. I was immune to the sleek beauty of it, having climbed into many expensive cars in my time. The interior smelt new, that leather and upholstery smell that took months to clear. The carpet looked like it had never had feet on it. Ajay climbed in the back without a second glance in my direction, so I retreated to the front. If I wasn't here, Ajay would probably still jump in Jax's car, which was wrong.

Jax swung out into the traffic with the ease of someone born behind a wheel then reared in a rally race and wove through the traffic as if the cars were parked. At a set of lights, he pulled headphones from his glove compartment and handed them back to Ajay.

"You'll hear some cool stuff if you put these on."

Ajay did as directed, effectively cutting himself off from our conversation, Jax's intention, no doubt.

"You said earlier you weren't allowed to have male friends."

I wish I hadn't. "What makes you think you have a right to ask questions about my life?"

"I thought some friendly conversation would be nice."

"You've done nothing but manipulate me so far. Where's the friendliness in that?"

"It was some of the things you said the other day at my apartment. I don't have a family anymore. I just want to help you with yours."

I looked across to him, but staring at his profile, I couldn't gauge his sincerity. "My dad brought us up to believe everyone had an ulterior motive, that few were trustworthy." I didn't believe he genuinely wanted to help, but I was weary. I felt weary every day now.

"A protective father. Nothing wrong with that. But it's a sad life if you never trust anyone. It keeps you closed to great opportunities. Great people."

"Are you including yourself in that description?"

He cast me a sideways glance with a lazy smile but didn't say anything.

I stared out the window to give me some distance from any further conversation. All I could think of was Dad's reaction on seeing me. What was I going to say to him?

"Dad's and my relationship is strained. I can't forgive him for what he did and for what he's done to our family." If only I could cork my mouth. Why tell him these things when I didn't like him?

"Understandable."

"I'm not sure how he's going to take the news about Mum. I almost don't want to tell him. It will gut him."

"No doubt. But aren't you doing this for your mum's sake?"

"I'm not sure what he can do about it, to tell you the truth. He's locked up. What can he do?"

"Sounds like you're talking yourself out of it."

"I don't want to hurt him."

"I thought you didn't like him?"

I leaned back on the headrest. How to unravel the turbulent storm that was my emotions toward my dad? "I loved my father more than anything. It makes what he did harder to accept."

Jax absorbed me with his eyes a little too long for someone driving. I couldn't read what was going on in his head from the look he gave, but the slight crease between his eyes meant he wasn't happy. I was getting used to the sorts of looks he gave. Most seemed to carry the weight of a dark secret too heavy to bear, which left me alone in an empty place where the real him did not exit.

This time I wanted to know what it was that stayed buried deep within him, so I continued to stare at him, hoping to glean small secrets of my own. I watched his jaw twitch as he clenched his teeth, usually a sign of someone saddled with conflicting thoughts. He shuffled around in his seat, glanced out the side window then back to the front. Next, with his wrist slung over the steering wheel, he danced his hand a little. His body wanted to move, as if agitated.

After a while, he said, "He wanted to protect you." Said like he resented the fact. "That's a father's job."

"You're right. I can't change the feelings I have for him deep inside. I still love him, but at the moment, it hurts too much to admit it. I'm sorry you don't have a father left to protect you."

Clutching the steering wheel, his knuckles whitened. For a moment he closed his eyes. What I said hurt. Why couldn't I reel the words back in?

"Maybe I shouldn't have said that. I was—"

"Don't. It doesn't matter. Perhaps he doesn't deserve your love, but just make sure there's nothing to regret between you and your father. It will only eat away at you in the end."

A locked tomb of untold stories rested between us. I would, perhaps, be left waiting an eternity for the key. I wanted to ask what it would take to get beneath his armor, to know what secrets he kept hidden, to know why he had suddenly appeared in my life and seemed determined to position himself center stage. Instead I stared out the window as the gulf between us widened.

———————

WHEN MY NAME WAS CALLED, Ajay leaped to his feet. I'd decided it was best he came with me and I would somehow manage to tell Dad what I had to say in code. I didn't want Jax anywhere near Dad. I would have to lie and say the neighbors brought me. But if Dad knew about me and a boy, the guards would likely cut the visit short because Dad went apoplectic.

The guard delivered us to the door and stationed himself just inside with his hands crossed in front of him. The wait was short and when Dad came through, Ajay leaped to his feet again and did little jumps on the spot as if he'd been injected with caffeine while Dad crossed the room toward us.

He wore a big smile and scooped Ajay up into a bear embrace from behind. Ajay giggled and my heart ached. This was how it should always be. Not an hourly visit once a week. Ajay craved Dad. He was never so happy as when he sat next to him in this dour room surrounded by unfriendly people on uncomfortable plastic chairs.

Behind Ajay, Dad's smile slipped and he gave me a look of concern. I replied with a weak smile.

He sat still holding Ajay by the hand. "Hey, honey, how you been?"

"Good."

"Where's your mother?"

"It's just us today."

He frowned, giving me an extra-long and heavy stare.

"This is what I drew today." Ajay pulled his school bag from the floor and undid the zip.

"Sure, champ, give me a look." He responded with his eyes set on me.

Ajay spread a crumpled sheet of paper on the table and described the scribble. Dad listened with half an ear. I could tell because of all the times he'd listened to Ajay before, with undivided attention, asking the right sort of questions and feeding Ajay with pride. Now he made trite noises. Once or twice, Ajay glanced up at him, no doubt noticing the difference in his responses. Dad smiled down at him and ruffled his hair or rubbed his arm but struggled to give Ajay any more of his attention.

When Ajay exhausted discussion on that drawing, he searched his bag for something else.

"How's your mother?"

"She's good. I think she's researching how to make us some money."

Dad stared at me like I'd spoken Japanese.

"She's out meeting people."

"And I did this in my book." Ajay pulled out his exercise book and looked up at Dad while he flicked through the pages. Dad pulled his attention from me when Ajay's palm rested on his chin.

"Show me." He nodded at Ajay's book.

Ajay launched into another detailed explanation of what he was doing on each page. I looked around the room as a way to avoid eye contact with him. Ajay needed his time with Dad first. God knows what I had to say wasn't worth talking about.

Dad did his best to give Ajay the attention he deserved and Ajay lapped it up with one long stream of talk.

I plucked up the courage to tell Dad while Ajay stuffed his book back in his bag. "I think Mum is meeting with some of your old acquaintances."

Dad stiffened and the temperature surrounding us rose ten degrees—I swear. His face did all sorts of transformations in a matter of seconds. It was painful to watch. The storm of anger that rode behind the genial facade he fixed in place when he looked at Ajay assaulted me. I didn't want to look at the writhing emotions so obviously suppressed below the surface. I ached to reach out and touch him, but a wall of judgment had destroyed the passage of touch between us.

"She's so scared you'll get in trouble if you do anything yourself. So she's decided to do it herself."

He jerked forward and, with his elbows on the table, sunk his head in his hands. I could sense the frustration and anger driving his sudden and forceful action.

"It's why I came. I wanted you to know. I don't know what you can do about it…but I just wanted to tell you."

A lump blocked my throat, my swallow painful.

For the first time in months, Dad grasped my hand. "You did the right thing. Don't worry, Sable. I'm going to take care of everything."

I'd yet to look in his eyes because I was too busy staring at his hand covering mine. Never before had his touch meant so much. A tear dropped onto the back of his hand. I wiped the rest away.

"I'm going to take care of everything, Sable. Do you hear me?"

I wanted him to. I wanted him to. I wanted him to make everything go away, the lies, the betrayal, the destitution, the fear, and Jax, because that's what he did. That's what he always did. I didn't want to be the adult, the only one holding my family together.

I nodded. Ajay rocked to and fro, sensing unease in the air.

"I think it's time we went."

"Who brought you here?"

Dammit. I thought I'd gotten away without having to lie. Just then, Dad's eyes trailed past me to the exit and his face contorted in rage. Next, he barreled past the table, toward the exit like a diesel locomotive without brakes, bellowing something akin to a war cry. Locked up in shock, I couldn't even scream his name.

At the window in the exit door, I saw Jax.

The rest unrolled like a nightmare. The guard at the door blocked his way. A handful more materialized out of nowhere, and Dad, fighting through them all, was finally subdued, cuffed, and led away. Ajay all the while shrieked himself hoarse until someone official came and shunted us out the door.

Ajay fought me all the way to the car, not wanting to leave Dad, forcing me to yell at him, until Jax intervened by placing a hand on his shoulder and whispering words I couldn't hear. Ajay stopped his ruckus but shrunk into himself with his bag against his chest. He wouldn't let me touch him, but he followed us to the car. I glared at Jax, thankful but resentful. At least we could go, but why was he the one to get through to Ajay?

Once Ajay clambered in the back, I leaned against the car as the tears burned behind my eyelids.

I tried not to relive the sight, but it replayed on a loop, determined to punish me. I'd made such a mess of everything. Dad's visitation rights would be reduced or removed completely, and god knows what else they did with prisoners to discipline them.

There was no way I would be able to hide my visit from Mum. Ajay was bound to withdraw for a while and refuse to go anywhere, including school. How would I explain his behavior to her?

I could feel Jax standing beside me. I opened my eyes and looked through a blur of tears.

"I'm sorry about that. I feel that was my fault. You warned me to stay unseen, and I didn't. I'm really sorry."

I turned away from him as I wiped the tears away. Dad was not the man I knew. Never had I seen him so angry, act with such rage. I collapsed back onto the hood of his car, using that to keep me standing because my legs wouldn't do the job on their own anymore.

After what he did, he wouldn't be able to help Mum. They would lock him away deep in that prison, leaving him no hope of contacting who he thought he could to keep Mum safe. She would end up dead or locked in a female prison. All I had was Ajay. This was surely the end of my family.

I pushed off the hood. "Let's just go."

"Sable."

"Forget it," I snapped and headed for the passenger door.

Chapter 11

THE DOORS SLID open to Elva crowding the exit, no doubt an intimidation ploy, and she succeeded.

"You're not too dissimilar to your mum."

The pit in my stomach sank through to my feet, while my brain, trying to register what had been said, turned to fuzz and mucked up any suitable response.

Elva waited with one hip flared, twirling the sharp stiletto of the other foot into the wood floor. With her hand on her hip, I saw the tattoo on her right wrist, different from Jax's.

"Oops. Was that something I wasn't supposed to say? It seems the cat's out of the bag." She joined me in the lift, bringing with her a rich citrusy, floral scent. "Don't worry, honey, we're all friends here." She settled her beautiful dark eyes on me. "And friends don't keep secrets. Lovers, perhaps, but not friends."

Rather than be poisoned by her, I scooted out of the lift. It closed on another one of her magnificent smirks. No one I'd met, except her, could make a smirk into a lethal weapon.

Jax had said he would contain Elva, whatever that meant, yet it seemed he'd revealed to her my confession about my family. And her last comment had to allude to her continual belief Holden and I were together.

I spun at the sound of footsteps. Jax analyzed my face, then halted. "What did she say?"

"Does it really matter to you?"

"Depends on what she said."

"She said I was like my mum. She knows nothing about my mum or me."

"Elva knows how to get under people's skin."

"But why would she make that comment?"

"You'll have to ask her that."

"Holden told me to stay away from you. He said you were a complete wanker, among other things."

Dangerous, manipulative, hard-hearted, I'd also add to that a smirk that trickled the creeps up your spine. His unforgiving stare coupled with the sneer, and I felt the butt of some terrible joke, one between the two of them.

"Holden will always think the worst."

"I wish someone would be direct with me about the past between the two of you."

"It's not your concern yet."

"Does she hate me because she thinks I'm Holden's girlfriend?"

"Aren't you Holden's girlfriend?"

I led myself into that without too much trouble.

"Elva's vindictive and spiteful, but someone you want covering your back when the going gets messy because she's loyal, courageous, and won't back down. She makes a habit of studying her competition and, I'm sorry to say, you're her competition. The only thing you did wrong was appear with Holden at the party. I'm not sure she'll ever accept you because she hangs on to negative emotions."

Just great. I wanted out of this mess. "Are we going to play this game? I've got better places to be. I'm not wasting my Saturday."

"What happened the other day once you got home?"

"Does it matter to you?"

"I wouldn't be asking."

"I made Ajay promise to lie to his mum. He disappeared into his room and wouldn't come out for dinner. Mum was worried he was sick. He's kept his promise."

"And you feel terrible for making him keep it."

"I feel terrible for ruining Mum's and Ajay's chance of seeing Dad again any time soon."

Jax folded his arms across his chest, drilling into me with his penetrating eyes.

"Can we get this over and done with?"

"Sable, I'm sorry—"

"Forget it. It's done. I should've known better."

He dropped his arms to his sides, hesitated a few moments, and I held my breath, waiting for more apologies I would refuse to listen to. Seeming to understand that fact, he headed for the gaming room.

"Am I a pawn in your vendetta?"

He stopped but did not face me. Staring at his back, now rigid with tension, I willed him to turn and face me so I could see the truth in his eyes.

When he did turn, his face was the schooled calm of neutrality. "Against who? If this is about Holden, we don't see eye to eye. We never will. But I'm not plotting anything against him. He's not on my horizon."

"I wasn't referring to Holden. I know this has nothing to do with Holden. I just don't understand. Why are you targeting me to play your stupid game? Why threaten me to join you? There are so many gamers out there who would love to join in on an exclusive game."

"I want special people."

I huffed a sarcastic noise. "You don't want me then."

He glanced sideways at me, the hint of that smirk cracking his otherwise emotionless face.

"You're exactly what I want."

"God, you're frustrating. You stalked me in that convenience store so you could force me to play your game?"

"There are so many reasons why I was there. One day you'll understand."

"Why did you dob me into that kid?"

"It's important to feel the consequences of your actions."

"As you will discover after you've settled your vendetta against the guy who—" I couldn't say any more. It was too horrible to repeat.

"I'm already in hell. It doesn't matter how deep I bury myself."

I slowed, allowing him to move farther in front of me. I didn't like him, I wanted to continue not liking him, but my hatred was being chipped away by his self-punishment and this confusing situation. Nothing made sense. And now I was stuck in the center of the triangle that was Jax, Holden, and Elva, and somewhere in the middle with me was a secret I was sure I didn't want to learn.

Jax pushed through into the empty games room.

"Tyren's been asked to leave too, has he?"

"What makes you say that?"

"Elva was on her way out just as I arrived. Tyren's absent. I hope you don't think this is a date."

"I don't need to blackmail a woman for a date."

"I'm glad you see this for what it is."

Wow, my first genuine smile. It made him look different, better-looking, more approachable. *He's still an ass.*

Jax started the computer while I looked around the room. There was little to see except for the desk with the computers and a cupboard by the right wall, which happened to be white like the rest of the room. "Why so much space?"

"You'll see."

"Not another cryptic answer."

"This one will be solved in a matter of minutes."

I came around to stand beside him. The screen fired up in seconds. Filling it was the word *Dominus*, which appeared in thick metal-colored capitals, the lettering bold and aggressive with sharp edging.

Jax left the word *Dominus* filling the screen and headed for the cupboard. He pulled out something small and silver, white gloves and socks and a white jump suit, all with silver dots over them. He gathered them in his arms and came back to me. "Put these on." He placed them on the desk. "Take your shoes off but you can leave your clothes on."

I held up the jumpsuit. "You want me to dress to play the game?"

"It's a necessity."

"Is it supposed to put me in a better mood to play?"

He flashed me a deadpan look while he flipped his boots off. *Right, don't speak, just do.*

The jumpsuit wasn't the exact fit but close enough, and I had silver dots running down my arms and legs and around my hips, same with the gloves and socks, which had spaces for each toe. Dots also ran down my fingers and toes and around my ankles and wrists.

"These are for...?"

"A real-life experience, or as close to as you can get."

"You guys are serious about gaming."

"You're only getting started. You can finish dressing while I prepare a few things."

Some silver dots much like the ones on my jumpsuit lay on the table once the jumpsuit, gloves, and socks were gone. Jax slid them to him while he sat down in one of the chairs. He tapped out some commands on the computer and the screen opened up into the game, or rather places for data input. He typed in my name and then swiped the silver dots in front of a red laser light at the bottom of the far-left screen. Once done, he rose from the seat and faced me.

"What are they?"

"The real surprise to Dominus." He came close and attached a dot on either side of my temples and one on my forehead. His proximity meant my air was filled with rich, warm tones, reminding me of hot spiced buns and mulled wine.

"I'm guessing the dots aren't for fashion."

"The computer will read the dots and record your movement. That's how you'll move your avatar."

"Move? We're not sitting for this game?"

"No. The screen is a soft introduction for beginners."

"That's me."

"You're more capable than that. Virtual's the best level for you."

"Not sure I agree with you. What about the ones on my head?"

"For the stats. This is for your eyes." He handed me small silver lenses, which fit snug around the eyes, like wraparound glasses, blocking out all vision. When on, I saw the word *Dominus* appear in front of my eyes, hovering in the air.

I pushed them up to my forehead. "Oh my god, this is incredible. I see what's on the computer screen."

"The fun hasn't even begun."

Jax slipped a belt around his waist. Across the front of the belt were what looked like silver studs. Seeing me look at it, he said, "This is my keyboard. It's the way I control the game."

"Do I get one?"

"No, the GM keeps the controls."

He pointed to the back of the room. "That's the virtual space. I'll begin the game from here."

Which had to mean I was supposed to go stand over there. I headed where he pointed while he started tapping on the keyboard. The deep blue mat stretched across the entire floor space, the only color in the room besides the desk and computers. It absorbed my weight and appeared to move ever so slightly under my feet.

"The floor just moved."

"That's its design. It will take getting used to, but once you have the hang of it, you'll find it's not too different from solid ground."

He joined me on the spongy floor.

"Try jumping."

I did and felt the impact of my fall absorbed by the floor, reducing the feel of my weight.

"The hardest part is leaving the mat after a session. Now run. This is the real magic."

I did, expecting to run off the mat in a matter of seconds, but instead I remained on the spot. The ground somehow moved like a conveyor belt with me marking time, and because Jax remained where he was, it meant the movement was discreet. I picked up my pace but remained in the same spot.

"What are we standing on?"

"Dominus has many secrets. The mystery's shattered if I reveal too many of them."

"This is like something I would expect in NASA, not in some guy's apartment, and it must've cost a fortune."

He dismissed my questions by looking down at his belt and fiddling with the silver dials.

"And the players you invite into the game. Do they get this setup?"

"This is only for us. Online survivors who reach the level cap are invited to join us here for the virtual experience, which is a whole different level again, but few make the cut."

"Where are these people coming from?"

"Everywhere. Being an MMORPG, there are no borders."

"And people are willing to come so far?"

"It's an honor to reach this level."

"Am I supposed to feel honored for jumping the queue?"

"You can tell me after our session. We'll go slow at first. There's a lot I'll need to run you through. But let's get you accustomed to movement first."

He slid his goggles over his eyes and I copied. My world turned white.

"I'll just load us a scene. You'll need reference points if you want to gain control of your limbs."

As I watched, the horizon came into view, darkening to gray, delineating up from down.

"That's enough for now. Too much else and it's distracting. Try jumping again."

I did, and the virtual environment mimicked the jump. Again the mat absorbed my fall.

"This is amazing, not to mention ridiculously advanced."

"The more you move, the quicker you'll become accustomed to the virtual world. It can take time to learn to manipulate your body in here. Gaining complete control of your movement is the secret to success. Try a few cartwheels."

I flipped into the first cartwheel. My vision altered, turning the gray upside down, then the right way up. I was off on the rotation and fell forward, but the mat was so springy my fall didn't hurt, and I was able to push myself up quick into another cartwheel with the same result. My mind was having a little trouble relying on the virtual scene, so I failed to land any of the cartwheels on my feet. "This is weird but fun."

"It's time to start."

The gray horizon disappeared as darkness descended across my vision, then soon filled with the word *Dominus*. It hovered for a few seconds before shimmering into the black to be replaced by columns of avatars.

"Choose an avatar. The only time you'll see yourself as your avatar is if you look down your body, but this is what other players will see. And there's no changing skin either. What you choose is what you have."

"Not sure what you mean, but do I have to choose?"

"The program reads the dots, not the suit, which means you'll be invisible and at a distinct advantage. So yes, you need an avatar. You can choose a name, but that's optional. You can also change your voice. For some, it helps set their focus for the scene. Again it's optional."

I scanned the figures. "I choose the hot chick in the red suit. She looks like she knows how to kick ass. And I think I'll stick with Sable."

"We'll skip weapons for now and focus on the basics."

I glanced down my body to see the white suit had disappeared. The first thing I saw were breasts spilling from a thin, flimsy bra, which was supposed to be my top. My waist looked like it had been pulled in with a drawstring and my bottoms were little more than underpants. Below the postage-stamp worth of fire-red material, my strong, muscular legs stretched for miles.

"Definitely a male-designed program."

"Tyren designed her."

"Really. Which ones did you design?"

"The men."

I looked across at Jax, not surprised to see him looking like Hercules or some Hollywood Viking-style warrior.

"You probably go virtual just to walk around like that."

"The costumes are pretty, but you've got to play the part. I'm not going to look good if I'm on my ass. You, on the other hand, will look good in any position. But if you're on your ass, pretty or not, you're out, meaning game over."

My pulse fluttered to quick time with his comment. I clenched my fists to force it back to normal. Firstly, his comment was directed at my avatar, not me. Secondly, who the hell cared what he thought?

"Then you better teach me so I won't land on my ass."

My vision changed. The black screen filled with avatars disappeared to be replaced by me soaring over a barren landscape. Dizziness racked my brain, and the next thing I knew, Jax righted me.

"Like I say, it will take some getting used to."

The world stopped moving below me, but I hovered in midair, the ground tens of meters below me. Again I felt Jax's hands on my arms as I pitched sideways.

"This is disorienting. I'm not used to looking down to nothing below my feet."

"You all right to stand by yourself now?"

"I think so." He probably wanted to distance himself from me.

"Focus on what you feel. The mat is underneath you. It's still there. Don't believe what your mind is telling you. At least not for now."

"Got it. My mind has no idea what it's doing."

Jax pointed ahead. His arm appeared in my view as the strong, muscular arm of a warrior with leather bracelets of studs and rings. The tattoo on his wrist was gone but the one down his forearm remained. I glanced at him and realized we were the same height, but his face looked like it had been carved out of granite. When he spoke, his lips moved like a real person.

"The Califax Dome. The end quest. The scene of the final confrontation."

He pointed to a tall tower rising up from the sprawling city below. Its beauty was unsurpassed in a land with muted colors of browns and gray. Glass panels caught the sun's light, shimmering soft hues of rainbow. It appeared an impenetrable place, something out of a fantasy, with glass spires and ornate carvings.

"It's beautiful. Made all the more beautiful because the rest of the scene is bland. Why is it the final confrontation?"

"It is where the seat of power resides."

"Got it. The enemy is inside and the aim of the game is to get in and topple those in power."

"Whose side you're on will determine whether you see them as your enemy or your savior. On the right side, the rulers are not your enemy."

"So whose side are we on?"

"Opposing factions."

"We're enemies?"

"The worst."

"That's a great way to start."

"The Califax Dome is ruled by four powerful factions, Persal, Aris, Set, and Negal. Alliances have been made to hold the peace and allow the four to rule in harmony. But alliances are always broken. Shifting allegiances will tip the balance. Some will choose to rule alone but require the help of other factions. The four are not the only factions, just the most powerful. Perun and Phonus are important although not powerful enough to sit within the Senate of Factions. Something they resent greatly."

"Do I get to choose a faction?"

"No. You're Persal."

"And you are?"

"Aris. Hold on. I'm going to change the scene."

I staggered, then hit the mat when we whizzed down from the sky, zooming to the ground. "I'd appreciate more warning next time."

I even lifted my knees up as we landed, expecting to hit them on the paving, when really I'd been sitting down on the mat the whole time. Jax's hand appeared in my periphery.

"Need some help?"

His avatar face revealed no trace of expression. If his lips could move like real life, then surely his avatar face would also mimic his real expression, which had to mean he shared no expression with me at all. Typical.

I accepted his hand and he pulled me to my feet, keeping a hold until I no longer swayed. "This is going to take longer to get used to than I thought."

"Don't worry, you'll pick it up surprisingly quick."

We were down amongst the buildings now, but everything looked dull compared to the Dome, and deserted, not a vehicle or person in sight. The streets were nothing more than empty cobbles and the buildings vacant monuments of unearthly fabrication.

"Each faction is warring by nature."

"Of course."

"Which makes it a miracle they are able to exist side by side at all. But along with their natural instinct to create war, they have a factional nature inherent in them since birth that does not become apparent till they reach puberty."

I looked down at my ample breasts. "I would say I'm definitely over puberty."

He ignored my smart comment, his face continuing to reveal nothing of his thoughts.

"Is this the part when I ask what the factional natures are?"

"It's extremely important to know the nature of each faction, for their nature is their power, along with any weapons they may gain."

"What's Persal's factional nature?"

"Destruction."

"Cool. How do I do that?"

"I'm not Persal, so I can't teach you. You'll have to learn it along the way."

"But you designed the game. You should know them all."

"I'm not about to give you the advantage."

"I'm so disadvantaged it's unreal."

"Then you better learn quick."

He was as annoying in the game as out. "What about Aris?"

"Bloodlust, rebellion, and thievery. It's usually an Aris that starts any feud."

"Why do you get three?"

"It's the way it works."

"What about the others?"

"Set is chaos and deception."

"So, no one makes deals with Set."

I couldn't puncture his concentration. He continued on as if I hadn't spoken. "Negal is pestilence and fire, Phonus rules the night, and Perun is thunder and lightning. They're the main factions you need concern yourself with."

"Destruction as a superpower sounds the best."

"Each faction will use their inherent nature in surprising ways. Don't assume any are more superior. And you're in luck because at the moment Aris and Persal have formed a secret alliance against the rest of the factions, which means I'm not going to kill you straightaway. At least not while you have your uses. But remember, there are no true ties between any of the factions. I could betray you just as easily as bed you."

My heart did a huge, giant leap. "Really…is that included in the game too?" And would my avatar reflect the flush rushing up my throat right now?

"Usually we're too busy fighting and deceiving everyone to bother doing much else. But anything is possible."

"Good thing because you'd get a slap."

"The best way to succeed is to trust no one. Everyone lies. Set are the best at it, but each faction has their agenda and none care about the other factions. It's all about power and ruling." Again he ironed over my comment without response. There was no shifting him from game mode.

"Not too different from reality then."

"Every move you make is for that goal alone. If you remember that, you're a quarter of the way to succeeding. Form alliances, harbor secrets, cheat, lie, and fight. That's the way to win."

"You have a cynical view of life."

"We're not playing real life. Yet."

I took that as him trying to be funny, but wasn't too sure.

He took my hand. I went to tug it back, but he said, "We're moving again."

This time we landed in a street with a bustle of people. Before I stopped myself, I gripped hold of Jax's arm, until we'd slowed our movement, then he released me at the moment I released him.

"Let's walk," he said. "This is Califax City. One of the few places the factions mix with accord. Behind us is the Dome. Everyone here is from one faction or another."

Jax and his design crew had obviously lost incentive to make the crowd fancy. Everyone passing us wore blank expressions, staring ahead like we weren't there except for their parting as we passed through. Their clothes were nothing but jumpsuits of varying dull colors.

"Step outside Califax and the factions are divided. They are forbidden to mix to keep the bloodlines pure. Can't have a mix of factional natures. Could give someone the edge they need."

He was so into this game. He and the other designers had thought up rules right down to bloodlines and ancestry. Perhaps it was a reflection on life where he grew up. To be honest, I could understand the lure of the game. Dominus had piqued my interest while I filed away all the information he fed me.

"How are you supposed to tell what faction someone's from?"

All the animated people coming toward us froze. "Come."

We approached a short woman in a dull green jumpsuit with thick, long red hair. Jax turned her head to the left and swept aside her hair. Behind the ear was a tattoo. It looked like an eye, a big, curving line at the base and another arching one over the top, with two bowing down in the middle.

Jax let her hair fall back. "The symbol for truth."

"She's a Set."

He stared at me. "Why do you say that?"

"Deception."

"You're catching on."

I turned his head so I could see his tattoo, the one he wore in real life. He'd even gone so far as to tattoo his gaming faction onto his skin.

"And this is Aris?"

He nodded. A fat bold line in the shape of a scythe, with a jagged handle, intersected a curved line tattooed to appear as if it was dripping.

"Bloodlust. Persal?"

The tattoos for the rest of the factions appeared in the air before me. Next to Persal was a fractured circle, boring for such a whopper of a power.

"Of course. The circle is symbolic of eternity, the universe, the cycle of life, whatever, but the circle's broken, meaning the end of all things. Total destruction."

"Congratulations. Most of the longtime players are yet to work that out. Every child is tattooed at birth according to the faction they are born into. For reference, each faction's nature and symbol will appear to your left when in game mode."

"Can we disguise or change the tattoo?"

Warrior Jax turned his expressionless face to me, leaving me at a loss to his thoughts.

He spoke the thread of my idea. "So you can deceive others into believing you have one power when you really have another? You sure you haven't heard of this game before?"

For some stupid reason, I swelled with pride at his compliment.

"You should be in Set. But the answer's no, the laws forbid it. But some don't follow the laws."

"Do we?"

"Yes. We never designed that feature in the program."

Weird. "Why did you say some don't follow the laws if you never put it into the program?" He was forgetting this was a game, made up and in his control.

He ignored the comment. "I think we should leave it there. There's too much to learn. It's impossible to cover it all in one session."

"We never got to fight the factions."

"When the factions fight, not a lot will be left. Therefore we limit how much fighting we do."

"I thought the purpose of the game was to fight?"

"If you were online, then sure. But virtual is different. Think guerrilla warfare. Stealth and cunning, learn each other's weaknesses while deflecting your own. You need to maneuver yourself into the best possible position before you engage in any skirmish. Remember factions fight with more than weapons. You risk too much if you attack without the best game play."

The scene disappeared and I was left staring at white. I pulled my goggles off and my mind took some time to adjust to staring at normal Jax.

"When do we do it again?"

His lips twitched into a smile. "Soon."

"Yes, I know I said one game, but we haven't played yet. It's kind of neat being involved in the game like that and not just hitting a button on the mouse. And I'm curious. It's complex."

So simple an explanation, belying the truth of my interest. One game and I was drawn into this intricate matrix. I walked a line thin as silk into a web of fiction woven tight with aspects of reality. If I played this game long enough, would I be left struggling to understand where the game finished and my world began? Like Jax?

Then what would I become?

He came toward me, hand outstretched. I stared at the tattoo on his inner wrist, a nonsensical design that looked like a cage, or a three-dimensional box, his enslavement, or so he'd said. My eyes wandered over the black marks swirling like snakes entwined on his forearm. Without a logical pattern, it was ugly but filled with meaning. *A guide when all is lost,* he'd said. Without thought, my eyes flicked to the mark of Aris behind his ear.

"Why did you tattoo the mark of Aris behind your ear?"

"You must never forget who you are."

"Sometimes I wish I could."

"You do and you'll fail. You'll be lost. Faction is family. It is who you are, your strength."

Why did he always come out with weird cryptic words? He was the one lost, lost in his own game. "Just as long as you don't expect me to get one of those."

He reinforced his offer of a handshake. This time I took it, my hand engulfed by the warm grip of his. Instead of shaking it, he held my hand firmly in his and looked into my eyes. "Welcome to the world of Dominus."

There was nothing welcoming or warm in the way he said it. But I was already beyond the moment of possible return. The doors had closed, and I stood on his side surrounded by the allure of mystery. But no matter how dark my containment, I wanted to be here. I wanted to learn his secrets. I wanted to learn Dominus's secrets. Most of all, I wanted to learn how to play to win the game of Dominus.

Chapter 12

My breasts oozed out of their confines. Luckily, no matter what I did, important parts remained covered, barely. I glanced down at my legs again, lifting each one out in front for a better look—long, creamy-white thighs, muscular without being butch. How long had Tyren spent designing me?

"How many players do you have playing at any one time?"

"Max we've had here is twenty. Online and it can be in the millions."

We stood on top of a cliff, a vast plane stretched below us. In the sky burned a red sun and a blue moon, spanning a good proportion of the horizon, both forever moving across the sky as polar opposites.

Moondine meant to travel in the direction of the moon; sunder meant to travel in the direction of the sun. Accetus was to head left if you were facing sunder and zendua the right. At the bottom of the chasm, a fast river flowed and was used, apparently, by Phonus to reach some of their towns situated farther downriver where the banks were shallower.

"Where are all the other players?"

"We're in the training sim. You're outside the game at the moment. Everyone you encounter is an NPC."

"Which are?"

"Non-player characters. They have no function at the moment."

"All the jumpsuit people I saw yesterday?"

"If you were online, there would be few NPCs as the players would populate the city. But we limit the number of players in virtual because we're looking for the best. We're not worried about how many we have playing at once but how good each player can become. In virtual, NPCs dominate. However, their purpose changes once out of the training sim. It's primarily PvP, player vs. player, so the NPCs will become your enemy."

"Playing virtual is a different game?"

"Yes and no. There are some things we've changed. It's more intense and harder."

Images appeared in front of me.

"Time to run through the weaponry. In the beginning, you are allocated a hand weapon. There is a choice of many, as you can see."

Everything faded from view except an assortment of blades, the image of each enlarged so I could see them clearly.

"Blades. Single or double-sided, or the three-bladed triplex."

"What are the ones with the spikes protruding from the tip?"

"Fancy, but that's all. They look lethal but you gain no edge over your enemy. Elva is responsible for those."

"Figures."

I think I saw a small smile creep through his animated face, but I could be making it up.

"If blades are not your thing you could go with clubs."

The blades disappeared and a row of clubs hung in the air. Long, short, spiked, or studded. Some even finished in a skull.

I looked at them without responding.

"Don't like? You can go swords."

Once again, I was faced with a huge selection of swords while the clubs dissolved into nothing.

"Do I have to choose something?"

"No. But you'll be the only one without a hand weapon."

"Do you use guns?" Shooting from afar sounded better than hand-to-hand combat. The idea of wielding one of the weapons that appeared before me turned my stomach. I was glossing through a lethal selection of weaponry so I could bash the hell out of someone physically, not metaphorically. Sure, it wasn't real, but I would be the one swinging the blade or club or stabbing them through the stomach, not a little animated character on a screen.

"No. A child can shoot a gun." The weaponry disappeared and once again I saw the cliff and the plain below.

"Why does everything have to be about being the best?"

"That's the only way you'll survive. It's the only way to win."

"So what if I die? I'll just choose another avatar."

"It doesn't work like that. In virtual, dead means dead."

"So, I'd be out of the game."

"If you're dead, you can't play."

"That's a stupid game. Thank god I didn't fly halfway across the world to play it."

"That's why only the best play virtual."

"Remind me again why I'm starting at this level."

"Because you can."

He turned his back on me and walked toward the edge of the cliff, and I had an urge to poke my tongue out at him.

"We can forget the weapons for now and start training."

"As in?"

"Hand-to-hand combat minus the weapons."

Jax was the most intense guy I'd ever met, both in and out of Dominus, but when in Dominus, his chiseled features and muscular body, including the ridiculous number of ridges on his abs, made him appear the epitome of intense, the game master, the unrelenting, uncompromising taskmaster.

He strode toward me with his fluid avatar fashion. "We're changing scene. Hold on." He held out his hand for me to steady myself with. I hesitated, not wanting to rely on him to keep me upright. "On your ass or on your feet, Sable, which one?"

Hopefully my avatar expression disguised the face I just pulled. I grabbed his arm as the cliff and plain shimmered out of view. The sudden appearance of white space, and I swayed sideways, but the tightening of Jax's hand on mine kept me from going right over. He became my reference point.

Jax gave us more features this time. The floor turned slate gray, the walls off-white, giving the area dimensions instead of infinite space, but no windows or door and I felt trapped.

"This is the combat arena, but don't freak. Tyren's responsible for the name. He likes everything to sound deadly. It's our training room while in the training sim. You can make mistakes here without threatening your life. Virtual is different from manipulating an avatar on a screen, so recruits spend time in here learning to use their body before they begin the game. When we use weapons, they appear on the walls for you to select."

Jesus, this was serious stuff. "Is it too late to opt out and play the game on the screen?"

"Yes."

Said with all seriousness, including that deadpan expression.

"Remember what you're standing on. Falls won't hurt. The floor will be stationary, which means we could run into each other, which is the point of this training sim."

He motioned for me to join him in the center of the floor.

"Playing online, you get buffs and debuffs, but in virtual, they don't exist, meaning you don't gain any skills or advantages or lose any, for that matter, unless you are injured or die. You enter and leave as you are. That's why it's essential you're the best before you enter. You train hard, you get good, and you get smart. Find your factional nature, it's the only power you'll gain, and learn to use it with cunning. In the end, you'll see size doesn't matter. It's your ability. Even the smallest can beat Goliath."

"That's a fable."

"What makes you think fables aren't based on truth?"

I rolled my eyes as Jax continued his instructions without taking time for a breath.

"We're going to start with some simple martial arts and get you used to moving your limbs in a virtual sense. All you have to do is follow my lead. Once you have the hang of it, I'll bring in a bot and you can practice on that."

"I never expected a workout."

"There's lots of things you'll encounter in Dominus you never expected."

A breather would be nice, but I doubted Jax would allow that.

"Let's begin."

The game swallowed me. I forgot about time while I practiced moving fake me and rewiring my brain so it read my virtual vision as the real thing. Jax was right about the falls; bouncy mat equated to nothing painful.

We ran through the basic moves that Holden had shown me. If Jax was surprised at my *somewhat* proficiency, he never showed it, but I was likely to miss subtle expression on an avatar's face.

After a while, Jax increased the level of difficulty in what he showed me, and that's when I began to fall apart. Jax was a hard teacher and soon became irritating as hell. He made me repeat and repeat and repeat. After the umpteenth repeat, I told him I would never make the Olympic team so there was no point in training me so hard. His face didn't crack a smile. He breathed out, told me to do the same, and started me again. Never—with a big capital—had I met someone with such ruthless determination.

He wasn't like my dad, he was worse. In both men, Jax and Dad, the calm belied a mind of steel and an indomitable nature that would accept no less than the best I could give. *Do it again, repeat.* Those two commands ground away at me until I just wanted out. My moves became sloppy as my enthusiasm disappeared into a sinkhole. It was like my life was on repeat. The unobtainable goal, perfection, forever out of my reach. Jax's barks chipped through to my soul until the unfairness turned to anger, which soured in my stomach and gave me a gut ache.

I continued with his training because I didn't know how to refuse, but the ache increased. My kicks became sloppier because I was dreaming more about kicking him in the nuts and watching him roll on the mat than the target.

Once Jax deemed I was ready, a female bot appeared before me, her face nondescript, her jumpsuit a dull green.

"Why can't I practice with you?"

Wound tight on adrenaline, I needed to release festering emotions.

Jax's persistent demands and brutal training cracked walls inside I was unaware I'd built and let a whole lot of dirty feelings out.

"This will challenge you. I can slow the bot's response at first, which will give you time."

"Screw the bot, I want to practice with you. You're better able to control your movements, I'm sure."

Coursing through my veins was a wave of anger I didn't want to stop and had rarely aired before, not out loud, especially not to my father. It's not that I was afraid of how he would react; I was afraid of what he would think. The dark emotions wanted wings, and I didn't care what Jax would think. Plus the idea of kicking him in the nuts had stayed in the forefront of my mind.

"It's better this way."

"I don't give a damn which way's better."

It was stupid to goad him. Of course he would beat me. At this point I didn't care.

"That's not—"

"I don't care what your training schedule permits."

In fact, I wanted to pull my goggles from my eyes and see the real him. I wanted to kick at the real him, exercise some of the real tension out of my real muscles. I was sick of staring at creamy, smooth, muscular legs that were supposedly mine but looked like a Marvel character. I was sick of being someone else.

"If that's what you want." His reply was measured.

I ripped the goggles from my eyes and felt a moment's wooziness while my mind adjusted to reality after so much time spent looking at a virtual screen.

Jax removed his goggles too. He stared at me, no question in his expression. It was like he expected nothing less than for this to happen.

"We do it this way. I'm sick of looking at a fabricated world."

Jax tossed his goggles off the mat. "You'll learn more if I'm not gentle." He fiddled with one of the silver studs.

"Whatever." I approached and took the stance he'd drummed into me for the last few hours. I had a pitiful arsenal of kicks at the ready, which I would perform subpar compared to him, but it made no difference to me.

I focused like he'd told me to, repeatedly—I was bound to hear the words in my sleep. I assessed his movement, where he placed his weight, what muscles he favored, where his balance sat. I attempted to blanket the amount of similar information I relayed to him. Then, when I thought time had stretched on long enough, I threw my first kick. He deflected with speed, grabbed my ankle, and sent me crashing to the mat, which wasn't necessary.

The fall didn't hurt but I still used a little venom in my voice. "Is that you going gentle?"

"Yes."

I pushed to my feet and inhaled deeply to release my stomach's knots and blow the tension from my muscles.

No dancing around this time. I launched into another kick from my short list only to find myself kissing the mat again.

I pushed up from the floor. If I was still animated, I'm sure steam would be seen pouring from my ears.

He waited, easy stance, poker face. I tried to stuff the frustration inside away from my face as I blew loose strands from my eyes. My racing heart rate and clenched fists told me I wasn't succeeding. This time I ran the short distance toward him, thinking the momentum would help add power to my next kick. Adrenaline powered my leg forward out from my hip joint at the same moment a blinding pain shot through my head like a long, thick nail had been rammed through my skull, the agony unbearable. I clutched my head, pressing it hard between my palms as if that would lessen the feeling.

I fell to my knees and bent low with my forehead on the mat, unable to do anything but cry out through the tears with seemingly no end to my torture.

Chapter 13

STRONG ARMS ENFOLDED ME, lifting me from the ground. With each jerk from the walk, I squeaked another weak plea. Jax lowered me onto the couch, and I huddled into a ball, knees up to my chin, arms shielding my head as if it would help ward off whatever had taken hold. Through the jags of pain, I became aware of Jax's hand resting on my thigh. To get me through the mental storm, I tried to focus on the warmth of his touch and the soft, subtle blend of his smell. I allowed my mind to wonder on his scent, fabricating images of cold winter's nights around the fire, drinking my fill of spiced warm drinks. The longer I focused, the more real my imagination became. We were both there, feet up on the couch, a hot mug of something spicy and sweet cupped in our hands while his other hand rested on my thigh, as it did now, and I imagined his imprint as a cleansing fire, capable of burning away the pain.

The headache persisted but I needed to escape my imagination. Despite a white light strobing behind my eyelids in rhythm with the throbs, flashing through my vision when I opened my eyes, I flailed about, trying to sit up. Jax grabbed hold of my hand to steady it.

"Relax." His voice was soothing.

"I can't see. There's a light."

"Just relax. It will go. But the more you fight, the longer it will take."

With a hand on my shoulder, he coaxed me back down onto the couch. I tried to calm down by taking big breaths but found it hard to concentrate with the pain. Again I focused on Jax's hand, releasing one from my manacle grip while the other stroked my side. His touch was enough to ease the panic.

Relaxing back, I allowed the throbs to wash through me. He was right, fighting it wouldn't change the problem. I focused on each beat, noticed where it started in my brain and where it ended, which didn't make it better but gave me an anchor. After a while, though, the throbs did lessen. And, with more time, dissolved into nothing.

At first I was afraid to move in case this was a false lull but soon grew impatient. I opened my eyes. The first thing I saw was Jax, peering down at me. With a gentle finger, he traced my cheekbone, and my breath crawled to a stop in my throat while he did so. There was no smile on his face, only concern, and something much deeper, an indecipherable but unpleasant understanding that haunted his dark eyes.

This was too intimate. He was too close. I sat up, forcing him to move back. "That came from nowhere."

"You feel better?"

"The pain's gone, but I'm afraid to move in case it comes back."

"How about I get you a drink?"

I watched him walk away while my mind jumbled up. What was going on here? I knew how to hate him and fight against him, but I didn't know how else to be with him, and I didn't want to learn a new way for us to interact with each other. Jax was a cryptic pain in the ass, intense, and scary at times. Enigmatic came to mind, but I banished the thought because to me it had always meant mysteriously alluring.

Rather than look at him, I glanced to the open door of the gaming room. From here I could see the white walls and the mat. Sitting out here, it was easy to believe the lie that none of the last few hours had happened. The surreality lay in becoming my avatar and joining the game, the physicality of each move, the complexity in the detail. When inside Dominus, it became more a reality than a fabrication.

Drawn to the sound of his return, I flicked a glance to the tattoo behind his right ear, although I couldn't see much of it from this angle.

It was there because of the rules of Dominus, a means of knowing everyone's factional nature, a rule of the game, not a necessity in real life, and yet Jax, as well as Tyren—and I'd bet Elva too—had bothered to brand themselves Aris, had chosen their family and wore their loyalty for all to see.

Jax handed me a glass of water. He sat on the coffee table in front of me and leaned forward to rest his elbows on his knees. "You look pale. Make sure you drink."

"I've never experienced anything like that before. I rarely get headaches."

After staring at his hands, clasped in front, he said, "It can be a side effect of the game."

"You're joking?"

"It happens at times."

"That's dangerous. Shouldn't you do something about it? You could really mess with people's minds."

"It only happens initially, then you adjust."

"Or grow a tumor."

"Ironically, it's the strongest who suffer. It's how we know who's worth keeping in the game."

"That's after you fry their brains."

He huffed a laugh. It was the first time I'd seen him in any way amused, or inching to it. I'm sure my face relayed my shock. And there was something else there as well, but I was not willing to assess the feeling. The headache burned the anger away, and Jax's bizarre mood, acting like he cared, then sort of laughing, and I needed to leave. I wasn't here to learn another side of his nature, especially one that made him appear more human, with a smidgeon of compassion.

"You must be shocked I was one of them."

"I would not have asked you to play if I didn't suspect you'd succeed."

Given his persistent stalking of me, it was a creepy thing to say. "I don't understand why you were in the convenience store?"

"You don't think it was a coincidence?"

"You suddenly turn up everywhere in my life, so, no, it wasn't a coincidence."

"What about Holden? The fact we know each other and him appearing in your life at the same time, is that a coincidence?"

My mouth dried. "What are you saying?"

"I'm saying you don't always know who your friends are, or enemies, for that matter."

He was crazy. "I think you're still lost in your game." It was complex enough, and if they were virtual most of the time, surely they would start to think and act like their avatars.

"What if the game was not just a game?"

Oh, god, I was right. "I'd say you have issues that need addressing. But I'm not qualified to help you."

Again with the half laugh. All of a sudden, I was funny, or a joke, probably the latter.

"You're not what I expected."

"I wasn't expecting you at all. Don't take this the wrong way, but I would have been happier if you'd never showed up. Nothing about you makes sense. And I haven't forgotten you threatened my brother."

"I wasn't after him. But you needed to be pushed."

"Why was it so important? It's just a game."

"There's a right time to reveal things."

I sat back heavy into the couch. Here we went again on a cryptic merry-go-round. "Maybe I should ask Holden."

"Holden will give you a distorted version of the truth."

"Distorted according to whose perception?"

"Holden can't be trusted. His loyalties are questionable."

"I wanted to ask him about your mental health."

Jax puffed out a breath, leaning away like he wished to escape the conversation. His sudden out breath released the elastic band stretched between us, which threatened to fling back and smack me in the face.

"You need me."

"No I don't."

"I'm the GM. It's up to me whether you survive."

"But I don't want to be a part of Dominus."

"It's too late. You already are."

"Is this you threatening my brother again?"

Jax sunk his head into his palms. "I thought it would be different. Easier."

"To threaten me, manipulate me?"

When he closed his eyes, his black eyelashes dusted his skin. I waited immeasurable moments for him to open them and look at me. Normally I couldn't wait to escape his unrelenting gaze, but this time it felt like his eyes, staring into mine, would be a lifeline, or at least the link to a mystery that would possibly save me.

"To be truthful. But it's the hardest thing to do."

"I have to leave. Am I free to go?" My sarcasm dripped from each word.

I stood, not waiting for an answer. Jax joined me, making our proximity between the couch and the coffee table tight. "I planned on telling you everything."

"Why don't you?"

"I shouldn't want to protect you."

I couldn't help it, I laughed in his face. "You think this is protection?" I couldn't find enough adequate words. "You're stuck in your world of Dominus, Jax. It's twisting your mind. I wonder if you know what reality is anymore."

"No, Sable, my world is reality. You just don't realize it yet."

Instead of salvation, his eyes plunged me into a turbulent sea.

Chapter 14

JAX WAS A LUNATIC, unstable and obsessed with dragging me into his delusional world. Wasn't being stripped of dignity enough? Not according to whatever dice had rolled against me.

"Cheer up. The problem won't be there forever."

I forced my face into something resembling calm neutrality as I glanced to the lady sitting beside me. Looking at her sorrowful smile and smelling her stale odor, like her clothes had been scrunched in the washing basket too long, I needed space. "True, but I may not survive its short duration."

I stood as I reached for the button. "Sorry," I said as I maneuvered past her into the aisle.

"My thoughts and prayers are you with, my child."

I couldn't even muster a smile for her kind words.

The bus left me on the side of the road, staring ahead as the cars flashed past me. The arguments in my head circled back to Jax's fixation with having me play Dominus. Everything he'd done so far had steered me to this point, to his game. That's how crazy he was. He was so lost he thought it was real.

Maybe I should speak to Holden. There were no guarantees he knew anything about what Jax was up to now, but there was history between them. Holden would know some of Jax's past and possibly what drove him to be such a lunatic.

I skipped through the traffic and up the curb, then wove through a scatter of tables with bright polka-dot tablecloths and a vase of daisies in the center of each table. The place brimmed with cheery chatter, laughter, and the smell of cheap floral soap from the pollen.

Catching sight of a woman's profile, I stalled my dash, only to be bumped by someone from behind, followed by the *chink* of glasses and a cold wash flooding across my back.

"Oh, god, sorry," the waitress said as I jerked away from the cold and turned to face her.

Rather than bothering to answer, I shook my head and waved my hand. Being soaked in wine was not my main problem. Mum was. What was she doing here? And who was she with? The cold from the drink seeped through my skin, all the way through until it reached my heart.

Perfectly trimmed mustache, good-looking for an old guy, strong features, square jaw, gray at his temples, dressed casual but neat, he looked at Mum like someone looks at a piece of succulent meat. I clenched my fist as I envisioned marching up and slapping him in the face.

Mum loved Dad. She'd never betray him, which meant this meeting was worse than a date. She was fishing for a job and this guy had to be an acquaintance from Dad's past. I wouldn't know because Dad had kept his secret life separate from his real life, us, or was it the other way around?

My world would not fall apart any more than it already had— already was. I marched over and stood at the head of their table.

"What're you doing, Mum?"

"Sable." Mom's cheeks flooded. "What are you doing here?"

"I asked first." I didn't want to interrogate Mum; neither did I blame her for what she was doing. She'd finally woken from her dark pit, which was fantastic, but she was climbing into an abyss she'd be lost in and we'd be dragged down too. Dad was at fault for treating us all like precious glass and keeping us locked away from the harshness of life. Mum had no idea the trap she was in, and I had no idea how to save her.

"And this must be your beautiful daughter." The guy rose from his seat, the perfect gentleman, with an outstretched hand. I looked at his hand and the thick gold band on his wedding finger, the manicured perfection of his nails, then up into his green eyes as a dozen phantom insects crawled underneath my skin. He was a shark, having sharp eyes that cruised with leisure, watching, analyzing, formulating a way to turn a situation to his advantage. I felt like I was waiting for the gallows and only this man's clemency would set me free, which of course would never happen unless he devised a use for me.

I ignored his polite welcome and turned back to Mum.

"I think it's time we left."

"But...honey..." she struggled to explain. "This is Carter." She looked at the shark, waiting quietly in the depths.

I refused to look at him. Instead I fed all my intentions, which were to get my mum as far from him as possible, into my stare. "It's time we left, Mum."

"Sable. You're being rude. This is not like you. I will come as soon as I've finished my conversation with Carter."

I could hardly drag my mum away, could I? I grabbed her hand. "Come on, we're off."

"Stop this." She pulled me back close to her. "You're embarrassing me." She sighed. "At least let me say goodbye to Carter."

I released her hand and folded my arms across my chest as a wall to his gloating expression.

"I'm sorry, Carter, but I must go."

"I understand." Carter extended his hand for hers, so obviously ready to kiss it. His lips would pucker next.

I pulled her hand away. "She doesn't need your slobber all over her."

"Sable!" Mom's shocked gasp wasn't enough to make me stop.

I pulled her along, drawing the eyes of the diners.

She hissed. "Stop this." She glanced back at the shark. "I'm so sorry, Carter."

"Don't worry yourself, Lila. We can finish our discussion another time."

Like hell they would.

Once we'd left the café, Mum yanked her hand away. "I don't know what's got into you, young lady."

Neither did I. That was not me back there. I was polite. I'd never argued with teachers or talked back to my parents. I followed rules. I had followed rules, until my life slid out of my control; now my personality slid the same way—desperation made a devil out of anyone.

"Who is he?"

"Honey, it has nothing to do with you."

"He's an old contact of Dad's, isn't he?"

"Sable...I'm not having this conversation in the street."

"Please, Mum. Don't do this. Dad's in jail because he dealt with these sorts of people."

"Look at us. Look what we've been reduced to. We're not a family anymore." She sucked in a breath, then covered her hand as if to hold back the sobs. With a swallow, she straightened and wiped at one eye. Calmer now, she continued. "We can't continue to live like this. We've barely any money and what we do have will run out real soon, and then where are we going to be? We need to pay rent, buy food." She palmed her forehead and spoke from behind her hands. "You have no idea how hard this is. No one is going to hire me. What can I do?"

I felt my own tears grow. The pain in Mum's voice killed me. That's why I couldn't be angry with her. She was trying her best to find a solution. Unfortunately her solution was all wrong. "I really think we should talk to Dad."

She grabbed me by the upper arms. "No. We're not telling your father. It would hurt him too much."

"All right, but will you promise me you won't see Carter again?"

She straightened and looked down the street, her fragility evident in the thin cotton material of her dress and the hollowness of her face pronounced by the dusting of a soft pink blush on her cheeks.

"He's offered me a job."

"What...Mum...no. He's a lying cheat. You can't trust him."

"He's a very wealthy businessman. He's offered me a job in the office. I don't know a thing about being a secretary, but he's willing to train me."

"Why?"

"I think he feels bad for everything that's happened."

One look at the guy and I didn't trust him. His eyes were too shrewd. Nothing about his smile was genuine. We were desperate, but were we that desperate?

"I've got to do this, honey. You understand that, don't you? It pains your dad to see us like we are. This is a respectable job. I'm doing paperwork and typing and answering phones. That's all. And I can start on a good wage. Normally you have to work for years before you start earning anything you would call decent, but Carter understands our situation and he's willing to help where he can."

I stared at Mum, at the fine lines creasing the corners of her eyes, a few running like forks on her upper lip. She looked like an innocent child, fragile, vulnerable, empty inside except for her fear, searching for her way home, for a savior. I was no longer the child in this relationship, but I wasn't her savior either. Instead I was contaminated, dirty, about to be swallowed whole by a secret, just like my dad.

Someone bumped into me from behind, sending my awareness back out into the street, the traffic crawling alongside us with the occasional horn blaring, to the pedestrians hurrying past us, moving in unison like robots, like bots.

A coldness wrapped around my heart as I looked without focus at the crowd, feeling the enemy inside. Lies, secrets, and betrayal had ripped our family apart and would do so again.

Chapter 15

ALL I SAW WAS Carter's green eyes leering at me like he wanted to suck me up and spit me out, that smile on his face greedy. My stomach shrank to the size of a pea just thinking about it. He loved this, loved playing the hero, loved having power over us, having us desperate and needy for his benevolence.

And how much did we know about the guy? Dad had kept that side of his life wrapped tight. We knew nothing about him, what he himself was capable of.

Jax snapped out his left leg and sent me flat on my back. Two steps and he stood over me. "Your mind's not on task."

A hot spike of adrenaline heated my core. Teeth clenched, I stared up at him.

"I'm not here to waste my time. If you're not going to concentrate, we go in."

I pushed away from his towering form and climbed to my feet. "I never asked for us to train for hours on end."

"Tell me, how do you expect to win?"

"Who said anything about winning? I'm here, aren't I? I came back to play your stupid game to fulfill my end of the bargain. I don't care if I win or not. I just want this over with so I can get out." I turned my back on him now that my fury had burned a hole through my core. Remembering more kindling for the fire burning within, I spun back. "You haven't fulfilled your side of the bargain."

His expression matched my own. "Now is not the time." His words sliced through the air.

"There will never be a time, because you never intended to keep your side of the bargain. You're not going to give me answers."

"Do I really have to baby you through this? I expected you to be more resilient, stronger, smarter. It disappoints me to see I was wrong."

He could've punched me hard and it wouldn't have had as strong of an effect. "I'm happy to disappoint. Now maybe you'll leave me alone." The thickness in my throat had me turn away. I paced to disguise the hurt and make it look like frustration.

"You came here again of your own free will."

"I came here with the belief in your promise."

"I never made a promise."

Never...what? "I can't believe you said that."

"Think back, Sable. I never promised to tell you anything."

"That's right, you threatened my family. That's why I am here. Well, you know what, you'll have to stand in line." It was none of his business, so why had I said it?

That stopped him. The smallest crease appeared between his eyes, the first twitch of a frown. "What's going on?"

"Oh, now you're interested in what's diverting my attention."

The tension and frustration pulling his muscles rigid snapped, sucking the fight from his body. He rubbed at his brow as he turned from me and walked away. The door to the games room flew open. Tyren filled the cavity. His eyes settled on me before tracking Jax as he paced across the mat.

"Tuesday."

Jax glanced over his shoulder at Tyren, nodded once, then turned his back. Tyren gave me one last look, wearing a solemn expression, not the cheerful eyes and smile of the guy I had first met.

I stared at Jax's back, his slumped shoulders, the defeat in the way he held himself, as Tyren backed out the door.

"You're probably not interested, but Mum has found herself a job."

Jax slowly turned around to face me.

Before I knew it, the rest of the story came out. "Sounds great, sure, especially since she's finally managed to get herself out of bed and dressed before sunset. It's one of Dad's associates, some guy called Carter. And I don't like it. Dad was mixing with some bad people. People capable of murder." My breath came out heavy. "Just like him. I'm worried she's getting herself mixed up with some bad people. It's like we're never going to escape."

Maybe I said what I said because of the way he appeared to be crumpling inside, leaving me behind. Why should I care? I didn't like Jax. Most of the time, I was uncomfortable around him. But other times, it felt like he was the only person who understood. Twisted logic —perhaps I was just going crazy after spending all this time with him.

I didn't understand the look Jax gave me, but the length of time he held my eyes walked a shiver up my spine. From the stress of moments ago, it felt like all our impactful and terse words shuddered to a halt, leaving a silent space, vacant, hollow.

"I'm attending a funeral on Tuesday." He jerked his head in the direction of the door, a reference to what Tyren told him. I hadn't realized I was offering an olive branch, but Jax had accepted it.

"A friend of yours?"

"Not quite, but someone who deserves my respect."

"When I met you on the train, you were exiting the cemetery. Another funeral?"

"So you did follow us." His tone was flat, not the light flirt of catching me out on my lie. "Life's a dangerous game." A typical Jax response.

"You have a very dim view of it."

"Don't you? After everything that's happened?"

"Sure, initially. I hated my dad for what he did and what's happened to us, but I can't afford to fall to pieces. Ajay needs me. And now I have to save Mum."

"You're willing to do that on your own?"

"If I have to. Dad could talk sense into Mum." I stopped and flicked a look at him before continuing in a soft voice. "Now I'm not sure what he can do."

"You don't need him. You'll work it out on your own."

I laughed but it was a sorrowful sound because of how much I wanted to cry right now. I didn't want to have to deal with this alone.

"I thought I disappointed you."

He rubbed at his forehead, looking zapped of any smart comeback. "You frustrate me."

"Thanks, good to know."

"I attend those funerals to pay respects to people who didn't believe in themselves, not enough. They were good people, but their weakness got them killed."

"And their weakness was a lack of self-belief?"

"Discipline and self-belief. Courage will get you so far. The belief you are good enough will get you to the end."

"Your childhood—" Oh, god, why did I have to start that conversation? The last thing I should be reminding him of was his family. "Sorry."

"We need to go in."

"Do we?" I wasn't in the mood.

"That's why you're here." His mood a finality.

He strode off to the computer, leaving me on the mat, powerless to protest.

WHEN I SLIPPED the goggles on, I was in Califax City. We moved along a crowded street. All the bots, in their nondescript jumpsuits, were heading in the opposite direction, but parted down the middle to allow us through.

Jax took hold of my hand. "Come."

I stopped looking around or following the layout of the street. I only thought of his hand holding mine. When I looked down, I saw the muscular forearm of his avatar with its wrist of studded leather and dangerous-looking rings. It was hard to equate what I felt to what I saw through the virtual goggles. His hand was warm and firm in mine, his skin soft, everything rendered amazingly accurate, down to the protruding knuckle bones and veining. But I was looking at an animation, a brilliant adaptation of real life, but still not real life. I had to remember that.

"In here."

Jax dragged me back to our virtual world with a gentle tug on my hand as he led me down a cobbled, narrow alleyway, past buildings slotted together like a jigsaw puzzle, metal doors of varying matte colors. Jax paused at a red door on our left. Above, the symbol of Aris glowed to life, the red of the circle appearing to drip down the wall. Within moments of standing there, the door *clunked* open, swinging in with a heavy, echoing metallic sound.

Inside, the walls hugged us on either side as we headed toward a bright, sunlit room. We stepped into a vast open space. Six pillars marked the corners of the hexagonal room, shooting stories high to a glass domed ceiling, which poured the sun through onto a mosaic floor. I circled the mosaic for a better look.

"We're in a house that belongs to Aris," I said.

Jax walked across the center of the mosaic, down the line of the scythe.

"A dangerous place for you to be if we were in game mode. We may have an alliance, but factions do not enter other factions' strongholds, even in a neutral place such as Califax."

"Why did you bring me here?"

"There is still much you need to learn. Since we're within the training sim, you're in no danger being here."

"If we weren't, could we still be with each other?"

"In Califax, yes, but only in public places and not all the time. The other factions must not know of the alliance. Outside of Califax, we would never meet."

"And if we were found together?"

"We'd be killed and the Senate of Factions would have a major battle on their hands determining what our connection meant. It would likely cost more lives before they were able to assure the other factions there was no alliance between Persal and Aris, all the while executing key figures within either faction."

"Nice game you've developed."

"There's no fun in anything easy. This is Aris HQ. Those arriving from outside Califax stay here for the time they're in the city."

"No motels then."

"Factions mingle but are not allowed to share the same accommodation."

"Does every faction have a place like this?"

"Yes."

"Where's Persal's? I may need it once we're no longer in the training sim. I gather it is one place we're safe."

"Yes. To attack another faction's stronghold is a declaration of war."

"And when factions go to war, not a lot will survive."

Jax walked past me with a passive face—in game mode once again—and down another dark corridor. Wall panels glowed a deep gold as he went, lighting his path. The panels illuminated etchings on the walls like cave drawings, twisting lines, wrapping and swirling back on themselves, a vast elaborate design, something I'd seen before. I slowed to study the markings.

Jax returned to stand beside me. I looked down at his arm as I lifted it. There appeared no difference between the virtual and real tattoo.

"What does this mean?" I looked at the wall and then at his tattoo.

He gently withdrew his arm. "I've already told you."

"Your guide when all is lost. It's a map. To where?"

"One revelation at a time."

He continued down the hall, then paused long enough for the door on his left to slide open. Inside, more wall panels came to life, casting a soft glow over a bed with flat pillows and dull green bedspread, the only item of furniture in the room.

My senses bounced to life as my steps slowed. "Is this your room?"

"No. This is how all the rooms in the stronghold look. Temporary accommodation doesn't need much else. But this is not what I want to show you."

He turned from the bed and crouched. "I wanted to show you this," he said, placing his hand on one of the tiles. Without seeming to do anything else, he stood and looked at the floor. I followed his gaze. Then the miraculous happened. The tiling fell away as if disintegrating in on itself, creating a vortex, which swirled in a chaotic vacuum, sucking the tiles, rocks, and dust in on itself with the sound of a brick wall collapsing. More and more tiles gave way to the force of the vortex, eating up the floor. I stepped back, thinking the tiles from under my feet would go too. When the chaos settled, we were left standing at the edge of a gaping hole.

Jax placed a foot in the hole and the dark pit illuminated, showing a staircase leading down underground. I inched over and peered in as he removed his foot from the top step. With his foot gone, the light disappeared, and once again I was staring into a black pit.

"What was that?"

His face remained avatar passive, his voice mute.

"Jax, what was it?"

"Something you don't need to know about just now."

"Then why did you show me?"

Jax was saved from answering by the floor remaking itself. Like watching a film in reverse. This time, instead of the sound of destruction, it was the sound of construction, tiles sliding alongside one another, rubble reforming, stacking, and joining until the floor was remade.

There was not enough light in the room for me to read any subtlety on his avatar face. I had only questions behind my stare, but Jax's walled expression deflected all of them before they left my mouth.

As he spun to leave, I grabbed his elbow to hold him back. "Why did you show me?"

"I don't know." For the first time, he sounded unsure of himself. "I shouldn't have."

A tug and he was free of my hold and out of the room. I quick-stepped to catch up as he led me down the dim corridor with enough time for one fleeting glimpse of the map on the wall before we were out into the lit space beneath the dome, then down another corridor. No panels glowed to life to mark our way. Instinctively, I reached out to balance myself with a hand on the wall. When my skin skimmed the smooth cool of the surface, I snapped it back, concentrating on the remnant feeling of cool on my fingertips. How did I feel that?

Ahead, a bright light flooded the corridor as Jax pushed out into the day. I hurried to catch up and found us in an alleyway with Jax striding away to the mouth of the alley like he hoped to distance himself from what he had shown me or maybe it was me he wanted to escape.

"How about we do something different, like give me a taste of game mode?"

"You're not ready," he barked over his shoulder as his strong, powerful legs carried him away.

"Sure I am. I know a kick or two."

"You're not ready." Yelled with a harsh finality.

"So you keep saying. The monotony is getting boring."

That got him. He gave me his attention. "Then we need to increase your training."

"I'm not scared. Enough with the training. Let's get this started. So what if I'm out of the game after one session?"

He spun so fast I ran into him. "Do you really want that?"

"Sure. I'm getting fed up with your somber mood. At least if I was fighting I'd be doing something exciting rather than listening to your monologue."

"You don't know what you're asking."

"Then how about you show me?"

"If that's what you want."

The scene around me changed. We remained within the alley, only the surroundings became more detailed, more alive. The sun cast shadows along the wall, now rich with weathered stone and textual irregularities. Fissures ran like rivers down the mortar, spreading across the stones in their own haphazard fashion. The giant moon hovered behind us, the blazing sun low in front. The cobbles beneath my feet were textured with grooves, cracks, and dirt. Staring at the dirt, my mouth filled with the taste of dust.

To the left of my vision, information appeared. As Jax had said, I saw the main factions' symbols to the right of my field of vision.

"What's all this running down the left and right side of my vision?"

"Come, we need to get moving. There's danger standing still."

"How do I get rid of it?"

"It's stats and other vitals. And you don't, you get used to it."

"It's a pain in the ass."

"Move it, Sable."

"Why?"

"You got what you wanted. We're in game mode, which makes you very vulnerable. The computer can sense your location. It will send an attack any minute."

"Cool, let's begin."

But Jax was already striding off down the alley to the entrance. I had to jog to keep up but only made it halfway when a shrill cry rent the air and a figure dropped in front of me, blocking my escape. The warrior was perfectly rendered, no nondescript jumpsuit man anymore. He wore an armor of deep green, his face covered by a mask. At his waist, tucked in his thick leather belt, was a blade, which he withdrew once my eyes settled on it.

He swiped the blade back and forth in front of his body with a sharp whistle as the blade sliced through the air. I felt the ripple of disturbance against my skin.

I shrieked and jumped back as my pulse swished through my ears. I didn't have a weapon. I was unprepared.

The warrior lunged for me. I only had enough wits to leap to the side. I crashed into the wall and staggered on my feet while small chips of brick work came loose and scattered on the cobbles around me. The warrior spun and lunged again. His sword sliced with the *whoosh* of a sharp blade cutting the air. I ducked and shrieked, useless against such onslaught. Although my mind seized with panic, my concentration funneled to this single moment. It helped whirl my brain into keep-me-safe plans.

This is a game. This is a game. Virtual was too real. My mind wouldn't believe my mantra.

Another swing with his blade and I ducked and dived to the other wall. Halfway there, something hard drove into my ribs, and I was sent tumbling sideways with a searing pain in my side. I hit the cobbles with a hard thud, which forced out all my breath.

The feel of wind, and I rolled to the side without thinking, while behind, a high-pitched chink as the blade sliced into the cobbles. Even the sound effects were too real to ignore.

I scrambled to my feet with the wall as my aid. My senses were attuned to the smallest breath of wind. Luckily I wasn't paralyzed by fear, but my mind couldn't fabricate a way out. Somehow, amongst the chaos, instinct took over and I balanced myself for defense.

The warrior dived toward me, and I lashed out with a kick designed to meet with his chin, but he dodged at the last, grabbed my shin, and hurled me across to the other wall, which I hit with a bone-jarring thud. He was nothing but a bot, so this shouldn't be hurting at all. Why was I hurting?

Aching in too many places, I rolled over on the cobbles as the warrior loomed over me. A part of me wanted to climb to my feet and continue, but I wasn't sure if my body would allow me to do so. Did this mean I was out of the game?

He remained passive, blade by his side like he'd won and the game had finished. I squinted up at his silhouetted body as a terrible itching creeped up my arm. I glanced down to see my skin writhing as if a million insects crawled underneath. As I stared, splits appeared, forming gaping wounds, and little black beetles spewed out, dripping blobs of crimson blood.

I screamed and screamed as a bolt of pain lanced me through the skull. I curled up in agony while the split in my forearm lengthened down to my fingers. The beetles and my blood oozed onto the cobbles. I could feel the tacky wetness of the crimson liquid on my legs.

My vision blurred, but the pain radiating through my mind kept me conscious. My head drooped, too heavy to keep up.

A clatter brought me back, and I forced my head up to see the blade lying on the cobbles and Jax riding the warrior's back. Unarmed, the warrior thrashed with his arms, but Jax leaned over and sunk his teeth into the warrior's shoulder as he pulled a small blade from a sheath.

The air was filled with cries of torment and stilled by imminent death. I tried to escape this place by curling inward into a ball, covering my ears, and scrunching my eyes tight. There was no escape. I was forced to endure, on the cold, hard cobbles, a moment of sustained terror.

Finally I thought to take my goggles from my eyes, but hands yanked me from the ground by my shoulders and pushed me hard against the wall. I moaned from the impact as my breath *whooshed* out and my head throbbed. I squinted at Jax with faulty vision as darkness threatened to take hold. All I saw was blood.

My head bobbed up and down a few times while I struggled to maintain my grip on consciousness. I opened my eyes and attempted to focus on him. But the horror of the vision made me recoil. Jax's face was covered with blood. It ran as trails down his chin, smeared his cheeks and neck. It was on his hands, his chest, and dripped from the blade of the weapon he'd re-sheathed.

I tried not to see, tried not to believe, tried not to smell the metallic scent of blood.

He shook me when my eyes closed and never opened.

He yelled in my face, "Look at me."

With a rough hand, he tilted my chin up. "Look at me." His demand harsh.

I obeyed.

His dark eyes were shot through with red. He grasped my head between his bloody palms and leaned in close, his chest heaving from the exertion of the fight, his metallic-smelling breath bathing my face.

"This is what I am." Intent for me to see, the pressure he placed on my temples hurt. "This is the face of Aris." He rested his forehead on mine and whispered though clenched teeth like it pained him to say it. "This is my true nature."

At once he released me and staggered away until he fell against the wall on the other side of the alley. My head swam and my vision tunneled. I wanted to rip my goggles off and escape this nightmare, but I was powerless. *But that can't be who you are* was all I thought as I slid down the wall, consciousness fading fast.

Chapter 16

I ROUSED myself and slowly pushed upright only to be punished by a dull throb in my head. Hands cradling my head, I moaned. This was the second extreme headache I'd suffered in a matter of weeks, a nd the inside of my mouth felt like I'd been drinking sand. I inched myself up to sitting, determined to get a drink, when I noticed the black bedspread. Mine was green, one of the few things I'd brought with me from my old life. This wasn't my bed. I peered around the room, seeing furniture that didn't belong. Jesus, this wasn't my room.

The austerity of the room and the smell, a faded musky scent, made me think a man belonged here. It was as if the owner had just arrived or was planning on leaving really soon. The room felt functional rather than aesthetic, with dark colors to dull the mood.

Waking in unfamiliar surroundings should've made me panic, but all I felt was pain and a hollowness inside that made me want to go fetal and hide under the covers.

This was all too confusing, and I wanted to lie down again and close my eyes, but there was something important I had to remember. The memory remained out of reach. When I fished for it, my head hurt.

I swung my legs over the edge of the bed and forced myself to dig deep inside my throbbing head. Somewhere in there was my reason for being here, wherever here might be.

I was so groggy I failed to jump with the sudden but gentle tap on the door.

"Yes." My voice croaked.

The door opened to Holden. "Hi, glad to see you're awake." He brought with him that fresh smell of a recent shower as he came and sat next to me on the bed.

"Why are you here?"

He grinned. "The question you should ask is *why am I here?*"

It was like I had to wade waist deep through a thick swamp to find any logical thought. "Is this your place?

He nodded.

"How did I get here?"

"What's the last thing you remember?"

I closed my eyes. "It hurts too much trying to remember."

"Don't worry, that won't last. I'll make you a coffee."

With my head sunk low in my hands, I felt him rise from the bed. "I'd prefer painkillers?"

He hesitated before replying. "It's best you don't take any for now."

"Why?"

"Sorry. It's going to be confusing for a while. Wait till you're able to remember a little more, then we'll talk."

"Do you know what happened?" I stood but swayed violently. My vision tunneled, so I closed my eyes and tried to focus on the floor under my feet. Holden grabbed my arms, which gave me something else to focus on.

"Steady. Best not move so fast."

He gently lowered me to the bed. "Stay put for a while. I'll be back with a sugared drink."

I caved forward, wrapping my arms around me as he walked out the door. Did I have an accident? Was that why I couldn't remember anything? Every time I delved into my memories, I faced a wall and a thumping ache that radiated across my forehead.

Some faint, unknown intuition made me pull my sleeve up to look at my forearms. They looked the same but for some strange reason I expected to see something different. I wasn't sure what, but this had to be a physical memory.

Holden returned carrying a large mug with tendrils of steam dancing across the surface of the coffee. He eased himself down beside me and handed me the mug. The smell was gloriously rich, caramelized, and nutty. Just the smell and the warm vapors flooding my nose and my head cleared a smidgeon.

"Thought you'd be better off with a large caffeine hit. It's going to be sweet, but you'll feel good afterwards, even if it tastes horrible."

I sipped, then screwed up my face.

"Once you've drunken half, I'll let you leave the bedroom. As it is, I'm scared I'll be carrying you half the way."

I held my breath and took another sip. "Why am I here?"

"You were unconscious. Jax knew I'd be able to help." His arm shot out and grabbed my cup. "Steady now. I don't want to change my bedding, and I want you to drink all of it."

"You said Jax. I was with him? What happened?"

He checked the contents of my mug. "Drink."

I did, as much as I could with it being so hot. He watched me sip away and nodded as if satisfied with the amount I managed.

"You were playing Dominus."

"I was?" A chunk of memory slipped through. "Yes, I was. I remember...you know about Dominus?"

"Something happened."

"What do you mean?"

"Jax told me this is the second time you've experienced a headache associated with the game."

I closed my eyes and shook my head. "Wait...hang on." My head hurt when I tried to make sense of what was going on. "I don't understand any of this. You haven't answered my question. How do you know Dominus?"

Holden's eyes dropped to the floor between his thighs. I wasn't sure if he was going to answer, so I had more coffee since he seemed so intent on me drinking it. He glanced sideways, watched me gulp what I could. When I finished, he looked at the ceiling, took a big breath, then looked at me. The melodramatics weren't keeping me calm.

"I'm a part of Dominus."

"You play the game?"

"Play…" His smile stayed away from his eyes. "Yeah, you could say that."

"Doesn't explain why Jax brought me to you."

Holden looked me directly in the eyes as he prepared to reply and icky feelings creeped up my spine.

"I'm one of you, Sable. I'm Persal."

"You play on the same faction as me?"

He stayed quiet. I had to fill the void and hopefully break his deadlock stare.

"I thought you two didn't get on, so I'm surprised he invited you to play."

"I'm one of the designers."

"You? But at the party, when you saw Jax, you looked angry. You moved us away so we wouldn't run into him. Jax said you hated each other. Elva backed it up."

He grimaced when I mentioned her name, but recovered quickly enough. "That's all true. But I'm still an important part of Dominus and there's nothing Jax can do about that."

"And that's why he brought me here?"

"Because of your headaches. An Aris can't help you with the sort of headaches you're getting."

With the mention of Aris, more chunks of memory came through, snippets full of chaos and too confusing to join together, a tiled scythe, a vortex in the floor, a stairwell into darkness, and black beetles everywhere.

Holden frowned as he placed his hand on my knee and leaned toward me. "What's wrong?"

"I'm remembering. I think I'm remembering. I just can't make sense of it. Why am I like this?"

"You're changing. But in a good way. You're finding yourself."

"What about myself am I finding?"

"Your factional nature."

Blood. It dripped from the long gashes on my forearms, smeared my legs, and coated the cobbles between my thighs. There was blood on

Jax. Mixed with saliva, it dribbled from his mouth, ran down his chin. Blood. I smelt it on his breath, saw it stain his teeth. It was on his hands and chest, all around us in the street. But not him, not Jax. It was his avatar. But I smelt it on his breath.

"Sweet Jesus, what is going on?"

Holden swiped the mug as I collapsed forward and cradled my head in my forearms. The warmth of his hand on my back didn't help.

"I guess you remember."

"But I was playing the game, that's all. Why do I remember the smell of blood?"

"The game taps into the neural pulses in your brain. That's why you wear the silver dots. Makes everything you experience real. You see blood, you smell it. You get hit, you feel it."

"Jax said it was his true nature. The way he...fought."

"There are only a few who can play the game. It takes time and careful selection finding them."

"Well, I stink at it. I don't know why he chose to take me in."

"Jax took you in too early. You never would've survived as you are now."

He pulled his hand from my back and, with a heavy scowl, looked at his hands now clasped together between his thighs. I could feel him slip away into himself and whatever troubled thought that pestered him.

"I don't care. I'm over the game. It's too violent for me. I can't do something like that again."

"No one can leave Dominus once they start."

"That's ridiculous. I'm not doing it."

"I wish it were that easy. Your only way out of Dominus is to play to the end."

"This is stupid. You can't make me. I'll tell Jax I'm not playing again."

"Jax doesn't want to see you anymore."

I felt like I'd been slapped across the face. "He said that?"

"It's for the best. He's Aris so—"

"Jesus Christ, this stupid game. Stop talking like that. Look around you, this is Earth. You can be Caucasian, Asian, African, or speak bloody French, but you can't be Aris or Persal in this world."

"You're getting headaches for a reason."

"Yeah, I'm finding myself. Meditation would've been a lot better."

"You're developing your factional nature. Your true nature."

I arched my head to the ceiling. "Yada-yada-ya. I think I'm going to go."

Holden stood with me and took my hand. "Jax won't play the game with you."

"Good, I don't want to play with him."

"I'll play it with you."

"You haven't been listening."

"Neither have you."

"Because nothing you say makes sense."

Holden paused to glance at our hands joined before looking back at me.

"You don't have a choice. You're in now. Your dad wanted—"

I withdrew from his touch, staggered away from him because his words transformed into a weapon of torture. "What?"

"Nothing."

"You said my dad."

"He would've wanted you to have choices."

"No, you were going to say something about my dad as if you knew him. Jesus, you work for him."

Holden's lips ruled into a straight line, lips pressed thin; he never meant to reveal that.

"You're a drug dealer, a murderer?"

"I don't work for him, not in the way you think."

"You were at the school to meet me. You made sure to position yourself so you could invite me to that party and to your club."

"Your dad asked me to keep an eye on you."

"Now I know you're lying. Dad wouldn't ask any guy to harass me."

"He was protecting you from people like Jax. But he can't do that now, so he's asked me to do it for him."

"I don't need your protection." I spun to leave.

"Sable."

I marched out of the room, ignoring his pleas. He caught me on the other side of the door, but I yanked free of his grasp.

"I won't protect you if you don't want me to, but I have to help you. Being Persal is not about the game. It's about you. About what's inside of you wanting to come out. You entered the game; now the process has begun. You have to learn how to control it."

"What process? Control what?"

"Your destructive nature."

"You're insane. I'm outta here."

"Sable, wait, please."

"I don't want to hear any more of this. You speak like this is real. They're characters on a screen. It's just a game. Can't you see how crazy you sound?"

Holden looked at the floor like a chastised child, creating a chasm into which any further angry words would fall. How dare he truncate our argument like that.

"I have to go."

"To where?"

"I need to talk to Jax."

"Leave it, Sable. He brought you to me. He can't help you."

"He owes me answers."

"I can give you those."

"Not all of them have to do with the game."

He quirked an eyebrow.

"Don't worry about it." I turned toward the door.

"You need to get home. You've been here a couple of hours. Add to that the time you spent in the game… Your mum will be worried."

"God, has it been that long?"

"I'll take you home."

I wanted answers from Jax, but I couldn't leave Mum to worry, and what about Ajay? He'd be worried too.

"Fine." It was like I'd just lost some epic battle. I didn't want to give in and be led home like a placid child. I wanted Jax to explain himself. How he survived the jump from the tower and why he wanted me in Dominus. And why…Jesus…why he revealed to me another side of himself, a shade of his personality other than the asshole I knew, a part of himself that was just like me, isolated by pain.

I reached for the front door handle as a tremor shook my hand. My body rippled with an unmet need, perhaps the effects of the coffee and sugar. Whatever it was, I felt wired for speed. I wanted to keep moving. There was no point in talking, or even arguing, as they would only slow me down.

I lifted my arms to see my hands shake.

Holden came close and covered my hands with his, calming the tremor. In his warm hands, mine felt clammy. I tried to pull them away but he firmed his grasp.

"Let me go." I became frantic. "What are you doing? Let me go."

"I can't. Not now. You're tripping again."

My heart raced above normal. "Get away from me," I screamed in his face.

Suddenly I felt so angry I wanted to hurt him badly.

As if sensing my need, Holden tightened his hold on me.

"This is a side effect, accelerated adrenaline. You end up with the shakes, hot flushes, racing heart. You want to keep moving, don't you?"

I nodded. I didn't like that he knew all of this, like he'd seen it all before. It gave credence to what he'd said.

"What's happening to me?"

"Something your father never wanted to happen."

"Did you put something in my coffee?"

He shook his head.

"How do I make it stop? I don't want any of this." I yanked my hands back.

"You can't make it stop. But I can help make it easier."

"No. You've done something to me."

"It wasn't me who did it. It was Jax when he took you into Dominus."

My racing adrenaline magnified the panic, turning it into an unreasonable terror. Tears blurred my vision. "What have you done to me?"

Holden snagged my elbow and reeled me in. I fought him like a girl, flailing arms looking for an inch of flesh to slap, but he overcame me and pulled me close so my arms were trapped between us. This felt like a prison and I attempted to break free, but Holden bound me tight. The violence with which my rage assaulted me burned hot through to the core of my body. I felt like I would explode. White-hot flares flashed behind my eyes, blinding my vision. Like the maze on the roof of the tower, I felt barriers in my brain shift, opening up new spaces. A strong compulsion drove my focus into those unexplored spaces, searching for something it alone knew was there, something tantalizingly strong that wanted to consume me. I craved to let it.

Polar emotions cleaved through me, desire to have, fury to destroy. I screamed for my freedom, but Holden's kiss shocked me silent and snapped my mind back to the room, to us, to him holding me, to his lips on mine, to the soft yet firm demand of his mouth. And I yielded because no guy had touched me like that before. The walls inside my mind shifted back into place. The yearning I'd felt not so long ago switched to a different sort of yearning. The opening of my body replaced the opening of my mind as exciting sensations took over, grounding me in this room with Holden.

I ached to fall deeper into this visceral spell but was yanked back from the edge when Holden entwined his arms around me and dragged me flush with him. I jerked back, then pushed him away. My body, tingling with something other than adrenaline, cried for the loss of our closeness.

I was panting and so was he. "What are you doing?"

"I'm sorry. But I couldn't think of any other way to bring you back. You were too close to doing something you shouldn't, not while you're feeling confused and angry."

"How did you know?"

"You and I are alike so I can sense it. It's like the buildup of electricity before a lightning strike."

"What was it?"

I didn't need to explain what I'd discovered locked behind the barriers in my head, because I was starting to believe his crazy story.

"Your true nature."

"Don't you mean factional nature?"

"They're the same thing."

"But it's just a game. It's not possible to have a fictitious power."

"Only a certain few do. But you won't survive virtual without it. That's why we're selective."

If I hadn't just felt a strong yearning to unleash that which I discovered in the depths of my mind, I would be laughing at him.

"Why did Jax allow me to play virtual if I lacked a factional power?"

By the look on his face, I could tell Holden didn't want to answer me, so I let it go since Holden wasn't in Jax's head and not likely to understand his motives. This was another reason I had to face Jax.

"And what I saw in Dominus. Is that Jax?"

"Jax when he's controlled by his factional nature."

"Is there a difference?"

"There can be. It depends on the person wielding the power. You can let it consume you or you can be the master. The choice is yours."

"I faced a warrior in green. He had me against the wall before my headache came. Just before I passed out, slits appeared in my forearms, which kept getting bigger, and all these beetles crawled out. Hundreds of them."

"The warrior you fought was Negal. Do you know the factional nature of Negal?"

"Pestilence and fire." I backed away from him. "Jesus, that's what it means to have a factional nature."

"Now you understand the importance of harnessing your ability. And why we don't play those in virtual who have none."

"This is a game. How can any of this be possible?"

"What you see in virtual is the game. What's in your head is not. It's very real."

"How many people know about Dominus?"

"Six of us designed it. But we have a few hundred now capable of playing virtual."

"What about Ajay? Is he like me?"

"Persal? Likely."

My heart seized. "That's why Jax wanted to meet him. He wants him in."

Holden pressed his lips together but never replied.

"He can't do that. I won't let him."

"Jax won't take him virtual yet. Ajay won't show signs of his factional nature until puberty."

"It doesn't matter. He still wants him."

"Ajay is their insurance policy."

A sudden cold invaded me. I couldn't breathe. "He'll be recruited if I don't play."

"It's likely he'll be recruited anyhow, in time."

"Who's they?"

The sigh he gave told me he wasn't going to tell.

"Who?"

He shook his head.

"You said six designed it. Jax, Tyren, and Elva, that's three from Aris. You, and who are the other two?"

"Knowing won't make a difference."

"I want to trust you."

"You can. I'm on your side, Sable. I'm Persal."

"I don't know what that means."

"Jax brought you to me because I know how to help you. Your faction is your family. There's no one else you can trust."

"If that is so, then tell me."

"I don't think it's a good idea. Not now. Not after everything you've been through the last few hours."

"Can you at least tell me what's so important about playing?"

"A lot rides on the success of those who play Dominus."

"What sort of answer is that?"

"The only answer I know how to give. I just don't know what to tell you or where to begin."

"At the start and the truth. It's that simple."

"Let's just say this is more than just a game."

"The game is designed to find those who have a factional nature."

Holden looked beyond me as if that would give him space from my questions.

"Right or wrong? Say the word."

He nodded. That was enough.

"But it's more than that, isn't it? It's like a training simulation."

"Smart."

"Training for what?"

"You figure it out. I mean it, Sable. I'm not saying any more."

"Why?"

"Because you're not ready to hear it. I want you to learn Dominus. I want you to live it like it was your world. Then if you still don't know the answer, I will tell you."

"That's not good enough."

"That's all you'll get."

I wanted to slap him, but since I knew what he was capable of, I perhaps wouldn't get that far.

"I need to go home."

Holden retrieved my bag from a hook by the door. At least it had come with me.

"I'll take you."

"I suppose you know where I live?" I quirked an eyebrow at him.

His guilt was in his silence.

"Who else knows everything about me?"

He shook his head.

"Don't bother. I'll find out on my own. And then I'll find a way to leave Dominus and take my family with me."

"I would help you if I could. I want you to believe that."

Yeah, whatever. To me his words were hollow.

We stared at each other long enough for me to discover Holden's iron will. I'd never had good friends, not really. I'd always wanted some, at least one close friend I could rely on who knew everything about me. It looked like that would never happen. Maybe it was time to stop worrying about something as mundane as making connections and focus on striving to be the best. Yeah, I sucked every time, but I had a damn good reason to not suck now.

Chapter 17

I slammed the car door without saying goodbye to Holden and walked the cracked paving to our door. Hopefully I wasn't about to ruin my grand exit by tripping on something in the dark. I was five hours late returning home from school—at least that's where everyone thought I'd been. And I'd missed Ajay at the bus stop. I'd never missed meeting Ajay at the bus stop. All because of this stupid game. Mum would go wild and then likely ground me. With everything going on in my life, hiding at home sounded like a great idea. But hiding was not the answer. Holden said once I started playing the game, I couldn't pull out, and with Ajay a target for Jax, I didn't want to give him an excuse to come knocking on our door.

I found a stranger in the kitchen, which stopped me dead in my stride. A portly woman of about forty with a long, straight nose pushed up from her chair at the table, leaving her magazine. She didn't look the sort to be connected with Dominus, the only thing that saved me from screaming at her to leave the house.

"Who are you?"

Little thuds down the hall disturbed her reply.

Ajay burst into the room. "Where've you been? You're going to cop it when Mum gets home."

"I'm so sorry, Ajay. I couldn't make it to the bus stop. Where's Mum?"

The woman must've seen this as her cue. "Your mother was invited to attend a function with her prospective employer. It was a last-minute invitation." She came toward me with her hand outstretched. "I'm Marleen. Your babysitter."

"Mum tried to call you," Ajay said.

I'd left my phone in my bag in Jax's lounge when we entered Dominus. From there I was out cold.

"I was a last-minute stand-in."

I ignored Marleen's comment because I didn't care. "Who did she go out with?"

"A man called Carter." Ajay looked up at me with wide, innocent eyes, something Jax would see lost if he got the chance.

"You met him?" My family was being attacked on two fronts, by Jax, Holden, and Dominus on the one side and Carter on the other.

"There's some dinner in the oven if you're hungry."

I barely acknowledged her friendly voice.

"Come, Ajay, I think it's bedtime. How about I read you a story?"

"It's only seven."

"I'll make it a long one."

"I told Ajay he could watch some TV until seven thirty."

I yanked Ajay around by the shoulder. "Thanks, but I'll read him a book."

"You sure you don't want any dinner?"

"Later."

I pushed Ajay down the hall, then tried to open his door, but there were so many clothes and toys blocking the way it took a few shoves before we were able to get in. Since the window was jammed, the smell of stale socks and shoes, not to mention unwashed clothes, brewed to a thick boil in the closed room. I flipped the light switch and got nothing. There was enough light from the hall to guide me across the obstacle-strewn floor for his bedside lamp.

"You need to clean your room."

"Whatever."

"Okay, buddy, sit." I patted a space next to me. "I need to talk to you first and then I'll read you a story."

He heaved a sigh and dragged his feet over. "This sounds like it's going to be boring."

"It's important, Ajay, so I need you to listen carefully."

"Is Mum going to marry this guy?"

"No. She loves Dad so much she would never do that. And I would kill her before she did."

He looked so relieved I ruffled his hair to make him smile. "Silly, did you really think that?"

He nodded, again with those doleful eyes. I wanted to tell him Dad would be home before Mum could get too lonely to look for someone else, but we'd both been lied to enough for me to add another on the pile.

"You remember how Dad always told you not to talk to strangers?"

"I'm ten, not two."

"Humor me, buddy. We're on our own now and we have to stick together."

"What about Mum?"

"Her too. But we have to be honest with each other. That's how we look out for each other. Remember Dad always told you family was everything, and that we were to keep an eye out for each other."

"You're acting weird."

"Ajay, I'm being serious."

"Are you going to read me a book?"

"I will once you listen to what I have to say."

He rolled his eyes, then swung his foot, rolling a shoe back and forth under his sole.

"You remember the guy who took us to see Dad?"

Ajay looked at the floor, kicking a sock onto another pile of clothes. Reminding him of that day was not the kindest thing I could do, but I couldn't spare his feelings. This was too important. "He's not a good guy, Ajay. This is me being really serious."

"I liked him. He was fun."

"He may be fun but he's dangerous. You're not to speak to him again if you see him. He may invite you to play a game."

"What sort of game?"

"It doesn't matter. You're to say no. Do you understand me? It's really important. And you're to let me know ASAP if you see him again."

"Okay." Boredom and annoyance dragging out the word.

"And tell me if anyone else talks to you."

"What about my teachers?"

"You know what I mean."

He pulled a face at me, but I needed him to understand how serious I was.

"If you're at school, you go tell the teacher a stranger wants to talk to you. If you're on the street, then look for a responsible adult, policeman, store owner, bus driver, in fact, don't even get off the bus unless I'm there waiting for you."

"Did Jax dump you? Is that why you're mad at him?

"What? No. Ajay this has nothing to do with—" I slumped, head bowed. I was making a hash of this, but I needed Ajay to be serious about this, cautious without being scared such that he didn't want to go to school. "Dad made us promise to always be there for each other. This is what I'm doing, Ajay. I'm looking out for you. I'm protecting you. And I think there are some people out there who want to get to us now Dad's gone."

"Why?"

"Because people can be like that. Adults do stupid things. Some do terrible things."

"Like Dad." Now it was Ajay's turn to look dejected. His comment wounded me too, mostly because I had never heard Ajay admit to thinking Dad had done a terrible thing. Dad was no longer my hero, but that didn't mean I wanted him to slip from Ajay's pedestal.

"Dad didn't mean to. Adults do stupid things, but they also make mistakes they would reverse if they could."

Closed hearts felt cold and isolating. Hating Dad hurt, too much.

My phone chimed a message as I was about to ask him to choose a book from his stack on the floor, which had toppled sideways. I'd ruined the mood and our special time together. I didn't want him going to bed feeling like this. Holden's name appeared on the screen.

"How about you choose a book and I'll answer this message."

What do u want?

Willing to tell u everything.

Truth or joke?

Truth u need to understand.

Finally.

Come to mine.

Before I could reply, another message came through. This time the caller ID was unknown, but I didn't need a name to know who it was.

Want to show u something.

Not interested in your games.

Funeral is for Salvador.

Why did he tell me that? Did I know a Salvador?
"Here, this one." Ajay thumped the book in my lap, upsetting my cell. It slid to the floor faceup.
"Looks good. Just let me finish this message."
From amongst Ajay's clothes on the floor, I read the return message illuminated on the screen.

Gamer

Of course, he was the guy playing with Tyren.
"How long's that going to take?"
"Not long, promise." I scooped my cell from the bundle of clothes as another message came through.

Dominus

The other funeral was for a gamer.

Was this supposed to be significant? Which meant…?

Do u want to know the truth?

Suddenly everyone was coughing up the truth.

u willing?

God, I hadn't replied to Holden yet.

Sure.

Tomorrow.

K.

"Come on."

"I'm almost done, okay?" Hearing the sudden harshness in my voice, I glanced at Ajay to catch his surly look in the dim light of the lamp. "Sorry, buddy, this is important, but I'm almost done."

Jax's next message came through.

It's time.

For what?

For u to know the stakes.

For who?

ur family.

I dropped my cell onto the book and palmed my mouth as the acid in my gut turned so acidic I was sure it burned holes in my stomach.

This was not about me replacing Ajay. Jax wanted both of us. Wasn't that what the message meant? And what about Mum?

The book and cell slid to the floor as I launched to my feet.

"What're you doing?"

"I'm sorry, Ajay, just give me a minute," I said as I paced.

Holden and Jax were both in on this. And Holden knew Dad somehow, and Carter worked with Dad. I slowed, my head buried in my hands.

The stakes for my family. It felt like doors were slamming around me, leaving me walled within, caged.

"Sorry, Ajay. I've got to go somewhere."

"You said you'd read me a story."

I dropped down in front of him, my knees cushioned by the mess on his floor. "I will, buddy, I will, but this is really important."

"You're not allowed."

"Mum doesn't need to know."

"But you promised me a story."

"I know, I know. I'm so sorry." I touched his temple with my own.

"I don't want you to go."

I sat back on my heels. "You like hero stories."

"So?"

"This is a hero story. What I'm doing. I'm going to save someone."

He slid backward, away from me, farther onto his bed, his expression closed. And I didn't have the time to try and pry him out of himself.

"I'll make it up to you. I promise. I won't ask you to lie to Mum, but please don't tell Marleen, okay? It's none of her business."

Ajay slumped down on his bed and refused to look at me. I thought of giving him an excuse to tell Marleen. Something about me being unwell and going to bed, but I wasn't about to have him tell my lies for me, not a second time. I would just face what punishment Mum gave when I returned.

I gave Ajay a kiss on the head and left before his mournful face made me feel too guilty to leave.

Standing in the hall, for a split second, I contemplated returning to the kitchen and telling Marleen I wasn't feeling well and would disappear to bed. In case she turned motherly and insisted on fussing over me, I decided to get going and face the consequences later. I tiptoed across the hall into my room, where I pocketed a couple of coins for the bus ride there and back, then opened the window and slipped outside.

It felt like I was stuck in Dominus, running from the enemy, attacked on every side. And I shouldn't think like that because I *was* stuck in Dominus, and I didn't know what that meant.

Chapter 18

THE LARGE SLATE-GRAY curtains of Jax's apartment were drawn. Only a thin line at the edges revealed any light from inside. At least someone was home.

On the bus trip over, I'd talked myself out of confronting him a dozen times, then a dozen times more talked myself into continuing. I should wait for tomorrow and listen to what Holden had to say, not Jax. Why was I listening to Jax? But I couldn't wait all night. I was not who I thought I was. The life I'd led was fictional, yet I knew nothing about the life I was supposed to lead, knew nothing about the person I was supposed to be. I didn't want to know. But regardless, whether I was strong enough or not, the truth was coming for me. Not knowing meant I would face it blind.

I stared at the intercom button for long enough to feel the cold creeping under my sweatshirt. Just do it. Everyone would be there, perhaps playing the game, maybe with other innocents like me. With that idea, I pushed the button and stood in front of the screen so he would see it was me. With the *clunk* of the lock unlatching, I pushed through and across the foyer to the lifts.

The lift doors opened to an empty room. The sound of my boots punctured the quiet as I left the lift and moved deeper into the apartment.

"Hello." The security door did not unlock by itself.

I listened for any indication someone was home, but the place sounded like a morgue.

"He isn't here."

I turned to find Elva standing in a doorway on the opposite side of the room from the kitchen, hands on hips. She wore her customary tight jeans, spiked-heeled boots, and lush lips painted a deep purple to blend with the thick black outlining her eyes.

"Where is he?"

"Anywhere you're not."

This was going to be a prickly conversation, but I wasn't leaving until I got what I wanted even if it was only directions to Jax. Elva scared me. I wasn't equipped to deal with people like her, but I possessed two qualities at the moment that fed steel into my legs and bolted them to the spot, determination and desperation; both made me bold. "I just want to talk to him."

She came toward me with her usual exaggerated hip sway. I refused to take a step back.

"Word of advice. Men don't like limpets."

"I'm not hanging on. He owes me some explanations."

"Want...owes. Tsk, tsk. No wonder he ran away. You're full of demands and he hasn't even kissed you."

Thank god. Had they discussed me?

"You're not his type, sugar." She looked me up and down. "All uptight and prissy. Daddy's little girl. You wouldn't know what to do with a man like him."

"I'm here for answers, that's all. I don't care about anything else. I don't understand any of this."

She snorted a hard laugh, strode past me to a chair, and sat with the grace of a feline about to stretch out in the sun. She eyed me from head to foot and pulled a face, showing me she found fault with every part of me along the way.

Her judgmental eyes took the words from my mouth. I felt two feet tall under her withering gaze.

"Trust me when I say don't ask questions, because the answers aren't anything you want to hear. Not someone as precious and cloistered as you." She settled back farther into her comfortable seat. "Life's been one smooth ride for you, hasn't it? Rich daddy, adoring mother, private school, best of everything. And then, oh, dear, life hits the skids and things aren't looking so pretty. A shabby rental, the worst school in the city, and your mum running into the arms of someone else."

"That's not how it is. You know nothing about my family."

"Is that so? Tell me, do you know why your daddy is in jail? I mean the real reason."

My silence told the story. I wanted to wipe the smug smile off her face because she was winning this argument. I thought I did, but the reality was I knew nothing about my dad.

"I've known your daddy for quite some time. What you know of him is nothing but a fabrication. What I know of him is real. You think he's the loving, supportive father. I'm sorry to say, sugar, but there's nothing to love about someone like that."

My blood sped like a freight train though my veins.

"Maybe it's time to take a good look at yourself, princess. Maybe you're just like your father, nothing but a lie."

"I think you've said enough, Elva."

Jax leaned against the banister looking down on us, arms folded across his chest. It was easy to see him as the enemy, as the reason my world was falling apart, but the truth was more sinister. Perhaps Elva was right. The more I dug into the belly of this mess, the more I'd regret I ever started, the more I'd realize I didn't know myself. Right now the truth seemed paramount, but maybe in the end, I would wish I'd lived ignorant in the lie.

Elva launched to her feet, making even that sudden movement look graceful.

"Just keeping the spot warm for you, sweetie." She air-kissed him and strode across the lounge toward the gaming room. As she strode past me, I caught the sight of the tattoo for Aris behind her right ear for the first time.

Jax remained like marble, a dark, unreachable presence. Looking at him now, I no longer saw the guy I'd first met in the convenience store.

That guy was a two-dimensional ass. The guy before me now was a convoluted mess, just like me.

"I didn't expect you to come tonight."

"Send a message like that, what do you expect?"

He snorted a *huh* sound, unfolded his arms, and left, heading back the way he'd come. I took that as an invitation and climbed the stairwell. At the top, I had a choice of doors, but none of them were open. Instead, at the end of a corridor were metal stairs, at the top an open door. I could open every door, or I could follow my instinct.

I climbed the metal stairs, my boots *clanking* on the metal grille, with the moon as my guide. Outside the chill caught in my throat, and I wrapped my arms around me because I'd rushed from the house wearing only a thin jacket. Around Jax lay an assortment of chairs and cushions but he made no use of them. Instead he stood next to a large metal bowl, warming himself by the fire. The scene was cozy and intimate, like a lovers' hideaway. Maybe staying in the entrance was the best place to be.

"You can come closer. I do bite, but I won't bite you, at least not now."

"That's not funny." The images of our last time in Dominus found their way into my memory with perfect clarity.

"Do you want a drink?"

I shook my head.

He jerked his head to one side, where a pile of blankets sat, stacked and inviting. "Grab a blanket or come stand near the fire."

If I stood near the fire, I could watch his face while he gave me answers, catch the subtle expressions before he shut them down. "This isn't a friendly visit."

"I'm rarely friendly."

"Why did you take me to Holden?"

"He didn't tell you?"

"He did, but it sounds like science fiction. And I want to hear your explanation."

"Why? What makes my explanation more important?

He stood in such a way shadows danced under his eyes. It should make him look spooky or sinister. It didn't; in fact he'd never looked so good-looking. "Does Aris exist outside of Dominus?"

His eyes ensnared me. But I was bound by more than his stare. I was bound by the secret hidden within me, but also in him.

"Do you really want to know the answer to that question?"

"There's no point in hiding it anymore."

"Yes. I am Aris, Sable. That is all I am."

"But you're a regular guy, you're not like that...monster in Dominus."

With the mention of the word *monster*, a muscle on the left side of Jax's jaw twitched. "I am Aris as you are Persal."

"I'm also a girl."

"No, you're Persal."

"What does that mean?"

"It means you shouldn't be here."

"You promised the truth."

"I promised something you don't want to hear."

If only everyone would stop assuming I was too scared to hear the truth. Seventeen years of lies. I couldn't live ignorant anymore. "You were so willing to get me into the game. You said I was good enough, but now you don't believe in me."

"Maybe I want what you have."

He was going cryptic again. "What?"

He returned his eyes to the fire, drawing himself back from me, creating a chasm between us.

"After what you've done, you owe me this."

"Ask me."

"Why won't you help me with Dominus?"

"I'm not Persal. I don't know how to help you master your factional nature."

"Every faction experiences their nature differently?"

"Yes. Only those within their faction can give the right guidance. Normally it's a parent or other more experienced members. It's important that you learn to control your nature, for a factional member without control is a very dangerous thing."

"I thought we were playing a game."

"We are. Dominus is a game. Your factional nature is very real."

"You designed Dominus to recruit and train those who have these abilities."

He didn't seem surprised at my guessing right. "Yes. There's you and then there's your factional nature. Dominus is the bridge. The mental stimulation of the game draws it out of you, sets it free, forces you to embrace what lives within. Holden will keep you from losing yourself in the process—maybe—but you need Dominus to rewire fast."

"Rewire?"

"Your mind is changing, being rewired to how it should be, which will enable you to be Persal. The headaches are part of it for you. For Aris, it is extreme muscle pain and an undeniable thirst."

"If our factional natures are a natural part of us, why do we need a game to force them through?"

"A person's factional nature will come through in time, in a slow and natural process, which doesn't involve extreme headaches or muscle pain, but as I said, Dominus speeds the process, forces the neurons to rewire as they should. It's the reason for the silver dots we place on your temples. But the process is fragile. If you pull out of Dominus now, the process will not be completed, the rewiring will cease. And what's left is not pretty. Not too many people remain sane when that happens."

"But why is this necessary?"

"So you are ready for the impending war."

Holy crap. "Did you just say war?"

"It's coming, and we need to be ready."

I laughed because there was nothing else I could do with the ludicrous things he said, but the laugh tinged to hysteria. His face hardened as he stared into the fire. Without looking at me, he replied, "You wanted my secrets."

"Yes, but…Jax, how do you expect me to believe you? Look around you. The world is not about to explode into a factional war. I mean, at the moment, there aren't even any factions, not according to the real world."

I didn't want him to be a loony.

"Explain what you are experiencing." He jabbed at his head.

"What…I…don't know."

"You won't because deep down you fear I'm telling the truth. You're developing your factional nature and it scares the hell out of you. But guess what, Sable, that's the real you. We're not nice people when we're consumed by our true nature."

I thought about his bloodstained teeth and the beetles that crawled from the gaping wound on my arm. He was right, fear rose up through my soul to sever any possible serenity I would ever have again.

"Did Salvador play virtual?"

"Yes." Jax kept his eyes on the fire.

"And what about the other gamers whose funerals you attended? Did they play virtual?"

Face bathed in firelight, there was little I missed of his expression, including the tension in his jaw. He chose to stare at the dancing flames rather than at me, nor did he reply.

"They played virtual, didn't they?"

"They weren't good enough." His voice was like a whip.

"Because they didn't believe enough in themselves," I whispered.

As quick as his outburst had been, he sucked the anger back in, all the way in until he seemed to be collapsing in on himself as his head sunk to his chest, eyes closing, like a shutdown, a shielding from my persistent demands for the truth.

No way would I give him the reprieve his body language cried for. "But what do you mean? Weren't good enough for what?"

"They didn't survive Dominus. They were strong but not strong enough."

"Are you saying they died because of Dominus?"

"The game uses your neural—"

"Holden told me that."

"The game convinces you everything is real."

"He told me that too." My throat constricted such that I couldn't breathe. I knew what he was going to say. I didn't want him to say it. I didn't want to hear.

"If you die in the game, you die for real."

"And you want Ajay to play." My sudden emotion sucked the last few words back into my throat.

Finally I had his eyes, and I would give him the full hatred of what now lived in mine. "I won't let this happen. I won't let you touch Ajay."

"We have you."

"You asshole," was all I managed through my tears, tears of rage. But they were more than that. I felt this great emptying inside of me as, bit by bit, my insides were being scooped right out, going further until my skin felt shredded and torn, leaving me exposed and vulnerable, with nothing holding me together. It was the same when the verdict was read in court and Dad was led away. It was an instability, like nothing was normal, nothing was all right, like an anchor holding me to this life, to me, had been severed, setting me adrift, alone.

Jax came around the fire toward me.

"Don't come near me." I backed up a few paces. "You're a monster."

He stopped, no gloating, no triumph, no anger in his expression. I turned away because I hated what I saw in his expression—the reflection of my own pain, eyes like hollow pits stemming from a heart shattered.

"I know." Uttered with sincerity. I wanted to launch myself at him, pound my fists at the wall of his own silent despair, because how could I fight against someone who was also bleeding?

"I'm not the one who makes the decisions. I want you to know that."

"Who does?"

"I don't want to tell you." He risked coming closer. This close I could smell the smoke clinging to his shirt; beneath that I could smell a hint of cologne and the faint sour smell of sweat. "Just do it."

"You don't want to hear this."

"No." I jabbed a finger at him. "You don't get to decide."

"Your dad and another man called Carter."

I shoved him away, needing space to blunt the suffocation I felt. "You're joking. That's not true. It can't be."

Jax reached for my hand, but I jerked it away, spun and escaped to the edge of the building. My family had been played better than I could have ever imagined. Poor Mum was inside the devil's lair. "Carter had him locked away so he could get to us, didn't he?"

"That wasn't the reason Carter did it. But it provided easy access to you, yes."

"Why were you in Dram Truckers?"

"To meet you."

"Was that because Carter told you to?"

"Yes. But I would've done it anyway."

"What does Carter want with my mum?"

"Your cooperation. He also wants to thoroughly screw your father over like he knew Nixon was about to do to him."

Since I was fast discovering how little I knew of the man I called Dad, I couldn't argue for his innocence.

He came to stand beside me at the edge of the roof and stared out over the skyline.

"You were right all along. I never had a choice."

"Your father never wanted you involved. He protected you for all these years." He spoke with a soft voice because he was standing close. It was the wrong voice for revealing such a brutal truth.

"It's too late to say that now."

"You can hate your father all you like, but he loves you."

With the fire at our backs, the lights from the city night below, his expression was not clear enough for me to see the nuance of his emotion. "Why are you saying this?"

"I know what it is like to lose a father. I was glad when Carter framed him, glad to see him suffer, but you're his daughter. You shouldn't feel the same way."

"So Dad is innocent?"

"Of those crimes he was convicted for, yes. The guy died because he was a recruit to Dominus. Your father didn't kill him, not directly at least." He turned to me, one side of his face lit by the fire, the other obscured by the night. "It was because of him you were kept out of Dominus."

"It's obvious you hate him, so I don't understand why you are sticking up for him."

"You have a father. I wish I still did."

I thought, after everything Jax had revealed, I would be numb, that all my emotions had already bled dry. But his simple words of pain kindled something inside my shattered heart. I looked down at his hand, extended for me to grasp, and a small shadow of emotion flared. Dominus was a bridge, he'd said. When I looked down at his hand, I also saw a bridge, a faint flicker that I wasn't alone. Instead of taking his hand, I ran a finger over the tattoo on his arm, the same as the one I'd seen in Aris HQ, his guide when all was lost.

I looked up to the tattoo behind his ear, revealed in the firelight, the symbol of his loyalty to his family, the symbol of strength, unity, and courage. "How strong is your conviction?"

"Unyielding."

"Your loyalty?"

"Unbreakable."

"When all is lost?"

"Until the end."

He took my hand. "I want to show you something else."

"I don't know if I can take any more."

"You want all of my secrets?"

Did I? I placed my hand in his and allowed him to lead me.

Chapter 19

Jax CLIMBED up onto the waist-high brick wall that demarcated the end of the roof and a four-story drop below. "Jax—"

"Come." He held out his hand. "I've told you my secrets; now you have to trust me." His voice was so gentle I couldn't refuse.

I followed him up. He held my hand firmly and it felt like an anchor.

"I don't like heights."

"Then don't look down."

"What are we doing up here?"

"You wanted to know what happened on the Adolphy Tower. I'm going to show you."

"I don't think I want to know anymore."

"This is your one opportunity to take command of your life, to be who you are meant to be. Are you willing to take that opportunity? If not, you can climb down off this wall and walk away. But if you want to see what's on the other side of your fear, then follow me."

I looked sideways at him.

He smiled the most perfect smile. "Trust me."

"We're going to jump?"

"I don't want to pull you off, so go with me. I know how brave you are. I know you can do this."

In the last couple of months, I'd been stripped bare. After tonight it felt like there was nothing left of who I'd been. I could turn away, choose to step off this wall, but if I did, it would be like I'd unplugged from Dominus and left my mind half rewired and me a fragmented mess. The alternative was that I choose to live a different life, choose to be a different person, choose to no longer exist but fight.

I looked across at Jax. "Yes."

"Yes what?"

"I want to be more than who I am."

He squeezed my hand. "On the count of three."

I closed my eyes and all I heard was the count of one, then my mind blanked out. Next thing, there was a tug on my hand. I left my scream behind as I plummeted over the edge and down. The ice wind caught my hair, slapped against my cheeks, ran down my throat, found hidden places beneath my clothes. I couldn't suck enough air into my lungs. This was not like flying. There was no sense of freedom, only falling, falling, falling to oblivion.

Would I feel that split-second impact when my bones splintered and organs were crushed? Would I be able to acknowledge for even the shortest moment the nanosecond before I died?

I lost myself, my body, my senses, my mind, my memory. Time became this single moment. I didn't even know if I was falling anymore. It was like everything had been compressed into a tiny dot. Then I felt a tug in the center of my stomach. Next it felt like I was about to fall apart —literally, like my skin had disappeared and the rest of me was about to float away. My pulse throbbed through my ears and the steady build of pressure in my head made me fearful of another massive headache. I couldn't reel my mind in or calm the panic attack, but at that moment, a hand squeezed mine. This was the one thing I needed to keep me sane. I focused on Jax's and my connection and used that to get me through.

A feather touch trailed along my eyelids and down my cheeks. The sensation dragged my awareness back, and that's when I noticed the cold wind had stilled. My body was no longer falling. I opened my eyes and found myself facing Jax. He rested one hand on my hip; the other hovered close to my cheek.

I looked around us to find nothing, just a dull, hazy gray, no distinction between up or down, no contours or detail. It was as if we'd stepped into the virtual game, or into a vacuum.

"Where are we?"

"It's a place of in-between, which means it's nowhere. It's nothing. And it's the only place we're free."

"Are we inside the game?"

"No. The game exists. This does not. But it's not a place we can stay for long."

"This is where you went when you jumped off the tower."

"It's like a seam, or a loop in time. It's an escape for a short while."

"How did we get here?"

"All the dimensions exist side by side. It's like when you make a choice to do something, which leads you down a certain path to a certain future. At that point of choice, there were a myriad of different decisions you could've made, but you didn't. Now imagine that those other possibilities didn't just disappear because you chose not to take them, but continued to exist alongside the reality you live that was governed by the choice you made. Now expand beyond possibilities to possible worlds. The dimensions exist side by side. If you are able to, you see them as discrete bands. All you need to do is select the band you wish to take. And that's easy to do when you know where you're going as you just need to focus on an element of your destination. It ends up almost like a luminescent light within the band you need to take. After you've done it enough times, you can start to catalogue all the luminesce into a mental map."

He moved away from me. "Shifting is like your body is being torn apart, but on a minute scale. Every molecule that is your makeup oscillates as it makes the shift. But you have to know what you're doing in order to make sure you take every part of you along when you do it."

"Is this really real?"

"It's more real than the life you live."

I laughed, then covered my mouth because it sounded crazy again.

"It's our connection that gets you through. As a shifter, I'm the one who activates the oscillation of our molecules, through this." He pointed to his temple. "I'm the one who gathers them all together and pulls them through. And don't worry, I'm good at it. I can shift us through fast enough gravity or the earth's rotation doesn't affect you."

"Shifter?"

"Blows your mind, doesn't it? But it can't be any weirder than learning about factional natures." He spun in a slow circle. "The in-between is the place you move to before you cross over. Normally you cross and you never visit the in-between, but if you want to, you can linger awhile. But not for long."

All I could do was shake my head as I looked around at the nothing-ness of the place.

"There's nothing bad about this. I find it calming. It's a place where we can exist as equals."

"And we can't anywhere else?"

"Everywhere else, you're one thing or another and never just you. Not like here."

"Is this all attached to Dominus?"

"The in-between always exists. But only special people can reach it."

"People like you, shifters?"

"Yes."

"How many of you are there?"

He paced away from me. "You don't want to be in my world. It's a cruel and lonely place. Unfortunately, you don't have a choice. I wish it wasn't the case."

What was going on here? There was a subtle shift in Jax's mood, a tensity to his tone. I wanted to change it back to where we were a few moments ago. "Thank you for bringing me here. I guess I trust you now."

"You shouldn't. I'm Aris, remember? And you can never trust those outside your faction." He'd created a chasm between us, not just in distance from his pacing but in his declaration.

"Now you've put us in categories. I thought this place was a place we were beyond that."

"You're right, it is. But like I said, it's a transitory place, and then you must be who you are again. There is no real escape."

"What would've happened when the green warrior attacked me had you not intervened?"

There was a moment's delay before he replied. "You would've been killed."

"In the game and in real life?"

"Yes."

I closed the distance between us.

"And an Aris saved me, a Persal."

"Don't mistake me for a hero. I'll only disappoint you."

With a hand on his chin, I turned his face to the side so I could see his tattoo. "Maybe there is loyalty beyond factions."

Jax gently withdrew his chin from my hold. Where had the mood of moments ago gone? When the softer emotions emerged, he slammed them down fast. When the gap between us inched a little closer, he ripped it apart once he realized it was happening.

"What are you afraid of?"

With his penetrating black eyes, he sunk deep within me. "It's you who should be afraid."

"Maybe I should be, but I can't help but feel gratitude toward someone who saved my life."

"Don't, Sable. Trying to find something that isn't will hurt you in the end."

Because you were hurt?

"We've been here long enough." He held out his hand. "Reality hurts enough without making it worse. Close your eyes."

"I don't want to. I'm not ready to leave this place." Away from here and I would have to face everything I'd learned.

"We can't exist here long because it's a transitory place. It's not bound by time or location, so we could easily become lost."

"That doesn't sound so bad."

"And what about your brother, your mother?"

Why did he have to destroy any small moments of peace? "Why do we all have to be enemies?"

"Because it's not our choice."

"Everyone has a choice as to who they want to trust and who they want to hate."

"Not everyone," he said as he took my hand.

"Not in my world."

"You're no longer in your world, Sable. You're now in mine."

My body was pulled. I closed my eyes as the gray slid across my vision and my stomach balled up in a knot. Soon the strength in my limbs weakened. Jax tightened his hold, but my body felt weird, like it wouldn't remain glued together. I wasn't sure if I was still holding on, if Jax was there, of where we were. I fought against the creeping tendrils of darkness sucking my consciousness away, fought but lost as the weakness took hold. It felt like I was being sucked through a straw, until there was little feeling anymore, until I slowly ebbed away.

Chapter 20

I JERKED awake thinking I was still holding Jax's hand. Instead I was in my bed. This was the second time I'd blacked out, the feeling disorienting, like I hadn't missed a thing, but really I'd missed a whole heap of stuff, such as how we returned from the in-between and how I got home.

I wasn't going insane. And if I was, I had enough company. In that company was my dad. For all these years, he'd been a part of this elaborate game, this elaborate lie. But not just him; I was a part of it too, and Ajay. What about Mum? If she was a part of this lie, she would not have turned to Dad's enemy, Carter. Mum was innocent, as was Ajay, for now. It was up to me to make sure he stayed that way. My being Persal would mean Dad was Persal, but who else? Holden, of course. He was a part of this family of factions I was supposed to hold allegiance to.

With everything unraveling as fast as it had last night, I'd missed asking so many questions. Like what was this impending war and the few things Jax had said about the in-between and other dimensions. I couldn't keep playing this game with my limited understanding. I needed to know what I faced, who my enemies were, and how I would save my family.

Mum and Ajay were in the kitchen. Pans clanked, the radio

announcer jabbered, and Ajay asked for the butter and a knife, a normal morning in any household. After months of living in a silent home that felt akin to living in a morgue, I should be grateful for what I heard. Mum had found a purpose, a way to support her family with a good job. Ajay's somber frown had transformed into a smile. To him, everything was shifting back to almost normal.

My life was worse than weeks ago. I thought Dad's imprisonment and our squalor were as bad as it could get. How about fighting for your life and that of your family? On a scale of one to ten, how bad was that? Off the scale. I couldn't even begin to plot where my life now sat. I wasn't good at working out life's problems. My world had been small and my dad was always there to make the difficult stuff go away. Now there was no one but me.

I rolled over and pulled the covers up around my chin. I didn't want to face this on my own, but I had little choice. Carter had Mum. He had me. Soon he would target Ajay. With Dad in jail, there was nothing stopping him.

I pulled the covers up over my head as I groaned, not wanting to face the jumble that was my life and my emotions. Dad wasn't a murderer. The relief would've been greater had it not been shadowed by everything else I had learned. Not a murderer but he was guilty nonetheless. As one of the game designers, he was as guilty as everyone else for sending innocent people to death for not being good enough. Elva and Jax hated him, but they were Aris, so their judgment was likely clouded.

I threw the covers back down to my waist. *Listen to yourself.* I was as bad as Jax, believing factions hated each other simply because they were different.

I closed my eyes and groaned again. Holden was just as bad, another designer, another guilty for all these teenage deaths. And I was supposed to trust him. Yet I'd been a pawn to everyone, had been all along, used to checkmate my dad. I curled myself into the fetal position and tried not to think about how stupid and innocent I'd been.

Covers thrown back, I rolled over to stare at the ceiling with a huff, then launched out of bed, sick of being on this merry-go-round in my head. This was not the way to survive. I had to stop blaming and doubting myself. I threw on clothes that would not impede me when I trained and headed to the kitchen.

Mum turned from the sink and put her dishcloth down as I entered. I took a subtle in breath and poured some milk.

"I tried to phone you last night to let you know of my sudden change in plans."

"Sorry, Mum. I saw your message too late. I lost track of time."

"Seven thirty, that's too late without a word."

"I know. I'm sorry, Mum."

"Don't make me restrict your freedom. I know I struggled with your dad's…" She flicked a glance at Ajay. "Anyway. I want to trust you. And that means keeping me informed of what you're up to. Ring me if you're going to be late. Have fun, make new friends, but if you give me a reason to lose trust in you, then we'll go back to the way it was."

I longed for my life to rewind and, unbelievably, have Dad back in our lives. "Sure. I understand."

"Good. Now eat some breakfast. Marleen said you went straight to bed without dinner. You feeling all right?"

"I'm fine."

Ajay's frown made me feel reprimanded again, so I busied myself buttering toast. Strangely enough, Ajay had had the maturity to keep his mouth shut about my disappearance last night from Marleen and Mum.

Mum eyed my clothes. "You wearing that to school?"

"I can't find anything clean."

"I'll put a load on before I go."

"Go where?"

"My first day, sweetheart."

Oh, yeah, dammit. But as long as I stuck with the deal, Carter wouldn't do anything to Mum, which meant I had to show I was keeping my end of the bargain.

"I want to make a good impression, so I'm prepared to stay late and finish anything undone from the day. I expect I will be a little slower than most, my first day and all."

So I didn't have to reply, I gulped my milk.

"Remember no plans are to be made for Saturday afternoon."

I nearly choked on the last of my milk. She was meaning our regular visit to see Dad, which we might not be able to do after his rampage. What could I say to Mum to explain why and how I got there? The truth, possibly, but perhaps knowing the truth would put her in danger.

I felt Ajay's stare bore into the side of my head. Another weird thing for a ten-year-old, Ajay had also kept his mouth shut about our visit, and Jax. He was acting bizarrely adult and smart about all the secrets I had him keep. My heart ached at what I made my little brother do. Normal ten-year-old boys shouldn't have to lie to their parents about important things that impacted upon everyone's survival. But then normal ten-year-old boys didn't have a ticking bomb inside their heads or the threat of death at the hands of a virtual game.

"Ajay, get dressed, honey, it's almost time to go." Mom reprimanded Ajay with a smile and he scooted off to get dressed.

Time I also disappeared. Being here was all too normal when my head was filled with the abnormal. Perhaps a day would come where being at home felt surreal and life in Dominus was my reality?

"I think I'll get going."

"Finish your toast."

"I'll take it with me."

I kissed Mum on the cheek. "Good luck today."

"Thanks, sweetheart. There's a lasagna in the fridge in case I'm not home in time."

I disappeared out the door before Mum could say anything else.

I'd just found my seat on the bus when my phone rang. Holden beat me to the phone call.

"I'm on my way to your club."

"I spoke to Jax last night."

"Was it civil?"

"What's between us is not as bad as you think. Besides, he understands the importance of cooperation. We're going there today. If you're closer to my club, we can go together. If not, I'll see you there."

"Are you going to be all right with Elva around?"

"This takes precedence over anything personal. Elva knows that."

"I wish I could blanket my emotions so easily."

"You will once you understand what we're doing."

That explained Jax's walled personality every time we entered the game. "Yeah, about that. Before I wear that dotted suit, you're going to tell me everything."

"I will, I promise. I owe you that."

"And Jax, will he be willing to share?"

"Not as much as me."

No surprises there.

"I also want to speak to Dad."

I knew the truth and I wanted him to know that. Seventeen years of lying, seventeen years of protection, and it made no difference in the end. Mostly I wanted him to know I was all right, that I would do my best, that I would survive.

"It won't be easy, but I'll see what I can do."

"I'll get myself to the warehouse. See you there."

I'd get off at the next stop and find myself the right bus, but for the moment I was happy to remain where I was, blanketed from my future for the short time it took me to disembark. Four months ago, I was worried whether my grades would be good enough to attend my choice of college. I thought about boyfriends and wondered if a day would come when I had one of my own instead of eavesdropping in the toilets to get my fill of romance. Here I stood now, not knowing if I would stay alive long enough to have a future and hoping I could keep Ajay and Mum safe.

The bus slowed and I leaped from my seat and clambered down the steps, beating an old guy with a walking stick, who no doubt cursed me under his breath for being rude.

I wasn't going to worry about trying to find the right bus. Instead I would run. The last few weeks vortexed around in my head. From Dad and Jax to Carter and Mum, also Dominus and the world's fate, Aris and Persal, tattoos meaning more than interesting pictures, stairwells that led to an abyss. Nothing made sense. The one thing most people relied on, reality, wasn't my friend anymore because even that was lying. People can't do scary, dangerous things with their minds, people can't leave this worldly plain for another; except they can and they do.

So I ran. I ran hard and I ran fast. My legs slammed against the paving, jarring me through, but I kept going. I passed one bus, then two, ignored both, and pushed through the wall of pain every athlete knew, down the curb, through fleeting gaps between traffic, up the curb on the other side of the street, and on. Buildings whizzed by me like a blur, people too, their faces jumbling into one. The jars went as far as my brain. Each pounding jolt sent a spasm through my head. It was like I was trying to punish myself for being who I was, for being so stupid as to fall into this messed-up alternate reality. I kept going, pushing harder, going faster, as if I wanted to outrun the truth, wanted to outrun my life.

When I reached the warehouse, I collapsed against the wall and gasped huge wheezing breaths. My legs shook with exhaustion and my lungs hurt, yet I was still in the same spot—that is, quite possibly doomed.

Once I thought I could string a sentence together in one breath, I rang the bell and the door clicked straightaway. When the lift doors opened onto the apartment, I stayed where I was because everyone was there and looking at me, everyone minus my dad.

Chapter 21

HE WORE A BLACK SUIT, which gave him rank amongst those in the room. "Welcome, Sable. It's been a long time coming, but I'm so very glad to have you here."

My steps were cautious, like I was ready for a fight, and I was. If Carter dared touch me, even a friendly pat, I would take out his eyes, at least I'd try, and damn the consequences.

They all looked at me, except Jax, who stared at the floor from his slouched position in one of the easy chairs. I couldn't decide if his ignoring me meant contempt or shame. Elva stood on the other side of the room from Holden, who came toward me and offered his hand. Being Persal, he was perhaps the only person in the room I could trust, but only a little.

"I was worried about you."

"Why?"

"It's taken you more time to get here than we expected. Thought you may have changed your mind."

He took in my look, face no doubt sweaty and red, and would've worked out why it took me so long.

"You all right?"

"Not sure. Ask me that in another hour."

He squeezed my hand and tried for a half smile.

I nodded toward Carter. "What's he doing here?" I didn't bother to lower my voice or sugarcoat my tone.

"You wanted the truth. He's here to give it to you."

"The truth according to him."

"It's the same thing any of us would tell you."

I looked Holden in the eye. "Why don't you? I'm not interested in hearing anything he has to say."

"Carter is a member of the Senate of Factions. He represents Aris, which means—"

"I'm King Dick around here. So sit and let's get on with this."

He did as he commanded, finding a seat that put him at the center of the gathering. He folded his hands in his lap and looked up at me. I remained in my spot, and that's where I would stay. I was forced to play his stupid game, but I would not follow his commands.

"What about my mother?"

"Your mother is finally living. You should be grateful for that. I've given her a chance no one else would've done for a woman her age with no experience. And as long as you play your part, she will stay where she is, earning her living and keeping her family fed."

The shark reappeared, cruising smoothly through my hidden accusations. How I wanted to smack that smug smile off his face. I wanted to watch him bleed. I wanted to hear him scream with agony, which wasn't me at all. In his presence, I became what he wanted me to become—a morally ambivalent fighter. I'd become his pawn, but he'd best be careful lest the pawn became his greatest enemy.

I didn't know what I was thinking, but I was now beyond my life, which meant I was free to become someone else, whether I liked it or not.

"What about Ajay?"

"Too young, for now. And if you want to keep him on the outside of Dominus, I suggest we get these questions done and start your training."

Fine. I mimicked him and sat heavy in the seat opposite with my arms folded across my chest. "I'm only getting started. This Senate of Factions, is that like the rockabilly community or something? Are you a bunch of people who like to pretend you live in the world of Dominus?"

Tyren transformed from a statue into a person and came to sit next to me, his expression encouraging and friendly. He seemed keen for me to be a part of their sick adventure. "We do live in the world of Dominus."

I snorted. "And this world, where exactly is it? I must have missed the label on the map during geography lessons."

Elva slammed her hands to her sides and huffed out the biggest breath. "Do we need to do this? Why can't we just throw her in the game and watch her sink?"

Holden sat beside me. Somehow this felt like a show of support for me against Elva. I didn't want to be stuck in the middle of their silent love battle. "Our world is not on the map because it's nowhere in this location."

"Yeah, right." My voice wasn't as sarcastic as I wanted it to be. I flicked a quick glance to Jax, but he remained as marble, looking at the floor. Perhaps I should drag the bright orange cushion I'd sat on out from under me and use it as a projectile, see if that would get me some of Jax's attention. Now was not the time for him to go icy. It annoyed the hell out of me that he should flip into one of his moods and feed me the silent treatment. He was the one who gave me to Carter, taunted Dad, gave me a glimpse of his softer side, showed me something at Aris HQ that had to be significant, threw me into the game without my factional nature, saved my life, took me to a place of magical serenity. Sometimes he drew me close, opened a part of his soul, and gave me a glimpse. Sometimes he treated me like a tool that Carter hoped to fashion to a weapon. It was as if there were times when he forgot himself and became real. Problem was, I didn't know which part of him that was.

One thing I knew for sure, after last night, I couldn't refute anything anyone in this room said with confidence, and that made the hairs on my arms and the back of my neck stand erect.

"So you're aliens?"

My voice sounded strained, inching up an octave at the end.

Holden smiled. "No. Not really. We call our world earth like you do. We look like you, we just live differently. And we happen to be across the veil in another dimension."

"You want me to swallow that crap?" The word *dimension* ran prickles down my backbone. Jax had mentioned it last night.

"I believe quantum physics covered it best. It's been interesting watching everyone argue over the theories through the years. Unfortunately, those in your dimension who understand the rules are unable to do anything about it. We, on the other hand, can. Dimension travel is… or should I say was…a common pastime." Carter sounded bored.

"And my dad?"

"Is…sorry, was a member of the Senate of Factions for Persal. I'm afraid his absence has been noticed and he's about to lose his seat."

My eyes fell to his white cuffs poking out the bottom of the sleeves of his shirt. Gold bars as cuff links finished the impeccable look, a wealthy businessman, organized, in control, powerful. What was under the right cuff? A tattoo like Jax's, the symbol of his unity with everyone else in this room except Holden and me?

"What are you doing in my world?"

"Recruiting and training. We need souls capable of fighting a very special war. So far your dimension has proved the best recruiting ground, but the process is slow and tedious."

"You're calling innocent deaths tedious."

I could've scratched the smirk off Carter's face. "Similar we may be, but there are significant differences."

"Such as our strong regard for life."

"Believe me, we value life."

"Your own, maybe, but no one else's."

Carter's laugh was mirthless as he looked around the room at the others. "What do you think?"

I followed his gaze to find no one met his eyes. Given the somber expression on everyone's faces, I would say they were uneasy discussing the lack of morality of what they were doing. Their silence pounded a restless beat through my veins. If they were all so uneasy, why weren't any of them speaking out?

Carter shifted his hard stare back to me. "There's a fifty-fifty split you're not going to make it. I was on the negative, but now, I don't know. Given you're Nixon's girl, we could be in for a surprise. What do you think, Jax? You ready to change your bet?"

The moment distilled to a single tick of the clock as my heart stalled in disbelief. I'd been rewound to the time in court, but instead of staring at my father's face, I was staring at Jax. A punch in the gut would've made me feel better than what I just heard. They were gambling on me surviving Dominus. But the sickest part was Jax had betted against me. I hardened my stare to nails, but they glanced off the crown of his head. All those tousled black loose curls acted like the perfect defense against my silent intent. *Look at me, just this once look at me, so I can see the face of deceit.* He stared stubbornly at the ground.

At what point had I started to believe in him? That was the only explanation I could find for how gutted I felt right now.

I bit back the sting in my eyes and focused on Carter. "What about Salvador and the other young gamers? How much did you win when they died?"

Carter's smirk remained solid, but the atmosphere in the room became taut with the silence. I made a point of looking everyone in the eye. Holden had the grace to sink his head to his chest. Tyren didn't look much better. Jax sat alone, yet to move. His were the only eyes I couldn't meet. Regardless, a knot of tension emanated from him and coiled around the room like a whip about to crack.

Were the lump in my throat and the sting in my eyes due to my anger or fear? I felt trapped in a cage with vipers, all watching and waiting for the wrong word or movement before they attacked. And with each in breath, I felt like I was slowly being bound by a wire coil.

Was this who my dad was? No, not the side of him I knew, the side that loved his family. He lied, but he lied to keep his family safe. I understood that now. How could I fault that? Because in his shoes, I would've done the same.

I addressed Carter. "How many others from your world are here?"

"No one else."

"How is Dominus a recruiting and training program?"

"It mimics our world."

"How much?"

"We want warriors who know how to fight. They need to understand the rules of our world."

"Aris and Persal have an alliance, right? Which means none of the other factions know you're here or what you're doing. Sounds to me like a takeover."

Finally Carter's smirk slipped. Tyren snorted an appreciative laugh.

Carter sat forward, the easy manner gone. "It's so easy to die. Just remember that."

He swept to his feet and buttoned the first hole of his jacket. "You've had your little talk. It's time to begin."

He strode past everyone without another word and disappeared into the lift. My eyes followed his back, so too my hatred. Surely it wasn't possible to carry so much hatred and not combust or turn into something ugly.

This was my enemy. This was the man who'd broken my family, would continue to break my family until he had what he wanted, and then he would go on to break my world. This was the man I had to stop. But how? I looked around me but no one would meet my eyes, strangers all of them. Were they all my enemy?

Tyren was the first to move. Looking at everyone, he said, "I say we do this," then to me, "This time you get all of us."

This I hadn't been expecting. "You're not all against me?"

I wanted to stay in my chair but rose anyhow.

"We play together against the computer. Don't you guys say over here, sink or swim?"

"That's a figure of speech. It's not meant to be taken literally."

"Whatever, you'll never learn how to be good unless you face the greatest challenge."

"How about I get a little better than totally sucks before I attempt that?"

"Babe, this is what we do. Trust us to get you through. And then you'll learn and you'll play better and get smarter. Once Holden helps you find your special talent, we'll be an unstoppable unit."

"And I thought you were the sane one of this bunch."

Tyren frowned, then burst out laughing. He came forward and clapped me on the back like we were old friends. "This is going to be fun."

Elva stopped short before following Tyren. "Don't think because you're Nixon's girl you're anything special."

I would take her friendly bit of advice to indicate she wouldn't be giving me any help.

They all departed for the gaming room, except Jax, who stood like he had aches that needed slow straightening. I should've followed the rest, but sucker me wanted to hear his explanation.

We stood alone in the room like strangers. After everything, we ended up like this. I wanted to pound against the barrier that continually formed between us. Why wasn't I ignoring him and following the rest through? Because at some point along the way, I'd started to rely on him. I believed he was someone who would help pull me through. Why had I done that, when so far fate had proved no one was reliable? The need to trust someone was greater than my logic, but Dad was right; no one was trustworthy.

"What we are is not always a pretty thing. You'll learn that once you allow your factional nature in. But it doesn't have to be the sum total of you."

"I don't care about that."

He wouldn't look at me. "Once you start, it will consume you. You need to know that. Not like you can do anything about it, but you should be prepared. You won't walk out of Dominus and be the same person. An important part of you will be lost forever."

We both remained where we were. As if the need to share and the need to hear had magnetized us in place.

"Why?"

"You can't face what you're about to face and remain untouched."

"That's not what I'm asking."

He stalled. His shoulders slumped as he looked at the floor. So brief was the emotion, it could've been missed, but I saw it and read it like a reflection of my soul, the understanding of inevitability. He wasn't a savior, he was just like me, a pawn. Neither of us was big enough to overcome the forces that placed us here. And now I became his mirror as I lost the most crucial parts of myself—the parts that made me believe and trust.

"You may not like this new part of yourself. Your father wanted to protect you from it."

"There's no point in saying that now. I'm here because of you."

It wasn't true. I would be here regardless of whether it was Jax who got me to this point, but my desolation made me angry, and he was the best person for my attack.

"You said you had a sister, so why Ajay? Why mess with him?"

Only the guilty turned their backs as he did right now. "You don't want to know my reasons."

"Because they're not good enough," I shouted at his back.

"Because you've been through too much. You have every reason to despise me. Most of the time I despise myself."

He walked away from me and I found myself stuck in place, unable to move because he'd taken my emotions and ripped through them with a Stanley knife, leaving me with nothing to help make my next decision. But there was no decision to make. Carter saw to that. I stared at the retreating form of Jax as he loped into the gaming room and out of sight. The door remained ajar, an invitation. Noises in preparation for the game flowed out to greet me. The distance to the room became a mile, or was it I was shrinking? I closed my eyes because that's the only wall I could create as the conveyor belt of my fate whizzed me forward; I would soon be ejected, ready or not.

I pushed everything important to me down deep until I was left numb and followed Jax into the gaming room.

Chapter 22

I WOULD LIKE to think everyone who stood around me in their dotted suits had an interest in getting me through Dominus alive, but there were no guarantees. I was going to stick to Holden like cement, which would only create a greater enemy out of Elva. Since I figured she was more likely to stab me than save me, what did it matter?

Jax had saved my ass the first time, but I wasn't about to rely on him again. Thinking about our crazy, twisted association gave me a head spin. One minute he was saving my life and giving me rare glimpses of his private side; the next he was betting against me surviving.

Carter appeared the boss, but I didn't know the group well enough to determine if the four of them were subordinate enough to listen to his commands or the sort to deal with matters as they saw fit.

If ever there was a time for me to find whatever inner strength I possessed, this was it. Unfortunately, my courage had taken a battering the last couple of months. Jax said Dominus was built on lies and manipulation, but after everything, I doubted my ability to shift through the fabrications to find the truth, and now I was forced to rely on people I didn't know or trust as I entered a game that gave the one-strike-and-you're-out policy a hellish new meaning; I had no second chance.

We stood in a circle, everyone's attention on Jax, which told me he was the one they considered the leader. Even Holden waited for him to speak. I searched everyone's faces, looking for a hint of understanding that what we were about to do was insane, but saw only determination.

My stomach coiled up tight, twisting right up to my throat such that I couldn't swallow. I didn't want to be here. This wasn't my fight. But I'd been dragged into it by virtue of my father and his other life, which was perhaps more real than the one he'd shared with us.

"We go in on game mode. But we have no objective today. This is a basic training exercise for Sable's sake. I'm keeping the level low. No heroics. Just make sure Sable comes out alive." Maybe I could relax a smidgeon now, and hopefully Elva would obey.

While the others put their goggles on, Jax approached me.

"Watch and learn, but keep alert. And stay close to me."

Holden came up alongside me. "I'll keep her covered." He sounded proprietary.

They eyeballed each other. I could sense both bristling. Holden was willing to give Jax the lead, but Jax wasn't technically his leader, being a different faction and all. Seconds ticked before a silent acquiescence took place between them. They broke and found a space, then slid their goggles over their eyes. I wasn't sure who won the steely-eyed contest, but I would stick with both if possible. I'd experienced what a warrior in game mode could do, and I wasn't prepared to find bugs crawling out of my stomach.

I slid my goggles down to find Jax had landed us right into Califax City. It was beautiful in game mode. The boring grays and browns gave way to an assortment of dazzling colors. The roads were cobbled and lined with trees whose leaves were turning deep amber, orange, or red. Garden beds of flowers turned the base of each tree into a colored quilt. The buildings appeared to be made of metal and glass, their architecture unique to anything found on earth. They sure liked to make everything imposing, including the overuse of spires, sharp angles, and thick metal beams. Perfectly rendered bots populated the streets, each original in design and scarily warrior-like.

Beside me, Holden looked set to fight a war single-handedly in black and orange with two decent-sized swords strapped to his back. Thighs of iron, a mean face to match. Elva looked only marginally better than her real self, which put her knockout fabulous in a deep purple bra and briefs set with a thick gold wreath around her waist. Bands with spikes wrapped around her arms. A dangerous-looking headdress of sharp points controlled her long, thick raven hair. Tyren was an impressive dark-skinned warrior dressed in black and gold. Like Jax's, his blade was small. After my last foray into Dominus, I understood why Aris only bothered with small weapons.

"You're without a weapon, but we'll leave it like that since you have no skill in wielding one." Jax then turned to the rest of the group. "Sable's vulnerable to the onslaught of her factional nature, plus her fighting skills are subpar at the moment, so no bot is to reach her. At level two, we're unlikely to be hammered, but there will be enough to keep us busy."

Jax focused on Holden. "Any signs of her tripping and she's not handling it, you let me know."

Holden nodded. After their mini showdown outside the game, Holden probably had words to add, but he kept those to himself, like any good solider.

He turned to me. "It's going to be hard at the moment to control your factional nature, but you should know that the arena of effect could be catastrophic should you lose control."

"What do you mean?"

"Most factional attacks in Dominus are done on the mind of the individual attacked, but for Aris and Persal, the effects are more tangible. Releasing your factional nature without control could create devastation on the immediate area around you or, if you really lose control, on a much wider scale."

"No pressure at all."

Jax ignored me and spoke to everyone else. "Since we have two Persal amongst us, we head for Persal HQ." He looked at Holden. "I think it best Sable is introduced to home base. You and Sable go first."

With a tilt of his head down the street, Holden indicated the way. So much for sticking to Jax.

I came alongside him, leaving the others behind. "Why are we going first?"

"Factions mixing will trigger the computer to attack. Milling together in the streets for a while is acceptable, but if we remain together for any length of time, the computer will read that as a threat. They won't be far behind."

I glanced over my shoulder, and sure enough, the rest moved meters behind us. Good thing Elva was an avatar. It meant I didn't have to see her wicked stare, which I'm sure she was sharing with me at the moment, simply because I was Persal but also because I walked with Holden.

"If the rules of Dominus match the rules of your world, it must've been hard for you and Elva."

"Very."

"You're so... She seems so..."

"We're opposites. Is that what you're trying to say?"

"So far you seem the nicest of all of them, particularly Elva."

"There's more to any of us, Sable. Don't be in a hurry to judge. Elva's not who you think she is."

"She hates me."

"She's strong, loyal, and fiercely passionate. The senate would've killed us both rather than allow our relationship to continue, and no one could've prevented it. I ended it between us because I was scared of the punishment. She would've stayed with me until the end."

She might have good qualities, but she wasn't about to favor me with any of them. But what Holden said gave her attitude toward me meaning. I couldn't help but feel humbled by her fidelity; risking your life for love was beyond something many were prepared to do. I would do that for my family; how about someone I loved who wasn't blood?

I glanced behind, my eyes finding Elva, stone-faced and warrior-like, looking less passionate and more fierce.

My pace slowed on seeing a wave of NPCs march toward us. In game mode, their strong, muscular thighs, nuggety biceps, and stern faces made me want to head in the other direction. Holden kept his pace and the bots broke around him. I doubled my steps to keep up with Holden, but a large, powerful-looking woman in yellow strode toward me. Being a bot, her face remained devoid of any emotion, including any recognition that I was in her way. She should move, but her strides remained unchanged. Just as I was about to dodge out of her way, she changed course. I tried to catch a look at the tattoo behind her ear but she passed too quickly for me to see.

"How do we know who the enemy is?"

"We don't. So it pays to be alert. Any one of these bots can transform into the enemy."

"Shouldn't you have told me that at the start?"

The others remained vigilant. Their faces scoured their surroundings, even looking up onto rooflines as if prepared for a bot to drop down over the edge.

"What's all this writing at the left side of my vision? Jax explained some things, but not all."

"Stats. Tells you vital stuff. The number at the top left is the number of kills you've made, the number next to it in green is the number you need to make before it's safe to exit the game. You don't get a kill-death ratio as you only get one chance to die in Dominus. The level you're playing is the number at the top right. The—"

"What? What do you mean, safe to exit the game?"

"Depending on the level you play, you have a kill quota you must meet before you exit the game. Pull out too soon and you suffer the consequences."

"Like what?"

"Level two, no consequences so don't worry."

"Don't you dare not finish."

"Focus on what we're here to do for now."

"No, tell me the consequences."

"Each level is different, increasing in severity each time you level up. People suffer differently too. Limb paralyses, extreme headaches, memory loss, unconsciousness. I won't touch on the more serious consequences."

"Tell me you're joking."

"Don't worry, I've got you covered. The three bars below show your skill, health, and power status; the silver dots on your skin allow Dominus to read these things. The one at the top is skill, how well you can fight, wield the weapons you have. Most players will usually choose a weapon and stay with it so they can become proficient. It's a handy marker as it makes you want to improve your skills when you start to see it shift. If your skill drops, it means you need to concentrate more or increase your practice."

How did he expect me to concentrate after dropping such a bomb of a revelation?

"The next down is your health status bar. Tells you how tired you're getting or if you've been hurt. Keep an on that one. You don't want it flashing red."

"And that means?"

"Nothing good. If you're experienced enough, you can push through red and get out all right. When it's flashing, it's critical. It means your brain waves are simulating the dive to death. That's why mental control is so important. If you can control your fear, then you can control your death in Dominus."

"You know what, how about you shut up now?"

He squeezed my shoulder. "The last bar is equally important. It's your power status bar."

"Mine's not even registering."

"It will. It's another one you want to keep an eye on. It's a valuable indicator for newbies, tells them when they're moving close to tripping. That's when your factional nature floods through to dangerous levels. Again, it will flash red when you reach that point. While in Dominus, it's critical. Since Dominus speeds up the rewiring of your brain, it can force your factional nature through too quickly sometimes."

"What does that mean exactly?"

"Outside of Dominus, if that happened, you'd destroy something, which in itself could be bad. Inside Dominus, you fry your brain, total meltdown, like melting electrical wires."

"How are you all right with this?"

"It's the cost it takes to achieve the outcome we believe in."

"You're willing to die for your belief?"

"Of course. Who wouldn't?"

"Hmm...let me see. Most sane people."

For once I saw an expression on an avatar, a broad grin. Don't know what he saw amusing about any of this.

"Seriously, I need to get you out if you hit critical either on your health or power status bar. At level two, that's easy as you don't have a requirement for a certain number of kills. And being Persal, I'll be able to sense that point before you trip—I hope."

"I don't think I want to know any more about this game."

Holden scooped me in for a shoulder hug. "It will grow on you." And left his arm there. Maybe she wasn't, but I imagined Elva's eyes boring holes into the back of my head. Was this Holden's plan? I shouldn't think like that. It only demeaned him.

We headed for a large obelisk at the end of the street. The pointy end was gold and, closer up, detailed designs emerged down the sides. The obelisk stood at the center of a radial of cobbled roads, which were filled with bots, not cars. I was about to ask how everyone in his world got around when an aircraft, a cross between a train and a plane with a sleek metal design, cruised overhead in the direction of a high column.

I glanced to Holden, unable to contain my wonderment, which was likely missed on my avatar face.

"A black skytrain. No cars in Califax, as you can see. The skies back home are crisscrossed with black, red, or blue skytrains depending on your direction of travel."

"How long have you been in my world?"

"Two years."

"So short."

"I'm a new recruit."

"How come Carter has three Aris to work with and Dad only has you?"

"It's not that easy getting here. I'm lucky I got through. Nixon's been on his own for most of the time. Somehow Carter's been luckier and found three of his faction able to shift."

"Why is it hard? Carter boasted about how easy it was for your kind."

"The Senate of Factions outlawed dimensional shifting about thirty years ago." He held up his hand and exposed the tattoo now present on his inner wrist, which was not there in real life. It was similar to Dad's, Jax's and Elva's. "Every citizen is grafted at birth. The graft suppresses their ability to shift. It also dulls their factional nature, although it's not always completely effective."

"Why do they do that?"

"Some say paranoia, fear of subversion, an obsessive need to maintain control. It took a long time for the grafts to become legal practice."

"It would prevent factions from moving to new worlds and raising an army of people like me whose factional nature is not suppressed."

"You're smart, but don't judge us until you've lived in our world. Our factional nature makes us dangerous, but we existed a long time alongside each other with our abilities intact. Many who remember that time see the grafts as an attack on their personal freedom. They believe we are now enslaved to the senate and say the senate has over stepped its mandate. I don't remember a time when I was free, but I don't buy into the senate's propaganda about creating a safer world for all to exist. I disagree with suppressing that which is so fundamentally a part of us. It's like saying we're all flawed when perhaps it's their expectations that are flawed."

"If you're grafted, how are any of you here?"

"The Senate of Factions' grafts remain inactive. According to them, it's a necessity to keep harmony within the factions and maintain peaceful relations with bordering dimensions, which is fancy speak for domination. This meant Carter and Nixon were free to move between this world and ours, but they had to find a way to bring us across. And of course, they did, but it's not an easy or safe process. There have been deaths on our side as well. It turns out there are only a rare few capable of surviving the nullification process in the crude fashion we were able to do it in. At the Dome, under proper medical attention, it would be different. That's why Nixon only has me. I was the only survivor."

"Why are you doing this? If it's killing so many people, why keep trying?"

"It's about freedom from oppression. We're sick of being made to live a certain way, sick of being stripped of our true nature. We want a say in our lives. Sometimes you have to make sacrifices to force change."

No one had the right to kill innocent people. If only he could see, but I said nothing because my arguments came from someone who'd never been forced to choose between love and death, who'd never had to deny the truth of who they were. I'd lived my life within the confines of my dad's protective love, but compared to Holden's life, I'd been free.

We walked away from the obelisk, down another cobbled street lined with amber-leafed trees. Topiaries of bizarre geometric shapes replaced the colorful garden beds. Not far along, Holden halted out the front of a tall building, the face of which was covered in tinted windows, darkened enough to obscure the view inside.

"HQ."

"I'm not going to find this place again." I looked around me. "There are too many metal and glass fronted buildings to make this one stand out."

Holden walked toward the building. At a certain distance from the entrance, a fractured circle shimmered in gold across the face of the windows.

He turned back to me and smiled. "The symbol will only illuminate for a Persal. You can't miss that."

Despite us all standing on the mat, I turned back to the others, moving up behind us, their leather-booted feet smacking hard along the cobbles. I couldn't begin to fathom the depth at which Dominus had meshed with my mind, twisting my senses and belief in what was real, turning everything around me into a new frightening reality.

"Show her around. I'll give you fifteen, then meet us back outside," Jax said.

Being in game mode meant Aris were unable to enter Persal HQ.

The light, airy rooms of Persal HQ contrasted with Aris's dark, gloomy, tunneled hallways. The large domed center of Aris was replaced by an expansive room at the front of the building, facing out over the street we'd just left. The comfort of the modular furniture looked questionable, and the decor of muted browns and creams made the space look soothing but boring, although a lot more welcoming than Aris HQ.

"We can socialize with other Persal in here. Mostly you will meet out-of-towners at HQ. Of course, I'm talking about our world. In Dominus, bots don't congregate within HQ, there's no point, so unless we're playing with a large number, you'll be on your own. Or you could be with me. HQ is also the meeting place for Persal leaders, and the conference room is directly above us." He pointed to the ceiling, which was a long way up.

"But there are no Persal leaders in Dominus, right?"

"There was your father. Sorry, maybe I shouldn't have said that. Come." He strode out of the room and down a wide and well-lit hallway, thanks to glowing panels running from ceiling to floor. Unlike at Aris's HQ, these remained glowing before and after we passed.

"Communal kitchen in there." The door slid open and he paused briefly in the doorway before striding off again. I stole a glimpse of the sparse room, gleaming metallic surfaces and walls, before the door slid shut again.

"There's not much else to see apart from the accommodations. But I'm sure Jax wanted me to show you something in particular."

He continued on his march and I remained dutifully quiet and followed. Halfway along the hall, Holden placed his palm over a section of the wall and it slid aside to reveal a cavity on the other side. The hairs on my neck prickled with the first hint of mystery. Any mystery in Dominus was likely to be dangerous.

Holden stepped inside and a large circular bulb glowed to life. We stood in an empty room—only empty for the time it took Holden to cross the small space and place his hands against the wall. The wall began to shimmer before collapsing to a vortex, a chaotic swirl that sucked the surrounding wall into its interior like a gaping black hole. It was like experiencing déjà vu with the noise of tumbling brickwork and fracturing plaster, then the sound of wind funneling down a tunnel once the collapse was complete. My hair flapped around my face, the long blonde locks nonexistent in real life. I even felt them tickle my face. Such was the strength of the wind, I was pulled toward the opening so grabbed Holden to use as an anchor. He tugged me close and we watched in an embrace until the violence subsided and left an abyss.

I let Holden go and took a few tentative steps forward, nervous the vortex would start again and swallow me. "I saw something similar in Aris's HQ."

Holden yanked my elbow to spin me to face him. "You were in Aris's HQ? When?"

"The time I developed my headache. We were in training mode, so Jax said it was all right."

"I can't believe he took you inside."

"Why?"

"That he would show a Persal." He shook his head. "Both Aris and Persal have these tunnels. We've been working on them for many years now."

"Just Aris and Persal?"

"Because of our alliance."

"Where do they go?"

"The Califax Dome. No one is allowed to enter the Dome that does not work there or is part of the Senate of Factions. To enter unauthorized is certain death."

"Why?"

"The Dome is where the senate maintains its power over our Earth. If the Dome was overrun and the senate defeated, they would no longer be able to suppress the people, but it's not easy getting in."

"So you're tunneling."

"Because neither faction could trust the other, we tunneled our own sections but kept our pathway secret from the other. Unfortunately for Persal, we hit an impenetrable rock that has slowed our progress. We've had to divert around, which has driven us far off course. But we believe Aris have had no such problems. We believe they are close to reaching the Dome."

"And if they are?"

"It's impossible for them to move around within the Dome alone. That is why both factions formed the alliance. The most important parts of the Dome can only be accessed with two faction members present. It's a way of reducing a possible threat to the senate's power. I guess they figured no two factions could hold an alliance long enough to succeed. This means it's likely Aris will share their tunnel success with us."

"But you can't be sure."

"No. In fact, I would count on their deception. If their tunnel is anything like ours, it's not a direct path. Before we were forced to divert, we created an underground maze in case factions other than Persal managed to find the tunnel. We hold the master plan; anyone else will only get lost."

"Aris have done the same. I saw a design on a wall in their hall. I think it's their master plan."

"You're probably right. Problem is no one from Persal can enter Aris HQ."

"Isn't it safe in training mode?"

"Due to its location, in Jax's warehouse, I can't enter Dominus without one of Aris present, which means I'll never make it into their HQ. Besides, Jax is GM, which means he controls the way the game is played and at what level anyone can enter. And the doorway to the tunnel will only open for an Aris, as this one will only open for Persal."

"Jax has the master plan tattooed on his arm."

Holden delayed his reply, drawing my attention. "Is that so?"

I missed the subtle expression because of his avatar face, but I didn't like the tone in his voice. Were we on the verge of scheming against Aris?

"I'm trying to understand why he took you to Aris HQ, why he showed you the tunnel. It makes no sense."

Best change the subject, somehow. As a part of Dominus now, I had begun to understand how the factions existed with each other. Their alliance was not for mutual benefit but for one to use the other and then finally win over them.

"Perhaps there is something between you two that we're all missing."

"What do you mean? I hate him." Something told me I was about to become another pawn.

"But why show you one of Aris's greatest secrets? If Carter knew, I would hate to think what he would do to Jax."

Was that a threat? "I don't understand either. I guess he did because there was little I would be able to do with the knowledge. Like you say, we can't get into Aris HQ, and I wouldn't remember the room—"

"What was in the room, the master plan or the tunnel?"

My mind swirled like the vortex, trying to think of a way to opt out. Holden no longer spoke like Holden.

"Shouldn't we be heading back? Jax gave us fifteen minutes."

"It's important, Sable. Your dad would want to know this."

Low blow, Holden. A fire sparked in the pit of my stomach. I turned from the vortex and stormed out of the small room. Behind me, the noise of the vortex remaking itself drowned out my frantic thoughts.

Holden, my faction, my supposed family, wanted to maneuver me into a position I did not choose.

Holden grabbed my hand and spun me to face him. "You don't understand yet what it means to be a faction member. Differing factions can't be friends. Differing factions can't be lovers. Sooner or later, the other is going to betray you. That's just how it works."

I wrenched out of his hold. "But you said the factions were able to exist side by side before the senate introduced their draconian laws."

"We did, but we still kept a distance from each other. There were still constant skirmishes, which sometimes got serious enough to destroy a town."

"You didn't keep your distance from Elva."

"It never would've worked, even if the senate hadn't intervened. Our factional nature makes all of us too unalike for any relationship to work."

"But Elva was willing to try. You said she was ready to die loving you."

We were close. The heat of the argument cooked the small space between us. I'd grab Holden by the arms and give him a good shake-up, make him see the twisted justification for what we were doing, if I knew it would make any difference. The steely face of his avatar robbed me of what I needed to see in order to know if what I said had any meaning to him. Perhaps I didn't want to reach his expression.

"You don't get it, Sable, because you've never lived it. We can't exist in this sort of fantastical harmony you want to create."

How could he say that?

"Then perhaps the senate is right to suppress your natures." I stalked away.

He jogged after me, then jumped in front to block my escape. "No one has the right to enforce their will on another. This is what the senate has done."

"They fear anyone more powerful than them."

"But we're not. That's the point. We still don't trust each other. That hasn't changed regardless of what the senate has done. Outside Califax there is no harmony. Factions never mix."

"From what I hear, it's because the senate is afraid of mixed children. They don't want powers concentrated in one individual."

"Isn't that enough reason?"

I leaned back against the wall, my argument punctured. I knew nothing about his world, what it was like to live in his world, which meant I wasn't confident in my argument. I had seen Jax succumb to his factional nature. It wasn't pretty, but I could understand Holden's desire to live free of shackles and be the person he really was. There was no black-and-white answer here, only misty, swirling gray.

"You've got to help us here. We're at a disadvantage, but it seems you may be our key."

"And what happens when you make it to the Dome?"

"We disband the senate, set the people free."

"And who will be leader? Who will make the new laws since you're adamant no faction can trust the other? And what sort of laws will they be?"

"I can't talk about that now because it hasn't been confirmed yet."

"Or maybe you're just blindly following."

I pushed past him and walked toward the front door. Holden let me go, which was good because I wasn't ready to continue our conversation. Outside, the sun washed across my face; god, even that was a physical sensation.

The others waited across the street—our enemy, Aris. Was Holden's argument valid? Was I being naive in my romantic belief in harmony?

Chapter 23

MY PERCEPTION HAD CHANGED and I didn't like the difference. At some point soon, I would change too, and I wasn't sure if I would be comfortable with the person I became. If Holden got his way, I would be a manipulating cheat. I looked across the cobbled street to where Jax and his crew waited. Born a different faction, they would do the same to us; they probably were doing the same to us—we just didn't know it yet. Dad was in prison because of Carter's deceit and, no doubt, guilty himself of deception. Between the buildings on this side and the buildings across the street, there stretched plenty of space. It didn't matter; I felt the streets narrowing, the game compressing in on me. The weight on my limbs threatened to sink me under.

Holden appeared at my elbow. "We best get moving. Staying stationary increases our chances of being attacked."

He headed off down the street the way we'd come, not waiting to hear what Jax had to say. I watched him go. If only it was Holden I saw and not his avatar, then I would know if the man who walked away was the Holden who entered the game or someone else, perhaps the truer version of himself.

The others came toward me. Elva's gaze followed Holden's back.

Jax looked at me. He could sense the change. I didn't need to see his real face to understand that.

"You all right?"

I nodded at him. "Sure. Is that all we need to do in this game? I think I've seen all I want to see."

"Soon we'll have to fight. Confrontation is inevitable." He glanced down the street. "He shouldn't be so far in front."

"That's my fault."

Elva's head snapped back to me. Missing the subtlety in Elva's expression was the only bonus about being an avatar.

Jax turned to Elva. "Bring him back."

She needed no more commands and set off at a lope down the street after him.

"Can't we just take our goggles off?"

"No. Once you're in, you must play through until a certain point before you can do that."

"What's the certain point in level two?"

"Victory or defeat. You must play at least one confrontation."

"If not?"

"I'm sure you can answer that."

"I can't fight."

The memory of bugs crawling from my arms spiked my adrenaline.

"We all need to fight at least one bot. But don't worry, one of us is allowed to intervene at some point on your behalf. You don't have to finish a fight, but you do have to start one. At least that's how it goes for level two."

"And higher levels?"

"The higher you go, the more kills you need before you can exit. Beyond level three, the kills must be your own and you need to complete certain tasks along the way."

"Do you have any idea how screwed in the head you are for designing a game like this?"

Tyren came up beside us. "I'm getting bored. Time to move, ladies."

Jax straightened. In that one gesture, he closed down to me and returned to being Aris.

"We head this way."

Following his own command, he strode off toward Elva and Holden.

Up ahead they were talking. I wasn't sure if the discussion was heated or amicable, but at least talking was an improvement. I felt sorry for Elva, knowing how much she still loved him and how much he didn't her. Unbelievably, it was Elva who gave me a faint glimmer of mortality in this world of fallen souls. Both Jax and Holden claimed she was loyal; she'd been willing to die for her love. I'm sure even now she would never betray him. And what would Holden do if he felt I wasn't playing how a Persal should play, if I refused to betray Aris?

We'd almost caught up with the other two when a savage battle cry sliced through the air. A warrior drew a lethal-looking club and raced toward Holden and Elva. The warrior had been close to passing them, so his sudden turn was startling. Holden reacted with lightning reflexes I'd not witnessed in our one training session. The swords were in his hands before I could gasp. Elva gave him space but remained at the ready.

The attack from one bot triggered the rest. Harmless bots walking by turned lethal. The others reacted like Holden, and I was surrounded by an invasion. Although engaged in fighting, Tyren and Jax stayed close to me, while Elva fought her way over.

I froze. That's all I did. My snapshots of training vanished in a void of fear. Clashing metal, cries of fury, grunts, and anguish, all the sounds of brutal fighting rained down. I glanced at the stats on my left to find they all remained at low levels, skills and health good, my power still nonexistent. The others moved quickly, eliminating the few that had appeared. Compared to the bot that had confronted me in the alley, these moved slower, which had to have something to do with level two.

When the job was done, Jax grabbed my hand and pulled me along. "Come."

He was barely panting, nor were any of the others.

"Keep moving. Remaining in one spot brings on the biggest attack."

We moved as one group. We'd been detected by the computer already, which was perhaps the signal to forego the stealth. But we didn't get far before another bot launched the next attack.

Holden and Tyren engaged the next two bots while Jax turned to me. "We can leave the game if you play."

"Meaning I have to fight."

He nodded.

"Okay." I sounded anything but confident. Visions of my last confrontation continued to echo through my head. "I don't want bugs coming out of me this time."

"If you strike quick, the bot won't get a chance to engage their factional nature."

"I can't strike quick."

"I'm here to help, but in Dominus, an attack by factional nature is a mental attack on the individual, which means I won't see what you see."

"I'm not reassured."

Jax could say no more because we were once again under attack.

A handful of bots turned menacing. Jax left one and launched himself at another. I took that to mean the big, muscular warrior in front of me was my opponent.

He wasted no time releasing his impressive sword. At the tip, two thick spikes increased the length of the blade by at least five inches. Instead of slicing it through the air, he jabbed it forward, hoping to skewer me on the end. I danced back enough to prevent myself from being speared in the chest thanks to my jacked adrenaline. Fight or flight, all I wanted to do was run. I fought a hard battle with my mind to keep my limbs from turning and fleeing, with me screaming as I went. Settle and focus. I rattled the mantra through my head. Remain alert, find weaknesses. All I needed to do was hold out long enough to satisfy the computer I'd fought.

He lunged again and I dived to the left. He was fast but not fast enough. I could outmaneuver him. The realization gave me courage. When he lunged again, I would dive to the left and kick him in the ribs. My attack would have minimal impact, but it would count. The bar registering my skill level remained depressingly low.

He tricked me this time by slicing the blade through the air, but his swing opened up his right side and I took the opportunity.

My leg jarred on impact with his side, but the effect was all in my mind. I had to remember that. He grunted like the whole thing was real, like he was real, which made it more than hard to convince myself it was only a simulation. My skill level increased by a smidgeon but remained too far to the left.

I readied myself for another attack when darkness descended. The only thing I could see was the information crowding the corner of my vision. We were black shapes moving through a black night. Jesus, was this what happened in their world, day turned to night without warning? Although my vision was clouded, there was nothing wrong with my hearing. The subtle sound of a blade slicing through the air was enough to propel me sideways away from the noise.

Because I couldn't see, my balance was off. Without the ground for reference, I was jarred when my foot hit the cobbles. I staggered forward but somehow managed to keep standing. A shape to the side told me where he was; in front there was open street, somewhere. All I wanted to do was run, the most natural impulse when faced with possible death, but to run meant I would be stuck within Dominus. Ironically the only way to save myself was to stand my ground and fight.

I spun and faced the dark shape front on. Before I had a chance to ready myself, he moved in a smooth motion toward me. The nighttime made his actions seem faster. All I could do was duck. The wind from his blade whizzed overhead.

Where are you, Jax? Isn't this enough? Perhaps fighting meant I had to attack him rather than dodge all the time. But how could I when I couldn't see him enough to kick?

I had to succeed or die.

I clenched my fists and gritted my teeth to dredge out the cold steel of determination. By now my body was used to the adrenaline and had found a happy truce. My mind was working for me, not against me. I corralled my focus and tunneled it so I felt finely tuned, alive—in time for his next onslaught.

My eyes had adjusted to the dark, so I was prepared for his sudden lunge, having somehow worked out a plan within the seconds I had before he struck. The plan was simple. It involved me dodging, but in such a way that I was positioned for a retaliatory kick, but as he drove his blade through the air toward me, his body dragged by his inertia, something hit me in the side of the head, enough to knock me off-balance. I fell sideways as he drove forward into the empty space where I'd been.

I hit the ground at the same time pain hit my head. The headache arrived. I looked to my stats to find the power status bar had moved to about one third. My factional nature was coming through. If I faded now, I would be vulnerable to the warrior. Somehow through the disorientation of the pain, I rolled and tried to scramble to my feet, but something hit me in the shoulder and swiped my leg out from underneath me so that my face hit the cobbles. I grunted from the impact and the agony pounding through my mind.

Something fluttered around my face. Disoriented, I raised my arm and helplessly battered the air to shoo it away. My hand hit fur. I shrieked and collapsed onto my back. The air around me filled with flapping sounds. Soft wind brushed my face. A sharp pain pinched my cheek and ran as a line down my jaw. Groggy from the pain in my mind, I wiped my face where it throbbed and felt wetness. I'd been cut, whether from the warrior's blade or something else, I couldn't say. My health status bar was on the move, inching up toward halfway. Below that my power status bar had reached halfway. Where was Holden? I needed to calm down. This was a simulation. It's wasn't real.

Small claws tangled my hair as sharp pinpricks worked into my scalp. My head was sensitive from the searing throb of the headache, and this made it feel so much worse. Fear wound its way up my throat and came out screaming as a chunk of my flesh was torn from below my eye. I cried the agony through gritted teeth.

The grogginess I'd felt slipped away as I found the last reserves of strength, perhaps not enough to save me, but I had to do it. I wasn't going to die being eaten alive. I flailed about, trying to dislodge the creature that held on to my face with its teeth. I felt fine hairs and leathery skin and my mind conjured grotesque images.

I screamed for Jax as I fell into a world of fear. Both my health and power status bars were moving beyond halfway. *Don't look at them.*

Blind, I was lost and terrified. My mind turned to chaos; there was nothing inside I could grab hold of to rescue me. My conscience collapsed inward and raced down pathways at lightning speed, funneling, funneling down to a central point. The barriers inside my mind slid aside as my factional nature rushed forth. My power bar now registered red. The bar began to flash. Jesus Christ, that wasn't good.

Behind my eyelids, everything turned white as my mind exploded. The brightness of the illumination burned my eyes but also burned the pain from my body. I felt renewed, invigorated, and ready to fight. Was I at maximum power? It felt good. I got up from the ground, only to feel something snap in my head. Like a plug pulled, my consciousness tunneled away fast.

Chapter 24

My consciousness filtered through, the softness below me the first thing I noticed. The smell was the next, a jumbled mix of fresh sweat and something else, clean smelling but not a fragrance I recognized. I would've been content to stay there feeling safe and comfortable if the pounding in my head didn't start as soon as I moved.

I nursed my forehead and groaned, pressing my temples as if that would alleviate the pain. I slid a hand down to my cheek and pulled it away and cracked an eye open only to find the light in the room too bright. "Jesus."

"Give it time. You'll adjust."

I jerked at the voice, then clutched my head again with another groan. "I feel like someone is cracking my skull open with a crowbar."

"It will be worse this time."

"What will be worse?"

"Yeah, your memories may take time to return as well. It was close. Too close."

Why was I with Jax? I tried to sit up, but the crowbar spilt farther down the center of my skull. "Oh, god. I want to die."

"We went in with too many too soon. Even though we were only level two, with that many of us together, especially two opposing factions in close proximity for the time we were, it resulted in a large-scale assault. You panicked. The result was a massive influx of your factional nature. Basically your power detonated in your mind. That's why you feel like you want to die."

"I don't remember any of it."

"You will. Memory is usually temporarily affected. It will right itself in time. I have something that will help, but I will have to move you."

On his saying that, I realized the softness I lay on was him. We were on a bed, or something soft. He was propped up, and I was lying back against his chest. The sudden realization and I launched up to sitting only to be attacked by a savage hammering to my brain. Energy abandoned me. I fell back onto him again, curling to the side and cradling my head, groaning.

"It's going to be intense, but at least your brain still works as it should. Any longer in the game and your brain cells would be like burned bacon by now."

His words came from far away, swimming through the agony clouding my concentration.

"I'm going to wriggle out from underneath you. It's going to hurt your head but you'll feel grateful once I come back with something to help."

Without waiting for me to protest, demand that he dare not move and make the crowbar split my brain in two, he was out, lowering me gently onto the bed. Without him there, I curled farther into the fetal position.

The feather touch of his hand on my hip brought me out of the fog of agony. He'd been gone for hours. The pain held me suspended, so maybe not.

"You'll have to roll over."

"I can't."

"You'll feel better once you do. Trust me."

I couldn't feel any worse than I did right now, so I did as he asked, inching onto my back, groaning all the way because it buried me deep in my misery, and at the moment I couldn't feel any hope of ever escaping this torment.

"I'm going to help you up. You need to drink some water to wash the pill down."

He held my escape from this torment in his hands, so I allowed him to help me up and opened my mouth to indicate he could pop it in himself. No way could I open my eyes right now to the light and feel yet more punishment. Jax placed the glass in my hand and helped guide it to my lips. The pill was small enough to disappear with one gulp. Once it was swallowed, Jax took the glass and lowered me back onto the bed, then started counting. When he reached ten, I blinked my eyes open, and not because he'd commanded I had ten seconds to open them but because my headache receded enough by that point I had the courage to try my eyes with the light.

"How do you feel?"

"Like I've got a mean hangover, which is a lot better than ten seconds ago. That's one hell of a painkiller."

Jax sat on the edge of the bed, behind him a stark white wall, the floor shiny white marble or a close approximation.

I pushed myself up onto one elbow. "Where are we?"

"My apartment."

"This looks nothing like your apartment."

"The apartment you know of. We're not in your world, Sable."

I launched all the way up to sitting, scanning around the room, to see nothing but white. The bed was the only piece of furniture, the only piece of color black, sheets and cover. "We're in another world?"

"My world."

I shuffled off the bed. The cool of the smooth floor ran up my legs and into my head, which still throbbed with the residual from the onslaught of my factional nature. The next thing I knew, the side of my body hit the bed and I crumpled to the cool floor.

"Give yourself some time." With his arms under my armpits, he hitched me back up onto his bed.

"I can't. We're in another world."

If I wasn't in shock from leaving Earth, I'd be in shock from another real smile on his face. A genuine smile that erased the hard lines and tension, wound him back to the young boy free of Dominus, world domination, lies, cheating, betrayal, and death. Drawing my eyes from his captivating smile, I glanced around the room once more.

"Was this where your family lived?" I knew nothing about him, except that he'd lost everything precious to him.

"No. Our family home was elsewhere."

I shouldn't have asked him. Now I'd lost the smile and the carefree boy, to find it replaced with the pain of what he faced, what we all faced, our reality. My eyes landed on the tattoo inside his wrist.

"Why doesn't Holden have one of those?"

"He had the tattoo removed by laser when he arrived in your world."

He fingered the mark. Watching him do it reminded me of all those times I'd watched Mum trace lines along the tattoo on Dad's inner wrist.

"You hate it so much, why didn't you?"

"I need a reminder of why I do this."

Along with the declaration was the shuttering of his emotions. It was always the same, so I sensed the moment it happened. His body language mimicked the closing of a door, the severing of a connection. Was the reason the result of his parents' murder or us being on opposing factions?

"Do you really believe in what you're doing?"

Jax folded forward, resting his elbows on his knees, and continued to rub at the tattoo, below that the graft, which was supposed to control his factional nature, now deactivated.

I slid toward him, placing my feet on the floor. "Holden sees it as a symbol of oppression. Is that how you see it?"

"Yes." He didn't look at me when he replied.

"How far are you willing to go to free yourself from that oppression?"

I looked around his room. While stark, it looked expensive by Earth standards. Back home, a high-polished stone floor would cost a fortune, and his room was not small. Oppression looked comfortable over in this world.

Instead of answering me, Jax stood and headed toward the wall, which turned into a door on his approach by sliding open. I rose to follow but was stopped by the view out of the glass wall. The whole one side of the room was glass, or glass looking, whatever materials they used in this world. Outside, the buildings rose like glass spires encased in massive exposed beams of heavy industrial steel…metal…whatever. Beyond those, crisscrossing the sky, were some of their skytrains.

The door *whooshed* closed, slapping me out of my daze, but as I neared, it *whooshed* open again. Jax was looking out of another window taking up the entire wall.

"Califax City," I breathed as I came up beside him.

Beyond the towers of glass and steel, the Dome rose like a majestic fork of savage spires, not a dome at all. Behind, a blue moon began its journey up the horizon, glinting its dirty-snow color off the glass. But the beauty of the sky was marred by the strange aircraft crisscrossing through the air, following invisible skyways. I pressed closer to the glass and peered down hundreds of feet below to a carpet of color, predominately green, but with splashes of vibrancy.

"I shouldn't have brought you here. I acted without thinking."

"Does everyone look like you? Human-like?"

The crinkle on his brow told me I'd asked a stupid question.

"I've watched a lot of science fiction."

"We are no different. It's how we were able to live amongst you on your world. We are a mirror image if not for our customs, culture, architecture, landscape—"

"World."

Our eyes held. The creep of my smile was matched by his own. "The only mirror we share is language and the way we look."

"And a love of our family, it seems," he finished for me, then looked back out onto his world, robbing me of his expression.

"I'm glad we share emotions."

This was awkward. I joined him staring out the window. Easier to do that than focus on the sudden uncomfortableness that saturated the air. I didn't know how I was supposed to feel toward him. Hating him was easy. I should want to continue hating him to continue making it easy for myself. *He's Carter's, remember that. They want Ajay.*

"I should take you back. It's as dangerous here for you as it is in Dominus. You don't know enough about our world to pass as a citizen and you have no tattoos, which will signal you as an anomaly. If the Senate of Factions discover you, they will start executing Aris and Persal until they find the truth."

"Why?"

"They will do anything to uncover dissent."

"Why is everyone so paranoid in your world?"

Jax turned to me and shrugged. "It's just how it is."

"If your governing body wasn't so scared of its citizens, maybe you'd all learn to get along. Fear leads to fear. Violence to violence. It's nothing but a circle."

"I wish it were that simple."

I turned back to the window, not ready to get into an argument over his beliefs as opposed to mine. Maybe I should. It could help me hate him again, and then it would be how it was before, and I'd know how to act around him. I was so far out of my comfort zone being here.

"Come, we need to head back. Everyone will be wondering where you are."

He held out his hand and once again I looked at the tattoo of his oppression.

"How is it there are people in my world with latent factional abilities?"

"When shifting was a normal part of our lives, many people spread out through the dimensions, much like when you go on holiday over-seas. And like traveling overseas, the process was strictly monitored. People had to register their intention and destination and register their return. All of this was held in a database. Carter and Nixon where able to sift through the database and record which dimensions were visited the most and by whom. It turns out your world was popular because the people there are almost identical to those on my world. And conve-niently for them, Aris and Persal in particular loved the place. I think that's why the two of them formed the alliance. They believed there were probably enough interludes between our worlds to give rise to offspring in your world with the talent. All they needed was something to kick-start the process."

"Dominus. What happened to get us here?"

"What parts do you remember?"

"Some bits are filtering through. I remember everything going dark in a blink."

"The warrior you fought was Phonus. They—"

"Control the night. So the creature that attacked me was a bat?"

"Bat. That's better than some of the nighttime creatures they evoke, but fitting for level two."

"It felt like my mind exploded."

"You destroyed the warrior. You saved your skin."

At least I did something right. "How did I do it?"

"It's likely the panic from the fight triggered your ability. The warrior disintegrated."

"I did that with my mind?"

"You're Persal, destruction, remember? It's easy to do with bots, not so easy with humans."

I looked back out over the city, to all the people who I couldn't see from up here but inhabited this world, filling the buildings surrounding us, riding their funny aircraft, walking the streets below, all these people who were capable of doing these things with one thought.

"Holden can teach you to call upon it at will and moderate the force."

The view out the window was the best place for me to look right now.

"The hardest thing you'll have to face is overcoming the desire to be that which you are."

I snapped my head around to face him. "I don't understand."

"Once destruction becomes your true nature, that is all you'll want to be. Holden can help you overcome this so you're not a danger."

I placed a hand on the glass, felt the cold seep through. The warmth from my palm kept the cold from moving straight through, but if I left my palm pressed on the glass long enough, perhaps the cold would break free and funnel right down to chill my heart. "And that is what it means to be free from the graft."

"Yes."

"I think I would rather be grafted."

"You believe everyone has a choice. You said that, remember? So you can choose to not be dominated by your factional nature. You can train yourself to command it, not the other way around."

I faced him. "I thought you didn't believe in choices."

"I have to believe we have some; otherwise there is no hope."

"But you don't want to believe that differing factions can be friends."

Jax huffed in frustration and half turned away from me. "It's—"

"Not that simple. Maybe that's because you don't want it to be that simple."

"That's why we fight. That is the point of Dominus. We want to change the way it is in our world."

"Change starts in the smallest ways."

He looked at me like I was speaking tongues. "You want to change the way the rules are in your world, and yet when given the chance to live differently in my world, you won't. There's no reason to treat Holden like the enemy, no reason for Aris and Persal to be the enemy in my world. And yet you both choose to keep the boundaries between your factions defined. Neither of you wants to trust the other. It has to come from in here first"—I pointed to my heart—"before it comes from here." I pointed to my head.

"You're talking about changing our culture. A history of habit cannot be wiped in a matter of months."

"How can you control your desire to become your true nature, which according to you is extremely difficult, yet you can't even stop yourselves from loathing each other?"

"You don't understand my world."

"I think I do understand your world. Perhaps it has more to do with what's really important to you. Living in freedom is very important to you—I can understand—but not so much living in harmony, or in love."

The sudden silence in the room underscored the heat in my voice. We stared at each other with a distance that seemed unreachable.

Jax broke the void created from our argument. "Those are ideals."

"And will remain that while you are all afraid of each other, hiding in your own quarters of the world."

He snorted a laugh. "You're nothing like your father. Being part of the Senate of Factions, he is very pro separation."

"If he and Carter are on the senate, why are they doing this?"

"For the same reasons we are."

"I don't believe that. People in positions of power rarely want change unless it's more beneficial for them."

"Maybe it will be."

"You say factions can't get on, but Dad and Carter made an alliance."

"And look where your father is now."

I pressed my lips together. "That was Carter's plan all along."

"Your father's as well. Carter just beat him to it."

"Neither ever planned for the other to rule with them."

"It would never work."

"But it does; otherwise you wouldn't have a Senate of Factions."

"You think any of them trust each other? And it works only because they suppress us all with these grafts."

"So you're willing to let Carter rule, because that's the plan, isn't it? That's why Dad's in jail, so that Aris can rule over your world. That's the true plan."

"Your father was no different. He planned on it being Persal."

"You told me when factions go to war, there isn't a lot left."

I stepped in close to him, drawn by the fleeting moment when his expression changed, when the conflict within twisted him up enough to make him look lost and shamed. The moment I reached for him, the shutter fell down, the iron of his conviction won through, and he stepped away.

I did too, allowing the space between us that was proper for Persal and Aris, which was what he wanted, what everyone seemed to want, without questioning the true cost. My headache from the game had receded, along with my strength, sucked away by the force of Jax's will. I couldn't match the armor of his determination, but it didn't mean I agreed. Dominus taught the players to fight in simulation with their factional natures so they could fight for real when the time came. Carter would have us become his puppets. He would turn us into monsters. He'd have us destroy each other so he could rule. Everyone was all right with that. And there was nothing I could do.

Chapter 25

I was curled up on the couch when headlights swept along the wall. Mum returned home late as promised. I jumped up and peered through the lace curtain. When the door opened, the interior light switched on, lighting up Carter's face. I tensed as a lightning rod stabbed me through the chest. I hadn't thought it possible to hate someone as much as I did him.

It wasn't enough for Carter to put Dad in jail. He wanted to hammer the nail in tight. Bit by bit, he would ruin Dad's world. He had me and Mum; it was inevitable he would take Ajay too.

I let the curtain fall back into place and went to reheat the lasagna. It was almost ten, later than the home time I'd expected, which I'm sure was Carter's fault. I stared at the lasagna turning on its plate while I tried to push my anger down to my feet. There was no use attacking Mum. She was the innocent in all of this.

Behind the whir of the microwave, I heard the front door open. What could I say to her to make her understand Carter was not the savior, that he was dangerous, that she needed to stay away from him?

"Hey, hon, I didn't expect you to wait up for me."

I looked over my shoulder and met Mum's eyes, but it was the eyes of the man next to her that made my organs drop to the floor. "I didn't expect you home so late."

Her smile faltered, and she looked to Carter. *No, Mum, you don't look to him for an explanation.* Carter's eyes remained fixed on me. The microwave pinged, the whirring silenced, and that silence extended throughout the kitchen. To avoid looking at the two of them again, standing side by side, like a couple, I removed the lasagna from the microwave and slipped it onto a plate.

"You haven't eaten yet," Mum said.

"It's for you."

"Oh…honey." She looked to Carter again.

I wanted to throw the plate at him, see the meat sauce run down his face and onto his shirt.

"We've already eaten."

We. My offer was for her, not them both.

"I hope you didn't stay up just to warm me some dinner."

"No." I drilled my eyes into Carter. "I stayed up because I thought we could have some alone time. Girl talk, like we used to."

From bright and jubilant to fallen, Mum's expression changed in a blink. I should feel guilty for dragging down her mood, making her feel ashamed, but I was too angry to feel anything else.

"I'll wait in the living room, shall I?" Carter said.

Mum fidgeted with the strap on her handbag, casting him a small smile.

Mum, tell him to go away. All that hate bubbling below the surface, I gathered it up and sharpened it into my stare. His smile deflected it back. And then the departing wink. The furnace in my heart brought tears to my eyes. I was caged, drowning, suffocating in a void, trapped within quicksand, helpless against an unstoppable force rolling over me, and that force casually turned his back and strolled into my living room.

"Honey." Mum came over and squeezed my arm. "I've told you, Carter feels bad for what happened with your father. He wants to help us out."

"Is that what he told you?"

"Stop this, Sable. You're being ridiculous."

"Am I? Why are you coming home from work at ten o'clock?"

"I have a lot to learn. I have no experience and Carter did me a favor by taking me on. It's going to take time for me to learn my job."

"Is it normal for the boss to bring his employee home?"

"Why are you acting like this?"

"Because…" *Carter's the devil. He wants to see Dad burn in hell and every-thing he loves destroyed. He wants to turn factions against each other, bring civil war, destroy us and destroy his world. He wants to win.* "I don't trust him."

"It's not about what you think, Sable."

"But I'm a part of this family, so don't I deserve to get a say in what affects us?"

She moved around me to the kettle. "Not in this instance, no. You're being unreasonable, and I don't understand why."

She put the kettle down and spun to take me by the upper arms. "Honey, Carter is the best thing that's happened to our family since your father's imprisonment. I don't need to tell you how desperate we are. We've run out of options. If not for Carter, we'd be on the streets soon. He's a gentleman. He's doing this because he cares."

I broke free of her hold and turned away. All the things I really wanted to say swelled up in my throat and not one of them I could put into words.

In my periphery, I watched her pick up the plate of lasagna. "As an apology for keeping me late, Carter took me out for a quick bite before bringing me home."

My hands fisted. "This isn't going to be a regular thing, is it?"

"Of course not."

Let it go. Punishing Mum wouldn't help. "I'll make us a drink."

She put the plate down, giving me a grateful smile. For the first time in these last couple of months, she'd found a purpose. This job was the best thing for her. She had a reason to get out of bed in the morning, a reason to care about her appearance. It was good for us as a family. We could climb our way out of destitution, ditch this rental, and move somewhere better. Great if it wasn't all built on a lie. Possible death was the payoff for all these rewards, siding with a psychopath, who would see his own Earth destroyed to seize control.

"Your daddy will be so proud of us. Once the paychecks come

through, we can buy a few new things for the apartment. Maybe in a few months, we can think about moving somewhere else, somewhere nice."

I inwardly groaned. Jesus, I was yet to confess about visiting Dad. I couldn't keep from her the part I played in having Dad's visits restricted. If there was one thing I could give Mum in all of this, it was that truth.

"I'm not sure they will allow us to see Dad. At least not in the contact room."

She smiled even though a small crease formed on her brow. "Why do you say that?"

"Ajay and I visited Dad the other day."

She laughed, but it sounded off, not a laugh at all. "Don't be stupid. That's impossible. How did you do that?"

"A friend took us."

"What? Honey…I don't understand. You went and saw your dad? Why didn't you tell me?"

I sighed. There was no going back now. "Something bad happened. Ajay was really upset about it, and I made him promise not to tell you. I didn't want to upset you."

She put the kettle down and faced me squarely. "Sable. What are you saying? I don't understand this."

"They may not let us see him."

"Why wouldn't they?"

"Dad went mental. Three guards had to restrain him." I hated saying it. Even now, a week later, my throat constricted.

Mom palmed her mouth. She whispered, "Why?"

"The friend who took me was a boy. He drove us there. Dad saw him and lost it."

"Jesus Christ, Sable." She closed her eyes. She turned away and I collapsed inside. It had been all my fault.

"Who is this boy?" She kept her back to me.

"A friend. His name is Jax. And that's all he is, Mum, a friend, or he was, maybe not anymore."

She faced me again. Seeing her tears made mine threaten at the corners of my eyes.

"Why didn't you tell me? I had a right to know."

"I'm so sorry, Mum. I never meant for that to happen. I just wanted to see him." And I choked. Mum was too devastated herself to react to my emotional outburst. She remained frozen, staring at the bench top.

"I've really made a mess of everything."

Finally she moved. She came over and swept me into a hug. Even though we were the same height, even though in the last few months I'd played the adult while she hid under the covers of her duvet, unable to face life, even though I was risking my life to save hers, at this moment, I felt like a child again. I wanted to be a child again, young enough so that a mother's embrace was all that was needed to make the world all right. I hugged her back so tight, like I would never let her go.

She whispered *shhh* against my hair as I cried on her shoulder. I didn't want to let this moment go, because it would be the only time in forever I would feel safe, the only time Mum could offer me any sort of security. Once she let me go, I would return to being the one who made the plans. Something I wasn't ready to do, but no matter, it was something I had to do.

"We'll sort something out. Even if we have to go back to noncontact visits for a while. We'll get through this."

Reluctantly I let her go when she stepped back. "How about you take a cuppa through for Carter?"

Hearing his name, a million pieces inside of me broke. But Mum wasn't looking at me, she was busy preparing his coffee. I forced a smile when she handed me the cup. "I'll be through in a minute." She turned her back on me to finish her own coffee.

I inhaled, then turned and headed for the lounge room. How much of our conversation had he heard? The part about Dad going apoplectic over Jax would've made him smile.

He'd seated himself in one of our cheap single-seaters, one leg thrown over the knee of the other, arms splayed on the armrests like he owned the place. His eyes followed me across the room with the hint of a smirk tugging the corners of his mouth. There was the accidental trip, or I could just throw the hot drink over him and not bother pretending. Instead, I handed it to him, because anything else would be a signal to him that he'd won, that I felt backed into a corner.

He reached out. I thought it was to take the coffee; instead he grabbed my wrist, turning it over to expose my pale skin on the inside. I gasped at the suddenness of his action. My pulse jacked in nanoseconds. His grip was a vise, holding my hand in place. "This is what makes you special." Green eyes looked up into mine. "An ungrafted source of strength."

If only it were possible to arrow a dart with my glare. "You have it all planned."

"It doesn't pay to start a war without already knowing the outcome."

"You planned on betraying Dad all along."

"As did he." He let my wrist go. "Your father and I are very much alike. So if you judge me harshly, then make sure to be fair and do the same to dear old Dad."

"Here we are." Mum entered the room bearing two more cups of coffee.

"I'm going to bed." I should stay and keep an eye on him, make sure he kept his hands to himself, but I couldn't bear to be in his presence for one more second.

I stormed down to my room, leaving Mum standing where she was, eyes widened in surprise. Once in my room, I swiped my phone from my bedside table and messaged Holden.

Are u available tomorrow to meet?

I sat on my bed, staring at the phone. This was the first contact we'd had since Dominus, since our argument. Fifteen minutes later, with my hand hovering over the buttons, ready to phone him, I received a reply.

Sure. At the club.

I was grateful he never asked what it was about. Perhaps he thought he already knew. We parted with tension. Thank god he seemed to have moved that aside and was willing to see me.

I'll be there first thing.

I threw the phone onto my duvet and stared at the wall opposite. My world had crashed, but I didn't feel small, because there was a fire now burning inside of me. Carter was not going to destroy everyone I loved.

Chapter 26

"You're making progress."

"But not enough."

"Sable, you don't have to defeat everything on your own."

Holden straightened, relaxing his stance, effectively halting our practice.

"I can't use my factional nature if I can't control it. Not if it means wiping out everyone around me. And I don't want to rely on anyone. I have to be able to fight on my own."

"You will, but give yourself time to reach that level of proficiency. People play for years on the screen before they move to virtual. We run them through months of training before we put the goggles on."

"I don't have time. Carter has a noose around my neck."

"Carter won't hurt your mum and Ajay. Not while he has you."

"No, but I don't want him around my family at all. Every day Mum goes to work, I want to be sick. She thinks he's the best thing that's happened to our family. He thinks he's won. I can't stand that."

"Winning this game is about patience. You go rushing in and you'll get yourself killed."

He came up close and tapped a finger to my forehead. "Mostly it's about using this, not your body. You've got to be smarter, not stronger. Your dad is in jail because of Carter's cunning."

He headed for the watercooler. I followed and accepted the cup he handed me.

"Dominus is not a game where those with the greater power win. Remember that."

"You need to teach me to harness my factional nature."

He sighed.

"Carter wanted me in. Well, I'm in, and I'm going to be the best, and then I'm going to screw him so badly he's going to wish he'd killed me."

At first my stare was combative, then I realized his wasn't, and I backed down. Once I understood it was sadness in his eyes, I stirred once more. "He started this."

And now I sounded like a child. I deflated for real this time.

"It's okay to rely on someone."

"Will you help me with my factional nature?"

"Of course I will. I'll help you with anything. I'm Persal."

Goddamn factions. Why couldn't he have said he would do it because he was my friend?

"What about Dad?"

"What about him? He's in jail."

"We have to get him out. Why can't he shift like the rest of you?"

"Carter activated his graft."

"Why can't you go in and get him out? You have the ability to shift."

"He wouldn't let me. If he disappeared, you'll all be at Carter's mercy."

"We are at his mercy." I slapped my hands at my sides. Holden and Dad were too stupid to see his punishment in jail had not kept us safe. "We have to find a way to reverse Dad's graft again."

"That will be difficult. Carter keeps the grafter he and Nixon reverse engineered safe."

"Which is where?"

"Locked up somewhere within his building. It will be located in his office. I can't see him wanting it too far from him."

"Where's his office?"

"Within the Amex. He runs his company from the fortieth floor. You can see how, for a Persal, it is nearly impossible to get inside."

"Mum works there. I could visit her at work."

"He'll be suspicious."

"I'm his new favorite toy. Anything to screw Dad, remember? Perhaps the idea of having two of Nixon's family in his building would be enough for him to welcome me in."

"Carter's cunning. He'll know."

"Not if I act right. Besides, I'm an earthling, remember? I don't understand the real meaning of factional segregation, which means my intentions for seeing Mum are innocent."

Holden scratched his chin while he paced the mat. "I'm not comfortable with this."

"What's your plan?"

He shook his head.

"So I guess we do it my way."

"What happens when you find the safe?"

"I break in and retrieve the grafter."

"How do you plan on doing that?"

"I'm Persal. Why are you asking me?

"You can't use your factional nature. The building will be full of people and you've yet to control your ability."

"Then teach me. Give me the control I need."

I wanted to pull my hair out. Why throw up walls when I was the only one making sense?

"It takes time and use."

"You say that about everything."

"Because it's true. Besides, using your ability will alert Carter."

God, I hadn't thought of that.

"It'll place your mum in a vulnerable position."

"She and Ajay will have to leave. Dad will make sure of that."

"Do you know what you're saying?"

"It's the only way. Dad is Carter's greatest rival, perhaps the only one capable of stopping him."

"You'll banish your mum and Ajay from this world, plus there's no guarantee of their safety in my world. If they are detected, it will raise questions in the senate. And they have a tendency to act negatively before they firm decisions."

"It's been three months and you're no further in getting him out."

Holden continued his irritating floor pacing. I felt tempted to seize his shoulders to still him. "This will also put you in danger. You're expendable. Carter wanted you because Nixon tried to keep you out. That's all. He would be just as happy to see you gone."

"There's no other choice. Carter is going to lose control of this, which could mean a war that will destroy your world and spill into mine. He underestimates our power of free thinking. Once half the recruits learn the rules of your world and discover they are from an opposing faction, they will turn on him. He will be forced to kill them or graft them."

"Don't you think I haven't thought about this?"

Then why was he going through with Carter's plan?

"You know as well as I do Carter won't release your people. He'll graft everyone who is not Aris. He'll be forced to do it because no one will accept a single faction ruling."

I closed the distance between us. He needed to believe in what I was saying, and it felt like the only way I could convince him was if I filled his vision, forced him to see only me, forced him to see my determination. "You need to teach me quick time."

"This isn't going to work."

"It won't if you keep saying so."

"Jesus, you're as stubborn as your father."

I took that as a compliment. The smile creeped in despite my best efforts to keep it hidden. Holden responded with a thin smile.

"What do we do first, fight with our bodies or fight with our minds?"

He hooked an arm around my neck and drew me to one side of the room. "There's no stopping you." Still with his arm around my neck, he guided me to one of his sparring dummies and positioned me in front.

"Sable, meet bad guy. Bad guy, meet Sable. These guys are expensive, so I hate to see him die, but it's for a vital course. Now tell me what you experience before you release your ability."

"You want me to do it now?" He was joking. Had to be.

"I thought this is what you wanted?"

"Here?"

"No better time."

And time was running out. I looked back to the dummy. "It feels like doors opening, barriers sliding away, and something is bursting to get out." With each explanation, the tempo of my pulse increased. Did I really want to do this, face my factional nature, something I saw as an evil side of me?

He nodded. "That's normal. The shifts will lessen in time. At the moment, your mind is holding it back. It's been locked away all this time. But once you get good at calling upon destruction, the barriers will disappear."

"But don't I need the barriers to hold it in check?"

"Yes, but it's not how it's supposed to work. Normally there is no barrier to your ability. It moves as freely through you as any mental thought. But it does mean it will become your desire. You'll be obsessed with the need for destruction."

"I don't want to be like that."

"And you don't have to be. But you must first release your ability from the binds of your mind. Only once you're consumed by the force of its power can you learn to master it."

"Or it will master me." And I would become like the monster Jax saw inside himself.

"You're too strong and stubborn for that to happen."

Did he really think so?

"Okay." He moved around to stand behind me and placed his hands on my shoulders. "I want you to focus on those barriers. Find a way to open them."

"But it comes rushing out when I do."

"The best thing to do when that happens is to try and channel it down into your body rather than outward. It's the only way to learn control. Use your body as the barrier once your mental restraints are weakened. Harness it inside."

I nodded.

He let me go, and I took that as the signal to start. I closed my eyes and focused on that place somewhere inside my mind that hid my factional nature. All I got was a load of mental images and thoughts about how much I was going to suck at this. I bit my bottom lip until it hurt as a way to force my concentration. Still nothing.

"I can't find it."

"I expected as much. In the beginning, it's usually triggered by extreme stress."

"What do we do?"

"We fight. You and me."

"That's not exactly extreme stress."

"You haven't fought me for real."

He took my hand and led me into the center of the room, leaving the dummy behind. "I'm not going to hold back…well, maybe a little, but don't expect this to be easy; otherwise we won't succeed."

"What happens when it comes through? I could hurt you."

He winked. "Try."

"Holden, this is serious."

"This is the best way for you to master your ability. Hold it in or destroy me. It's up to you."

"No, I can't do this."

"Do you want to help your father?"

"Yes, but there has to be another way. Why can't we go into Dominus? I can fight bots."

"Without Dominus, you wouldn't be this far along, but it's the worst place to be while you're trying to master control." Because I could fry my brain. But wasn't a fried brain better than killing someone?

I backed up, holding my hands up in surrender. "No, not with you. It's too dangerous."

"You pull back and Carter wins."

"He won't because I'll find another way to control it."

"Ajay's a ripe age, easily manipulated. Carter plans to replace the vacuum in your family with himself."

"He won't get a chance. I'll stop him."

"He will make your mother forget about Nixon. She'll fall in love with him instead."

"She loves Dad too much."

"Your dad's locked away. At some point, your mum will get lonely. She'll crave company, the touch of a man."

I shook my head. "No she won't."

"Are you so sure?"

"Stop it."

"You know I'm right. Her life is empty now. Ajay will want a father. Someone who can take his father's place. Perhaps you will too at some point when your father's memory slips away."

"No."

Holden nodded. "I think so. Perhaps it's happening already."

The barriers exploded in my mind, leaving me feeling like I'd been smashed across the head with steel piping. The power tunneled out in a voluminous rush, like a great channel of water. In my mind, something took over, something dark and dangerous. It rode on the back of the wave through my body until it infected my heart—the dark, delicious desire to destroy.

This wasn't me, this feeling that took over. If I let it become me, I would kill Holden. But the torment in refusing the calling to become my factional nature tore me apart.

I fell to my knees as the dizziness took hold. I was losing control, and in the process of fading, I was going to kill Holden. I had to be stronger than this, had to be better.

The agony on Jax's face when he told me how much the bloodlust consumed him flashed through my mind. He was better than this.

I fought against my yearning. I grunted with effort as I tried to draw my power back in, tried to funnel it into my body, where I could hope-fully contain it, but the effort was enormous. All I felt was the power coursing through me and out. I lost control.

The noise was so loud it felt like my eardrums burst. With the blow-back of the explosion, I was sent onto my back, an invisible pressure at my chest. Debris rained down on me, across my face, grit sticking to my eyelashes, slipping into my mouth. I coughed through the dust as Holden crawled over and patted my arm, then drew me in for a hug. I turned over to look at him, seeing white in his eyelashes and a fine casting of dust covering his face and shirt.

"I'll take that as a positive start."

I looked around us at the aftermath, then up at the sky, which I was able to do because the roof was no longer there.

Chapter 27

WHEN THE LIFT doors swung wide, Jax turned to face me. Seized mid-stride, his body language poised like the guilty, I too froze in the entrance to the lift. What was it I read in the silence surrounding him, the taut twist of his body, and the hollowness behind his expression? Unfamiliar voices spilled from the gaming room. This was not nerves, surely?

"How many new players are there?"

"Six more."

"I hope they're on our side." I managed to find a small smile, not sure where it came from.

"We play together. If that's what you mean."

"Is this Carter's doing?"

"Everything is Carter's doing. I hope you always remember that."

Jax was being his usual intense, somber self. No surprises given we were about to enter Dominus, but this time, something in the way he stood, avoiding my eyes, looking like he wanted to be elsewhere, and I wanted to back away to the lift. Most of what Jax said made me feel angry, frustrated, or helpless, usually all three at once. Him standing there, stalled on what he was about to say like the words were a burden to speak, I wanted to be anywhere but in this apartment, alone with him.

"Shall we get started?" I left him and headed for the gaming room.

"Sable." Weighted like lead, my name sunk in the air once out of his mouth.

"What?" I could see the effort it took for him to say just one word.

"Carter was right, I did bet against you surviving Dominus."

My legs itched to turn me around and lead me to the gaming room. The wild beat of my heart said *leave now*. This was not the conversation I wanted to hear; but this was the conversation we had to have.

What he was about to say would change a lot, if not everything, so I gave him all the time in the world to say it.

His deep sigh carried all my fear and pain along with his. "We're about to enter Dominus. I shouldn't have started this now."

"Don't you dare. Finish what you were going to say."

Emboldened by my harsh tone, he fisted his hands then relaxed them by his sides. "Remember when I said I wanted to take everything precious from the man who murdered my family?"

He was right; this was not the conversation to have just before we entered Dominus. Because I knew. I knew what his next words would be, and I couldn't bear it.

"I thought it would make me feel different. Make everything better. But you were right—"

"Stop."

"I agreed to recruit you because I wanted my revenge."

"Stop it."

"I can't now, Sable. I have to say this to the very end. It's why your dad went mental the day he saw me at the prison. He knew I'd gotten to you, and he was afraid."

"Shut up. Just shut your mouth."

"I planned for you to fail. Then I planned for Ajay to fail. And I would be the one to tell your father."

"Why are you telling me this?" It was nothing more than an agonized plea.

"You needed to hear it. You need to know the monster in me. You've seen my true nature, and now you know what I planned for you. I'm not the sort of person you should want to be with. No one should want to be with an Aris, especially not me." His strides ate the distance between us. "We harness fury and turn it into a weapon with which to destroy those who are not like us. We don't need weapons because we kill with our hands and teeth. We bathe in the blood of our enemies." He grabbed me by the upper arms, dragging me close. "We crave death in all its beauty." He rested his forehead to mine. "Bloodlust is a torturous thing."

Knowing the truth was also a torturous thing. He let me go when I pulled away from him.

"I wanted to see you fail, but instead I've done nothing but protect you. I despised your father for what he did, and I wanted to despise you. But I can't."

My dad had killed everyone Jax loved, not just his dad, but his baby sister and his mother, leaving him alone, without family.

"Your father punished the innocent, but I cannot do the same. I can't hate that much."

My strength drained, with it the will to stay standing. The sofa close by cushioned my fall as my legs weakened under the strain of supporting a body too heavy to keep upright. I sunk down onto the armrest, then curled further until I was hidden behind my hands, but that was not hidden enough.

Behind my wall, I heard the door to the gaming room open. "Are we doing this?"

Normally I would hate for Elva to see me feeling raw, but Jax had peeled everything from me.

Elva gave us both the escape we needed.

THERE WERE ten of us in all, three extra Aris and two Persal. The idea was to slowly populate the game with people instead of bots, giving me time to learn how to work with more active players to achieve our end goal. I glanced around at the newcomers, expecting to see another face from school. We all stood off the mat dressed in our regulatory white suits with silver dots.

I flicked a glance at Jax, but he avoided my eyes. Everything was moving too fast. I'd no time to think about any of what Jax had said. For so long I'd believed Dad a murderer. Turned out he was. The courts might have charged him with the wrong murder but it didn't make him innocent. I'd already been gutted by his lies, learned to harden my heart against him, so this new revelation did not tear me apart, at least not where Dad was concerned. But what about Jax?

We were about to enter Dominus at a higher level, so I didn't have time to think about what this revelation meant for us. If the vendetta was still in his heart, why bother training me and saving me? Why tell me the truth if he planned on using me to crucify Dad? Should I trust him in Dominus or did I stick to Holden?

My eyes dropped to the floor and everyone's socked feet with silver dots, the safest place to look. At least I could control my emotions better while looking at neutral ground.

"Sable, new to your party are Reg and Malvo. On Aris are Sam, Nuke, and—" Jax said, like he hadn't just revealed a crucial shocking truth.

"Striker." He smiled sheepishly at me. "Might as well know my game name. Real name's Patrick."

Patrick was on the thin side and not much taller than me, but his smile was genuine, although a smidgeon too eager for my liking. None of the others had bothered to take a new name in Dominus. No doubt he liked to be someone other than himself when playing.

"You got a game name?" He bled excessive energy. No one should be keen to play Dominus.

"No."

"You should. Focuses your drive. You know what I'm saying?"

Jax came between us, ending the conversation. "We go in at level five. Our task is to capture the Central Airways terminal and lock down the area. No one arrives at the terminal and no one leaves. And I'm setting the clock on this one."

"Is that wise?" Holden glanced at me.

"Carter's orders."

All eyes met mine, telling me I was the reason for the order. Patrick's smile split his face, as if raising the stakes was the best part about playing.

"And that means?" I said.

"It's a time-sensitive task. How long have we got?" Tyren said.

"One hour," Jax said.

"Whose time limit is that?"

Jax eyed me. "Carter's."

Tyren slung an arm around my shoulder and led me onto the mat. "Don't sweat it. It's as good as done."

I extracted myself from under his shoulder. "If we're not successful?"

"We will be." He flicked me under the chin, winked when I stared up into his eyes.

I knew little about Tyren, about any of them. Since I had to rely on these guys, blanks in my understanding of them weren't good. Important details, like what brought them to this point, instilled their belief in Carter and his plan, were vital pieces of a jigsaw. I'd have more confidence in trusting them to help me through Dominus if I understood their history, passions, goals, and beliefs. Surely they had family, people who'd be wondering where they were, what they were doing, if they were all right.

The rest followed us onto the mat, finding a position clear of everyone else.

Since the gulf between Jax and me had grown too great, I turned to Holden. "Do we get out if we fail to capture the Central terminal before the hour?"

A smile his only reply, which meant no.

"How many kills do we need?"

"Whoever gets in your way."

"But I can't control my ability and that's the only thing I have. What if one of you guys gets in the way?"

He ran a hand down my arm, a soothing gesture, which fell way short of his intention. "I'll be there. I'll help you."

"It's time you chose a weapon," Jax said.

"I haven't trained with one yet."

"Start small, like a dagger. They're easier to wield."

"And useless."

"There's enough of us to keep you covered for the most part. You do need your own kills and that's where your ability can help. Holden will keep a close eye on you. You also have Reg and Malvo. Both are experienced Persal who can help guide you through. Just remember, it's a matter of keeping control."

Sure, no problem.

"Yeah, we all want to survive." Patrick snorted a laugh. Did he know that at least two people had died playing Dominus? Patrick was from my world. This wasn't his war. Neither was it Sam's, Nuke's, or Reg's, or any of the other hundreds they claimed to have already recruited.

I glared at Jax, which wasn't going to help. This was not his call. Carter had earned himself some more hate points from me. I glanced at Holden, then around me to each of the others, who were already slipping on their game faces, stoic yet withdrawn, each doing whatever was needed to prepare themselves for entering the game. Had anyone told them the truth of Dominus? If so, what was the bribe that won their loyalty?

Soon I found I was the only one not wearing goggles, the only one who seemed to understand what it was we were really doing. Half the party held no allegiance to this other world, yet they were willing to slip their goggles down and risk their lives to fulfill the ideals of a madman.

The hardest thing for me to do was lower my goggles, commit myself to level five of Dominus.

A row of weapons appeared in front of my vision, blades decreasing in size from left to right. Nothing interested me, but I had to select something.

"Can I see the tri-blade on the far right?"

The blade enlarged while all the others faded into the background. I couldn't wield a single blade, but perhaps I could throw. Since this weapon had three blades radiating outward, I was bound to hit my opponent with one of them.

Jax walked toward me with the blade flat in the palm of his hand. "Interesting weapon. I hope you have a good arm for throwing."

It was smaller than I expected, but the perfect size for my grip. The handles were made of jade, cold and smooth to the touch, according to my mind, which was busy fabricating signals for something that didn't really exist.

"Use a pinch grip, like this. Make sure when you throw it you keep your arm in line with the target. Don't move it across your body like this."

"Got it." Without hours of training, there was no way I would throw effectively, but I listened hard all the same.

Jax focused on the rest of the group. "Nothing changes, guys. You know what to do."

An impressive warrior in sea green, scarred across his shoulder and down his chest, strode toward me. "Pretty cool, huh? The scars make me look rough, don't you think?"

Since he'd changed his voice in Dominus, to a deep rumbling tone, the enthusiasm bleeding through his voice was my only glue to who it was—Patrick. "You're looking pretty hot."

"It's an image. I'm not very good in Dominus."

"You wouldn't be here if you weren't good."

"That's a matter of opinion."

"Holden, your party approaches from sunder. I suggest keeping Reg and Malvo at the bottom. You and Sable can secure the top with Elva and me. We'll enter from moondine. I want everyone coordinated. Once we're in, no one enters, no one leaves."

That was what it meant to be GM. Holden subordinated himself to Jax's command, as did the other Persal. Without another Persal at the top of the hierarchy, it meant Aris ruled.

"We split as soon as we're in game mode. I want you at Central no later than thirty. You run into trouble, you sound the warning. We'll hang back until you arrive."

"Gotcha," Holden said.

Orders delivered, Califax City appeared in front of us, rendered in the beauty that was game mode. I was beginning to pick out landmarks, like the obelisk and Dome, plus a mountain range bordering the city on one side, running moondine to sunder. I would perhaps be able to pick the direction of Persal HQ, a handy backup in case things went terribly wrong. At least at Persal HQ, I wouldn't be attacked. A digital timer on the right of my vision now joined everything else on the screen. Already the numbers were counting down.

"Why didn't you guys give us virtual maps?"

"Ups the stakes," Holden said as he patted my back.

A looming monolith of metal and glass rose above the buildings surrounding it. In the background, the Dome was the only piece of architecture taller than the Central Airways terminal. Tiered platforms stacked ten high serviced a myriad of skytrains, which came and went like bees swarming a hive. Air traffic converged from one side; the other was for departures. Once away from the terminal, the skytrains diverted onto their path and zoomed off around the city and beyond.

I moved up beside Holden. "How do we stop the skytrains from coming and going?"

"There's a coms room in the glass bulb at the top. We'll breach that first with the help of Jax and Elva and divert all traffic. We've lost minutes already. Let's go." He sounded like Jax when barking orders.

Reg and Malvo followed Holden as stone-faced avatars, their powerful legs striding down the paving. Remembering the last time we'd played and how neutral bots could turn nasty real quick, I quick stepped to catchup with Holden. Jax and the Aris party were nowhere to be seen, meaning there were only four of us to deal with any trouble along the way, or maybe I should say three since I would not include myself as a fighting force.

With his long legs, Holden kept the pace high. I knew the reason. The longer we were in transition to the tower, the more likely we were to be attacked. Right on cue, a harsh cry came from behind. Malvo responded swiftly and buried his sword into the bot's chest. I looked away when blood seeped around the blade and down the warrior's chest to his stomach. Why did they have to make that part so real?

Holden grabbed my hand. "Pick your pace up. One attack tends to trigger the rest, and I want to reach the tower before the horde descends on us."

So did I. Would four fighting be enough to survive level five?

Malvo caught up within seconds and he and Reg dropped behind, both with their swords at the ready. I flicked a glance all around, darting my eyes from one bot to the next as they kept appearing out of nowhere, a ceaseless wave directed at us. Something inside my mind shifted like a slider door opening. I glanced at my power status bar to see it had shifted to orange, but my skills and health status bars remained unchanged.

A female bot dressed in a small yellow leather fight suit spun in front of us and raised her ball and chain over her head while bellowing a war cry. On instinct, I reached for my tri-blade, held within a belt that appeared at my waist the moment I chose it.

As if her cry sounded the alarm, a few more bots hurled toward us from the side. Reg and Malvo, coming up the rear, confronted those, leaving Holden and me to deal with the lethal-looking female.

Everything ran through my head in one nanosecond, a dozen defensive moves, counter offenses, and attacks. My skills status bar turned orange, which meant I was thinking the right sort of defense. The ball and chain she swung around her head formed a protective shield; I wasn't getting close. I risked a distracted glance sideways to see Holden hung back, giving me the clear.

"Make this your kill, Sable. It will give you a good head start."

It sounded wrong—my kill. This wasn't how it should be, but in Dominus there was no way out except to play through to the end or death. It didn't matter how I felt or what I wanted. I needed to make this my kill. My skills status bar had not increased, but at least it wasn't back in green. My power status bar was the one to keep a watch on. Already it was tinged a deeper orange. The result, perhaps, of all my training with Holden, my factional nature sliding through more readily without too many barriers.

The woman approached, eyeing us both, swinging her ball and chain from side to side, swapping it from hand to hand as if to show us she could handle her weapon from either hand equally well. Two enemies made her cautious.

The tri-blade felt light. I positioned it into a pinch grip at the tip of one blade and waited with my blood rushing through my ears, adrenaline spiking, sending a tingle through my limbs. One inhale and I forced some calm into my body and channeled my focus on my opponent, noticing the minute detail, like the way she favored the right side for her weight, which told me she would likely use the right hand to wield her ball and chain. The computer liked my tactic as my skills status bar increased, sliding farther to the right.

Her move opened up her left side. My dominant side was my right, which couldn't be more perfect.

Our moment stretched to infinity, but the mission niggled at the back of my mind. One hour was all we had, not enough time to waste on every fight we encountered.

The ball and chain swung like a pendulum in front of her. I followed its arc while, inside my head, gears churned and barriers rattled. My factional nature wanted out. Heat tunneled through the recesses of my mind, expanding, forcing through cracks in the defenses I mounted to keep it in. The training with Holden strengthened my ability to access my factional natural, but it also welcomed it in, made my restraints weaker.

My power status bar inched up farther, melding the orange with the red. If I released destruction now, I would end this, but I would also end my party. I dug my nails into my palm to force my concentration, force my factional nature behind whatever barrier I could find. My heart jumped around in my chest, and I could feel myself losing my grip, feel fear sliding through. It would make me sloppy and the unleashing of my factional nature chaotic.

Her attack was so sudden, I froze for the split second it took my mind to catch up. A flood of adrenaline seared through my body, burning as it went, weakening my hold on my power. Pressure built inside my head, hot, sharp lancers, as my factional nature nudged to the surface. My power status bar edged up to red. If it flashed, I was done for. I couldn't get out of the game without frying my brain for not reaching my kill quota nor completing the mission, but if I remained inside with a flashing power status bar, my brain would also fry.

The tri-blade left my hand, an unaimed throw as a force knocked me sideways. I crashed to the ground with Holden coming down heavily on top and the *whoosh* of something heavy splitting the air above my head. With the loud *crunch* of the ball and chain hitting the cobbles, we looked to the warrior on her knees, the tri-blade protruding from her chest. Blood pooled around the wound and spread fast, stained her yellow outfit red, then dripped to the paving.

Holden climbed off me, then hauled me to my feet. "That was close. Another second and you would've been wearing the ball as a headdress. Good shot though. One kill down. You're on your way to reaching your quota."

I looked away from her bloody chest, then spun and bent double as my stomach threatened to release. "Why does that not please me?"

My skills status bar sat in the red. The computer disagreed with my mood. With the threat over, the pressure inside my head eased, decreasing the color on my power status bar from the light red back to deep orange. To my left, the kill score changed to one. To the right, the number changed to nine. Nine more kills were needed. I pressed my hand into my stomach and inhaled to soothe the shake in my hands.

"You'll have to get used to it. It's part of the game."

"Do they have to die so realistically?"

"It's just a game."

"No, it's a desensitizer."

Holden rested a hand on my shoulder. "You stress too much. Come on, let's get to the tower."

I glanced to the digital counter to see the numbers whizzing down too fast.

Feeling sick with seeing so much blood was *stressing too much*? This was a side of Holden better hidden.

In an instant, the warrior vanished along with any trace of her—like the blood that had pumped from her chest—leaving my tri-blade to clatter to the cobbles, clean. I stared down at it, hesitant to pick it up, clean or not, but Reg swooped in and did it for me.

"It gets easier," he said, handing me my weapon.

Why should it? How was it right to train to find killing easy? If I wasn't feeling so depleted and flat, I'd make an argument of it. If the clock wasn't ticking toward our demise, I'd refuse to move until I made everyone realize the reality of Dominus. This was a game now; soon it would be reality. Instead I kept my mouth shut and followed the rest of my party. The people who were supposed to be my family.

"You did well to contain your power. But it's all right to use it," Holden said once we were striding away from the kill zone.

"I still don't feel confident in controlling it."

"You'll only get better if you try."

I kept my eyes ahead, unable to look at his avatar face, a fabrication, just like the game. But underneath the game was a reality, so too underneath the avatar was a man willing to reach deadly limits to fulfill his belief.

"Not with you guys around."

"I have more faith in you than that."

"Shame I don't have it in myself."

I couldn't help but glare at him. Feeling my eyes on him, he turned and winked, something that came through on his avatar's face, but kept silent.

"Can I just say this game sucks."

"You'll grow to respect it once you see yourself improve."

He strode on, which I took to mean end of conversation.

I'd somehow managed to divert my powers from harming him the other day and instead blew the roof off his club, which Holden thought a major success. With no club left to train in, and the authorities scratching their heads over what happened, we retreated to an abandoned graveyard on the outskirts of the city, where I accidentally demolished a historical church, built turn of the century, and half the headstones. To me that said I was dangerous; to Holden it was progress.

With the next bot attacks, I found myself caught in the middle of the skirmish as Reg, Malvo, and Holden surged forward and engaged. My tri-blade rested in my hand, but I stayed paralyzed, mind and body betraying me. Blood oozing from the female warrior's chest kept replying through my mind. I couldn't do this. There was no satisfaction within me at being the victor, relief I wasn't dead, maybe, but no triumph at my achievement. While the guys clocked up an impressive kill count, I fell behind. If I didn't reach my target, I would be unable to exit Dominus.

That we were all desperate to amass our kills was the sickest part. It was a game for now, which made it fun for the three of them, but I'd been to this other dimension, to Califax City, filled with people just like us. Carter would see it destroyed along with us. The bots we encountered in Dominus would become real people.

Chapter 28

AT A JUNCTION BETWEEN THREE STREETS, Holden stopped and pointed in the direction the moon traveled across the sky. "Central Airways terminal. Right on schedule. Our way up is off to the left side."

I looked both ways before I stepped off the curb, habit from my world, but since there were no cars in Dominus, it was a waste of time. Like a horse bolting for home, Holden's pace quickened, forcing me to jog-walk to keep up. It meant we'd reach our destination without too many more disturbances, which I wouldn't complain about. At the right corner of my vision, the number of kills I needed to exit the game loomed like neon lights. I would have to fight to kill nine more times. Bots disappearing after bleeding onto the paving made what we did only marginally better. Next to my kill quota, the digital numbers said we'd lost twenty-five minutes already.

At the end of the street, the paving opened out onto a large pedestrian space surrounding the base of the Central Airways terminal. Three massive legs formed a tripod base upon which the tower was constructed. See-through lifts raced up and down the metal legs, ferrying bots to and from the terminal. I scanned the base for the Aris party. If they were there, they'd blended well with the surrounding bots.

"Come." Holden strode forth toward the first metal leg and the mass of bots scurrying around the base like ants.

I craned my head up the side of the tower to the glass bulb at the top, which disappeared up into the sky—heights weren't my thing.

At the base, everyone remained vigilant for possible attack. We couldn't enter the lifts until Aris arrived, but the longer we remained here, the more vulnerable we became. I still needed nine kills before I was out. Nine times I would be forced to embed my tri-blade into some-one's chest.

"There," Reg said.

I scanned in the direction he looked and saw Elva first, behind her, Striker and Nuke. At the third leg, Jax, Tyren, and Sam moved in line to the lift.

"Things could turn at any moment, so stay alert," Holden said as he strode toward the remaining tower leg.

Jax and his party hovered toward the front of the line. At the other leg, Elva and her party had muscled to the front, preparing to board the lift. With one swift downward motion of his arm, Jax signaled our ascent up the tower in the lifts.

Holden unhooked a small black canister from his belt and turned to the other two. "When the fireworks happen, you two secure the entrance."

Reg and Malvo nodded.

He took my hand. "Up we go."

"I feel queasy."

"Then don't look down."

He pulled me into the lift with some bots but maneuvered us both so we were toward the front. With his elbow, he hit the screen to our left and we shot skyward so fast I left my organs behind. I shrieked and grabbed Holden's arm. He laughed and swept me close.

"Sad thing is, it will all be over…now."

Despite our speedy ascent, the deceleration of the lift to a halt was unnoticeable.

We stepped out into a large open space, the rest of the bots spilling out behind us. The sun's rays shone off the smooth marble surface and the bots, scurrying about the platform like they were real people with a real need to get somewhere. On one side, skytrains arrived; on the other, they departed. Bots climbed up stairs to the platforms and disappeared inside the doors of the skytrain while others disembarked in steady streams and joined the chaos. Moments later, in a well-choreographed dance, the arrival side turned to the departure side and vice versa.

Holden tugged my arm, and I turned to see Jax and Elva heading for a lift on the other side of the large open space.

"That's our ride," Holden said of the lift that descended on their arrival at the base.

Not waiting for my questions, Holden pulled me through the crowd. At this point, the only benefit to being in Dominus was the cleared path we made as we headed across to Jax and Elva. If they weren't attacking us, the bots diverted from us.

The expanse of the platform was such my heart had plenty of time to crawl up into my throat as my eyes flittered from one face to the next, until all the NPCs blended together into a potential lethal opponent. Tracking the assortment of weapons adorning those passing by raced my nerves faster than a bullet train. I refocused on the lift we were meant to take, then to Holden, marginally comforted in seeing his diligent attention to the bots surrounding us. We were in the center of enemy territory. Around us milled hundreds of bots, who could became potential warriors at any moment.

"Get in," Jax said once we reached them, no congrats on making it this far, no quick words about what we faced in the coms room.

It was only once inside did I realize the lift was not made of glass and the railing that ran the circumference was all that kept us from falling hundreds of feet below. I turned and moved to the center of the lift, away from the edges.

"It's worth the look." Holden stood at the edge, with the front of his boot in space.

"I don't think so."

He held out his hand. I shook my head, so he wiggled his finger as a *come on.* "Seconds are ticking away."

"We can reach the coms room with me standing here."

"Master your fear, Sable."

Elva sauntered past me to stand next to Holden. "Quite a view," she said as she leaned over the railing.

Childish. Holden as well. But he was right. I wouldn't win if I stayed lost in my fear.

I accepted his outstretched hand, and he reeled me in, slipping an arm around my waist as I drew near enough.

Look. My eyes stayed closed. *Just look, dammit.*

Below was a skytrain hovering at a platform, below that was another, and then another, ten platforms in all. I wavered and the railing dug into my stomach. Holden pulled me away, and with hands on my shoulders, he gently shook me. "Not so hard. You're doing just fine."

"Time is running out. Once we take control of the coms room, the computer will recognize the challenge and change tactics. Sometimes it will hijack the system and override our commands." Jax had to be saying this for my benefit, although I'd rather he said nothing at all if the news was that bad.

"How is that fair?"

"It's not meant to be fair. The simulation is meant to be real. How many kills do you have?"

"One."

He frowned. "That's not enough. Once we complete this objective, we have fifteen minutes, then we need to get out or hell will break loose. And you need—"

"Nine more kills. The number's pretty clear. What's your definition of hell breaking loose?"

"I'd rather not say." Jax looked to the other two. "With the others in position, there's no stopping now."

"It will be tough securing the coms room, so there should be plenty of opportunity for her to gain more kills," Holden said.

Jax eyed Holden as if to say it was all his fault I was so low on my tally. I glanced at Elva but she was looking down, removing herself from my predicament, or smirking, the latter more likely.

Because we didn't have as far to ascend, the lift moved slowly, which allowed plenty of time for the view. I remained focused on Jax's back because that was the best place to look for someone with height issues, but I couldn't shut out the thick metal beams in my periphery, beyond them to the blur of a passing skytrain.

Soon, but not soon enough, the lift slowed. Jax turned to me. "No one's allowed in the coms room, so we're going to face an attack the moment the lift doors open. You ready?"

"Yes." No. I closed my eyes, giving myself the time to escape for one micro moment. With the feeling of a gentle breeze across my face and the sound of the lift door sliding across, I opened my eyes as I pulled my tri-blade from its belt and balanced it in my hand. I couldn't be any further from being ready. The fight with the warrior on the street still needed to make its way through my nerves and out the other side into a long-to-forget memory.

Before Holden and Elva entered, they released their canisters and the flairs erupted, turning the sky a kaleidoscope of colors. The three of them rushed into the coms room in battle mode. I lagged, overwhelmed by the chaos that erupted.

Twelve bots inside launched into action. While Holden wielded his weapon, Elva and Jax kept theirs sheathed and instead used their hands and teeth. All three whirled with lightning speed, decapitating, slicing, stabbing, or mutilating their opponents, but as the bots died, more appeared. There was nothing but the ugly sounds of grunts and cries, the wet squelch of torn flesh and cracked bone. This was the brutal and savage truth of Dominus.

With the initial attack, the bots on the platform below raced around like disturbed ants. The computer had registered the attack and was in the process of mounting its defense. And I needed my kills if I wanted to be free.

I moved into the coms room, doing my best to avoid watching Jax and Elva fight. I knew why Jax had paused to speak with me before we entered the game after our talk with Carter. He wanted me prepared to face what he would become. Was it shame that had driven him?

A bot disengaged from Holden's ferocious slashing and raced toward me. My throwing arm went limp, and I dodged to the side and scuttled around the circular room, placing Elva and her bot between us. I'd been caught off guard by the warrior's sudden attack and my first instinct was to run.

My brain scrambled as it flipped into panic and my heart jumped into my throat. There was too much going on for me to concentrate. Something whizzed past my head and embedded into the wall behind with a *thunk*. I ducked too late as a warrior dressed entirely in black with a hood covering his eyes leapfrogged over the control panels and flew toward me with giant strides. I fumbled for my tri-blade, but he kicked it out of my hand and it spun off across the floor. Next a boot caught me high in the chest. The wind was knocked from me as I hit the wall behind. My health status bar moved to light orange as I wheezed to breathe and my skills status bar inched farther down toward green. The black warrior pulled his axe from the wall and raised it above his head to strike when a fist punched through his chest from behind. The warrior sank to his knees, then vanished, leaving Jax in his place.

With a rough hold, he jerked me forward to my feet. Elva punched buttons on the controls on the coms panel.

"We're leaving." He breathed on my face, and I turned away from the metallic stench on his breath. Hand still vised on my arm, us going nowhere, I turned back to meet his stare. There was nothing on his avatar face to read, but the red stains on his teeth and down the front of his tunic had mercifully disappeared. He jerked his arm back and stepped away, shielding his eyes from mine. He could not have read the disgust on my face, not an avatar face, surely, but my actions spoke for him to hear. Or maybe he'd distanced himself from me because he was disappointed in my lack of kills or ashamed his were so many.

The lower we descended into the chaos below, the higher the pressure built within my mind. My power status bar inched up to halfway. On the right, the digital numbers flicked down. We had twenty minutes left in the game. I had twenty minutes to reach my kill quota.

The skytrains closed their doors but did not depart. All the skytrains approaching changed course. Bots were clashing with each other as if the computer was unable to recognize us from itself.

"Now we subdue this level. The guys on the ground will prevent anyone from leaving via the lift."

I yanked Jax's arm for his attention. "There's too many. How can you hope to win?"

"All we need to do is prevent anyone from leaving for the next fifteen minutes and we can classify our mission a success." He turned to Elva. "You and Holden secure the skytrains on the left side." He then looked at me. "We'll take the right. Remember no one is to board; otherwise we fail our task."

"What about the lifts going down?"

"Elva disabled them from the coms room."

"And the platforms below us, how are we going to deal with those?"

"With only ten of us in the game, they're disabled. We only need to secure the top level and the ground. You must make your kills."

There was no hiding when the lift door opened, but with every bot lost in a fighting frenzy, I felt able to duck amongst the crowd, chasing Jax to the platforms on the right. The other two fanned out, defending when attacked with swift, merciless strikes. I was left in the rear with too many kills still to make. If I remained hidden, as I was behind Jax, I would be stuck inside Dominus and the computer would win; I wouldn't make it out sane.

Jax fought his way to the first platform and checked the doors of the skytrain to make sure they were secure. Bots wanted in but he disposed of them quickly enough. It was time I took the initiative. God, I didn't want to. I didn't, I didn't but I had no choice. *Face your fear or die.*

Diverting from Jax, I headed for the next platform, keeping low so I could reach the platform without incident. I climbed the stairs as a bot to my left broke from fighting on the platform and hurled himself at me. I wasn't prepared for the sudden attack, so ducked and used another bot, busy fighting his own opponent, as a shield, which the computer didn't like as it wiped any color from my skills status bar. If only my power status bar would do the same. Instead it kept inching up, as the burn inside my head increased from the back pressure of my factional nature surging through. I couldn't block that and become an effective warrior at the same time as both used all my concentration. There was still fifteen minutes left in the game. Beside the digital reader, the number nine stared at me. Nine kills. I wasn't going to make it.

The warrior who'd launched himself at me abandoned his attack and sprinted across the platform, slashing at anyone who got in his way, and then dived through the skytrain doors that had just slid open.

Oh, god. The computer had overridden Elva's programming, and thanks to my cowardice, I'd just let a bot escape.

"Jax." I struggled to be heard over the noise of the fighting, but I did manage to gain his attention. He was too far away to do anything. If the skytrain departed, we would fail. While no one had made the outcome of that clear to me, we were in Dominus, so it wouldn't be good.

My feet were running before my mind told them to go. I cleared the stairs, jumped over a fallen warrior, ducked under the swing of a blade, my attention fixed on the doors. They were closing. I had to make it. I busted my lungs as I sprinted over hurdles of bots and dived through the doors. My momentum was such that I crashed into the wall on the other side of the narrow skytrain, then was crushed against the wall even further when something heavy hit me in the back. Before I could struggle free of the sandwich I was in, the skytrain pitched sideways and shot off away from the terminal.

Chapter 29

I ROLLED across the floor and collided with a seat as the skytrain tilted on an axis and did a swift U-turn. My health status bar mirrored the way I felt, creeping up into the orange. Too many places hurt as I tried to right myself. The floor of the skytrain was a grille-style metal, uncomfortable for rolling around on, but the seats looked plush enough. Only problem was, the plush seats were filled with bots, which meant I didn't have long to wallow in self-pity; any moment they were likely to turn nasty.

Someone tugged my foot and I spun to see Jax. It was like seeing a ghost. How did he make it onto the skytrain so fast? Didn't matter. I crawled toward him, threw myself at his chest, sending him backward with my momentum, suffocating him with my hug. "We failed." Thanks to me. I buried my head in his chest.

He set me back. It was hard to stare into the eyes of an animated character, hard to see the true emotions within. "If the skytrain arrives somewhere, then we have, but while it's in the air, we still have a chance."

Either he didn't know this was my fault or he was more interested in righting the situation than apportioning blame. The only way to stop the skytrain from arriving was to do something radical like blow it out of the sky.

"So we're stuffed."

Jax pushed me down, flattening me to the metal grille, then leaped over the top of me. I rolled to see him engage with a warrior, when two more bots launched from their seats, weapons at the ready.

I ducked low and kicked out, hitting the first warrior, a woman, in the stomach, causing my skills status bar to change direction and inch upward. The force of my kick buckled her forward, and I took the advantage to knee her in the face and heard a satisfying crack, perhaps her nose. She staggered but recovered quicker than I would've liked and barreled toward me with her blade extended. I dived left but she was fast and elbowed me in the temple. I stumbled sideways, seeing stars, and hit the side of the skytrain. The jolt ran through my shoulder to my spine. The handrail jabbed into my waist and I moaned with the double onslaught of pain. The spike to my temple turned my mind fuzzy.

I looked to my power status bar to see the color slide through into a deep orange. My health status bar increased too, moving up to halfway, triggered by the throbbing through the right side of my body. The female warrior, seeing her advantage, raised her blade.

My hand came up to shield my face, mind frozen in terror. The blade cut down through the air toward me. No control over my body, I could do nothing but watch. The noise of the wind sliced in half followed the blade down. The sharp edge of her weapon became my vision. A blur. Jax appeared from nowhere and finished her off with a slash to her neck, decapitating her. Blood spurted from her neck as she folded forward. I shielded my face again, thinking it would splash me, but she was gone before she hit the floor, as was her blood.

I collapsed against the wall as my factional nature fought to tear down my restraints, my power status bar now red. No, not now. I couldn't let it free. The unruly power would annihilate the skytrain, us in it. We wouldn't survive Dominus if that happened.

As if sensing my trouble, Jax fought close beside me, ripping warriors apart. It seemed bloodlust came with super strength, which allowed him to destroy with his hands alone. But I still had to fight if I wanted to escape Dominus.

I pushed off the wall, feeling woozy from my failed fight while struggling with my power. I pulled my tri-blade from my belt. There was no use hiding anymore and no way I was going to be stuck in this game for any longer than I had to, which meant I had to fight with courage and strength to make it out.

I glanced around only to find the skytrain empty except for us. Jax had killed all our opponents.

"I still need kills."

"And you'll get them."

He grabbed my hand and dragged me to the front of the skytrain. "There are only five minutes remaining until it's safe to exit. But only if you make your quota. The bot that boarded the train is behind this door. We get through and he's yours."

"Do you know how to fly one of these things?"

"Not a skytrain, but I'll learn quick."

"You want me to kill the only person on board who can land us?"

"We don't need to worry about landing. You get your kills."

"Jax, there's one bot on board."

"Not for long. The computer will supply more soon, once it registers we're alone."

I glanced around the empty skytrain, expecting them to appear. "How do we get through?"

"That's the problem. The doors are high-tensile alloy, a mixture of alum and tyrite."

"I'm guessing those are tough metals."

"Unbreakable. The door opens with retinal recognition."

"Great. So we're not going through the door then."

"That's precisely how we're getting in."

I totally missed the crux of his plan.

"Or should I say that's the way you're getting in."

"No. I can't do it, Jax. The last time I used my factional nature, I blew up a church. I have no control over my ability. I'll destroy us along with the skytrain."

"You won't. I have faith in you."

"Don't say that. I can't do it."

"You're our only hope. If the bot manages to land the skytrain, none of us are getting out. We'll be stuck inside Dominus, fighting until we're too exhausted to fight anymore."

"I can't believe you guys even thought of those rules."

Jax spun me around to face the door. With his hands on my elbows, he spoke into my ear. "You have to do this. You're the only one who can. Think of everything Holden told you."

I stared at the flat metal door while Jax's breath played in my ear. Was this where my life would end? In a game I despised? But if I didn't do this, more lives were at risk; we would all be locked within Dominus. I turned my head to Jax, whose face was inches from my own.

"I believe in you," he said.

I looked back at the door. His trust was misguided. But I was not going to be stuck in Dominus.

This was going to be messy.

"Wait." Jax squeezed my shoulders.

I flicked a look to the digital countdown. We'd passed the ten-minute mark.

"Why?"

"Just wait."

I turned my head to look at him, but he was looking elsewhere. That's when the skytrain filled with bots. Jax set me free. "Do it, Sable."

My ability itched for release just below the surface. I concentrated on inching the barriers of my mind aside, but once the walls began to shift, the energy rushed forth, an unstoppable force. I tried to stem the flow but felt like a stick trying to withstand a tornado as my power bar rushed to red.

My ability exploded outward as the world around me blew apart. The noise of the explosion deafened. The force of the power slammed into my chest, punching the wind out of me and crushing my lungs as I was thrown backward. With nothing to hit, I tumbled through the air, blind.

I fell and fell and fell. It was only when my throat began to hurt that I realized I was screaming. My chest hurt from the compression of the explosion, and my ears rang. But at least I was still alive.

It took moments for me to realize I no longer fell. I felt for the arm around my waist and exhaled the fear, knowing Jax was still with me. I opened my eyes only to see a hazy film across my vision.

"Jax?"

"I'm here." He ran his hand down the side of my face.

"I can't see properly."

"Your vision will return. You've just got to give it a little time."

"What happened?"

"Apart from you destroying the skytrain?"

"I told you—"

I jerked when he placed a finger over my lips. "I wasn't sure if you could control your power. It was worth a try. In fact, it was the only hope we had. All the same, I was ready to get us out the moment the explosion began. Your vision's blurred because I wasn't as quick as I thought I could be. The explosion set off a reciprocal event along your neural pathways. Any longer in Dominus and your brain would've fried; as it is, your vision is temporarily damaged."

"I told you I couldn't do it."

"But you did. We're out of Dominus because of you. You got your kills and we beat the computer."

I slumped forward, exhausted, only to find Jax's chest there to support me.

"Unleashing my ability sucks the energy out of me."

"It won't once you're proficient."

"Where are we?"

"The in-between."

I let out a deep sigh and relaxed into his embrace. I was too exhausted to feel awkward with him holding me or care how he felt about me being so close. At first he kept his grip on my upper arms, the support I needed to hold me firm, then slowly he slid an arm around my waist.

I closed my useless eyes and inhaled his familiar aroma, the combined smell of our sweat. Normally it was something I'd feel embarrassed about, but we'd made it out. I'd totally screwed up blowing up the skytrain, but we were alive. We defeated Dominus.

All too soon, Jax set me back, keeping ahold of my upper arms. "We've been here long enough. It's time we went back."

"What happens if we stay here too long?"

"We lose our way. Finding home becomes impossible. We'll end up drifting through the in-between for eternity."

"Right this moment that doesn't sound like such a bad thing."

"How's your vision?"

I opened my eyes and could make out Jax's outline but his features were still blurry. "It's coming back."

"It won't take too much longer."

"Will the others be wondering where we are?"

"The in-between's not bound by time. When we exit, it will be like the explosion just happened. You ready?"

No. "I guess I have to be."

"Let's head back to celebrate."

Chapter 30

Jax assured me there were nine other people in the gaming room, which meant we were all out.

"Hey, little lady, good to see your face again." Someone patted me on the back. "You responsible for the fireworks in the sky?" Patrick's face was a blur, but by the sound of his voice, I knew he was wearing his cheery smile.

I nodded. "And I lost my vision because of it."

He sucked a breath between his teeth. "Lucky you got out in time or you'd be putty brains by now."

"Thanks to Jax."

"Sticking together is the only way through. Going it alone is the quickest route to disaster."

"I need to sit down."

Someone took my hand and led me out of the gaming room, the touch a warm comfort while I was lost behind my blurry field of vision. I listened to the footsteps of everyone following, but no one spoke. Whoever held my hand guided me backward until I felt the couch at the backs of my legs, then sat heavily. All I saw was the outline of furniture and people. The bright colors blended; the rest faded into the hazy background.

The couch dipped next to me as someone sat down. "We have you to thank for getting us out," Tyren said.

"I was the reason we were nearly caught in Dominus. The bot who escaped did so because I was too afraid to fight. If I'd destroyed him before he got on the skytrain, we would've been out sooner, and my vision would be fine."

"No matter. We're all here now because you righted an issue you created." I could pick out Holden's voice.

"I'd say that was a brilliant success." Patrick threw himself into a single-seater opposite me and slung his legs over the edge.

I leaned back into the couch and closed my eyes. No one seemed to care it was all my fault we were close to being stuck inside the game. My dramatic ending made up for my lack of courage.

"Drinks." As she was the only other woman within the party, I could easily pick out Elva's voice. She'd remained silent since my return, perhaps the only one of the group who'd happily blame me for our near miss.

"What do you say, Jax, not a bad run?" Patrick said.

"Five minutes under the hour, which is acceptable."

I kept my eyes closed and listened to him speak. Jax had fought the bots while I released my factional nature, somehow managing to remain close enough to save us both from the explosion. He didn't have to. It had been his choice. He could have easily shifted through to the in-between without me. Did that mean he wanted me to survive, that I was no longer a part of his vendetta against my father?

"I'm happy with your effort. Everyone held their station well." He wasn't meaning me. He couldn't be meaning me.

"I hear things were a little chaotic on the ground," Holden said.

"Nothing we couldn't deal with," Reg said.

"Elva, I was impressed with your speed in the coms room," Jax said.

"Surely you didn't expect anything less?" There was mocking humor in her voice.

"Of course not."

This was the debrief and he'd left me out of it. Good, I wanted to forget I'd even been involved.

Someone touched my shoulder. When I opened my eyes, I found my eyesight was clearing. A soda hovered in front of my face, Holden behind it.

"Thanks."

"How're you feeling?"

"Tired."

"Dominus takes a lot out of you. But you'll get better and find it less tiring as you go. Right now, sugar is the best thing for you."

Jax crushed his can and headed for the kitchen, leaving everyone to continue their debriefing without him. Reg and Malvo drew Holden into conversation about their tactics at the base of the tripod, which left me to myself.

After a while, I grew tired of hearing stories of what had happened. We were out, game over. Couldn't we forget about it, not feel cheered by our success? But I guess this was what happened when you came out of the adrenaline-high stakes of Dominus. Everyone needed to share the joy in the survival.

I stayed quiet and watched as the conversation moved beyond Reg, Malvo, and Holden to sweep in everyone else except Jax, who had his head inside the fridge. Here was Aris and Persal sharing grizzly stories, at times laughing and joking without any care to the factional mix. In the face of possible death, where the party was forced to unite, factional differences meant nothing. Why couldn't it be the case in friendship and love?

With no part for me in the conversation, I rose from the sofa, slowed to clear the dizziness swamping my head, then headed for the kitchen. Jax still had his head in the fridge, and I ran my eyes over his back. Inside his athletic frame lurked a violent killer. The few times I'd released my ability, I'd felt the overwhelming drive to become my factional nature. It had felt so natural, like I was only half a person without it. The strength of the yearning scared me. How would I come back from destruction once I gave in to my desire and merged with my factional nature, once it became me?

The Jax I knew was not the Jax underneath. He called it his true nature, but to me it was another part of him that hovered on the side and not the total of who he was, which meant I had to overcome my fear of my ability and learn to control it too. I wouldn't be the hindrance I'd been today.

I dropped my gaze to the counter and the slices of bread spread across it when Jax turned, his arms full of sandwich stuffing.

"You want one?"

"Sure."

He spread butter on one side of a pair.

"I haven't said thank you yet for what you did."

He shrugged, allowing the compliment to slide from his shoulders. "It's all part of the game."

"I know. But thanks all the same."

"You want some ham?"

I nodded. "If Dad can shift, does that mean I can too? If I can do that for myself, then no one else needs to risk themselves for me. I could take care of myself."

"There's no guarantee you'll be able to do it. Apparently every descendant born from a union of our world and yours has a factional nature, but few can shift as well."

The news was like a slap to my face. "But if I can't shift…"

While closed off in my small, blurry world, listening to everyone recap the game, I had decided to learn to shift. I was the weakest of the group. But that had always been me, the one who never got it right. Only now I was a hindrance to everyone, not just myself, and hindrances in Dominus could be fatal. I wouldn't risk anyone's life because they were too busy saving me and not themselves.

I'd assumed I would be able to do it, which meant I could easily move between this world and Jax's, or wherever Dad took my family. Without the ability to shift, I would become dependent on someone. I didn't want to be dependent on anyone, not anymore.

"It's just the way it is. But you're right. It's important you know now whether you can or not as it will influence the way you do things."

"I have to be able to do it." Dammit, I never meant to say that out loud.

"I understand. You don't want to be reliant on another in that way. I would be the same. Reg is the only one that can from this group. It doesn't impact how the rest play the game, but it influences how I see them within the game. To me they're the vulnerable ones because they have no back door if things get really bad."

"How will I know?"

"I'll help you," he replied, then hesitated and his gaze flittered past me to Holden. "If you want...I'm sure Holden will also be willing to help if you asked."

"If you're offering, thanks."

"How about tomorrow?"

I'd hoped to see my dad tomorrow. But I was desperate to learn if I was one of the unlucky ones.

"I'll be here. Make it the afternoon."

Jax slapped ham on the butter side of the slices while a silence descended between us like a guillotine, slicing off all the words building in my head. The conversation we'd had before entering Dominus hung between us. I didn't know how to begin it again. Perhaps Jax wanted it to remain a dead topic, but I was the daughter of the man who'd killed his family. Less than a month ago, I was his revenge. Did looking at me remind him of his greatest pain?

He continued to build the sandwiches, burying his concentration in the task, keeping me at a safe distance, or maybe my interpretation stemmed from my guilt for being alive while his family were dead.

Guilt had fast become a part of me. Holden and I were plotting against Aris, like the good, loyal Persal we were. I loathed the idea of betraying Jax, of convincing him once again that he should never trust another faction. But I couldn't let Dominus continue, nor Carter succeed. Dad was my only hope, which meant I needed the grafter. The worst part of this was I didn't know if I could trust Jax with this secret, if I could trust an Aris.

Chapter 31

I FOLLOWED the guard under a harsh fluorescent light along a narrow, uninviting corridor that smelt of recycled air. The scuffing of our shoes followed us as an echo, which was soon disturbed by a door clanging shut farther ahead, the sound of incarceration and isolation.

In here, every door slammed shut on entering, driving you farther and farther into the labyrinth that no doubt sucked hope and vitality from your soul. The guard escorting me kept his smart pace, not bothering with small talk because that would be welcoming.

My unfriendly escort pushed open the door to the noncontact visitors' room, then stood aside as I passed through, feeding me a glare as I walked inside that voiced his judgment on my family and myself. My family was tainted because of my dad.

Seconds later a guard led Dad into the room and directed him to the seat opposite me on the other side of the glass petition. On seeing me, he sunk into the seat like the weight of his body had become unbearable. Even the expression on his face mirrored the departure of his strength.

He picked up the phone, an indication I should do the same.

"You're alive," he breathed into the receiver, sounding like someone having received a holy revelation. "They wouldn't say who my visitor was. I…" He shook his head, closing his eyes as if gathering the strength to continue. "I thought the worst after your last visit."

For the first time, I saw stress on his face, the shadows under his eyes, a weathered hollowness that came from living with tragedy. As with every other time I visited him, the duality of my emotions sucked my energy dry. He made me feel too much. These extremes of hatred and love, how could I feel two opposing emotions for one person?

"I know everything," I blurted out.

A shutter came down over his expression. The energy sap he'd experienced moments before on the relief at seeing me alive vanished, and my father resurfaced in full strength. I faced my dad as I had never faced him before, as an adult. Gone were the fanciful stories he would tell me as a child to hide behind his lies. We were playing adult games now, and my dad had never been a man to hide. He straightened in his seat as his mouth hardened. He nodded slowly to himself as his eyes stayed leveled on me. Good, he had no intention of hiding now.

"Holden."

"Jax. I know you killed his family."

He didn't even blink, no twitch or flicker in his expression. "I'm grateful he decided not to return the favor."

I couldn't maintain our stare. Instead I sought refuge by looking at the tattoo on his wrist, a symbol of his enslavement in his own world. And now he was enslaved in this world too. He'd removed his factional tattoo, the one that signified his factional family alliance, but had chosen to keep the tattoo that marked him as a prisoner.

"You need to understand the reasons why."

"You've given me nothing but lies. There is no excuse for murder."

His out breath was forceful. "Sable, please, you cannot make judgments on something you don't understand. It's not as straightforward as you would think."

"Then help me understand."

Seventeen years I believed in my dad, adored him like I thought I would no one else. The day he was led from the courtroom, my heart was severed. After learning the truth behind Jax's family's deaths, my heart was destroyed again. But despite this, I still loved him. I didn't want to, but I couldn't stop myself, couldn't eradicate that part of my soul that needed him.

"Carter was always going to deceive me."

"And you him."

"I had something in this world that became more precious to me than our plans, something that divided my loyalties to our goal."

This was the reason I'd come, the reason I couldn't turn my back on him, because I knew, with all the lies he'd told us, what he said now was the truth.

"Carter's goal never shifted, so he needed me out of the way. It turns out Renus, Jax's father, was also causing him a few problems back home on our world. Given my love for you, Ajay, and your mother, it was easy for Carter to find a way to rid himself of Renus. He fed me a lie, said Renus had agreed to deactivate his graft and come through. The deactivation process is dangerous. There have been many deaths."

"Holden told me."

"Renus elected not to attempt it. For all these years, he remained in our world, unwilling to take the risk. Then Carter said he was coming through. His reason for doing so was to remove the obstacles that hindered my concentration on our goal."

"Us." I was drowned in the convoluted ugliness of deceit.

"I had to get to him first."

"But his whole family?"

"If I didn't bury him and bury him good, there would have been others. It was a necessary lesson, or so I thought."

I sunk forward, elbows splaying outward on the petition bench, head resting on my hand. How was I supposed to feel? Dad's love for us had made him a murderer.

"Carter lied, of course. Renus had no intention of coming through. But it was too late by the time I had learned the truth. Carter's plan worked. He'd rid himself of brewing discontent at home while keeping his hands clean. I regret my decisions, Sable. If nothing else, I want you to believe me on that."

I believed he killed Jax's family to protect his own, but I couldn't believe that he regretted it. He'd do it again given a similar situation. The strength of his love for us drove him, but his moral ambiguity gave him the ability to kill. I loved the man who would do anything for his family. I loathed the man who would go so far as to murder innocent people to prove a point.

"What has Carter made you do?" Truth revealed, Dad was eager to leave his guilt behind or maybe he didn't have enough guilt to hold him there. Was there any point in reliving what was done, refusing to move forward until I made him bleed for his crime, when a greater atrocity loomed ahead? Carter would bring war to both our worlds.

"Holden's teaching me to use my factional nature. So far we've played to level five."

He closed his eyes. "And you survived. Thank God." Spoken like a prayer.

"Thanks to everyone I went in with, but I need to learn how to shift."

"Not everyone can, hon."

"I know. Jax told me."

A deep frown gouged down the center of his brow. "You need to stay away from him. Stick with Holden. He's the only one you can trust."

"Jax has helped me more than anyone else so far."

"He's Aris, Sable."

"I'm sick of this factional division."

"His loyalty is to his factional family. He will betray you the moment you're no longer needed."

Stop. There's no point. He won't hear you. "Holden told me Carter has hidden the grafter in his office."

"It makes sense. It's the only assurance he has. Why is that important to you?"

"I'm going to get it, then I'll be able to set you free."

"No, it's too dangerous."

"I'm gaining control over my factional nature. It's not easy, but I'm doing it. I can use it to get into the safe where he keeps it."

"Sable, listen to me." He hunched forward, leaning close to the glass as if about to tell a secret. "Do not do this."

"Carter has Mum working for him."

"I know. Holden told me."

"He visits you?"

"He's Persal. He understands factional loyalty. He's kept me informed."

"Then you would know why I must do this. Carter has Mum; next it will be Ajay. I won't let him win."

"I'm working on a plan. Please wait until I can come up with something that is guaranteed to work. Please, Sable, for yours, your mum's, and Ajay's sake."

He didn't trust me to succeed because I never had before. But I had a damn good reason to succeed now.

"I'm not going back into the game."

"I don't want you in Dominus. But have you truly mastered your factional nature? Do you know the consequences of pulling out of Dominus if you haven't?"

Dammit, he was right. I still did not have complete control over my factional nature.

"Stick with Holden, Sable. He will do what it takes to get you through to the end. He's Persal. You can trust him. Let him be the guide I cannot be." Dad raked his hands through his hair. The knuckles on the hand holding the phone turned white. Any minute I expected the phone to snap. Watching him, a fragment of my heart cracked, allowing the love I felt for him to flood through. I understood anger born from helplessness. It had been my only emotion these last couple of months.

"I'm a different girl from the one you knew."

Dad's face emerged from behind his hand as he lifted his head to look at me. "I knew that the moment I saw you."

"I'm going to do what I think best."

There was no reply he could make. He knew it. I saw it on his face.

"I don't question your love for me."

"I want to keep you safe, always."

"You can't, Dad. You never could. Now you just have to believe in me."

He touched the glass dividing us. "I do, honey. I've always believed in you." The tips of his fingers turned white pressed up against the glass.

Damn stupid tears. I gave myself the time to swallow the blockage in my throat. "I'll never forgive you for what you did to Jax's family, but I can't leave you here. I'm going to finish this, Dad. I have to."

"I know you do, because you're my daughter."

Chapter 32

WHY DID Elva have to be the first person I saw every time I came over to the apartment?

Her lip curled on seeing me. "Shouldn't you be running to Holden? Didn't he tell you how toxic we are?"

"He never said that."

"He didn't need to. It's in his eyes."

She turned away to protect her vulnerability, but it was too late. I had already seen the wound in her eyes. I had thought they were doing fine after our session in Dominus. It seemed I was wrong. What had happened between then and now to hurt her?

"Holden is—"

"Save it, Mary Poppins, it's too late." She glided up the stairs with her typical feline grace, passing Jax coming down. He stopped to watch her pass, then descended, eyes fixed on me like I was the cause of Elva's distress.

"It wasn't me. Being so close to Holden's not working for her."

"She's stronger than you think. She'll do what needs doing regardless of what she feels."

"I will never understand how easily you people suppress your emotions."

"Because there are bigger things at stake than love."

"I'm only playing Carter's game because of love."

"Then let it make you stronger."

An olive branch? I'd take it as that. My love for Ajay and Mum would make me stronger. It had to.

"Shall we begin?" Jax called me forward with a curl of his finger. "Just remember, no matter what happens today, you're still capable. Shifting is an extra gift and not the sum total of who you are."

"You know I will be gutted if I can't do it."

"Then you will have to deal with that and move on. You can't change whatever outcome is about to happen."

Was he so sure I would fail?

I must've relayed the thought in my expression, because he took a step back as he glanced away, hands finding their way to his hips, looking like he wanted to say something but had no suitable reply.

I'm not as big a failure as you think.

"I know how much you want this. I feel it." He placed a hand over his heart when he said it, and I felt swept up in an invisible embrace. So simple a gesture and yet with it he made me feel heard, felt, understood —my enemy, Aris. "I'd be the same too. But you must be prepared to fail."

"I always fail. This time I can't."

From feeling cocooned by his gesture of moments ago, my throat choked up, and my heart felt squeezed, making it feel like I was sucking in air through a pinhole.

"No one's done level five on their second go in virtual. You did it and succeeded."

I rolled my head back as tension wound like a coil inside of me.

"Don't wall up, Sable. It's true. You're more capable than you wish to accept. No one will judge you for not being able to shift. No one except you, that is."

"Judgment is not my fear."

"I know," he said as he came alongside me. "It's about relying on yourself, surviving without help. I understand that desire. It's my own. But you will never survive Dominus on your own."

"Nor Carter."

His eyes were so dark. This close, they reminded me of black holes, where nothing escaped. Only this time he opened the shutters and revealed himself to me. I saw fragility, vulnerability, and fear but also strength, determination, and humility. After long seconds, he looked ahead at the couch. If not him to break the link, it would have been me. The moments between us became too intense, too confusing. It would be easy to fall in love with him and yet it was the hardest thing to do. Factions, Dominus, our worlds, and war stood between us.

"Like your ability, it's not something you will get straightaway because you have to learn to see beyond this world. You have to learn to focus a different way, to see with different eyes. The dimensions are seen as a series of bands. We are surrounded by them, but only those capable of shifting can see them if they choose. Close your eyes."

Staring into the black space behind my eyelids, I heard the thrash of my pulse sending my blood through my ears, felt the heavy beat of my heart pounding against my rib cage. I needed to be able to do this.

"I want you to take a few deep breaths to relax yourself. When you feel calm enough, I want you to open your eyes. Try not to focus on what you see in front of you. Allow your eyes to remain soft. Don't try and see detail. How do you reach for factional nature?"

"I focus on the walls inside my mind that form a barrier to my ability. Once I see them in my mind's eye, I can pull them back."

"Try to do the same for releasing your vision from everything around you. Don't try to look at what is there; focus on nothing in particular. When done right, your surroundings will wobble and then slowly compress. Diagonal rays will dissect your vision, interfering with what you see around you. Then the room will disappear and all you will see are bands like horizontally stacked folders. That's when your vision has slipped from reality to the dimensions. After three slow breaths, I want you to open your eyes."

I looked inward as I always did when I searched my factional nature, being careful not to touch the walls of my barrier; I didn't want to be grappling with my ability while trying to see the dimensions. With each inhale, I focused on diving deeper inside of myself, holding the breath for as long as I could to force my heart rate to calm, my nerves to soothe.

At the end of three breaths, I opened my eyes and saw the couch opposite me. I tried not to look at the detail, like the color or pattern of the weave. I shifted my focus to the armrests and back of the couch, but my eyes were drawn to the bright-colored cushions plumped at the corner. Was that Elva's feminine touch?

Jesus, stop that.

I screwed my eyes to blur my vision, but nothing appeared in place of the couch, no horizontal veining or stacked folders, just a blurry couch. My eyes then wandered to the lush black throw draped over the left armrest. We had a similar throw once upon a time ago before we were forced to change address.

God dammit. You're doing it again.

I delved further into my mind and hit the protective wall. Inside, my factional nature stirred, rippling along the seam between freedom and confinement. I felt it as a wave bumping against a pier. I snapped my consciousness back. In doing so, I became aware of the couch again.

"It's not working."

"You haven't given it enough time."

"I can't stop staring at the couch."

"It won't just happen. It takes time and practice."

I turned back to the couch, closed my eyes, and counted to ten under my breath. But the frustration was already bleeding through. I fisted my palms, digging my nails into the flesh. *Concentrate.* When I opened my eyes, the bright cushions called my attention. "How can you look without focusing?"

"It will come to you."

"What sort of an answer is that? I see a couch. That's all."

Jax paced back and sat down on the single-seater behind us. "Keep trying."

He was right. If I wanted to make this work, I had to try again and again.

And I did, until the light streaming through the skylights on the cathedral ceiling turned a murky gray. And in all that time, with Jax sitting silent and patient behind me like a panther, I tried, but all I saw was the couch, the cushions with their tasseled borders, and the throw with the last two weaves loosened.

The weight of my heart slid through to my stomach. I slumped down into the chair adjacent and finally managed to stare without focusing but only because I was lost in my disappointment.

I'd failed. I was not one of the few from my world who had a factional nature and was able to shift. Never had failure left me so empty.

Jax moved in my periphery, his jeans making a *shushing* sound on the fabric of the sofa as he sat forward.

"It's not going to happen," I said. I could hear the desolation in my voice.

"You should've noticed something by now. Even just a glimpse. When your factional nature comes through, the sight that enables you to shift does too. You would've noticed it already."

"Why didn't you tell me?"

"I had hoped it would be different for you. You needed to try, at least, to convince yourself you did your best."

I could not have found the strength to rise out of my seat. All I wanted to do was curl into a ball and leave fate to swallow me whole.

"It's not a failure, Sable. Few from your world are capable. It doesn't make any of them weaker. And now you know. It's time to move on."

I turned away, curling my legs up on the sofa so he couldn't even see my profile. If I could move, I would leave the apartment, as I couldn't bear to share my failure. No matter what he said, nothing would lighten the heaviness in my chest.

"We're going in again the day after tomorrow."

If there was one thing to bring me back, it was that. "Dominus? Why?" I said, unfolding myself as I turned back to face him.

"Carter's flown in more recruits. Some have already arrived. The rest will be here tonight."

"Other people from this world?"

"People we've recruited over time."

"How many?"

At the edge of his seat, Jax looked ready to pounce into the air. Flowing out of him and into me was the indomitable force of inevitability, the tsunami of an impending catastrophe. "Fifty all up."

"Fifty. What are we supposed to do?"

"We play against each other, Aris and Persal."

I palmed my mouth, unable to speak.

"The objective will be tough. But I'll ensure strict rules."

"What factions are they from?"

"Mostly Aris and Persal, but there are a few Phonus and Negal."

"Who will choose sides?"

"The other factions can choose their side, since there is not enough of them to form their own party."

"What level?"

"Carter has given me some leeway. Nothing below level seven."

"What's the kill quota for level seven?" With those words slipping from my mouth, I collapsed forward. My stomach felt as though someone had turned it into origami.

Jax leaned down too, lowering to my level, elbows spearing into his knees. "The way through this is with control. You annihilate the NPCs. That's your kill quota. I'll keep the others away from you."

I closed my eyes, shielding myself behind my hands. "You can't, Jax. How can you do that when we're fighting on opposing sides?"

"Sable, look at me." A command, but offered in a tone that sounded more like a request.

I peeled myself away from my hands. There was no point hiding or stopping the end now racing toward us.

"You can't leave Dominus, Sable. Not until you master your factional nature. Tomorrow, you've got to let it go."

The earnestness of Jax's expression made me want to crawl onto his lap and bury my head into his chest. Dad would look at me like that, like he could give me the best parts of himself, his courage and his unconquerable will, when I fell apart.

"You've got to embrace who you are. It's the only way to break free of Dominus. It's the only way you will win."

The truth was the only gift he could give me, and nothing frightened me more.

Chapter 33

TOO MANY STRANGE faces stared back at me. How many of the people standing on the mat saw this as an honor, thought they were the lucky few who'd made it this far? We were about to fight to survive or give our lives to Dominus. How many thought about that? We were now allies or enemies, but none of us were given the chance to choose that position.

Dressed in the regulatory white jumpsuits, we blended with the white background. Our heads and the silver dots were the only things that stood out, a bunch of dismembered body parts hovering in the air.

Jax joined us on the mat, positioning himself center. Everyone else gathered in a circle around him. Male, female, large, small, dark-skinned, or light, Dominus had no borders, neither did prejudice, hatred, and deception, nor conviction, love, and loyalty. Hopefully everyone present tended toward the latter traits rather than the former.

"As you know, the strategy for this game has changed compared to what you've played before. The enemy are no longer just NPCs. You will also be pitted against PCs, each other. Persal and Aris have the greatest numbers; therefore they will be the two opposing parties. Those of you who are not of those factions may choose the faction you wish to fight alongside."

Jax had made it clear to all fifty players, before they committed the time and expense of coming here, the strategic change. All fifty came. Not sure what that said about the players or the addictiveness of the game.

"The objective of today's game is extraction. The Senate of Factions has gathered at the top of the Veulta Plaza to celebrate decades of rule. Invitation is exclusive and security is tight. The objective is to remove the four senate members from the Veulta and secure them in a defined location."

Jax focused on Holden. "Your party will be on the offensive. It is up to Persal to extract the senate members. Aris will try and stop you. The winner is the party who succeeds in their objective. Remember all four members must be extracted alive. We enter at level seven, which means your kill quota is thirty. We also have a time limit of two hours."

"But how are we supposed to play against each other?" The question came from a small brunette standing before Malvo.

"By being smart and following the rules I have put in place. I have changed the game mode in order for today's session to work. Your kill quota will be earned from the NPC players, but you will be forced to engage with PC players as well. Fight skills and nonlethal use of weaponry is permitted in those cases. Leave your factional nature to the NPCs. Once in the game, you will all notice you have an extra belt carrying tags, which look like flat black discs. You are to use these on PCs. Once you have gained the upper hand forcing your opponent's surrender, tag them with one of the flat discs and this will remove them from the game even if their kill quota has not been reached. I must warn you there will be consequences if you are removed from the game early."

"Such as?" I said.

Jax decided to look at everyone else when he gave his reply. "Most of the usual, but nothing permanent or life-threatening. It may lay you up for a few days though."

"Well, that's a relief," I breathed, not bothering to hide the sarcasm.

"Do we still need to reach our kill quota?" someone asked.

"Yes. To make it easier for everyone to distinguish NPCs from us, I've marked the NPCs." He looked at Holden. "A specialist tactical unit will form part of the NPCs. They will provide most of the security at the Veulta along with my party." Directing what he said to Holden had to mean the specialist tactical unit had some meaning to Holden. Dominus was a simulation of their real world, which meant so was the specialist tactical unit. Was this Jax giving Holden a nod to what was ahead?

"You will be given limited control over the game mode in order to make necessary plans to meet your objective. If you do not succeed with your objective within the two-hour limit, the win goes to Aris. Whether your party wins or loses, all players will be able to exit the game without too many severe consequences. Any questions?" Jax took everyone in with one sweep of his head.

Silence was his answer.

"Keep an eye on your stats. Don't let anything get out of hand." With the last comment, he cast a quick glance toward me, meaning if anyone was going to lose it and cause mass devastation, it was me.

"Play safe, everyone. Let's begin."

When my goggles came down, I found myself in familiar territory. To the right of my vision, the digital counter was already running down. To the left, the number thirty glared out at me. The number of kills I needed, unless I was eliminated from the game first, the most likely thing to happen to me. I had to be the least experienced, which equated to the worst player here.

It took me seconds to recognize the street even though I'd only been here once before. "Persal HQ," I said, running my eyes up the face of the headquarters.

Without a word, Holden strode across the street, fiddling with the belt at his waist, not something that was normally there. I glanced down at my own new addition to my avatar. The flat black discs Jax had spoken about hung from small metal clasps. Before entering the building, Holden glanced over his shoulder. "I've tweaked the game mode, which will enable any who are not Persal into Persal HQ without triggering an outside attack."

He headed into the building with the rest of us filing in behind. Carter had made sure there was an even split of Persal to Aris players, but the few Phonus and Negal unbalanced the game. More seemed to have sided with Aris, which would have something to do with the Aris party having three native players in Jax, Elva, and Tyren as opposed to Persal's one.

Holden paused in the entrance, allowing us all time to enter. Once everyone was inside, he said, "We'll head upstairs."

A lift door detached seamlessly from the wall in the corridor, *shushing* open to reveal a metallic-colored space like a large tin can. Our reflections warped off the surfaces, making us look like an army.

The lift doors open after a short few seconds to a vast room, centered with a long, imposing table surrounded by high-backed chairs. As with the front room downstairs, glass comprised the entirety of the face of the building overlooking the street.

"We've got fifteen minutes to strategize before we initiate our game plan."

I glanced to my digital clock to see the countdown had not slowed in our favor.

"Do we have one?" The avatars blended into a mash of angular features and muscle, each man as warrior-like as the guy sitting next to him, each woman just as deadly. I recognized Reg and Malvo from our last game, but the rest were a bunch of fake faces. It would be so easy to pretend they were nothing more than bots. What had Jax said about the NPCs being marked?

Holden again fiddled with the sets of controls at his belt, the ones Jax had given him so he could coordinate Persal's attack. A digital image appeared in the center of the table.

"The Veulta Plaza," Holden said, leaning forward with his palms resting on the table.

The plaza reminded me of a wedge of cheese or a slice of cake, blade narrow at the street frontage, thickening as it receded back to the block behind. Tubular beams of metal formed the corners and a lattice of windows covered the face either side of the wedge.

"The senate will be located in Descaros, an exclusive restaurant located at the top level of the plaza. We can assume Aris will maintain a large contingency of warriors on the street and ground floor of the plaza, covering all entrances."

"So how do we get in?" Another avatar face concealed the person underneath.

Holden narrowed in on the street, zooming the view of the digital image in close like a video camera until the people on the street became clear. Instead of exotically dressed warriors, the bots were dressed in black jumpsuits with heavy-duty boots and an assortment of gadgets hanging from the belt at their waist—the specialist tactical unit.

"Never seen them in a game before," said someone else.

"Specialist tactical unit, nickname sweepers, highly skilled people."

"Let me guess, personal bodyguards to the senate," replied the same guy.

"They're much more than that."

"They're swarming the place. How are we supposed to get past them?" a woman asked.

"We don't. At least not from below."

The image moved again, whizzing up the face of the Veulta until it hovered above, looking down on the plaza to reveal a row of large glass panels dissecting the roof. "We're going in from above."

The Veulta disappeared to be replaced by something resembling the skytrains, but smaller and sleeker with a few extra bits hanging off, looking like weaponry; I'm sure I didn't want to know. "We hijack two STU utilities. Fly over the top and abseil down through these sun vents. The STU utilities are equipped with what we need to extract the senate from the air. Back home these utilities are used for a multitude of tasks, such as airlifting personnel out of dangerous situations. Once on board, I will give you all a harness. I, Sable, Reg, and"—Holden scanned the room—"you. What's your name?" He pointed to a small brunette sitting two seats down from me.

"Marijane"

"The four of us will be responsible for the senate. All of us will get an extra silver disc. These are for the senate. It will disable them from the game while not removing them from it, enabling the four of us to extract them.

He directed his next comment to the three of us extracting the senate. "Before you jump, I will issue you a second harness. This must be placed on the senate member in order for us to pull them out. We're taking them up the same way we go down. Sable, you take the Persal senator. I will take Aris. Reg, you can take Set, and Marijane, Negal. If one of us fails, the rest of you must take our place."

"Two problems, who's going to fly them, and who here knows how to abseil?" I said. Given no one in this room had seen the STU, I doubted any of them would know anything about their skycraft.

"Malvo, if you're up for it, you and I will each pilot a utility. The real fight will take place within Descaros; therefore we take everyone with us once we secure our transport."

"Slight snag," Malvo said. "I have no idea how to fly one of those things."

"You will," Holden said. "We'll separate into parties of four and approach from differing directions. There will be six in a party; the extra can come with me. Malvo, I want you, and Sable, stick with me. Reg, you too will be in my party."

"I got no problem with that," Reg said.

Holden pointed to the people sitting next to Reg, one guy and two girls. "You three will join my party. The rest of you form your parties now before we leave."

"You haven't answered my second question," I said.

"It won't take long to learn. You'll have the equipment necessary when the time comes."

With minimal talk, everyone decided who they would join and shuffled into their respective parties. Holden then went around each and allocated the direction they would approach the Veulta, any of the four compass points, moondine, sunder, zendua, and accetus.

"The rest of you will create a diversion allowing Malvo and me to access the skycraft. Once inside, we will be able to provide cover for everyone else to climb aboard. I want the diversional attacks to start in no less than half an hour. That should give all parties time to deal with any difficulties en route and to be in place at the right time." Sweeping everyone into his gaze, he said, "Does anyone have questions?"

When no one replied, Holden's attention turned to me. "Sable, you need another weapon."

"Is that because I suck with my tri-blade?"

"Level seven you get a maximum of three weapons. I figure another wouldn't hurt. Three may be pushing it."

The weaponry screen appeared in front of me. Rather than a selection of all the categories of weapons available, the daggers hung in the air before me.

"A dagger would be best, I think. Small and light, it won't get in your way. Anything else is too difficult to wield."

"Fine. I'll have the one with the jade-looking handle and the curved blade." For no other reason than it looked nice.

All the other blades faded, leaving my choice hovering in front of me. I plucked it out of the air, understanding the rules of Dominus enough to know what I saw was what I felt. The blade fit into the leather pouch strapped to my belt, which appeared the moment I touched its hilt. Weapons on my left hip, tags on my right, I was ready to fight—at least in theory.

"Malvo, if you're ready, I'll load you up with the information necessary to pilot one of those craft."

"Hey, what? You can do that?"

But Holden was focused on his controls and didn't bother looking up or answering. I glanced between Holden and Malvo, catching the sudden rigidity in Malvo's avatar. His arms straightened by his sides, his head jerked. Being an avatar, his face hid any secrets to what he saw or felt.

"Wow, this is freaky stuff. Amazing," he said.

His body relaxed, head bowed, followed by a deep inhale. "All right. That was awesome."

"Last time for questions." Holden scanned the length of the table. "Good. Let's begin."

I wasn't ready to leave Persal HQ. The place felt like a sanctuary. No one could attack us here, but hanging around meant Aris would win. And I didn't want to leave the game shy of my kill quota and suffer whatever consequence Jax did not make clear.

The digital clock informed me we'd killed twenty minutes since entering the game, which left us with one hour, forty minutes to win. Let's hope Aris failed to put up a good fight. Call me pessimistic, but I doubted that would be the case.

Before exiting onto the street, Holden turned back to his party. "Large parties trigger the computer to attack, even if we are from the same faction, so we move in lots of three through the streets, but keep your parties together. The two of you who are Phonus, you best stick together behind your party. We want to minimize the amount we have to engage before we reach the plaza. It's level seven, so expect the worst. It's likely coming for you." With that soothing comment, Holden left HQ.

Behind, the parties moved in different directions, breaking down to smaller groups of three and disappearing down side streets or heading back down the road.

"One hour, thirty-five minutes, guys. We're losing ground with each second we stand here."

A yellow line ran down the center of the paving. I looked down to see it end at my feet. "What is this?"

Holden took off at a jog, forcing me to quicken my stride to stay alongside him. "I took the liberty of adding it in so we all knew where we were going. Since I'm the only one who knows the exact location of the Veulta, I added a guide for the rest of you. That means the other parties won't waste time finding their way."

"What did you do to Malvo back there?"

"Loaded him with a flight manual for the skycraft."

"If you can do that so easily, why not load me up with every martial art skill there is?"

"Remember the reason for Dominus. You learn nothing if you fail to truly inhabit the skill."

"Neither you or Malvo knew how to fly until now."

"Both Jax and Tyren are skilled pilots. Carter has every contingency covered for when the time comes."

"Let's hope it never comes, right?"

Holden glanced down at me as he jogged along. "It won't." His avatar face was not enough for me to see the conviction on his face.

As we continued jogging, my eyes wouldn't stop wandering to the digital clock, noting each minute passing, which did nothing for the adrenaline boiling acid up my throat. Beside me, both Holden and Malvo cast sweeping glances around them as they ran. Of course, stay alert. Any of the bots appearing before us could turn nasty. And now I understood what Aris meant by marked. A digital reading appeared above each bot, naming their faction, but on us, the PCs, there was nothing.

With the first cry, I drew my tri-blade as I spun to see the four behind us pulling their own weapons and engaging the bots. Holden and Malvo jumped forward, wasting no time to eliminate the threat. Thirty kills needed, I couldn't afford to waste this opportunity.

But I needn't have worried, as a large male warrior with a spiked collar and wrist cuffs separated from a group of approaching bots, targeting me. Before he reached me, he ripped his spiked club through the air with an audible *whoosh*, rippling the disturbed wind toward me. It washed across my exposed skin, hot, like a blast from a furnace. His factional symbol danced above his head. I couldn't remember whose factional symbol his was, but it had to do with fire.

I was about to glance at the digital list of factions and their symbols squeezed along the top of my vision when he attacked in earnest and I was forced to defend, dodging each swing of his club. My skills status bar remained low because I wasn't engaging, just dancing around his club. But just as I was about to release my tri-blade, a sword sliced the air in front of my nose, millimeters from its mark. The club gone, he swung the sword again. I dodged to the side, then released a kick, aiming for his knee. His hand came out and swiped my leg aside, sending me to the paving. The jar ran through my hip, spine, and up into my head and ignited the tethers on my factional nature. With the heat in my head, it felt like the binds holding it in were burning. My power status bar rushed up to over halfway. But my skills status bar dipped as did my health status bar thanks to the pain in my hip.

I rolled away as the sword came down with a chink onto the paving. I rolled farther to counter the next swing of his sword when a roar sounding like a violent wind rose up around me. I shielded my eyes from the intense heat, as the blaze encircled the two of us. Now I no longer needed to look at the digital display to know Negal ruled pestilence and fire.

It's only in your mind. I repeated the mantra as I climbed to my feet, but it didn't lessen the heat of the fire. Confronting a factional nature made my own reply with a savage need to break free. Jax said I had to let it go. I had to become what I truly was in order to escape Dominus for good, but not here, not now. I'd not gained adequate control. The area of effect was such that I would kill my party.

I released my tri-blade, but with shocking speed, the warrior danced to the side, avoiding the blow. The tri-blade disappeared into the flames, leaving me with my dagger and factional nature; I was not about to include my fighting skills. The miss caused my skills status bar to drop, but my power status bar moved up to an early tinge of red. Fear and panic drove it forward. Mind control—Holden was right, Jax too. I felt scattered, my mind unable to stay on one logical plan, and I had yet to master moving instinctually as I fought.

The warrior roared, bunching his muscles up to his neck. Another sword appeared in the other hand, which he wielded through the air, slicing each in sync with the other as he advanced on me.

I glanced at my small blade. This against his two swords. Then my gaze moved to the backs of my hands. A black mark formed along the veins, spreading out like roots fast taking hold. It crept up my arm, snaking along a winding path, forking, then forking again until the dark mark looked like a spider web, all the while progressing ever forward up my arm.

Negal. Of course. Pestilence and fire, that's what Negal controlled. This was nothing but a mind game. *Not real. Not real.* I scrunched my eyes closed, but when I looked again, the webbing had progressed to above my elbow. That's when the burn started. My health status bar filled rapidly, moving through the colors, stopping at the start of red.

It's not real. Not real. Dammit, I needed to concentrate. The hairs on my arms singed. The smell of them burning reached my nose. My skills status bar sunk, my immobility not doing me any favors.

A wind picked up, flaring the flames of the fire toward me. I shielded my face with an arm that felt like it was already on fire. My power status bar shifted into the red, deep red. My factional nature was there, right there, wanting out. If I didn't release it, my mind would be cooked. If I did release it, I might also cook my mind.

I had to do it. Had to do it. *Face it. Become it.*

The restraint was unbearable, as I gritted my teeth, attempting to withhold the bulk of what was inside of me. A white light flashed across my vision. It felt like a tunnel was gouged through my head. And then it was gone. The fire, the burning, the black veining mark. The others were there. The fight won, the bots disappeared.

"We've lost time," Holden barked as he jogged off down the street.

Ten minutes according to my digital display. Only ten minutes. It felt like hours. All my levels had stabled. I'd won. No casualties beyond the Negal warrior. My kill quota was down to twenty-nine.

We'd not made it far when our next attack came. I reached for my dagger only to find my tri-blade hooked in place on my belt. Defeating the warrior must have earned me my weapon again. This time I would not hang back, waste time in fear.

I released my tri-blade and caught a warrior through the side. A lethal blow if the spurting blood was anything to go by. She fell to her knees, releasing the tri-blade. It clattered to the paving the moment she disappeared. I dived for it, while swiping my dagger up and around, catching another warrior, engaged with one of my own party, in the side of the neck. God, I was getting good. I shouldn't feel happy. Competency felt great. I couldn't help but swell with pride. Until a boot met me in the middle and sent me backward onto my back. The wind *oomphed* out of my lungs as the pain radiated through my joints.

The warrior loomed over me. My blade and tri-blade were gone. My punishment for getting so cocky. My factional nature lashed out, swiping my mind with a hard flick. I shouted my shock, anger, frustration and released it along the squint of my eyesight. The warrior detonated before my eyes.

Holden peered down at me, hand out to haul me up. "Stay on your feet," he said as he turned and continued the mad dash for the plaza. With my jubilation resized from the boot to the stomach, I limped along behind everyone else. One quick look at my belt showed my tri-blade and dagger had returned. All status bars good. Number of kills four. No doubt everyone else already had thirty.

At the end of the street, Holden signaled our stop. With a hard sweep of his arm, we formed a group behind him as he edged his head around the building we sheltered behind. After a quick survey, he signaled both Malvo and me forward.

"This is what we're after."

Malvo and I edged our heads around as Holden dropped back to give us space. The entrance to the plaza swarmed with STU, an impossible entrance point. I saw only bots with their factions digitally displayed above their heads, which had to mean Jax kept all his team at the top, expecting the showdown to take place within the restaurant. Three STU skycraft waited on the street to the left of the plaza.

I pulled back and turned to Holden. "How did you know the skycraft would be here?"

"It's protocol back home. These utilities are loaded weapons. Explaining all their capabilities will take us the next hour. And we only have one hour ten minutes left."

I flicked a look to my digital counter. Damn, he was right. "Let's hope within the hour we can fight our way to the skycraft without too many attacks slowing us, get to the top without being shot out of the sky, abseil down into Descaros without incident, something I have no idea how to do, fight our way through Jax's party, all of which have to be in the restaurant, and haul the senate out. I might add none of us knows how to use this equipment you say will get the senate out." I hated that I sounded pessimistic. We had to complete the task. We had no choice, so adding the sarcasm didn't help.

"Both Malvo and I do. It was part of the upload I made. We're proficient with all systems and equipment on the utilities."

Time to stand by my party and do what needed doing. "Okay then. Let's do this."

Holden held up his hand, indicating patience. The other teams needed to attack first, draw the diversion.

"Where are our bots? Don't Aris have their own NPC attack to deal with?"

"Wait until the attack begins. The place will swarm with the bots from both sides. A range of factions will appear. Any faction but Persal will be our enemy. Feel free to eliminate them."

I was about to ask another question when a skirmish broke out to the right of the plaza.

"This is it. Malvo and Sable, stick with me. The rest of you clear us a path."

The other four moved around us and broke out into the street at a sprint. We followed in the rear. With the sudden surprise of our party, a group of bots, both warrior fighters and STU, broke away from the diversion the rest of our party had created and charged toward us. As they did, to the side of us, a wave of Persal bots appeared, keeping pace with our sprint. I'd never been so relieved to see bots appear.

Holden grabbed my hand and pulled me sideways, veering toward the skycraft, leaving the oncoming defense to our friendly bots and remaining party. We didn't go far before he dropped my hand to fight off an attack. Malvo headed for the second skycraft but was soon halted by an unfriendly in the form of a savage-looking woman bearing a lethal-looking ball and chain.

"Sable, behind," Holden shouted.

I ducked and spun, lashing out with my leg in a low sweep as I came around, striking a bot across the ankles, pulling him down. By the time he hit the ground, my tri-blade was embedded in his stomach. I closed my eyes for a brief moment to avoid looking at the aftermath of my strike, waited the moments before I could open my eyes and retrieve my blade, which appeared clean on the cobbles once the bot had vanished.

My kill quota flipped down one less, and my skills status bar moved up to light red. One look at the digital clock. One hour to go. We needed to be in the air.

Holden made a dash for the STU utility, enemy bots not far behind. My tri-blade and dagger flew from my hands as easily as blinking. Amazing what confidence could do for you.

Yards more and Holden would reach the utility, but he was slowed when three bots appeared from the left. He dealt with all three in one shot, clearing his way. More appeared like a relentless wave, diverging their course and aiming right for him. Too many for my weapons.

I tackled the edges of my factional nature, which danced along the seams of the bind I'd placed around it. Too many and I needed to release more destruction than I had so far. If I let that much go, I'd lose control.

The digital clock appeared to have sped up, flying through the hour and winding down to fifty minutes remaining.

If I didn't give it a try, Holden would be slowed once more, or worse.

You can do it. Destruction wanted out. Withholding it felt as though the pressure swelled my brain to twice the size.

Wasting time.

I tried to funnel destruction out in a controlled stream but it slipped my binds and gushed forth like a tornado. In desperation, I focused on capping the onslaught, clutching my temples as I did as if that would hold it all back.

I turned my head from the impact, the immediate bots eliminated, but so too those farther behind, friendlies and not so friendly.

NPCs only, Sable. It's okay. It's cool.

When I turned back, I saw Holden activating the door on the closest skycraft. He'd made it that far. Adrenaline-fueled relief surged through me. The other two skycraft were hidden from my view by the first, so I couldn't see how Malvo had fared.

I was about to run for Holden when something heavy crashed into my back, sending me to the cobbles. My back cracked and my head snapped back on the impact with the ground. No time to check my stats, I rolled just as a bot with the digital display of Aris above him mounted me, pinning me to the ground with legs splayed either side of my waist.

Bloodshot eyes, leering smirk of bloodstained teeth, he was Aris, all right. But not a PC. I attempted to buck him off as my factional nature surged through the channels of my mind like an injection of thick, hot fluid. The suddenness of it shot a searing pain through my head.

The Aris warrior placed his hand over my chest. I lifted my arm to chop his hand away when he tightened his thigh muscles around my middle and pressed his palm down firmly on my chest. Done so quickly, the surprise of his move momentarily froze me. The delay was all he needed. With his other hand, he pinned my left arm to my side, then pushed farther with his palm. Agony so great blotted out my thoughts. What was going on? I tried to lift my head to look down at his hand on my chest, but the torment was too much. My health status bar peaked at deep red. Any minute it would flash. My power status bar was also peaking, but I couldn't gather my thoughts coherently enough to release it with enough restraint to contain its impact.

A piercing cry filled my ears, one long, drawn-out wail of agony spilling from my lips. Through the daze of pain, I lifted my head to see his hand had punctured through my chest down to his wrist, gushing blood from the raw wound. A crack of bone, a wet squelch, and agony flared. Throbbing welts of pain radiated outward from my chest to the rest of my body. Flashing red lights filled my vision. My health status bar blinked its lethal warning. So too my power status bar. Everything blinking. The digital clock ticked down. We had four-one minutes remaining, but I had only seconds.

Pain stripped my capability, my strength, my courage. Death wove a dark spell across my eyes, funneling my vision down a long, dark tunnel. Was this death? The power in my limbs drained; the fire in my mind vanished. And I'd failed at mastering my factional nature. I'd failed at saving Ajay and Mum. I'd failed. That's all I'd done. Failed.

I couldn't. I just could not die, could not abandon those I loved, could not let Carter win.

The red warning flashes became my vision. I focused on my power status bar. The flashes blurred, then swam back into view. My factional nature was always there. It was within me, part of me. My enemy could hold me down, take my freedom, but he could not chain the truth of who I was.

I refocused on my enemy. His face loomed close, teeth stained, mouth red like a lipstick outline, eyes the color of free-flowing blood. His hand encircled my heart. I could feel the cool of his touch, feel my heart seize and body spasm in fear. My vision blinked, faded. I bit my lip, the small sharp pain dull in comparison to the rest of my body but enough to remind me I still had to win.

I raised my free arm. His face was near. I wedged my fist into his gaping mouth and shot a rod of my factional nature down my arm and into his head. It exploded in a fine spray. I shut my eyes, shielding my face with my arm. When the pressure of his weight relented, I rolled to the side, gasping, panting, moaning the shock of being alive.

"Sable." Someone shook my shoulder.

I glanced over my shoulder to Reg.

"Get up. We need to get in the utility."

I looked around at the rest of the party rushing for the first skycraft. Some were racing around the first and heading for the second.

Reg pulled me to my feet and dragged me the final distance to the open door and half threw me inside once we reached it.

I tumbled in on my side, landing at the feet of one of our party. The door clicked tight with a heavy thud behind me, blackening the interior. A light flicked on as the sound of engines fired.

I rolled onto my back and spared the time to check my stats. My health status bar was on its way down, skills status bar a nice red, power status bar also red, which was all right by me. It was good to know my factional nature waited with me, just below the surface.

Chapter 34

With no windows, we were blind to what was happening outside, but with the sharp angle of the skycraft, nose high in the sky, I could imagine us racing up the face of the plaza. I'd scrambled to a seat and strapped in as we'd hovered off the ground, thank god, or I'd be down in the back of the skycraft pressed against the metal railings and other uncomfortable-looking equipment. Some had not been so fortunate and were slowly making their way, with the aid of others, to spare seats.

Had Malvo succeeded in taking off? If only we could see out. Maybe it was better if we didn't.

Holden's voice came clear through a sound system above our head. "Above the door either side of the utility, you will see a black metal bracket housing the high-tensile abseil line. I'm deactivating the lock for it now. Lift the bracket and release the line once I've leveled out.

"If you look now, you'll find a chest harness on each of you. When it's your turn to jump, you'll hook the carabiner at the end of the line through the clasp on your chest harness. Your descent will be controlled automatically by the utilities system, but I warn you it will be fast."

I looked down to find the harness Holden had mentioned during our briefing at HQ.

"One of you will remain onboard to secure the utility and collect the senate as we bring them up. Sort it out who that will be amongst yourselves now."

Malvo's voice overrode Holden's. "We've got a problem."

He'd made it, but the tension in his tone made me edgy, not something I wanted to hear on the cusp of a fight.

"What is it?" Holden said.

"The utility is not responding. It's banking left, and I've got a row of warnings. Auto controls have engaged, and I can't override them."

"Dammit," Holden hissed. "Aris. They've sabotaged one of the utilities, if not all of them."

"Fuel's dropping rapidly."

"I'm coming after you," Holden said.

The utility rolled left as Holden chased after Malvo's skycraft.

"You'll have to evacuate. I'll pull us as close as I can alongside you. Everyone will have to jump across."

I glanced around the confined space. Hopefully we weren't about to exceed our maximum load.

The acceleration of the turn pressed me into my seat. With the strain in my fingers, I looked down to see my knuckles had turned white as I gripped hold of the seat either side of my thighs. We weren't in the turn long before the craft dipped the other way, or so it felt. Not being able to see out any windows, I wasn't sure if we were horizontal to the ground or still going up, and how far from the plaza we'd deviated. A quick flick to the digital clock and my pulse zoomed up to lightning speed. Thirty-three minutes left.

Heights weren't my thing, and now we were in a chase through the sky. How air-worthy were these things? They looked sturdy enough, but what if Jax had done something to this one as well? Jax was the only other person who could control the game. This had to be his doing.

"Navigation systems down, cell pressure's dropping, and stabilizers are malfunctioning," Malvo said.

"I'm coming alongside you now. You need to hold it as steady as you can."

"I'll try, but with the stabilizers gone and the auto controls banking me in random directions, it's going to be tough."

I glanced to the digital clock. Thirty minutes remained. Christ, we weren't even going to make it through the roof of Descaros at this rate.

Holden jerked the skycraft right, and I was swung forward but caught by the harness I'd flung over my head before I lost my seat. Not being able to see out and his jerking maneuvers as he tried to pull us alongside Malvo confused me as to which way was up. And we were supposed to fight after all of this.

I closed my eyes and tried to concentrate on my breath, anything to slow the beat of my heart. Had Jax sabotaged this skycraft as well? He wouldn't, not all of them. This was not something I needed to think about right now. Would plummeting down to Earth be enough to make us all think we were dead, to end us in real life? The thought was enough to end me right now. But he wouldn't do that. He just wouldn't. I had to believe he wouldn't.

Get a grip, Sable. My fingers cramped from holding the seat so tight.

I checked my stats. Everything looked good. My eyes could not help but wander to the digital clock. The sight made me feel worse. The numbers seemed to turn with rapidity. What consequence would we suffer for losing?

"Open your side door now and try and hold her steady. We'll have to do this quick."

There was a *clunk* and a metallic *whirring* as our own right-side door opened, the door sliding sideways to reveal the interior of Malvo's skycraft and the rest of our party gathered at the entrance. Soon Holden's voice disappeared under the roar of the rushing wind.

One by one, each party member leaped the short distance between us. Once onboard, hands grabbed each avatar that made it across and pulled them clear for the next to jump across.

Malvo's skycraft jerked left and rammed into the side of our own with a horrific crunch, and I couldn't help but shout out something nonsensical, feeling like my heart vomited out with the words as those without a seat smacked into the side of the skycraft. My grip on the seat was a vise. At any moment, my fingernails would pierce the upholstery. Holden reacted defensively, banking us hard left with a curse. Even with the roar of the wind, I heard it. Those without a seat tumbled around inside. This was all going horribly wrong.

"I've managed to gain control," Malvo shouted, "but I can't say for how long."

Holden responded by moving us in close again and shouted for everyone to make it snappy. As close as he dared go, Holden bridged the gap to about a meter, and the rest of Persal jumped, two at a time to speed the process up.

"Malvo, your turn," Holden yelled.

I ate my heart. How could he make it? Once he relinquished control, the skycraft would bank away, perhaps drop from the sky. God, I couldn't think. I didn't want to think, but I could not take my eyes from the open door.

From inside, I saw a shape, which fast turned into Malvo making a dash for the open door. Without slowing, he reached the edge and leaped at the exact moment his utility banked away. For one brief moment, which slowed to infinite time, he flew through the air, pinwheeling his arms. The distance seemed too great. The guy closest to the door was out of his seat as Malvo hit the side of the skycraft. His hands clawed the floor as he scraped to find a foothold. Unable to find that, his arms glided backward as he slid out, but the guy out of his seat latched on to one arm. Someone else leaped to the rescue, and between them they dragged Malvo onboard.

Holden banked us away as the door slid closed with a heavy suction seal and loud *clunk*.

Everyone was safe inside and we all glanced around at each other, but I doubted anyone, including me, pierced the avatars' features to read the true feelings underneath.

"Twenty-seven minutes," someone said.

I glanced at my own digital clock to confirm it. I don't know why I bothered.

I sunk my head, followed by my shoulders, falling into the black depths of defeat. Did we have to continue? The word *surrender* already formed itself on my lips. Holden would never give in. Maybe most here felt the same. I said nothing because it's not how this game worked. Play it to the end. That was the only option in Dominus.

Eyes closed, I counted to ten. When I reached it, I counted again, and again. No stopping, the loop my sedative.

"Prepare for our first drop," Holden said over the intercom.

My eyes flung open, my heart stabbed out of my chest as again the loud *clunk* of the activated door pounded through my head.

Jesus, I couldn't do this. My vise grip would see the seat coming with me.

Either side, the two closest to the door prepared the line, then hooked themselves on. The roaring wind meant I couldn't hear what either said to each other, nor could I hear Holden through the intercom. If I couldn't hear him, I wouldn't know what to do.

They were gone. The two either side jumped. Coming up from down below, a roaring shatter of glass. The wind funneling upward around us brought with it shards that rained into the underside of the skycraft with a loud hammering as the utility rocked gently side to side. Splinters of glass shot through the air, small fragments finding their way inside, falling onto the second four lining up at the doors.

And then the next four were gone. A blink and they were over the side with the black line zooming them over the side and down.

I looked away, stared at the avatar opposite me, looked at my hands, then to my stats. My factional nature sat in the red. Once it would've made me panic to see it there. Now it gave me steel. The digital clock said twenty-five minutes. My pulse fled through my veins.

Another four went, and another, another, and another. There were few left inside. The wind continued to roar. I couldn't move from my seat. I stared ahead with a lump thickening in my throat. One blink and another lot went over the edge. I forced the sting from my eyes.

Holden appeared in front of me. "Get up, Sable."

I wanted to shake my head. I bit my lip hard enough to draw blood. *Please don't make me.* I stood.

"Move to the door." He took my arm and moved me there himself. "Look at me," he yelled above the roaring wind.

I glued my eyes to his face. As he tied me up to the descent line, he said, "Your descent will be fast but controlled, remember that." He squeezed my upper arms with his fingers. "Once inside, you fight. The Persal senate is your target. The Persal senate and only the Persal senate." He slapped a hand over my heart and just about sent me out the door. "Your factional nature is in here, Sable. It's you now. You're destruction. Remember that."

He spun me around, grabbed my arms, and folded my fingers around the line. "Your anchor, so hold it tight."

Below me was space. Space, space, so much space. The wind smacked my cheeks, caught my hair and tugged it away. I couldn't breathe. I was choking. The scream welled, clogging my throat. I closed my eyes. *There is no space, there is only ground. You're on the ground, you're on the ground.*

A hard shove at my back and I was falling, leaving a scream behind.

Falling, falling, falling, but it was over in the blink of an eye as I shot through the roof of Descaros and into a world of chaos. My feet hit something that wasn't the floor. Underneath all the sounds of fighting came a clatter and tinkling, which sounded like cutlery hitting the floor. I was on a table, messing up the dinner setting. An avatar flashed past my vision, then another, and I was knocked into action.

I unclipped from the line and placed my hand down to steady me, but I felt a sharp pain and I sprung my hand up again, a shard of glass lodged in the soft fleshy part. This wasn't real, but my mind didn't agree.

Wasting time. I scanned the room while I flicked the shard of glass from my palm, eyes searching for my target. Avatars everywhere, total chaos, too many to discern one from the other. Friend or foe. Along with the digital displays to indicate an NPC, there were plenty who wore no digital display at all. Wound like a spring, the humans scared me the most. NPCs were easily dealt with; PCs took caution unless I released my factional nature.

Aris would get the senate members out of Descaros. I kept low, searching for possible exits, and my eyes landed on Holden, fighting his way toward the far-left corner of the room. Three Persal moved with him, cutting through the swathe of Aris. As I'd expected, I found the senate members being hastily ushered to opposite doors. My eyes landed on the word *Persal* dancing above an avatar dressed in what resembled something like a suit. The clothes screamed importance as did the way four Aris STU surrounded him, one of which was human.

I was off the table and running only to be blocked by a female Aris

PC, her sword already in her hand. I ducked low, dodging to the side as she swiped down with, what appeared to me, a lethal blow. The strength in her swing would've gutted me had it made contact. Could she not tell the difference between NPC and PC? Or maybe she was locked up in fear, her actions beyond her.

Swiftly she corrected her wild swing, bringing her second weapon, a dagger, out of her belt with smooth efficiency—not a newbie like me. Eyes sawing into me, no way was she letting me go. I wheeled around, bringing my tri-blade up, releasing it before my arm was halfway, before she could calculate my aim. The tri-blade came up low, spinning through a dozen rotations before embedding just below her knee. I fell with her, turning my head from the pool of blood gushing from the wound. *Not real, Sable, not real.* She would feel it though. Maybe not as intense as a real wound from a blade penetrating the flesh, but close enough. Horrible as it was, terrible as I was for daring to do it, I had to finish the job or I'd lose my tri-blade. I crawled across to her as she clutched her wounded leg, screaming her pain, reached for one of the flat black discs, and slammed it into her chest. Her eyes flicked to mine.

"Sorry." I breathed the words but she was gone, taken from the game.

A *thud* beside me and another avatar hit the ground, an NPC writhing in pain, but with no apparent injuries. In a blink he disappeared. My arm was wrenched from my socket as I was dragged to my feet. A woman, Marijane, shoved her face into mine.

"The Persal senate." I caught a quick glance at the tattoo behind her right ear as she shoved me in the direction I'd been heading, something like a fork with three wavy lines radiating outward from the ends of the prongs—Negal, pestilence and fire.

I staggered forward on my way, pulling my blade from my belt so that I carried both weapons in my hands. In my periphery, someone shot upward through the roof of Descaros. I spared a glance to see a slumped Aris senator harnessed and heading out. Holden had succeeded. A quick look to the digital clock. Fifteen minutes remained.

Two steps and I was forced to engage again. An NPC this time, worse, he was STU. Without thought, I unleashed my factional nature, a slither to reduce the area of effect. The stream of it came naturally, the control like silken thread sliding through my fingers. The NPC disintegrated in a shower of... I doubled over as I ran on, feeling the wetness rain down over me. The bile in my stomach rose quickly. I palmed my mouth. Carter was going to pay for what he was doing to us.

Surrounded by four STU, one a PC, how the hell was I going to succeed? Thirteen minutes, that's all I had.

My attention was caught by another senator going through the roof. Negal, Marijane's catch. Two down, two to go. Dammit, I wasn't going to make it.

Never had my skills status bar looked so good, but my eyes couldn't help but wander to the digital clock. Hands now shaking with adrenaline, I rushed into the crowd, releasing my tri-blade with timed strikes, slashing up and out with my dagger from the other hand as I went. My kill quota flipped up as fast as the clock flipped down. Was this what it was like to play the game to win? Was this what it was like to become Carter's tool? I couldn't help but crave the feeling, the adrenaline of the fight, the power of making a kill. But each strike was also like an incision made into the heart of my soul. Slowly I was losing myself; slowly destruction was winning through. I could feel it as an energetic wave rippling through my body, pressing up against my skin with every strike I made, tantalizing my desire like a drug. I felt taller, stronger, no longer the girl who'd entered Dominus less than two months ago. This was me, who I was really meant to be.

Something hard thumped me in the stomach. I bent forward with a groan as my body sailed backward, colliding with a table behind. I tilted over the top, legs going up over my head, then shoulders first onto the ground. Before I could roll to safety, a hand grabbed my fancy warrior bikini top and lifted me off the ground. The Aris guy who'd formed part of the STU guarding the Persal senator shoved his face in mine, ran his tongue down my cheek like a dog, then hurled me away. The wall caught my fall, taking the wind from my lungs. I staggered, gasping for breath, getting nowhere when I was slammed back against the wall.

"What do you want, Persal?"

The guy was in my face again, leering down until we were nose to nose.

"According to my clock, you have ten minutes to get the senator out." He backed up, giving me a foot, curling his fingers up as a taunt. "So what you gonna do, Persal? Show me what you got."

He was a PC. I couldn't use my powers. Keeping my eyes on his face, I reached for my tri-blade to find it gone. So too was my blade.

"Looking for these?" he sneered, holding up my weapons.

I darted a look to the left. Where were Holden, Marijane, Persal, anyone friendly? Where were my fighters helping clear a path to my target?

A sharp sting to my cheek and the sound of smacked flesh brought me back to his face.

"No good looking for help." His stride ate the distance between us. In my face again, he said, "It's you and me." His lip curled. "Take me on, bitch." His breath the foul metallic aroma of blood, his eyes the reddening of Aris.

Something pressed into my stomach, harder, harder until I felt the smooth, cool edge of a blade pierce a line across my stomach.

"And with your own weapon too. Humiliating or what?"

Snapped around my neck like a vise, his hand squeezed tight, pressing my windpipe slowly to the back of my throat. I couldn't even cough.

His mouth pressed against my cheek. "Beg for mercy while I drip your blood at your feet." He licked my face again, his hot breath and warm tongue running over my nose and down my lips to my chin.

"It would be so easy to take a bite." This time I saw the red stain of his teeth.

I clenched my teeth, clenched them until I felt they would shatter, clenched them to keep my factional nature in. The sight of him, the smell of his Aris lust and destruction bled through my eyes to be the only sight I saw. It was filling me, swallowing me, drowning me, becoming the only thing I was. The force… I thought I would fragment while releasing the power through the open seams.

I stared into his eyes, his craziness, his desire to be what he wanted to be, bloodlust without restraint. And through my eyes, I poured myself out, the deep fear, the deep power, the well of destruction. It came out and went into him so easily, so readily, straight in through his eyes, pouring, pouring in a solid stream. Soon his eyes rolled back inside his head, his head arced back, back, and back, in an unnatural bend. His grip on me loosened, but as it did, someone wrenched me around.

"Sable, stop it," Jax shouted at me. Hands digging into my shoulders, he shook me. "Let it go."

With a sudden gasp, I sucked the air into my lungs, sucked destruction back inside too. It snapped back like an elastic band, slamming me into the wall. Dazed, it took me seconds to come back from where I'd been, lost on the precipice of my true self.

The first thing I saw was my stats, excellent, the clock. *Oh, god.* One minute to go.

Then I looked to my feet. Jax was on the ground, lowering his head toward the guy who'd pinned me to the wall, now flat on his back. I sagged, my legs giving out with the memory. I palmed my mouth, frozen for a terrible heart-shredding moment. It was like I was back on the Adolphy Tower cast into the abyss of nothingness from Jax's dive. The chaos around me died as my attention shrunk inward to what was immediately in front of me, to the guy with his listless eyes staring to the ceiling, his body unresponsive to Jax's attention.

The room evaporated, the chaos stilled. Whiteness filled my eyes.

Game over, we were out.

I inched my goggles down to find myself crumpled on the mat. Jax was close in front, the guy too. Unmoving, unblinking eyes to the ceiling filled with a hollow emptiness, the vacancy of death. Next I looked at my stomach. There was nothing there, no bloody mess. It had been all in my head, a fabrication of Dominus. But his death was not. That was very real.

A piercing pain shot through my head. I clutched my temples between my palms and collapsed sideways to the mat. This was the consequence of losing. Around me, Persal and their allies fell to their knees, crying out the agony that was our punishment for not winning. I curled into a ball, knees up to my mouth, embracing the agony and wanting more, needing the torment to erase the understanding that I was a killer.

Chapter 35

THE DARK FOUND me with my back against the waist-high brick wall, legs folded to my chest, forehead on my knees. Solitude and darkness were my escape. I could pretend I'd already fallen into hell. The blissful empty space of numbness left me long ago, about the time the headaches tormented me for real. Which was good. Pain was my due. The fact I did not feel it now was no mercy. My heart was tortured; my body should be tortured too. But I felt good, strong. Destruction flowed beneath my skin, a lost part of me now found. Rather than loathe the invasion, I felt united, whole. It would take nothing to touch that part of myself, to unleash it and revel in the strength it gave. And this was my torture, for I'd become what Carter had desired to make, and I wanted more.

I'd questioned what I would do when the game turned to *us* and *them*. Where *them* was no longer NPCs and the stakes were defend or death. I'd thought I was moral enough to find another way, an escape from the devastating choices, but in the end, I didn't. Faced with my own mortality, I panicked. I chose me over someone else.

The *clunking* echo of boots on the metal grille reverberated through my head, but I kept my forehead buried, shutting out the intruder, nor did I look when he approached, but I followed the sound of his shoes across the cement roof until he was close. Eyes closed, I felt more than heard him sliding down the wall. I could feel the warmth from his body, the soft disturbance of the air around me as he took up space alongside me.

Little had been said between us. Mind emptied, I had nothing to say. Hours later, I still had nothing to say. I was burning with shame and the horrible understanding of what I had done, filled with feelings too ugly to share.

"No one blames you," Jax said.

"They should."

"We're all guilty of the same crime."

I whipped my head up to stare at him. "Are you really?" My words were cruel, I was cruel. I was a killer.

"I saw how it played out. I saw the blade he held against your stomach."

"That didn't happen. Not really. I'm not hurt, but he's dead."

"He had you by the throat. I saw him lick you."

I hid behind my palms. "It was nothing. Not something that could kill me."

"Sable, you can't bury yourself in this. You acted on instincts. Everyone would."

"That doesn't excuse it or make me innocent."

"No, you're not innocent. You're not guilty either."

"Don't say that. There should be no excuses. It just gives a person leeway to do it again and again."

"You were always going to experience your factional nature at some point, you and everyone in the game, Dominus or no Dominus. It's the way it is."

"But without Dominus, I would not have used it to kill someone."

"You've felt the compulsive pull your factional nature can have over you, so don't be so sure."

"Dad would not have allowed that to happen. He would have guided me."

"Are you sure about that?"

When the silence came, it wasn't gentle. I dropped my head to my knees. Jax finally said, "Forget it. I shouldn't have said that."

The distant noise of the street filtered up and settled between us.

"His name was Harris. Thought you would want to know."

"Thanks." It did help to know at least his name, but it didn't rewind time, change what I had done, didn't stuff destruction back inside the cage. "It's out for good."

Maybe it took him awhile to find any meaning in what I'd said. I didn't help him because the rest was too ugly, too shameful to share.

"I know."

Did he have to be so understanding? Did his words have to be so gentle that they felt like a loving arm slipping around my waist? Why couldn't he hate me like I deserved to be hated for desiring the destruction inside of me?

"Don't loathe yourself for what you are. Trust me, it will twist you."

I found the courage to surface from behind my knees and found us in nothing but shadows under the half-moon light. Jax mirrored me except his head rested back on the brick wall. He looked straight ahead to the small strip of light running horizontal at the bottom of the door that led inside.

"What else am I meant to do when all I want to do is destroy?"

"It doesn't matter what's inside of you. It's your choices that define you."

"Don't give me platitudes unless you really believe in them."

He dropped his head forward and allowed the noises from the city below to fill in the gaps. He believed in what he said as much as I believed in it, and I had no belief in innocence anymore.

"Do you still plan on following Carter?" I said.

The dark shared little of his features. His eyes looked like sunken pits. "Why do you ask?"

Did I reveal what Holden and I planned? If I didn't, I would be the same as all the rest, enforcing the belief in factional loyalty over everything else. "What do you want, Jax?"

A light would be good. Having a conversation in the dark robbed me of the precious ways people communicated beyond words. In many ways, not seeing Jax clearly made it easy, less personal, less confronting.

"Truth? I want this over. I want to return home."

"And see your world destroyed? That's what will happen if you don't stop Carter. He'll see to it."

"I don't know what I want anymore." I couldn't see his features, but there was no mistaking his hand rubbing along the tattoo at his wrist. "If you loved your world, then you wouldn't want this. Where is the justice in one faction suppressing all others?"

"I'm in too deep."

"Look what he has done to me." He didn't deserve the harshness in my words, but I couldn't keep it in. "No one is ever in too deep." I swiveled on my ass to face him.

"We're too far along. There is nothing that can be done now," Jax said.

I pushed back against the wall again. If I told him our secret, he could ruin everything. Did I dare continue? Of everyone, I wanted to trust him the most. But could I? "There is." One more breath and I blurted out, "I have to free Dad."

"I won't help that man. Besides, it changes nothing, just the faction ruling."

"No, it does more than that. Dad will never suppress your people. It would be how you want it."

"Don't be so naive, Sable. I understand your loyalty to your father, but the only difference between him and Carter is Carter beat him to it. Your father had no intention of sharing the power just as Carter didn't. At some point, he would've disposed of Carter as Carter did him."

"But Dad's not interested in their plans anymore. That's the real reason Carter made sure he was out of the way. Dad was happy with his life here, his family. He wasn't interested in overthrowing the senate anymore."

"If that's true, then why has he allowed Dominus to continue for all this time?"

I had no answer because it was my question too. "I can't leave him there."

I was on my feet, unable to stay still any longer. "There is no other way. Dad will be able to stop Carter. He's the only person I can think of with the power to do it." I stopped my erratic pacing. "I won't go back inside Dominus. I can't."

"You don't have to. You're your factional nature now."

The truth was consuming. I was destruction. I was my real self, no longer hidden, no longer contained or suppressed. I was more than what I'd ever been before. I was capable, powerful. I was a killer. "Carter will force us in again and again until he bleeds the humanity out of us."

Jax rubbed the tattoo on his wrist, withdrawing into himself. The force of my conviction ran through me like a thousand volts of electricity, and I was wired to argue with him, wired to throw some destruction around. No way would I allow him to go silent on me; no way would I let that beast out.

He beat me to it. "How do you propose to get him out?"

"The grafter."

If he was surprised how I knew about the device, he never showed it, at least not what I could see in the dark.

"Dad will take Mum and Ajay somewhere safe and then he will stop Carter, and Dominus." I tried to sound convincing, but I'd been pulled apart. I might be whole, I might not doubt my courage or strength, but I doubted those within my world and doubted my ability to be good.

"What about you?"

"That's why I wanted to be one of the lucky ones to be able to shift."

"You've already planned all of this."

Perhaps I'd been a fool in telling him.

"Does Holden know?"

I nodded, then not sure if he saw, I said, "Yes."

The seconds slowed, during which I questioned my sanity yet again in telling Jax. He wouldn't tell. I had to believe he wouldn't tell.

"I will not help you free your father."

I tried to ignore the disappointment from his refusal. And now I'd revealed our plans, it felt imperative I began. "I have to go."

Jax grabbed my arm before I made it to my feet. "I'll keep your secret."

But you won't help. I pushed up, losing his grasp.

I turned and managed two steps, then swiveled back. "By not telling, you're helping in a way. I'm grateful for that, but I don't know why."

"I don't want to be this."

I retraced my steps toward him.

"I don't want to be what's inside. Every time I become my true nature, I find it harder to come back. You're right. I don't believe in what I say. It gets harder and harder to believe we have any choices. What Carter is doing, what the game makes us do, is changing us, changing me. When I'm in Dominus and become my true nature, I feel powerful, unstoppable, invincible. The lure is consuming. Sometimes I don't want to hold it in. I think how easy it would be to rid myself of these human qualities and simply exist as Aris. When out of Dominus, as I am now, here with you, I loathe that part of myself. It's not how it should be. It's Dominus. It's turning me into a monster."

His words moved into my soul, became the mirror of my own emotions.

"No, it's Carter."

"I don't want to be the monster inside of me."

"Then I will save you from being that monster."

I would save myself.

CARTER TOOK one day to review the results and deemed the game a failure. He'd wanted all the senate taken, not two.

I reread the passage Jax had messaged me from Carter's debrief.

The boy's death was an unfortunate but inevitable consequence of our fight for freedom.

Carter had managed to turn the word *freedom* into a lethal weapon.

I have been unsuccessful in achieving the outcome needed because of a persistent fatal flaw I have as yet been unable to excise. For our success, it is imperative this weakness is eradicated.

Our humanity was the weakness, our unwillingness to kill each other.

All players will enter Dominus again for an extended duration. Level ten.

Carter wanted us to play like NPCs. Just like the digital clock in Dominus ticking down, so too did my window of opportunity to steal the grafter.

No one would enter Dominus again. That was my silent promise.

Mum had disappeared into the bathroom, saying she needed to relax in the tub after a stressful day and we weren't to disturb her for anything. I was more than happy to follow that request and headed for her bedroom. Dad would have to remove Mum and Ajay quickly, which meant some things would need to be prepacked or they'd leave with nothing. I should be telling them the truth, but the timing sucked. Mum was a hopeless actor. Once she knew, there was no way she could pretend she didn't. She would refuse to return to work, and I needed her there if my plan was to work. Unfortunately, Mum's and Ajay's ignorance assured their safety for now.

I opened the door on the small secondhand cupboard we'd picked up cheap. Not all of her clothes from her former life had made it inside. Most still remained packed in boxes and stacked along the wall. I fingered what she had, not knowing what to grab. I doubted the people of Dad's world walked around dressed as warriors, like they did in Dominus, but what did they wear? If we were to fit in, we would need to dress exactly like them.

I dithered for valuable moments before I pulled a few things from their hangers and stuffed them into a plastic bag. Next I went through her smalls, grabbing as much as I could stuff into the bag. Those were more important than what went on the outside. There were plenty of other things in her room she would hate to see left behind, like the photo of the four of us smiling for the camera, which sat on the makeshift bedside table. I picked the photo up and stared at it. I couldn't even remember when it had been taken. I looked about the same age I did right now, but our smiles appeared genuine, so it was before the tragedy that sent our family spiraling into the black pit of Dad's imprisonment. I stuffed the photo in the bag with the clothes. There were, perhaps, whole photo albums of us around, or images stashed on sticks somewhere, but were they important compared to the larger picture of our reality?

Leaving Mum's room, I headed to Ajay's. He sat on his bed reading a comic.

"Can I come in?"

He nodded.

"Can you do something for me, Ajay?"

He put the comic down.

"I want you to go through your draws and pick out your second-favorite clothes and pack them in here. Anything you would like to take with you on a holiday and don't mind not seeing for a while."

He climbed off the bed. "Why?"

"Because we might be going somewhere soon. But it's a surprise for Mum, so you can't tell her."

He didn't look satisfied with my answer.

"Not another thing I have to keep secret."

"This one is a good secret."

He took the bag and opened his wooden draws, which were also secondhand and stiff to open. I helped him when they got stuck halfway.

"You can only take a few things, okay? And make sure you leave some room to take some of your favorite toys. But they can't be heavy, or it will make the bag hard to carry."

"You're weird."

I ruffled his hair. "Thanks, buddy. When you've finished, leave the bag under your bed. Remember it's a surprise, so don't tell Mum."

"What's in that bag?"

"Some clothes of Mum's."

"Has this got anything to do with Dad?"

I inhaled deeply. "Why do you say that?"

"'Cause you say it's a surprise, and I can't think of anything that would be as surprising as going somewhere with Dad."

"You know that surprises can't be mentioned or they lose their specialness, so—" I mimicked zipping my lips.

Ajay was unimpressed. He rolled his eyes with slumped shoulders, like I'd asked him to repeat his homework three times, and picked through his clothes.

I left him to it and headed for my room. There was so much I wanted to take, mementos of a life I thought I had left behind when Dad went to jail, but now meant so much to me. This wasn't like leaving for another town. It wasn't even like moving to another country. How were we supposed to pack for leaving for another world?

I collapsed onto my bed and sunk my head to my chest. I didn't want to leave. I didn't want this reality. I didn't want to be a killer. But I was. I could never, never take that back. His sightless eyes would be the memory I carried until my death.

The desolation that welled in my stomach made my body feel heavy, my limbs useless. If only I could will myself away. I felt caged and desperate for breath. The compression on my chest made me gasp. Then the tears came. One long, silent stream absent when Dad was led away from the courtroom, when we stood aside for the vultures to pick over our possessions, when we moved into this beat-up rental, when I learned how to kill someone with my factional nature. But now they came, a wave so great it felt like my insides were emptying out. With the tears came all the pain of the last couple of months and all the pain of what was to come and all the pain of who I was and all the pain of what I was yet to do. I drowned and drowned, then sawed in horrible hacking breaths, then did it all over again and again until the bedcover was wet and inside of me felt dried out.

In the silence that followed my great outflow, I sat up and wiped the wet from my cheeks. Just like in Dominus, the clock was counting down. I had no time left to feel sorry for myself.

Chapter 36

"You sure you want to do this?"

"I have no choice."

"Once you take the grafter, there's no going back. You know that, don't you? Carter will hunt you down. He won't stop until he finds you and your family."

"Dad will protect Mum and Ajay."

Was Holden's sudden quiet a lack of faith in Dad succeeding or a lack of faith in me?

Rather than be consumed in his solid stare, I ran my eyes up the face of the Amex to where the windows turned from imposing to small squares as they disappeared up into the sky.

I didn't want to live life looking over my shoulder, fearing Carter's reprisals. More so, I didn't want Carter to win. I wasn't about to let him curse both our worlds into a living game of Dominus, curse me into being a soldier. Turning away now meant he'd won. "I'm going up."

"I can't come with you."

"I know. Just make sure you're here when I come down. I'll give you a ring when I've succeeded, so make sure you're ready. Once I get Mum and the grafter, we go get Ajay and Dad."

"Good luck. If you get in any trouble, call. I'll come and get you." His voice was strong, his words solid, but neither matched his grim smile.

He leaned down, angling his head close to mine, close enough I saw the radial patterning in his eyes, a lighter blue toward the center, deepening as it moved out. Motionless I stayed as he pressed his lips to mine, light, inquiring. A few seconds more and I pulled away. What was the intent behind that?

"Remember, call me if you need me."

He squeezed my hand as I pulled away farther. Why did I feel like we were parting for the last time?

Much like the Adolphy Tower, the interior of the Amex was extravagant and sleek. I skirted around cappuccino drinkers, their tables spilling across the smooth tiled floor, assailed by high-volume chatter and the addictive aroma of freshly brewed coffee, to the lifts. A double checked the shiny silver placard next to the lifts and confirmed I would find Hampton and Bougher on the fortieth floor.

I rode the lift alone, staring at the silver door, breathing deep into my stomach, then hitched my breath as the lift slowed to a stop. The doors slid open to a man waiting to enter. His eyes perused over me, halting at my face as eyebrows wandered up his forehead. Wearing denims, T-shirt, and trainers, I didn't look like I belonged here. He stood aside, giving me room to exit, while tracking me with his stare. Bot or human? *God, did I just think that?*

For a second, I flicked a glance to the left of my vision, curious about my power status bar, but, of course, there was nothing there. Nothing in my vision because that was particular to Dominus, but my factional nature was all me, and it stirred beneath the surface, the nudge running below the skirting of my skin. I turned my back on the guy who'd passed me into the lift and looked down my arms, expecting to see the skin ripple or glow, some visible manifestation of the surge I felt roiling below the surface. Was this what it meant to become your factional nature, to have the energy invade every part of your body?

At the end of a long, wide corridor with slate-gray carpet, smelling freshly laid, I found a small Asian lady tapping away on a keyboard and speaking into her black wireless headset. After a brief smile to let me know she wouldn't be long, she turned her head side on and dropped her voice. A high ponytail revealed bare skin unadorned of tattoos behind her right ear. Of course there would be nothing. Jesus, stupid. *Real world, Sable.*

Half tempted to drum my fingers on the desk, I resisted and instead turned away, staring back down the corridor to the lifts. There was always the chance to back out. But no one else was prepared to end Dominus.

"Can I help you?" came a friendly voice from behind me.

I spun back to face the receptionist. "I'm here to see Mrs. Cross."

A flicker of expression flared, then vanished so fast I couldn't attach an emotion. The instant jacked my pulse. I looked at the smooth, unmarred skin of her inner left wrist. But Holden had his tattoo removed when he first arrived in this world. *Get a grip. The enemy's one person, not everyone.*

"She works for Carter," I said because she'd not replied. And what was Carter's last name, Hampton, Bougher, or neither? "I think she's his personal secretary."

"Can I have your name?"

"I'm her daughter."

She blinked, twice, in rapid succession, which meant nothing. It couldn't. This was my guilty mind, me in freak-out mode.

"Please take a seat."

"Thank you."

I crossed the wide expanse to the three hard-backed plastic seats, which looked inappropriately placed along the long corridor with no other furniture to blend them into the decor. The seats were as welcoming as they looked, like the rest of the space, austere and sterile.

The rhythm of the woman's fingers tapping on the keyboard irritated the hell out of me, but only because my blood ran a marathon through my veins. I glanced to the lift once more then the other way, another long corridor leading farther into the devil's lair. Did it really take that long for someone to reach the reception desk from elsewhere in the office? Destruction played a nice tune along my skin. I could pull it out and strum awhile. But I was the sum total of my choices, not the victim.

Finally Mum came, looking every bit the competent secretary in her figure-fitting dark navy skirt and dusty pink shirt finished off with suitable office shoes. I inched to standing, watching her come toward me, looking like the woman she'd been when Dad still lived with us. Carter was right about one thing, Mum was finally living. This job gave her meaning, focus, passion. With each day, she developed a new skill, discovered her competency, and found her self-esteem. My heart skipped for the woman she was becoming yet fractured because of the man who gave her this gift.

"Honey, what are you doing here? Why aren't you in school?"

"I wanted to see you."

I accepted her hug with more enthusiasm than she gave and found it hard to let go. If I managed to succeed, we would be together. If I failed, we may never see each other again. Soon my hug became awkward. I had to let her go.

"Is everything all right?"

"I wasn't feeling well. The teacher sent me to the nurse's station, but she was busy, so I thought I'd go home, but I'm feeling better, so I came to see you."

I gave her my biggest smile so she would forget about the me-being-sick part and the weird way I'd greeted her.

"I want to see where you disappear to every day."

"Most normal teenagers couldn't care less where their mum went to work."

I shrugged. "I'm not normal." I headed the way she'd come. "Nice place." I glanced around like I thought the decor worth noting.

"It's great to see you, but I'm in the middle of a few things, honey. I'm not sure of the protocol for social visitors. I'm not sure if they have one."

"Carter won't mind. I think I should apologize for the way I acted the last time we met."

She grabbed my elbow, gently pulling me back toward her. "You're not going to make a scene, are you?"

"Why would I do that?"

"You're not exactly Carter's fan."

"Like you said, without his help, we'd be eating off the floor."

"Okay, but you can't stay long. I'm really busy."

"Can you give me a tour?"

"Sable—"

"Just a little one. Will you introduce me to Carter? I haven't met him properly yet."

"He's not here."

"He's not?" Fantastic luck. "When will he get back?"

"He's due back in half an hour, but don't think you're hanging around until then."

"I'll make sure I'm gone, don't worry."

How many people in this office were in on Carter's charade? How many would be fighters, armed with a special but lethal gift? Thinking like that filled me with jitters and lit a fuse under my factional nature. How many times had I been inside Dominus, four, five, and my factional nature was already tuned to fight? Of course it would be. I was destruction. You didn't go around handing out bouquets with such a time bomb writhing inside.

We rounded a corner to imposing double doors. To the left of those, a desk with little on it but a screen and keyboard.

"This is my station."

"It's tidy."

"We're a paperless office."

"So no messy desktops or filing cabinets."

"Not much of anything, as you can see."

It looked like a place to get bored real quick. My attention directed to the doors. "What's behind the doors?"

"Out of bounds."

"Carter's office?" I picked up my pace, heading for the doors. Half an hour—less now—that's all I had. I couldn't help but flick a quick look to the right of my vision. *Stop it. You're not in Dominus.* A digital countdown would be handy though.

"Out of bounds, young lady."

"Just one peek inside."

Having never been good at laying firm boundaries, she shadowed me to the door.

At the door, I paused, hand on the silver knob. "I bet it's impressive." I beamed a broad smile conjured out of nowhere because there was nothing inside of me wanting to smile. "Just one peek."

Mum held up a finger. "One. And don't touch anything."

As expected, his office was bigger than our rental, with an expansive window, which made the room appear as though it flowed out onto the rooftops of the adjacent buildings.

"Wow, impressive." I stepped into the room.

"Yes, wow. Now you've seen it, let's go."

"I'll be a good girl. I promise." I flashed her a smile as I continued into the room. If I moved in far enough, she'd stop pretending she could turn me around.

"I'm going to need Carter's schedule for the launch tomorrow." We both jumped at the sound of an intruding voice. A woman stood in the entrance, dwarfed by the shear size of the doors. Her deep green eyes settled on me even though she'd spoken to Mum. A quick shot of adrenaline burned its way through my stomach, igniting a tickle running along my skin. I forced myself not to look at my arms, though I was sure the skin would be rippling with the disturbance underneath. The woman's long, straight hair hung forward over her shoulders, covering the skin behind her right ear, and a fitted jacket of deep green kept the secret on her wrist well hidden. If there was any secret to be found there.

"Oh...umm...sure." Mum glanced at me, hesitant, then glanced back at the woman. "Sure."

Attention back to me, she gave a small jerk of her head in the direction I should go, as in out the door.

"It's fine, Mum, I don't want to interfere with your work."

I beamed another smile when two forks indented between her eyes, and held up my hands. "I'm a good girl."

She flared her eyes and gave me a meaningful look, which said, *We'll be talking once I get rid of this woman,* then hurried out of the office.

The numbers on the digital clock would be flipping down in rapid succession had I been in Dominus.

A horseshoe-shaped office desk with loads of draws, an imposing leather suite centered around a weirdly designed coffee table, a bookcase wall filled with volumes behind which you could hide a safe. A dozen places to look.

Holden had never mentioned a safe. I'd thought of it, and a good place to hide a safe was behind a painting, like the large one behind his desk. Large enough to make it immovable, but also to make it inconvenient to reach when you wanted to get inside.

The carpet muffled my hurried steps to the set of draws on the left. The first wouldn't open. Something to hide? But I'd try the rest before I took up time busting in. I wrenched the next, expecting it locked as well, and the draw flew out, spilling its contents on the floor. "God dammit," I hissed. The horror of what I'd done echoed through my chest.

I fell to the floor, scooping up handfuls of draw junk. Out of a short-lived habit, I flicked another glance to the right frame of my vision, then squeezed my eyes shut. *Real world, Sable.* Was there no clock in here anywhere? Not on the desk.

Forget the mess.

The rest opened to nothing interesting. Stepping over the mess, I yanked open every other draw, my thumping heart growing louder with each failed search. Before I could stop myself, I darted a look to the absent digital clock, no numbers counting me down, but time still disappeared.

I raced across the room to the shelving, shifting books aside as I skimmed along the rows. This was ridiculous. The top draw was the only logical place.

I crossed back to the desk. Treading on draw junk, I yanked the top draw a couple of times. Each time it caught on the lock, my frustration arced. On my knees, I searched through the mess on the floor and then the next draw down for anything that could act as a lock pick. Finding nothing, I sat back on my heels. A slither of destruction. That's all it would take. A cry welled in my throat at the thought, as a greedy sensation filled my heart. But before I could caress the surface of my factional nature, my eyes settled on a thin seam, door sized, running down the wall adjacent to the desk.

The sniff of success gave me wings to cross the room in a nanosecond. Close up, I found a small square panel, colored white to blend with the wall.

The softest sound of fabric rubbing against fabric stilled my hand as I reached for the panel. Draw stuff all over the floor, me caught snooping, how did I explain this to Mum? I looked over my shoulder. But I didn't find her.

Chapter 37

RESTING on the corner of his desk, arms crossed over his chest, Carter looked like a school principal ready to delve out punishment. He'd closed the door behind him when he entered, shutting me in and Mum out. A captive, caged, forced to endure the dissection of his eyes, the malicious creep of his smile. "Predictable."

One word backed with a punch, which hit me square in the gut.

How fast could I harness my factional nature? How fast could Carter harness his? If I acted too fast, I'd lose control of destruction. Mum. She was on the other side of the door. Too close. And what if the grafter wasn't even behind this door?

"I'm waiting."

Sweet Jesus. I was screwed.

"Your mother said you were here to apologize."

"You're not going to play that game?"

"Only because it seems you are."

He slid off his desk and headed around to his chair. "I'm flattered you should care so much about my feelings." He gazed down at the draw discarded and the mess on the floor.

Eyebrows arched, he glanced up at me. "You have been a naughty girl. I'd expect no less from Nixon's offspring." He waved a hand toward one of the seats on my side of the desk. "Please sit. There's something I want to talk about."

"I can hear it standing."

He didn't bother to disguise the smirk. "Suit yourself," he said as he slid down into his seat.

Elbows on armrests, he entwined his fingers, rested them on his stomach, and leaned back into his chair. "I'm curious. What does it feel like to kill?"

So unexpected, the question slammed into me. "You're such an asshole." Restless energy roiled within, feeling like a wild sea. A powerful wave surged over the top. I could end him now. A nudge, an open stream and I could feed what he'd wanted from me into him. I could win.

It would be so easy. "You're a lying cheat." It would feel so good to let destruction free.

"Harsh words from a girl who never knew what her father was for seventeen years."

It would end the suffering.

"You would know what it's like, so why don't you tell me?"

"You're mistaking me for your father."

It would end me.

Killing once could be an accident. Killing twice was a pattern. There would be no finish to what I began.

I closed my eyes as I sunk inward, funneling down into the deep pit now forming at the well of my soul. There was no more left of me to strip bare. I was already raw.

"You have a fair amount of innate skill. Has Jax told you that? Few would make it through level five without the necessary skill. Recruits take years to train. Level seven, now that's impressive. I thought we'd lose you. Instead you lost someone else."

Every moment spent with him forced me closer to who I was. But every word he spoke reminded me of who I'd become. A barb speared into my soul.

Carter swept out of his seat. "Don't shut down, Sable, thrive." He approached, the eagerness lengthening his strides. "You have what it takes. It's instinct, yet more. A will of steel, uncompromising."

TERINA ADAMS

"You want weapons."

"I want soldiers. Selfless service, duty, honor, loyalty, the belief in what is right, the courage to see it through."

"Mindless determination, soulless decisions, heartless actions."

He pulled back, slipped his hands in the pockets of his jeans. "There is only one way to win."

"You're so willing to destroy so many."

"Nixon did wrong by you. He should've told you the truth. Opened your eyes, then maybe you wouldn't be so naive. You can't bring change by playing nice."

"And you won't create loyalty by ruthless control."

"No, you create fear, which is more powerful."

"You should've read our history books. They're full of people like you who spent the rest of their lives growing insane with paranoia. You'll only breed hatred amongst the people of your world."

"That is not something I need be concerned about."

I stepped back as he continued closer, then to the side when I realized he was heading for the concealed door. One press of the white panel and it opened to reveal a drinks cabinet inside.

"Talking is thirsty work. You want one?" He didn't stop to see if I nodded, instead grabbed the scotch and poured himself a shot. Drink in hand, he returned to his desk, leaving the concealed door wide open to show how stupid I'd been. Stupid, Stupid imbecile. Did I really think I stood a chance? That I could've outsmarted him? If Dad had told the truth all along, I would be smarter, stronger, better able to face him, defeat him, but I would also be like him.

"Jax and Holden know what your real plan is."

Carter downed the scotch in one gulp, then sat heavily in his seat. Once he slammed his glass down on his desk, he said, "Of course they do. But they understand the significance of Dominus. Unlike you, they know what it means to live as we do." He sat forward. "Don't ever think you have an ally in Jax. It's one thing you must learn, my girl, if you are to survive in my world. You can trust no one. Do you think Jax is your friend? That he really cares for you, a Persal? That in all of this, he will stand by you?" He eased himself back. "As for Holden, I'm not worried about Nixon's dog. He is one against many. Besides, Nixon keeps the

318

leash tight because he knows what I will do if Holden interferes with my plans. But you're a rogue. Someone I've kept an eye on. I'm afraid you've chosen the wrong man to betray." His feet went up onto the desk, elbows back on the armrests, fingers entwined. "Did you think you would succeed with this ridiculous plan of yours?"

He could not have known. Which could only mean… I didn't want to believe it. Holden would not have betrayed me, which left Jax, the only other person besides Dad and Holden I had told.

"One day you will learn to trust no one but yourself. It's the only way to get things done. It's the only way to survive."

The door clicked open. A solid guy in a pinstriped suit led Ajay inside. *Sweet Jesus, Ajay.* My heart thumped so hard I swore it would punch out of my rib cage. He knew everything, which was why he'd brought him here. I searched the pinstriped guy for the telltale sign. Sure enough, it was there behind his right ear. Aris, easy to see with his short-cropped hair. He was from my world but had tattooed himself a loyal supporter of Aris, of Carter.

Carter lowered his feet from his desk. "Here he is. Sable and I were just having a conversation about you. Weren't we, Sable?"

"Hey, buddy." I threw open my arms to draw him near, meeting him halfway across the room.

"What are you doing here?"

I snagged him close for a hug, ignoring his question, and stared over the top of his head to Carter. There was so much hatred inside of me, amplified by the ever-restless desire of destruction, but the strength that gave was not enough to overcome my emptiness. My glare would've been hateful if I'd not felt cored out and defeated by deceit.

"Now all we need is the mother and it's one happy family. If you come here, Ajay, I may have something for you."

He unlocked the top draw with a key from his pocket and motioned for Ajay to come and look inside. I kept my hand on Ajay's shoulder and squeezed it tight when he went to move.

"Ouch." Ajay yanked his shoulder from under my hold.

"You don't need anything from Carter, Ajay."

"Why not?" He was already walking away as he asked the question.

A pressure built within my head, pushed against my rib cage and down along my arms. I couldn't, not now, not with Ajay here. If I released destruction, I could lose everything. Carter would win. He could shift; Ajay couldn't.

Carter watched me while Ajay came around to his side of his desk. The eyes of the shark were back, the ultimate predator. They glistened with triumph, gloating over my defeat.

"Oh, cool." Ajay drew the last word out and all but dived into the draw to retrieve whatever Carter hid in there.

My heart exploded in my chest when Ajay pulled out what looked like a gun—a fat, bulky gun. Carter took it gently from Ajay's hand and placed it on the desk.

"I believe, Sable, you were looking for this."

The grafter. I stared at it like it was the holy grail while swallowing my heart back down.

"What is it?" Ajay's enthusiasm made Carter laugh.

"It's not a toy, I'm afraid. It's a valuable piece of equipment. Priceless beyond measure. You could say it's the secret weapon the bad guys are after. That's why it's so important we keep it safe." He winked at me.

Standing beside Carter, eyes saucered as he stared at the grafter, Ajay looked innocent, vulnerable, blackmail for my good behavior, an example of my failure. It was too much. My anger burned a hole through my heart right down to my stomach. The acid then poured out to liquefy my muscles; I couldn't move.

I shredded Carter with my stare while my mind zinged about, wildly thinking up plans. No tri-blade at my belt, destruction was my only weapon, but it was too risky with Ajay in the room and the way I felt. Death for Carter was too good. *Please don't let it be because of me.* I had a kill quota of one in real life. I'd trade my soul for success if I reached two.

If I could shift, I would grab Ajay and launch for the grafter, but that left Mum behind. Holden waited down below, which didn't help because I had no way of alerting him that Carter wouldn't see.

"Why is Ajay here?"

"Ajay's here for instructional purposes." Carter ruffled his hair. My hand itched to slap his away. Ajay's nose wrinkled but he kept still.

"Is this the surprise you were talking about?" Ajay said, once Carter stopped messing with his hair.

I frowned at him, meaning *shut up*, but I doubted he got the message. I wanted him over here with me. "No. That was something else. Where's Mum?" I said to Carter.

"Running an errand for me. She won't be long, but it's not necessary for her to be here. I think we can come to an understanding without involving your mother." He quirked an eyebrow as if that added extra weight to his threat. "Close to eighteen years I've been here, in between reinforcing my presence in my own world, of course. That's how long it's taken for me to reach this far. In the meantime, I've built a successful empire. This world has been good to me. But I have never lost sight of my goal. It means too much." He rose from his seat and came around to lean back on the front of his desk. "Did you really think I would let anyone prevent me from succeeding? I will forgive your little stunt because of your naivety. You cannot understand the importance of what I hope to achieve."

"The only people who will benefit from this are Aris."

"You say that because you do not know the laws of our world, what the senate have done to the people."

I looked to Ajay when Carter said *world*. At least he might think Carter was nuts.

No one, no matter how young, would miss the tension brewing in the room. "Ajay, come here." I waved him over because the tension was strumming my nerves. I needed Ajay near me.

"When's Mum coming?"

Carter looked over his shoulder. "Soon, my little buddy."

"You've proved your point. It's time he left."

In my periphery, the pinstriped guy flexed. I glanced over to see him position himself in front of the door, a show of force. Carter wanted Ajay to stay.

"I'm sure Ajay would like to hear the parts of the conversation that involve him."

"You've got nothing to say that's worth him hearing."

"On the contrary—"

We all glanced toward the door as it opened, bumping Carter's man aside. I expected Mum, or someone else from the building. Instead my eyes met Jax.

My emotions jumbled up into pieces. A burst of relief, but someone had betrayed my plans to Carter. Please let it not be Jax, but there was no one else. I wanted to have hope, but I couldn't keep lying to myself. Had his vulnerability on the rooftop the other night been a lie?

"Jax. What a pleasant surprise, and what perfect timing."

Ajay shifted his eyes from Jax to me to Carter, no doubt trying to connect the dots.

Jax sauntered over. He flicked a glance at the grafter, then at Carter; he'd yet to look at me. Could it be guilt kept his eyes from meeting mine?

"I was unaware of any meetings." Was this him playing a game for my benefit? If he'd orchestrated the deceit, why play around like this?

"An impromptu one. But I'm glad you've arrived. There are a few issues I wish to clear up."

The way Carter spoke, he didn't sound like he was expecting Jax either. I glared at Jax, hoping the intensity would travel the distance to him and irritate him enough to look my way. Perhaps naïve, but I believed if I could look in his eyes, I would know if he was the one who betrayed me. But if not him, who else? Elva had been around when I'd disappeared upstairs to the roof. Maybe she'd overheard.

Jax refused to meet my glare; instead he sat in the chair opposite Carter and slouched back like a rebellious child. He pulled some coins from his pocket. "Ajay, there's a vending machine on the ground floor. Perhaps you could get me something to drink."

He flipped Ajay a coin.

"Ajay doesn't need to go that far. I've got plenty here. Besides, I think it best he's involved in the conversation. I see no point in keeping Dominus a secret any more. We're all one big family."

"What's Dominus?" Ajay asked with keen interest.

"It's nothing. Something for adults." My legs twitched to move.

I glanced at Jax. He tapped his steepled fingers on his chin, reminding me of a lethal predator biding its time before it struck. Seeing him galvanized the fight within me. I wanted to scratch out Carter's eyes, see if he retained his smug smile.

The air thinned with tension. The barriers holding my destruction within rattled with the fear and desperation welling inside of me. My power status bar would be red, I'm sure. Dad had always taught me to believe in myself, and I hadn't. He'd said I had to go deep within if I wanted to be the best. Any emotion that held me back, I was to face it, hold it, befriend it, breathe it, become it, and only then would I control it. Only once I became that which I avoided the most could I then master it.

I turned my attention inside, felt the heat of destruction caress along my mind, soothe down my body, tingling and exciting all my nerve endings. There was no need for me to funnel my power down into my body to keep it harnessed, as Holden had once taught me, for it was already everywhere within me, snaking its way along my back, down my neck, around my muscles, and down to my feet. The fine hairs on my body stood erect as every part of me zapped alive, because destruction was my tool.

I was still unsure whose side Jax was on, which meant I had to do this on my own and allow him to reveal his intentions.

I had one chance to do this right.

My pulse thudded through my ears as I gathered destruction and focused on tunneling it outward in a single stream toward Carter's desk. I gritted my teeth with the energy it took to restrain the amount of force that came through.

A fissure ran down the middle of the desk, then it exploded into pieces with a loud *crack*. The computer torpedoed into the wall behind while chunks of wood splintered outward like mini spears. In the chaos, I dived for Ajay, who'd thrown himself to the floor with lightning reflexes.

"Jax, the grafter."

Please be on my side.

It didn't need to be said. The grafter had also launched into the air and lay on the other side of the room. Jax was across the room in seconds and scooped it up.

For one horrible moment, our eyes locked, time seized, my breath too. Was my belief in him my greatest mistake?

"Take it."

He threw it at me. As it left his hand, his eyes changed. Red began to soak his irises as he became bloodlust. A roar from behind and I spun to see the guy who'd escorted Ajay into the room pounding across the floor, lost in his own factional nature. Jax and the guy collided midair with a sickening crunch of bone. I grabbed the grafter and pulled Ajay close as Carter climbed to his feet and threw the desk that had landed on him aside, shattering its legs into the window. His bloodshot eyes glared wildly around. How sane were Aris during bloodlust?

I tried to cover Ajay's eyes—after what he'd already witnessed, it was too late—and tunneled my ability, focusing on the back wall. As I released destruction, I sucked a little back, creating an inward vacuum, forcing the wall to explode inward. Large chunks flung forward amongst the billowing fine powder and pummeled down on Carter.

I had to get Ajay out of here.

Jax and the other guy were locked in a merciless battle. Conscious of Ajay by my side, I spun him around to shield him from the terrible sight of Aris in motion. I could protect him from seeing, but I could not blanket the sound of fighting, the agonizing cries of pain, the guttural howls of fury. I didn't want to leave Jax, but Ajay was my priority.

I ran for the door as a chunk of plaster embedded in the wall close to the exit. I dragged Ajay low as Carter bellowed his rage.

The door opened and a man stepped in and froze on seeing the chaos inside. Two security guys came barreling up behind him, but the guy blocked the doorway, trying desperately to escape back the way he'd come.

My mind spun ahead a million seconds an hour, making plans to get out. The door was blocked by the idiot, so I made an exit by redirecting the destruction within and blasted a hole through the wall in front of me. This time I forced all my destruction outward, raining debris down into the next room. The guy sitting behind his desk dove for the floor and crawled under his desk.

"You gotta go, Ajay. Take this." I shoved the grafter into his hand. I pulled my phone from my pocket, flicked through my contacts until I found Holden's number. "When you're in the lift, call this number. The guy's name is Holden. He's tall with blond hair. He's waiting outside the building. Tell him he must take you away. See here." Again I scrolled through my contacts list. "This is Mum's number. Ring her and tell her you're down on the street below waiting for her. Make sure she comes to meet you. Holden must take both of you with him. Do you understand?"

He shook his head. "What's going on?"

"I can't tell you now. Just do this for me, please."

Ajay pressed his lips firmly, then yelled, "No."

I yanked him toward me and shouted at him. "Don't be a baby, Ajay. Dad didn't raise a baby. Dad would never approve." I was being a bitch, but I had to make Ajay listen. "Be strong like Dad taught you. Get Mum, then get out." I shoved him away hard. "Go. I've got to help Jax. Holden will take you somewhere safe, where I can meet you. You can trust him."

He froze in fear, eyes welling with tears.

"Please, Ajay, you've got to do this. And don't give that to anyone but Holden. He'll make sure you're safe."

I shoved him again. He stumbled, then turned and ran.

Chapter 38

CARTER'S LOOK of triumph was not a pleasant sight. *I could end you.* The thought like a drug, but I would kill what was good about myself.

On the ground in front of Carter was the guy who'd blocked the door, possibly out cold, or dead. The two security guards lay next to him; blood pooled around the middle of one guard. Playing Dominus, I'd seen enough blood, but this was not a game. The other security guard lay on his side. Apart from his woozy, uncoordinated attempts to sit up, he appeared fine.

The bloodlust had drained from Carter's face. He looked calm and in control. "It's time we slowed this down."

Large gashes tracked from Jax's face down his throat. His shirtfront was slashed and colored crimson red. Hopefully most of that was from the other Aris, but judging by the way he wavered when the guy released him, he had to be in pain. Any minute, I expected him to crash to the floor. A small justice came when his opponent, looking somewhat worse off than Jax, collapsed to his knees and coughed up blood. I turned away, not wanting to see. This was Carter's doing—the satisfaction he must gain from seeing us fight without humanity in our soul.

I glanced at Jax. He looked out of his one good eye, the other fast closing. Blood trailed into his bad eye from a long, deep tear above his eyebrow.

"You cannot win, Sable. You must know that."

"My chance of success is as likely as yours." *Because I could end you now.*

Sweet Jesus, don't think it. Don't let this become you.

"And what do you hope to achieve? You've turned my best against me, but he is one amongst an army."

"Do you really think Persal recruits will stay faithful to you? You'll lose control of this fight."

Conscious of Ajay making his escape, I had to keep Carter chatting. Ajay needed time to get Mum and find Holden.

"They will remain loyal long enough to complete the goal I set for them. I've found the minds of your kind particularly susceptible to brainwashing. You were not in Dominus long enough to benefit from the tweaks I made to the game, but most others have played for years. My view is the only view they have. They are incapable of questioning their actions."

I looked to Jax, but his face was too much a bloody mess for me to tell if he knew or not. Likely not.

Carter looked at Jax. "Unfortunately, my tweaks do not work on those from my world." He focused on me. "So, you see, it's hopeless. As we speak, recruits from around the world are converging to the warehouse. Tyren is waiting there to greet them. At any time, I can signal the beginning."

"It was Tyren who told you I was coming here." The relief washed out through my voice. Elva was also innocent.

Carter's answer was a smirk.

Not only was I overjoyed it wasn't Jax, I was also weirdly pleased it wasn't Elva. She still hated me, but I admired her loyalty to Holden. To betray me was a betrayal to Holden. I needed at least one person in this screwed-up reality Carter had created to act with integrity. Besides Jax, I'd pinned my hopes on Elva; I wanted to believe love could mean that much. Somehow this revelation settled the destruction inside of me from a turbulent storm to a few gusty winds. "I thought it was Elva."

"The bitch has a loyalty problem."

"I've never found her loyalty lacking." Jax staggered toward me, then stopped and rested a hand on his knee for support while he struggled to take a breath. I took his arm, indicating I was willing to take his weight. He looked up at me. "Elva warned me of what Tyren overheard last night and of what he told Carter."

"Perhaps we should all sit down and relax. My men will arrive soon with your brother and mother. And Holden too, I hope."

If the ground cracked open and swallowed me up, I would welcome the escape. Was there no end to Carter's reach? He huffed a triumphant laugh at the expression I portrayed. *It would be a pleasure to wipe that from your face.* But not the way I wanted to. I would not sacrifice myself for what he desired.

"Only now do you learn the extent of my power. In fact, this is only the beginning. With one call, I can end your family, little girl. Just like dear old Dad. Jax tell you about that? How Nixon killed his dad for betrayal, then went on to eliminate the rest of his family because killing one wasn't enough?"

"It was you all along." Jax's voice was weak. The effort it took for him to speak was written across his ruined face. "You pinned your betrayal on my father. The way I see it, you're as guilty of their deaths as he."

A man appeared at the door wearing black combat fatigues. Jesus, he had his own SWAT team, more lethal than anything the government could provide. Hair razored to his scalp, his tattoo was clear for anyone to see, a broken circle, Persal, one of my own, brainwashed to see only Carter's truth. Unlike me, he would perhaps attack without thought to anyone in the building.

With a jerk of his head, he motioned for Carter to join him out in the corridor. Undecided at first, Carter glanced to us, his expression tight. He didn't want to leave us. Likely deciding what the guy had to say more important, he stormed across the room and out into the corridor, making sure to position himself where he could see us.

As if only Carter's presence had held him up, Jax sank to his knees. I crouched with him.

"Jax, you've got to get out of here. There's no point in the two of us staying."

"I won't leave you."

With the hem of my shirt, I wiped some of the blood from his good eye so he could see better. "Don't try and be heroic. Just be safe."

"You have no way of getting yourself out of here."

"Neither will you if you stay any longer. You're bleeding too much. You'll lose your strength. I doubt whether Carter will be forgiving."

Jax's head drooped, shoulders following. The other Aris lay on the ground, his chest rising and falling.

"I have to make sure Ajay and Mum got away. I can't go with you."

Finding some strength, he looked me in the eye. "I'm not leaving you."

This is what loyalty meant. Something Carter didn't understand, didn't care about.

"I won't be long."

Carter's conversation wasn't going well, hands gesticulating, the other guy standing back like he expected Carter to explode. Seeing his anger fed fire into my belly. If Carter was upset, something had gone wrong with his plan. There was hope.

I left Jax half kneeling on the floor and ran to the wall, sliding myself along until I reached the door, then inched my head around. Carter's voice was low, a loaded threat. Elsewhere noises of chaos as people yelled, crashed about, tried desperately to evacuate from something they had to believe was a terrorist attack. Good thing too, but I needed to make sure everyone had gone. I scanned the area around Mum's desk, then back down the corridor. What I looked for was on the wall near the entrance to the lift.

This would take precision and a lot of pain holding destruction in, but I could do it. My dad had said so. I focused inward and touched the thread of my factional nature. It flared up in response, eager to wreak havoc. I clenched my teeth with the effort it took to release a fraction of my potential. Using my finger as a directional guide, I pointed to the small red box mounted on the wall, feeding a snippet of my destruction along my finger in one thin shaft straight down the corridor. The glass of the box shattered, releasing the alarm.

No one fled from the rooms because they'd all been smart enough to escape when the fighting first began. However, the alarm would sound around the building, initiating a mass exodus, perhaps not the entire building, but at least the immediate floors below.

My eyes locked with the deep green of Carter's. His mouth opened as his face screwed up about to yell something, but I was pinwheeling backward into the room, back toward Jax as the doorframe splintered behind me.

Something thumped across my shoulders, punched the wind from my lungs, and sent me sprawling across the carpet. A sharp burn singed my chin as I grazed my face along the carpet. I pushed up, coughing, gasping for air I couldn't suck in.

"Jax, give me your phone," I gasped, then turned over onto my back to see someone who was supposed to be my family, a Persal—loyalty thicker than blood, or so I'd repeatedly been told by everyone—stride through the remains of the door toward me, destruction in his eyes.

No thought, just instinct. I funneled another splinter of my power, ripping the carpet at my feet, sending it up into the air in a long sheet to descend on the guy now pounding toward us. Power released, I half turned to Jax. "Cell." My voice come out nothing more than a squeak.

The carpet exploded into strips as something small hit me on the arm.

I crawled backward on my ass, swiping the phone as I went. The guy strode through the falling strips of carpet.

"Is that all you're going to give me?"

I looked at the cell screen. "Password," I squeaked to Jax, gasping breaths because my lungs still wouldn't work how they ought to.

The guy darted his eyes over me to Jax. "You should see the state of your boyfriend. He ain't looking too pretty."

Jax's broken voice came to me as I continued to shuffle backward on my ass, reciting six numbers that sounded like the hardest things for him to say.

Behind our tormentor, Carter sauntered through. "It's a shame to lose competent players. You, I'm not too sad about, but it wounds me to say goodbye to my game master."

I lay backward onto the floor and stared at the ceiling, a long way up. This time it wasn't a nudge, a gentle tug, a slow release. I sent destruction up and yanked that sucker down. The explosive force shot backward as a roar filled my ears. I rolled onto my stomach as bits of ceiling came down. Shielding my head with my hands, I peered ahead to Jax as a jagged spear of plaster smashed down beside him.

I'd pulled part of the ceiling down without thought, down on us as well as them. The air filled with a cloud of debris and fine powder, clogging my throat, blocking my nose as pieces of plaster pummeled my back and tore through the skin on my arms.

Jax was right behind me, one eye swollen closed, the other a slit filled with blood. White had settled around him, through his hair, a coating of powder clinging to the blood on his face. Thankfully most of the chunks of plaster had found me, missing him. The tear above his eye was an ugly weeping wound. He'd collapsed down onto his side, propped up by an elbow, head sunk as blood dripped from his nose to the carpet, soaking through the moment it hit. Another dark stain pooled around his middle from wounds hidden under his shirt, wounds better not seen—or else I would fall apart.

I forced my eyes away, swallowed the panic down into my belly, and punched the code into the phone, then Mum's number once I had access.

Jax barely moved. He would have nothing left in him to shift to safety.

Two rings and Mum answered. "Who is this?"

Someone coughed behind me. "The last dying fight of the helpless." Carter coughed again.

"Mum."

"Sable, where are you? What's going on?"

"Are you and Ajay with Holden?"

Jax lifted his head, his face a hand's reach from my own.

"Sable, tell me what is going on."

"I applaud your effort. But I cannot let it go unpunished." Behind me, Carter crunched his way through the debris.

"Just tell me," I said into the phone.

I looked at Jax. He met my eyes, and I fed into my stare my plan, which wasn't the best way to tell him, considering what I was about to do. *Please have the energy to make this work.*

"Sable, I want to know what's going on."

"Tell me."

"Yes, yes, I am. I don't understand what—"

I ended the call and gripped his cell in my hand.

"Jax," I whispered. "Take my hand." On my elbows, I crawled closer to him.

"You will be a lesson to anyone else who chooses their own path."

I looked over my shoulder to see Carter had made his way to within yards of us.

"You've won, okay?" I said, hoping to placate anything the Persal guy could think to do in retaliation as I pulled myself closer to Jax. Close enough I hugged him to me as I slipped his cell into his back jeans pocket.

Carter sighed. "This is a pitiable sight."

He was covered in white. It dusted along his eyelashes and formed an arc below his eyes. Blood trickled from a small cut left of his mouth. Other than that, he looked unharmed.

I turned to Jax. His head was bowed, so I lifted his face to meet my eyes with a finger under his chin. This wasn't going to work. One look at him, and I knew it wasn't going to work. But this was our last chance, our only choice. When I was sure he was looking, I nodded once.

"Your end will come sooner than you think," I said, staring up at Carter.

I released my destruction.

Chapter 39

I WAS COMPRESSED into Jax by the shockwave of the explosion as it flung us outward, away from the blast. Hot wind blasted across my face, suffocating in its speed. The heat scorched to my lungs, but it soon turned to an icy-cold chill, freezing me inside.

Flashes of kaleidoscopic color flittered through my vision. It hurt to look, so I closed my eyes and clung on to Jax, my only solid connection, while we were buffeted and tossed in free fall to our deaths or somewhere else? Had Jax been strong enough to get us out?

After the wild lashings of the wind, the roar of it rushing past my ears, the impossibility of breathing, the sudden quiet slammed into us. Tranquility and silence, coupled with the sudden cessation of movement and the cold, cold creep of a smooth, hard surface underneath and I opened my eyes.

A white floor, white walls, sparsely furnished room. I hitched to one elbow. Jax lay on his back, a fast-spreading pool of his blood turning the high-polish stone floor a bloody mess.

"Jax." I scrambled toward him, my hand touching his first, feeling the warmth still on his skin. Thank god. "Jax." I was over him now, peering down into his shut eye, then to his chest, searching for the rise and fall of life, but his chest was too much of a bloody mess to see. This close, there was only the metallic smell of blood. One hand at his cheek, I called his name again. "Jax."

"Give me a minute." Words slurred and faint.

"What can I do to help? Can I get someone?"

His hand touched my side.

"Do they have ambulances here? Is there a number I can call for help?"

"Bed."

It was only meters away, but without his help, I wouldn't stand a chance.

"We need to stop the bleeding."

"Bed," he whispered again.

"It's going to hurt."

He rolled, grimacing, but kept the groans in. Watching him ease himself upright onto one hand and his agony was my own, his moves slow, with a lot of effort. I slid under his shoulder, inching him up to standing. It took eternity, a lot of blood on me and the floor, before I could help lower him down onto his black sheets, where he sat, head bowed, hands hanging limp on the bed.

"I need to stop the bleeding," I said as I moved to the bottom of the bed and gathered the top sheet into a ball.

It made a terrible bandage around his middle, and he had no strength to press it in place. I had to remove his shirt and take a proper look. Through the shredded strips, I saw vicious torn flesh and gaping wounds.

"I don't know what to do, Jax. I know nothing about this world."

"Bathroom, there's a cabinet."

A clumsy wave of his hand pointed me to the adjacent wall. At first I thought the pain of his wounds and subsequent blood loss confused him, leaving him without strength to give me proper directions, but I tried it all the same, walking toward the wall. I was within feet when the edges of the door appeared. It sunk inward, then slid aside with a soft vacuum-sealing sound. Inside, the walls shimmered an aqua blue like the sun's rays on the ocean. If I stared hard enough for long enough, I swore I'd see some fish moving not far below the surface. I stared down through the basin to the white floor below. Captured inside the glass—

perhaps—were weird three-dimensional geometric shapes like fossils embedded in rock, preserved for eternity.

Bottles, creams, anything that looked like it belonged in a first-aid bag, I swiped from the cabinet shelves, gathering them in the cradle I formed using the hem of my shirt. On the way out, I grabbed a towel slung over the handrail.

Jax remained where I'd put him, although his head had sunk lower. I inverted the cradle I'd made of my shirt, dumping my gathered supplies next to him and placing the towel beside them.

"You'll have to help me here. Nothing looks familiar."

Jax turned his head, peering down at the assortment of supplies. "The bottles."

I sifted through everything else, pulling each bottle out and holding the labels faceup for him to see.

"The red label."

I dropped the others and unscrewed the lid on the one he'd selected to find small white pills inside.

"Do you need water? They look small enough to swallow dry, but I'll go find a glass if you want."

A slow shake of his head, so I tapped a few out onto my palm, my dirty palm, but there was no time to worry about racing back to the bathroom to wash my hands.

"Two," he said, which I took to mean *feed them to me*.

I slipped them on his tongue, and he grimaced as they went down. The stream of blood down his throat rippled as he swallowed.

"I need to lie down."

"I should clean and bandage your wounds first."

He shook his head. "I'd rather lie down."

"Jax, I need to take a proper look at your wounds. They could be deep. You'll get a bad infection if you don't bleed dry first."

"It's okay." His voice grew softer. "I need to rest."

Rest and never wake up. "I'm afraid if you close your eyes, you'll never open them again."

He lowered himself down, which spurred me forward to help him. Damn him. He was so stubborn, and I was not about to fight with a badly wounded guy. I surrendered and eased him down onto his pillow.

The bottles and other supplies clanged together as we moved about on the bed.

"The pills were coagulants." He inhaled before he spoke again. "Fast-acting. Give me the white-labelled bottle."

I sat back and rummaged through the remaining brown bottles. "There's two." I brought them up close to read the label. "I think they're the same thing."

"Give me one."

The pills were large oval tablets like something you'd give livestock, not humans, large enough to stick halfway in your throat without half a glass of water to flush them down. Jax didn't appear to care, opening his mouth like a baby waiting for the spoon.

I slipped it onto his tongue and he crunched it up before swallowing. "Painkillers." The parts of his face not swollen, bruised, or torn reflected the horrible taste. "It will take effect soon."

"Is that all? I feel I should do something else. Maybe clean your wounds, stitch something."

He slowly shook his head. "No, give me some time to rest."

The sight of him made it hard for me to resist falling into action. I slid onto the bed, moving up to rest back against the wall, giving Jax the silence he needed. The fight, Carter's triumphant sneer, and the explosion reeled through my mind when I closed my eyes. Mum and Ajay were safe. That was all that mattered. Dad I'd free in time, once I managed to contact Holden, once Jax had recovered.

I rested my forehead on my arms and accepted the firestorm of memories and images so real I could be experiencing them over and over again. I'd felt as desperate and panicked as I'd done in Dominus. The whole scene we'd just played out felt like nothing more than a level in the game. The game had poisoned me. Carter had poisoned me. Dad had poisoned me; he'd been a part of Dominus too.

The feel of Jax's hand touching my side drew me out of my macabre thoughts. On his back, he looked up at me through his one good eye.

"Oh my god," I said as I turned to my side and peered down on his face. "The wound over your eye looks much better. It's not bleeding anymore."

"That's the pills at work."

I looked down his body. It was half-concealed by the sheet I'd bunched at his waist in a useless attempt to stem the bleeding.

"I'll be fine," he said, catching where my gaze fell. "You should know Carter will still be alive."

I blew out a breath and looked away. "I thought as much."

"He would've shifted the moment we did."

Maybe it was a good thing. I didn't want to build my kill quota.

"At least Mum and Ajay escaped. Would Holden bring them here? Maybe he freed Dad first. They'll be at Persal HQ, I guess, or Holden's apartment. Does he have one?"

Jax closed his one good eye.

"Sorry, I'm asking too many questions."

"I don't know where Holden would go. Persal HQ is not a good choice to take your mum and Ajay, unless he plans on uncovering Carter's plan. Unlike Dominus, the place will be full of people. Real-life people, not bots. There's no way he will be able to hide them. Without tattoos, they are easily spotted as foreign. It's also likely he's taken them to his place, which is in the Persal quarter of Califax."

"How will we know?"

"Factions only communicate through work portals. Carter and Nixon devised a means of communicating personally beyond the normal channels. If Holden's listening in, I could contact him that way. We may have to move around the streets of Califax. We'll get you some tattoos. You'll need those if you don't want to draw attention to yourself."

"Then tattoo me with one of these." I touched the tattoo behind his ear, now covered in blood.

"Why would you want that?"

"I don't want to be forced to separate from you in a world I don't understand."

"Using the tattoo of another faction is a death sentence."

"How am I supposed to act like a Persal? I don't know your rules."

"Once we find Holden, he'll keep you safe within Persal. We'll find your family, Sable. I promise, but I need rest first. The pills are fast-working, but not that fast."

My muscles ached to get going, but as I looked at Jax, the urged petered out. Even though he talked clearer, his voice stronger, he still looked like he'd been mauled by a savage dog.

"I'll take a shower and change my clothes once I've slept. Do you think you'll get some sleep if you lie down?"

"God no. Not until I see Mum and Ajay."

"Fair enough."

Jax rolled slightly to his side, reaching behind. He pulled out his cell and dumped it on the bed between us before settling onto his back again. I stared down at the screen, illuminated from the movement. A message had come through at some point while we were in my world. With confronting Carter, fighting one of his loyalists, and the explosion, Jax had missed the notification.

I scooped the phone up. The message displayed only the first few words.

"There's a message," I said as I typed in the number password Jax had given me, then opened the message screen. "It's from Holden."

My eyes skimmed across the words, then again, then one more time as I tried to make sense of what Holden had said. I couldn't believe it. No matter how many rereads, they still said the same thing, still held the same meaning.

The cell fell from my hands, landing on the bed between my knees.

"What is it?"

"He's gone."

"Who, Holden?"

"He's taken the grafter."

Beside me, Jax rolled over to his side, then rose up to his elbow. "Taken it where?"

"He doesn't say. He had no intention of freeing Dad." The words felt distant, not from my mouth. "Oh my god," I moaned, rocking forward. I curled down until my face hit my palms, my palms my knees. "He deceived us. This is what he wanted when we made the plan. He made his own plan. I don't believe this."

I felt Jax move beside me, sliding up to sit with his back against the wall. He shouldn't do this. He needed to lie down, but there was not enough emotional strength in me to voice what I thought.

"What about your mum and Ajay?"

"He promised me they're safe."

"He's decent enough for that to be the truth."

"A decent person doesn't betray you." I surfaced from my palms. "Where would he take them?"

"I don't know. Here, someplace on your world, it's hard to say."

"He had a day to plan this."

"Sable, they could be anywhere. If we want to find them, we have to find Holden."

"What about Dad? And Carter?" I slid forward and dragged myself off the bed. "I don't believe this," I fisted my hair. "How could he do this? He was so full of factional loyalty." My pacing ignited the turbulent heat pooling in my belly. "He was so insistent on factional loyalty over blood loyalty, over everything. And here I am with an Aris while a Persal has cheated me." If my words were a tangible thing, they would've cut my mouth on the way out.

"We're here, Sable. We got out. Your mum and Ajay are safe. Holden doesn't matter. Forget him. I'll free your father for you. I'll make sure nothing happens to him. And we'll find a way to release him of his graft. This is not the end. Carter has not won. As long as you hold that in your heart, Carter won't win." Softly spoken, a soothing elixir to blunt the edges of my thoughts.

It worked. The anger fueling my mad pacing evaporated from my limbs. I sunk onto the edge of the bed.

"You would do that?" I looked over my shoulder to Jax's ruined face, one side a bloody, swollen mess, the other marginally better. He'd come to the Amex to warn me, to help me, while Holden waited below to deceive me. This was the man who'd dragged me into Dominus to see me fail, who then fought alongside me to stop Carter. "You're choosing to side with the opposing faction. You're choosing to save the man who killed your family."

"I won't pretend I don't hate your father. I always will. But at the moment, I hate Carter more. I've lost everything. I don't want that to happen to you."

I turned toward him, sliding a knee up onto the bed. If only I could see his features better, but the swelling and coloring distorted his face, disguising any subtlety in his expression. "I've never heard anything so selfless." I held his eyes.

If only I could release my emotions and allow them to flow across the space between us like I could destruction. Words were inadequate, a shadow of what I truly felt.

I crawled up the bed, sliding down alongside him, and took his hand, placing it over my heart. The Aris bot in Dominus had pierced my chest with his hand to remove my heart. I wanted Jax to do the same, pierce my flesh so that his hand might reach my heart, so he might cradle it within his palm. And then he would know. There would be no barriers between us, not even flesh. And he would know what this meant to me, the sacrifice, the loyalty.

Jax dropped his gaze to his hand, covering my heart. "For so long, I've been driven by my revenge. I feel empty without it. I don't know what I want anymore. All I know is your fight gives me direction. Your passion gives me purpose. You give me purpose."

"Thank you." Two words inadequate for the emotion I felt.

It seemed so natural to slide my head down until it rested on his shoulder.

Surrounded by blood, over him as well as me, my clothes, my pants, my hand, staining the sheets, smearing across the floor, footprints of it following us to the bed, we remained silent, together amongst a macabre picture of death. But we'd survived because we'd stayed together, fought together, trusted each other.

Dad was right, betrayal was inevitable. But he was also wrong. The one person who had every reason to betray me, a guy from an opposing faction, had turned into my greatest ally, had turned into the one person I could trust.

Thanks to Jax, this was not the end. Carter would not win.

Author's Note

With all the millions of titles on Amazon it's great you found mine. If you would like to know when I have a new release, instead of leaving it to chance, you can sign up for my newsletter. There are three free reads already waiting for you, plus two chapters from Jax's point of view

Type in terinaadams.com into your search engine

This story was my passion. I hope you were gripped while reading Dominus as much as I was in writing it. If this was you, please let me know in the reviews on Amazon. If this was not you, please still let me know.

Thanks heaps. See you in Califax.

Califax

In a world built on lies, fear and deceit I must learn what it means to be destruction.

Betrayal and deceit. That's what Dominus taught me.
But it has also taught me how to be strong, how to fight and how to unite with the darkness inside.

Two men have deceived me. One has saved me.
But what will happen when I enter Jax's world, a world where the people know little but fear and factions are killed for loving each other?

In Jax's world, right and wrong blur and the only important lesson is survival…

About the Author

When I wasn't riding a camel through the Rajasthani desert, white water rafting the rapids on the Zambezi, bungee jumping off the Victoria Falls bridge or hiking the peeks in Pakistan, I was piloting a twin prop into remote aboriginal communities in northern Western Australia or staring down a microscope in a laboratory.

Now somewhat tamed, the microscope has morphed into a computer and I spend more time plotting dire situations for my protagonists than being in them myself.

I am the author of books that won't stay normal.

www.ingramcontent.com/pod-product-compliance
Lightning Source LLC
Chambersburg PA
CBHW030240120726
47903CB00005B/1558